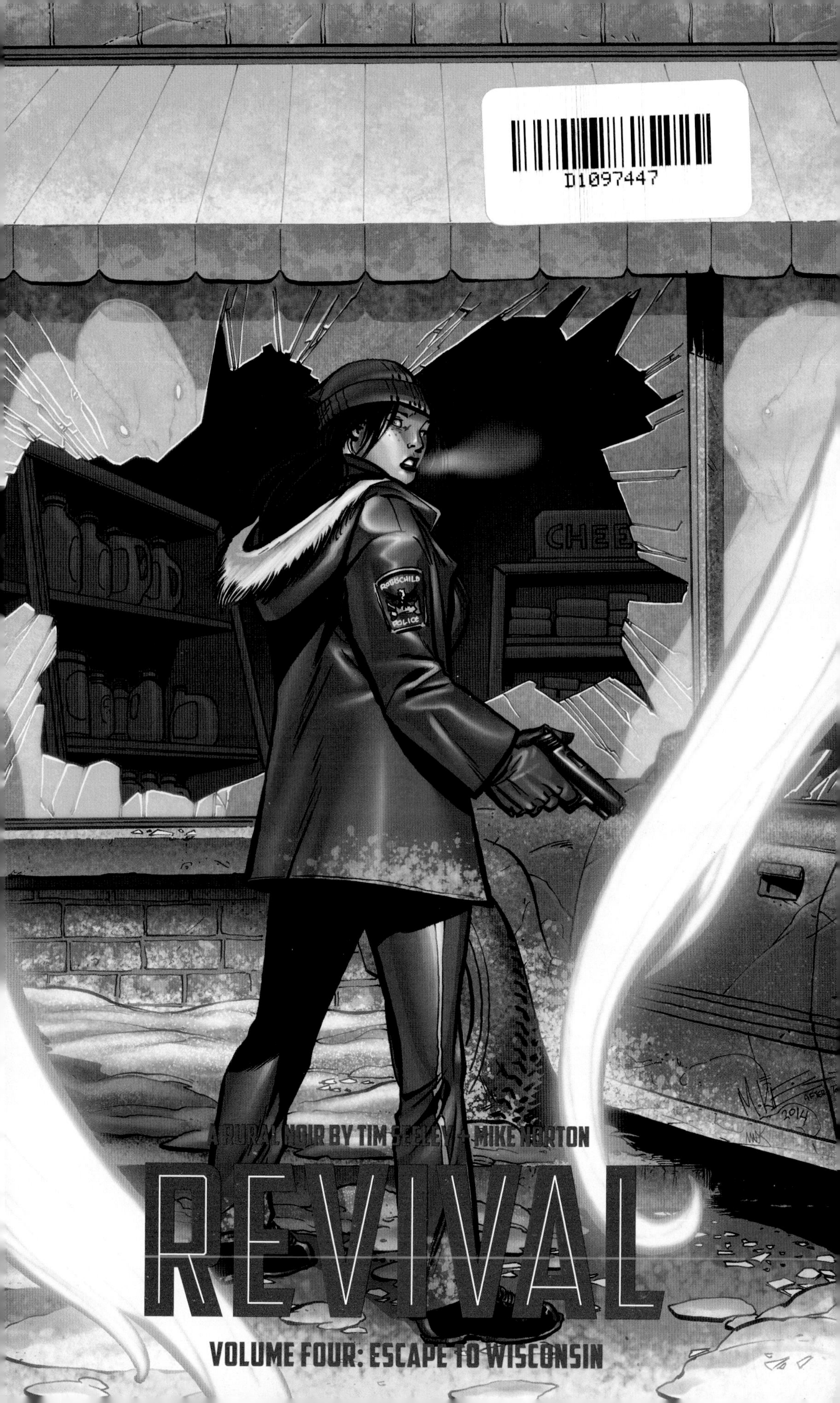
CHEE
ROTHSCHILD
POLICE
A RURAL NOIR BY TIM SEELEY + MIKE NORTON
REVIVAL
VOLUME FOUR: ESCAPE TO WISCONSIN

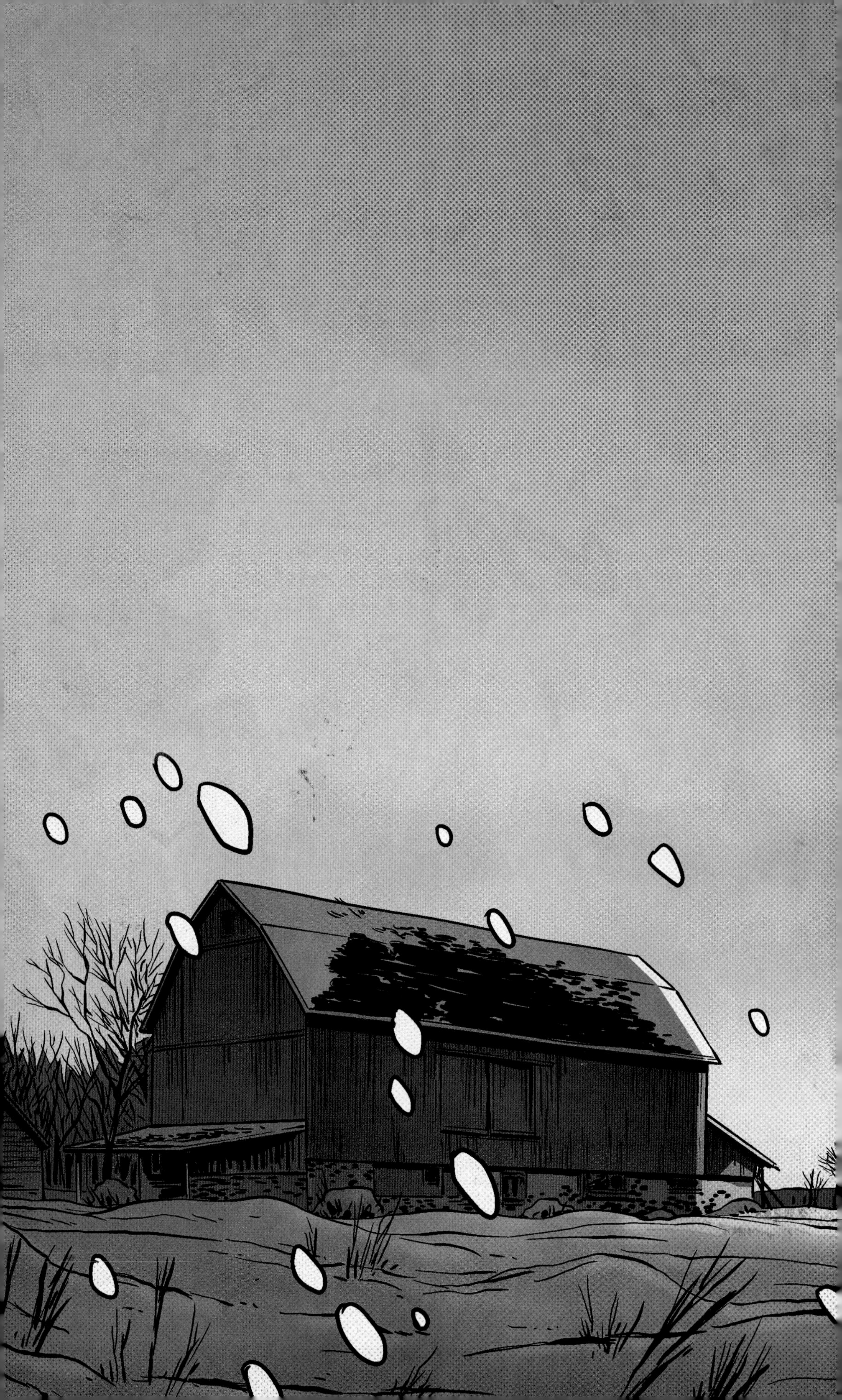

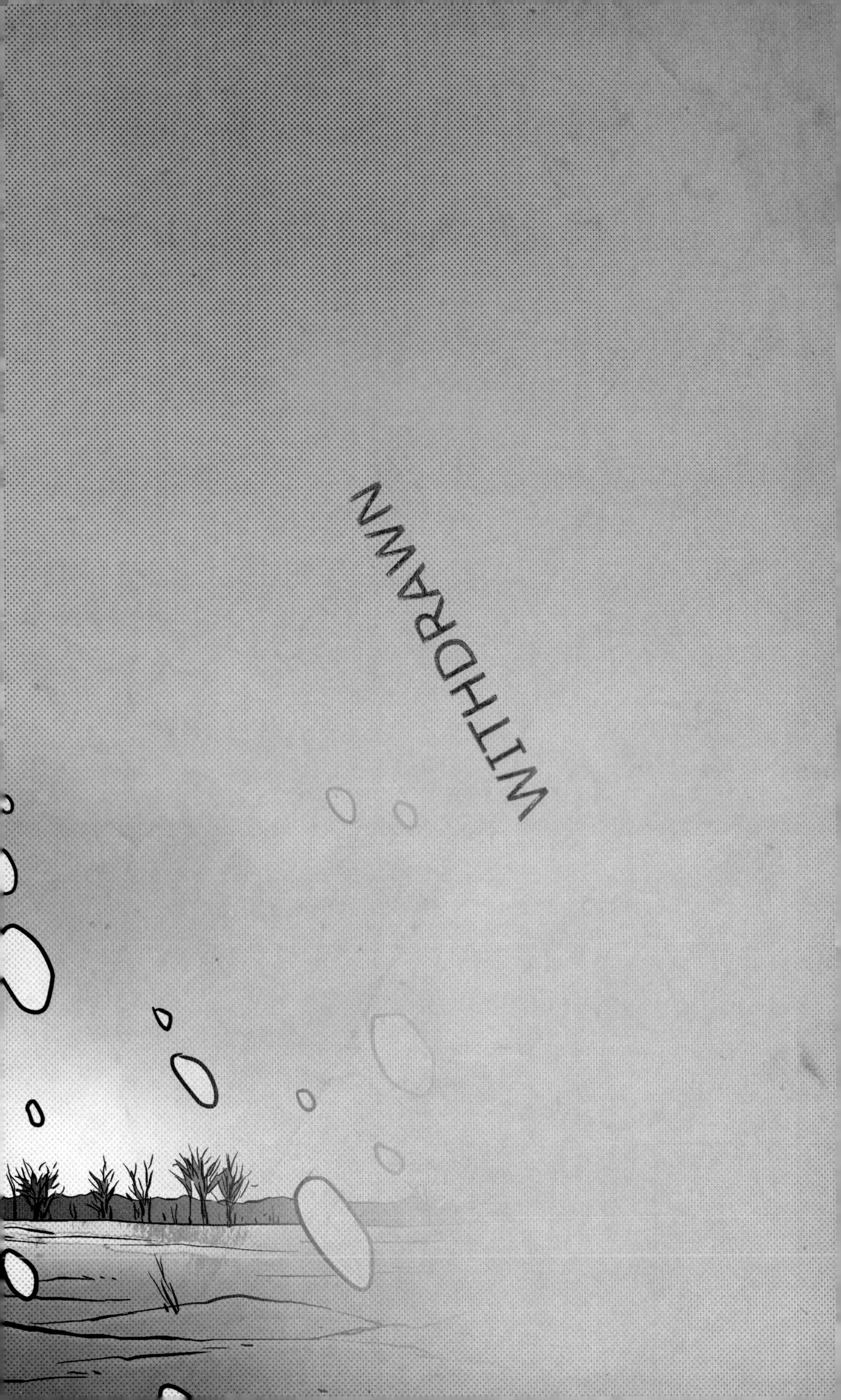

STORY BY
TIM SEELEY

ART BY
MIKE NORTON

COLORS BY
MARK ENGLERT

LETTERS BY
CRANK!

CHAPTER ART BY
JENNY FRISON

EDITED BY
4 STAR STUDIOS

DESIGN BY
SEAN DOVE

FOR MORE INFO CHECK OUT
WWW.REVIVALCOMIC.COM

ALSO CHECK OUT THE SOUNDTRACK BY
SONO MORTI AT **SONOMORTI.BANDCAMP.COM**

IMAGE COMICS, INC.
Robert Kirkman – Chief Operating Officer
Erik Larsen – Chief Financial Officer
Todd McFarlane – President
Marc Silvestri – Chief Executive Officer
Jim Valentino – Vice-President

Eric Stephenson – Publisher
Ron Richards – Director of Business Development
Jennifer de Guzman – Director of Trade Book Sales
Kat Salazar – Director of PR & Marketing
Jeremy Sullivan – Director of Digital Sales
Emilio Bautista – Sales Assistant
Branwyn Bigglestone – Senior Accounts Manager
Emily Miller – Accounts Manager
Jessica Ambriz – Administrative Assistant
Tyler Shainline – Events Coordinator
David Brothers – Content Manager
Jonathan Chan – Production Manager
Drew Gill – Art Director
Meredith Wallace – Print Manager
Monica Garcia – Senior Production Artist
Jenna Savage – Production Artist
Addison Duke – Production Artist
Tricia Ramos – Production Assistant
IMAGECOMICS.COM

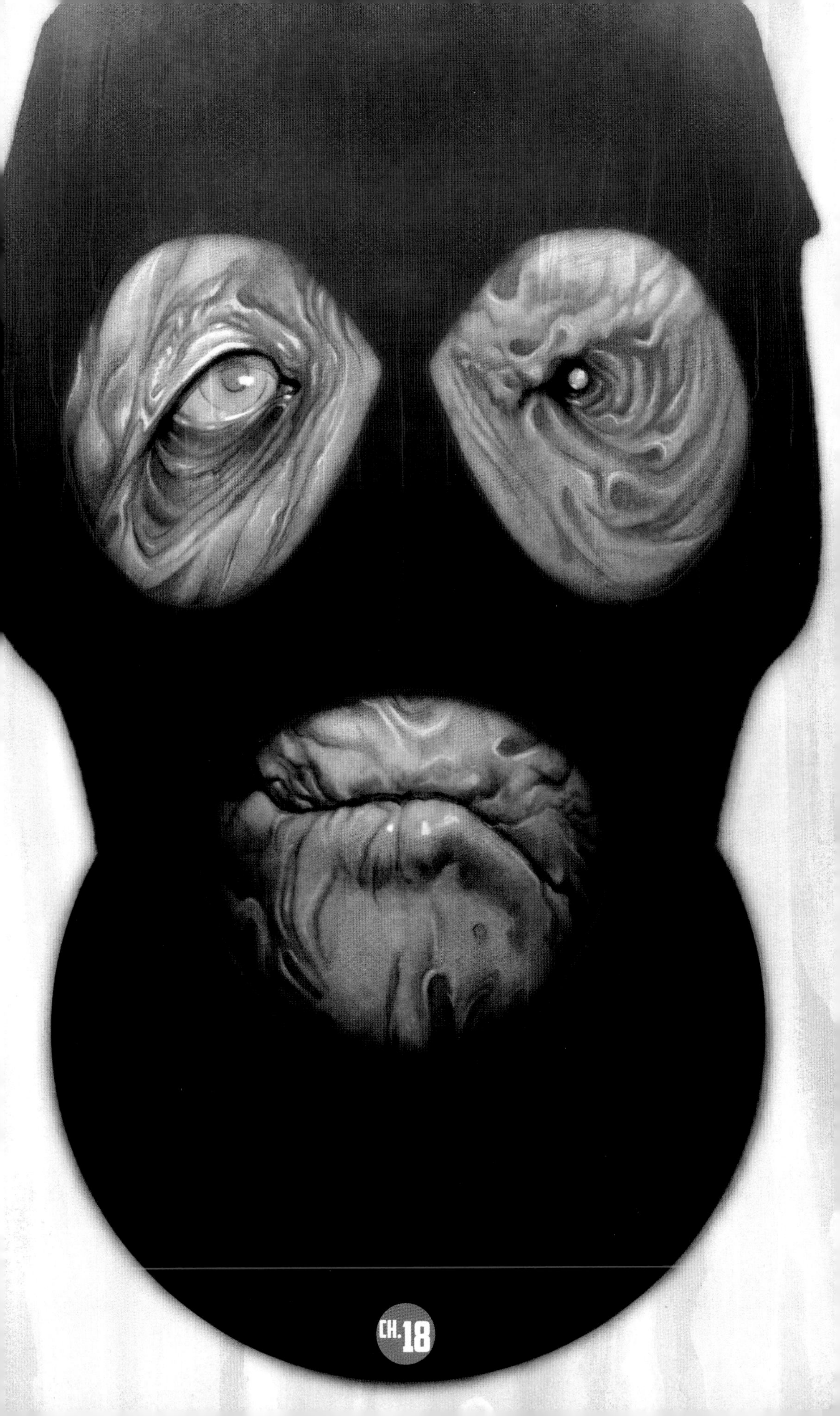
CH. 18

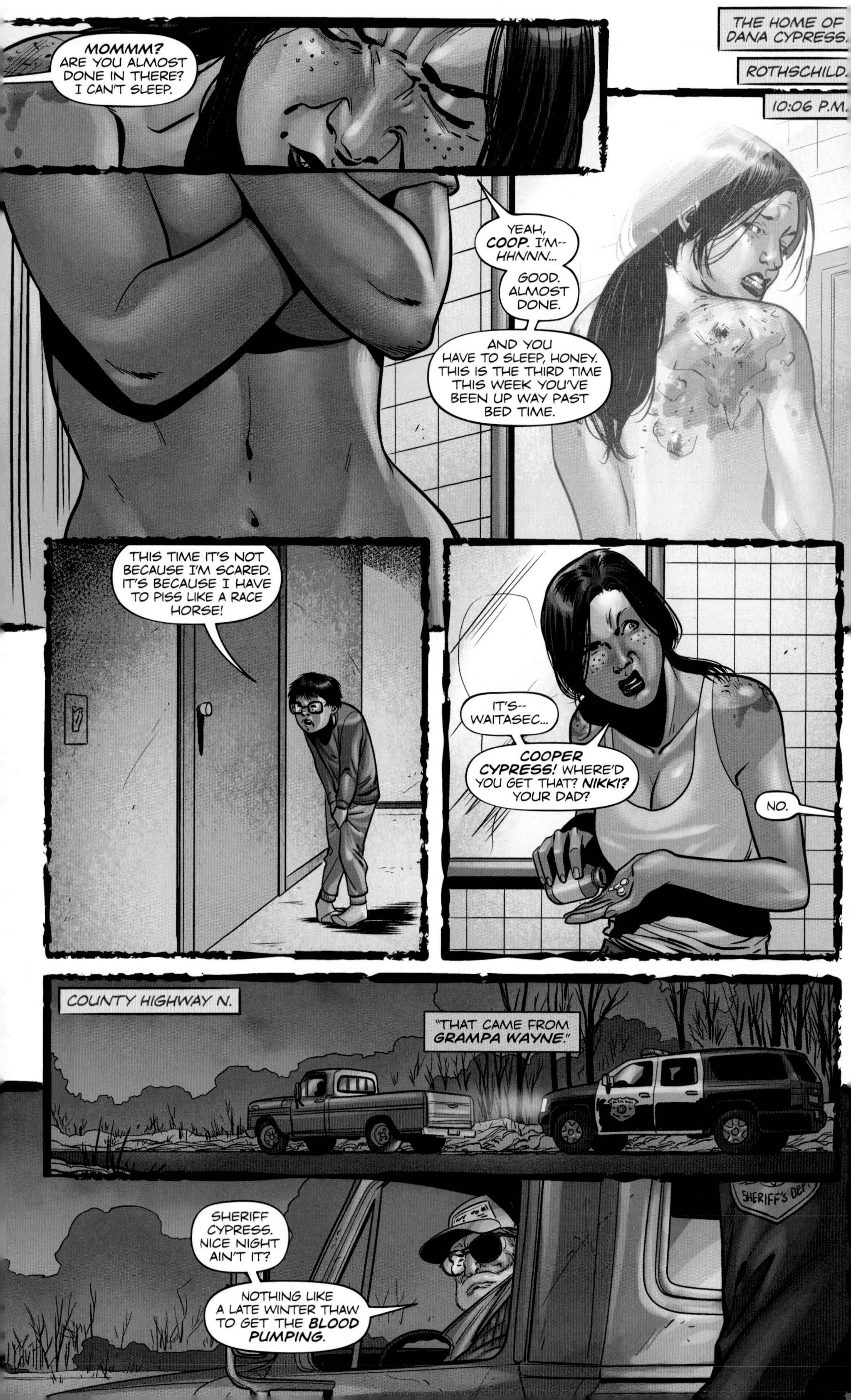
THE HOME OF DANA CYPRESS.
ROTHSCHILD.
10:06 P.M.
MOMMM? ARE YOU ALMOST DONE IN THERE? I CAN'T SLEEP.
YEAH, COOP. I'M-- HHNNN...
GOOD. ALMOST DONE.
AND YOU HAVE TO SLEEP, HONEY. THIS IS THE THIRD TIME THIS WEEK YOU'VE BEEN UP WAY PAST BED TIME.
THIS TIME IT'S NOT BECAUSE I'M SCARED. IT'S BECAUSE I HAVE TO PISS LIKE A RACE HORSE!
IT'S-- WAITASEC...
COOPER CYPRESS! WHERE'D YOU GET THAT? NIKKI? YOUR DAD?
NO.
COUNTY HIGHWAY N.
"THAT CAME FROM GRAMPA WAYNE."
SHERIFF'S DEPT
SHERIFF CYPRESS. NICE NIGHT AIN'T IT?
NOTHING LIKE A LATE WINTER THAW TO GET THE BLOOD PUMPING.

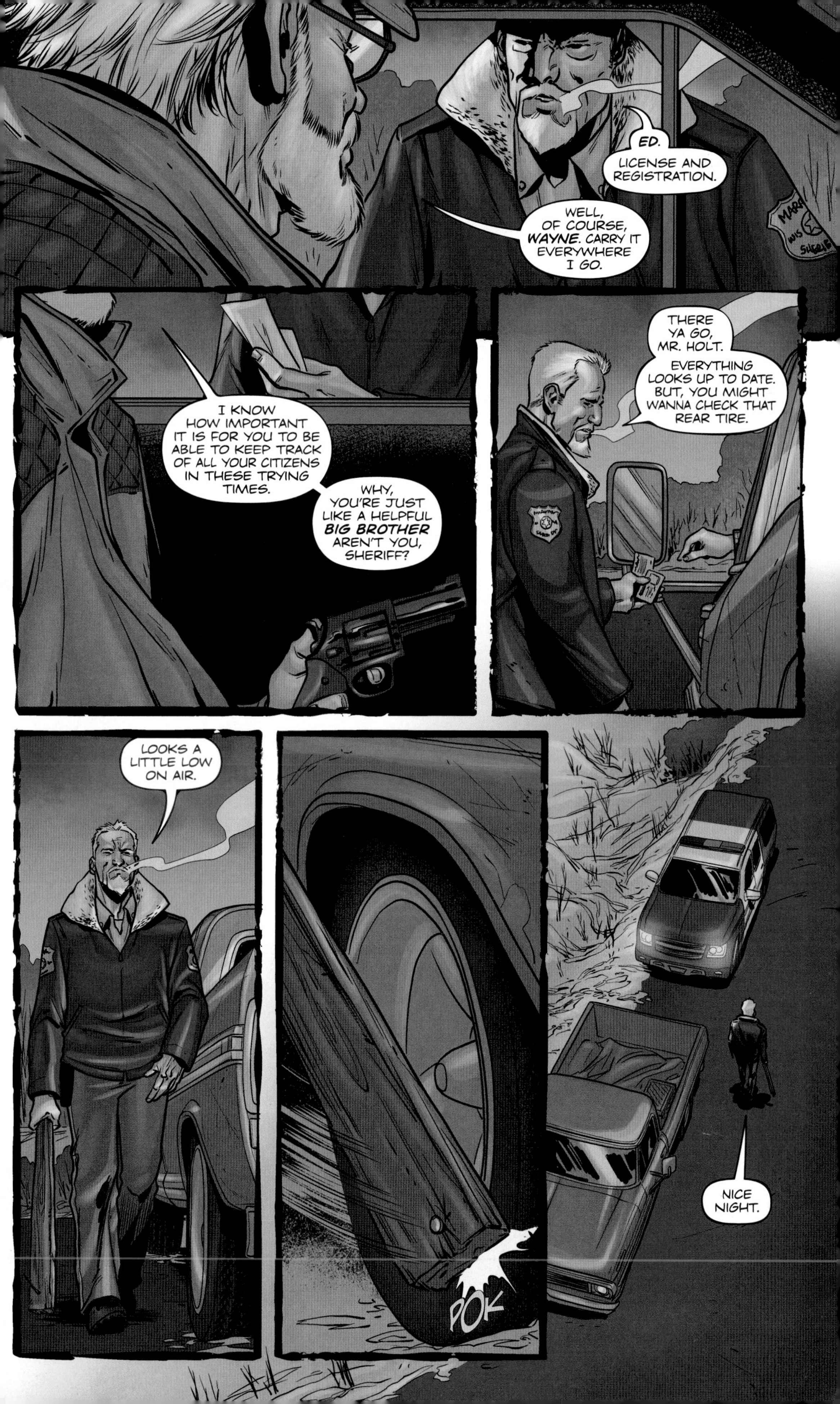

ED.
LICENSE AND REGISTRATION.
WELL, OF COURSE, WAYNE. CARRY IT EVERYWHERE I GO.
I KNOW HOW IMPORTANT IT IS FOR YOU TO BE ABLE TO KEEP TRACK OF ALL YOUR CITIZENS IN THESE TRYING TIMES.
WHY, YOU'RE JUST LIKE A HELPFUL BIG BROTHER AREN'T YOU, SHERIFF?
THERE YA GO, MR. HOLT.
EVERYTHING LOOKS UP TO DATE. BUT, YOU MIGHT WANNA CHECK THAT REAR TIRE.
LOOKS A LITTLE LOW ON AIR.
POK
NICE NIGHT.

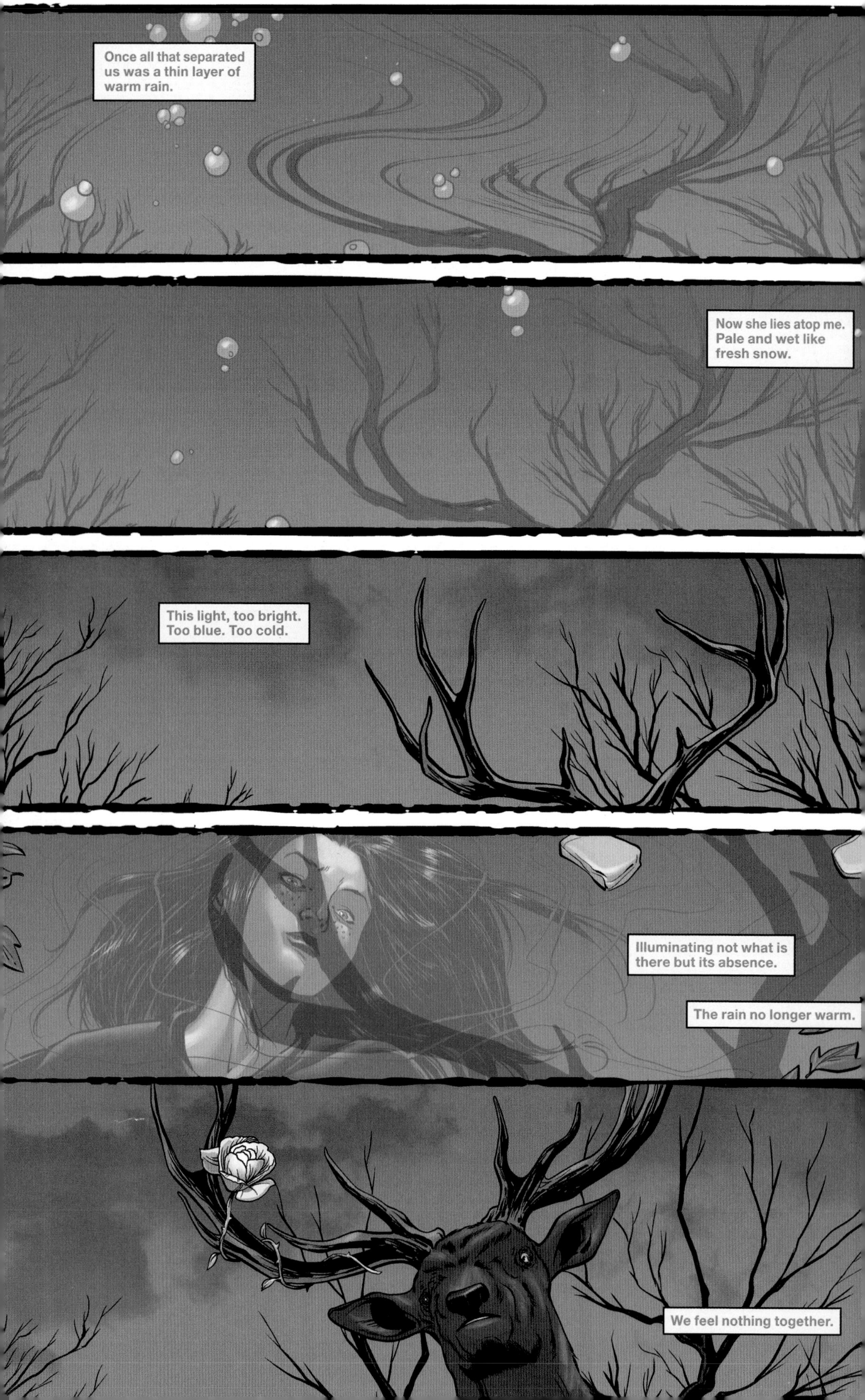
Once all that separated us was a thin layer of warm rain.
Now she lies atop me. Pale and wet like fresh snow.
This light, too bright. Too blue. Too cold.
Illuminating not what is there but its absence.
The rain no longer warm.
We feel nothing together.

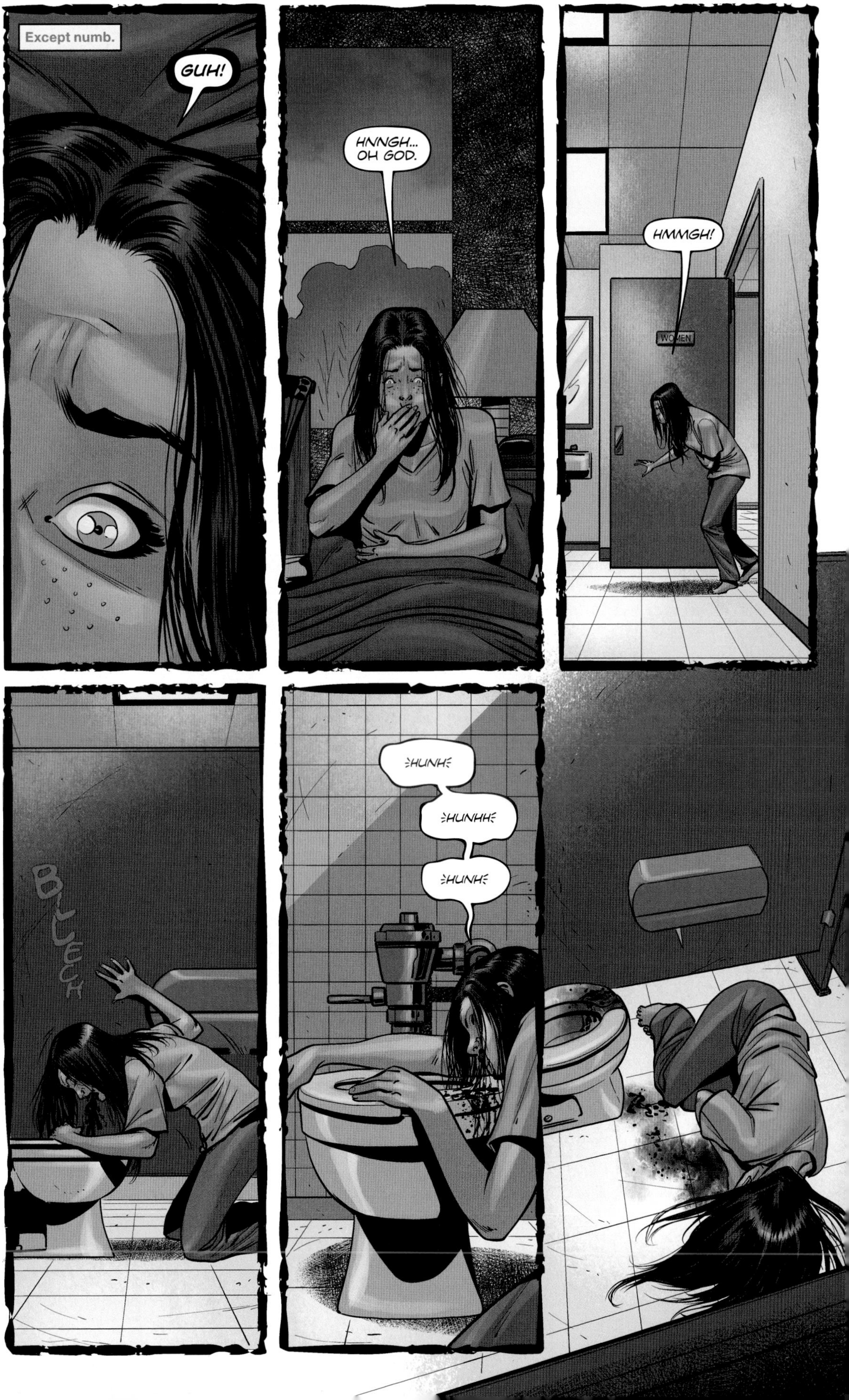
Except numb.
GUH!
HNNGH... OH GOD.
HMMGH!
WOMEN
BLUECH
HUNH
HUNHH
HUNH

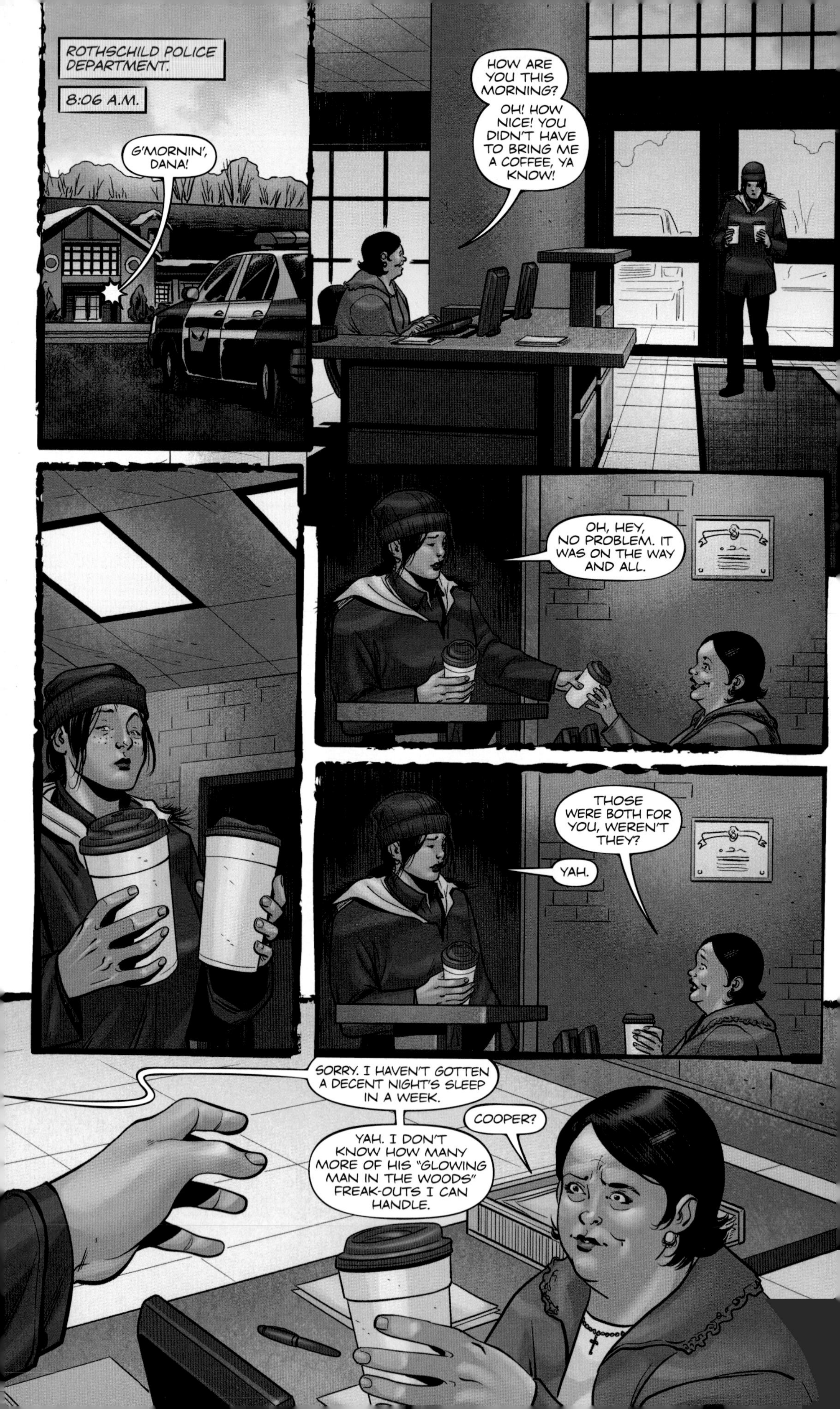
ROTHSCHILD POLICE DEPARTMENT.
8:06 A.M.
G'MORNIN', DANA!
HOW ARE YOU THIS MORNING?
OH! HOW NICE! YOU DIDN'T HAVE TO BRING ME A COFFEE, YA KNOW!
OH, HEY, NO PROBLEM. IT WAS ON THE WAY AND ALL.
THOSE WERE BOTH FOR YOU, WEREN'T THEY?
YAH.
SORRY. I HAVEN'T GOTTEN A DECENT NIGHT'S SLEEP IN A WEEK.
COOPER?
YAH. I DON'T KNOW HOW MANY MORE OF HIS "GLOWING MAN IN THE WOODS" FREAK-OUTS I CAN HANDLE.

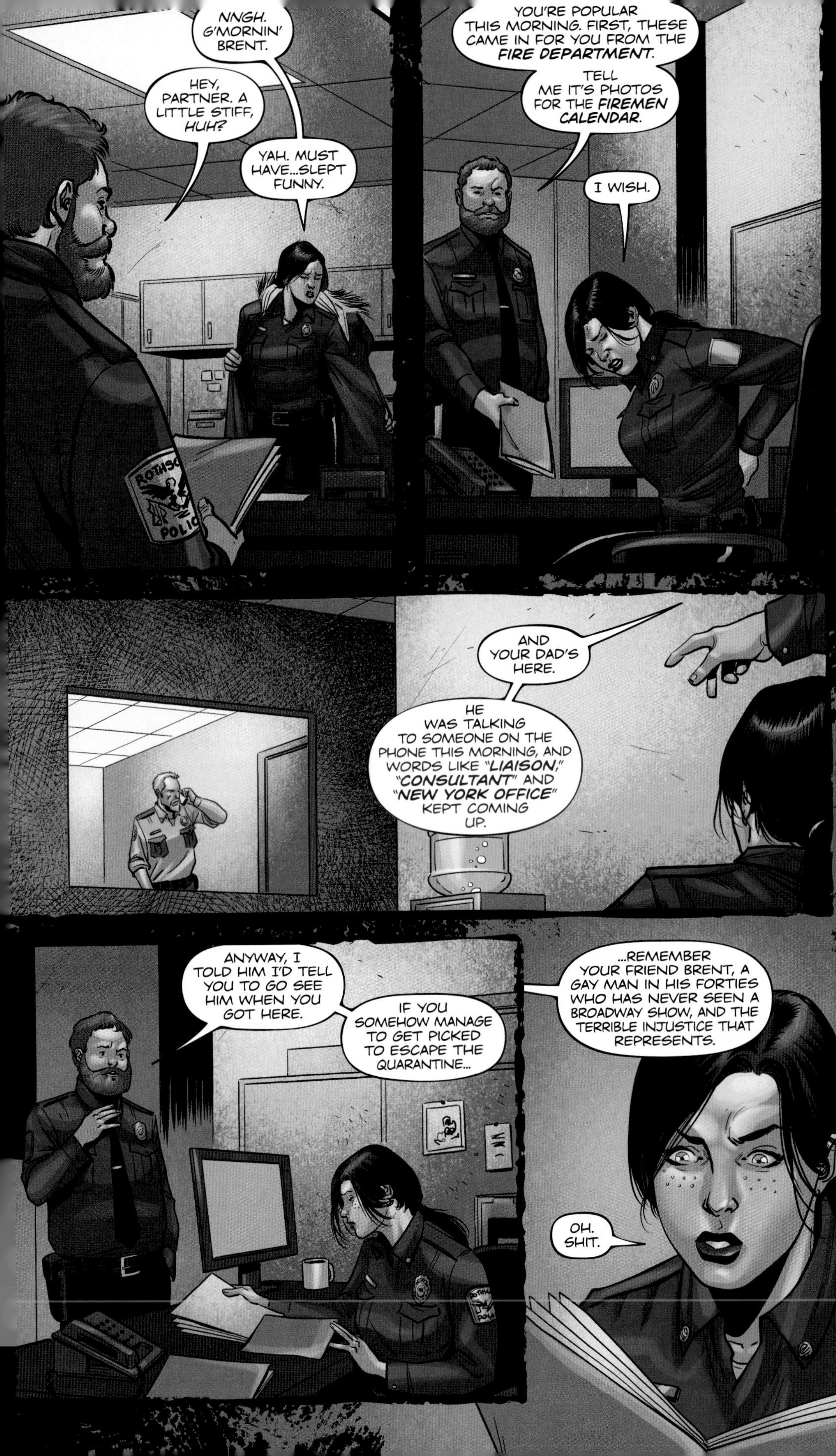
NNGH. G'MORNIN' BRENT.
HEY, PARTNER. A LITTLE STIFF, HUH?
YAH. MUST HAVE...SLEPT FUNNY.
ROTHSC POLIC
YOU'RE POPULAR THIS MORNING. FIRST, THESE CAME IN FOR YOU FROM THE FIRE DEPARTMENT.
TELL ME IT'S PHOTOS FOR THE FIREMEN CALENDAR.
I WISH.
AND YOUR DAD'S HERE.
HE WAS TALKING TO SOMEONE ON THE PHONE THIS MORNING, AND WORDS LIKE "LIAISON," "CONSULTANT" AND "NEW YORK OFFICE" KEPT COMING UP.
ANYWAY, I TOLD HIM I'D TELL YOU TO GO SEE HIM WHEN YOU GOT HERE.
IF YOU SOMEHOW MANAGE TO GET PICKED TO ESCAPE THE QUARANTINE...
...REMEMBER YOUR FRIEND BRENT, A GAY MAN IN HIS FORTIES WHO HAS NEVER SEEN A BROADWAY SHOW, AND THE TERRIBLE INJUSTICE THAT REPRESENTS.
OH. SHIT.

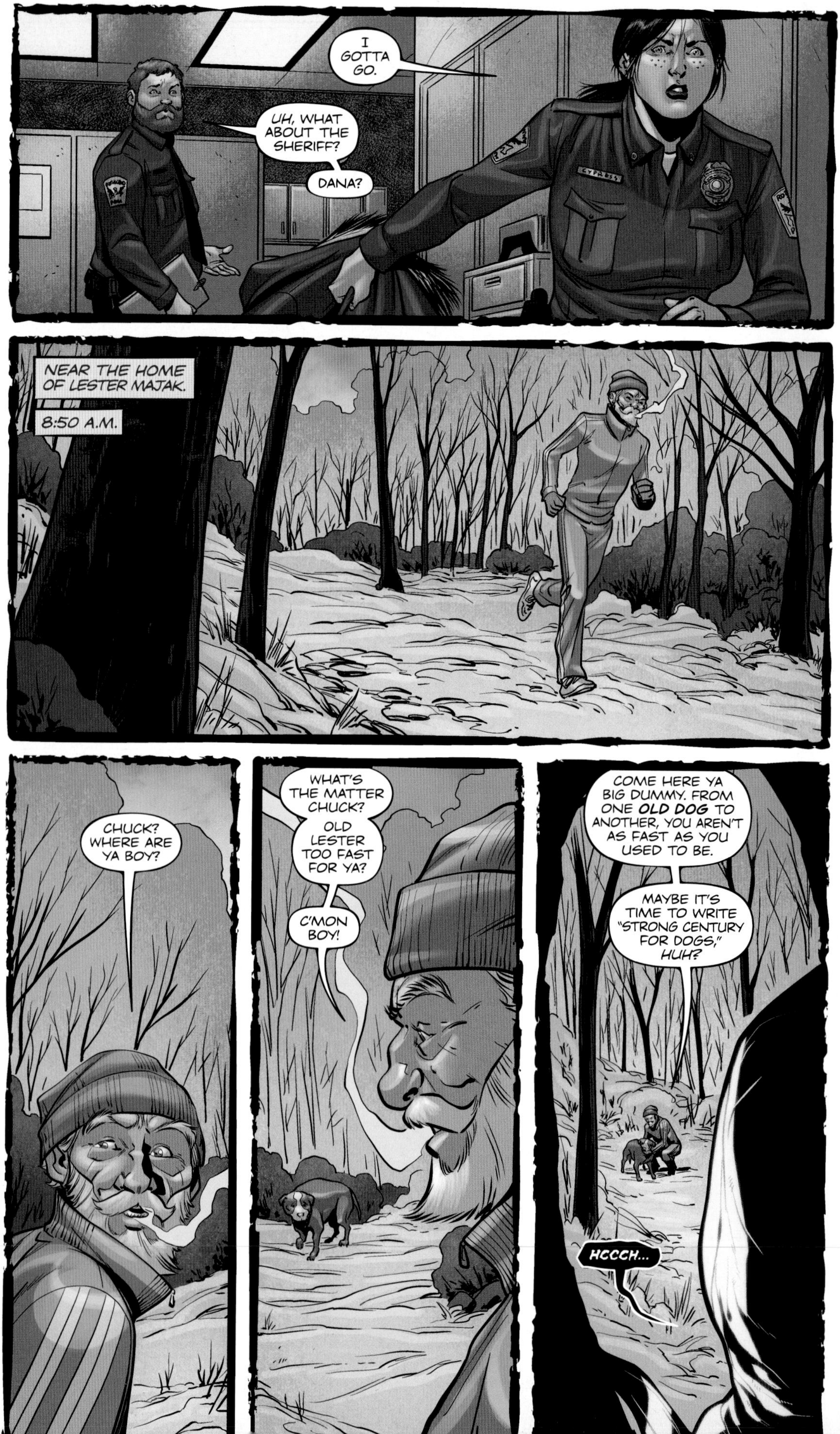
I GOTTA GO.
UH, WHAT ABOUT THE SHERIFF?
DANA?
NEAR THE HOME OF LESTER MAJAK.
8:50 A.M.
CHUCK? WHERE ARE YA BOY?
WHAT'S THE MATTER CHUCK?
OLD LESTER TOO FAST FOR YA?
C'MON BOY!
COME HERE YA BIG DUMMY. FROM ONE **OLD DOG** TO ANOTHER, YOU AREN'T AS FAST AS YOU USED TO BE.
MAYBE IT'S TIME TO WRITE "STRONG CENTURY FOR DOGS," HUH?
HCCCH...

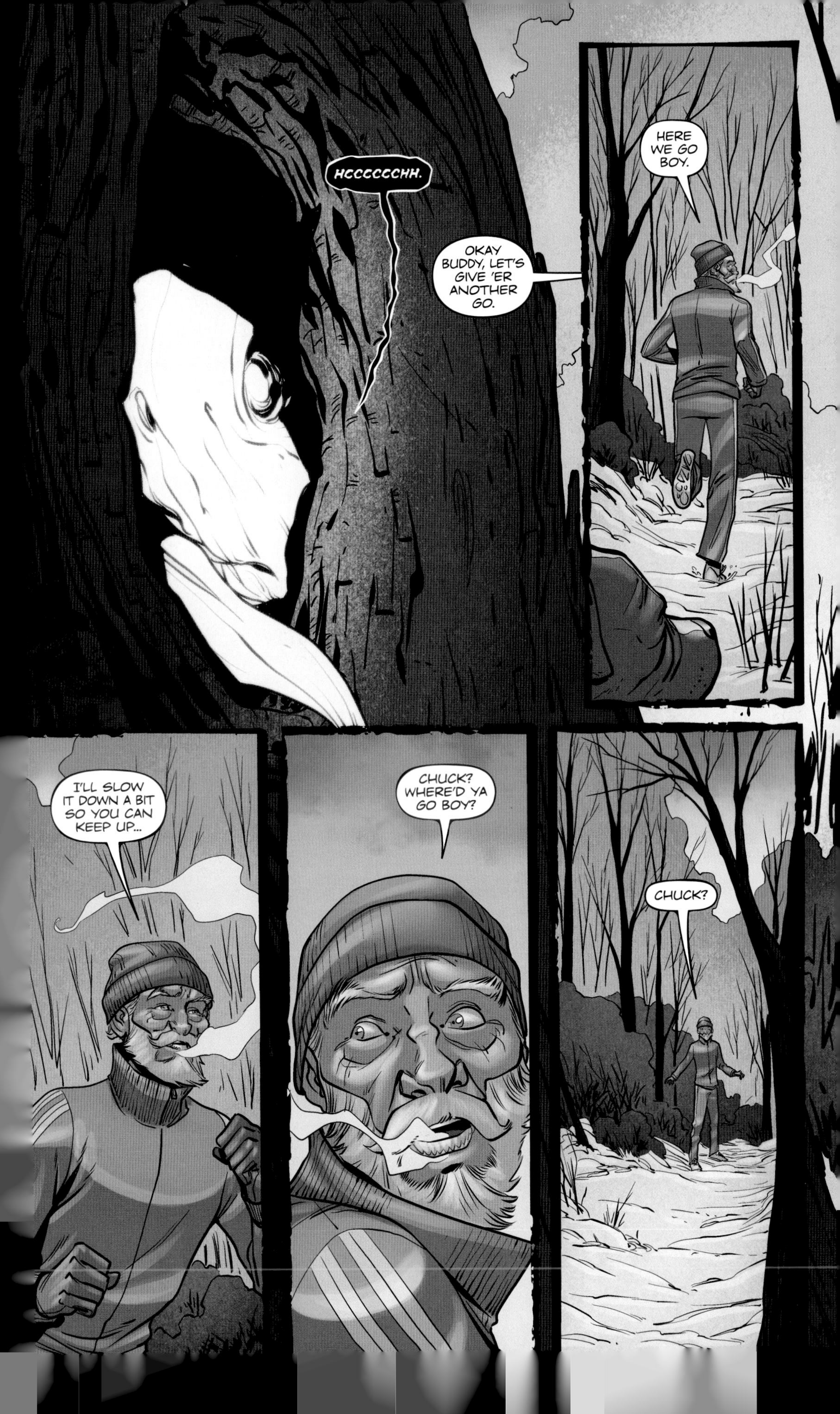
HCCCCCCHH.
HERE WE GO BOY.
OKAY BUDDY, LET'S GIVE 'ER ANOTHER GO.
I'LL SLOW IT DOWN A BIT SO YOU CAN KEEP UP...
CHUCK? WHERE'D YA GO BOY?
CHUCK?

TIMBER LANES.
ROTHSCHILD.
11:28 A.M.

"ALL COMPOSITE THINGS ARE IMPERMANENT, THEY ARE SUBJECT TO BIRTH AND DEATH."

"PUT AN END TO BIRTH AND DEATH...

Sean Sez...
Bowl—FOR HEALTH!

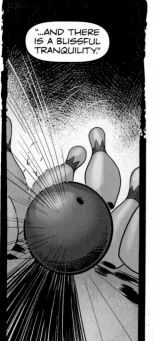

"...AND THERE IS A BLISSFUL TRANQUILITY."

ZEN BOWLING.

RANDY DECKER?

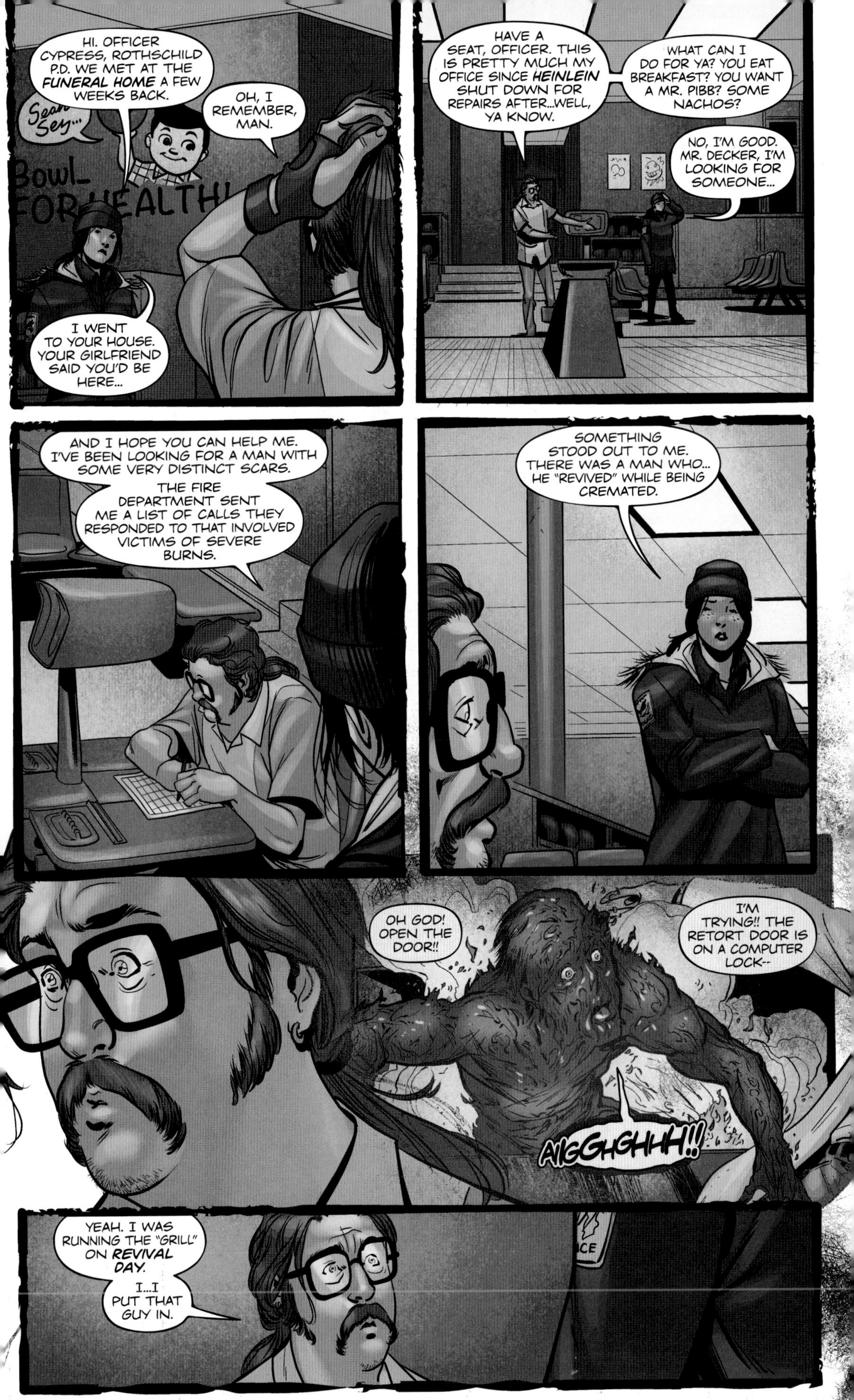
HI. OFFICER CYPRESS, ROTHSCHILD P.D. WE MET AT THE FUNERAL HOME A FEW WEEKS BACK.
OH, I REMEMBER, MAN.
Bowl FOR HEALTH!
I WENT TO YOUR HOUSE. YOUR GIRLFRIEND SAID YOU'D BE HERE...
HAVE A SEAT, OFFICER. THIS IS PRETTY MUCH MY OFFICE SINCE HEINLEIN SHUT DOWN FOR REPAIRS AFTER...WELL, YA KNOW.
WHAT CAN I DO FOR YA? YOU EAT BREAKFAST? YOU WANT A MR. PIBB? SOME NACHOS?
NO, I'M GOOD. MR. DECKER, I'M LOOKING FOR SOMEONE...
AND I HOPE YOU CAN HELP ME. I'VE BEEN LOOKING FOR A MAN WITH SOME VERY DISTINCT SCARS.
THE FIRE DEPARTMENT SENT ME A LIST OF CALLS THEY RESPONDED TO THAT INVOLVED VICTIMS OF SEVERE BURNS.
SOMETHING STOOD OUT TO ME. THERE WAS A MAN WHO... HE "REVIVED" WHILE BEING CREMATED.
OH GOD! OPEN THE DOOR!!
I'M TRYING!! THE RETORT DOOR IS ON A COMPUTER LOCK--
AIGGHGHHH!!
YEAH. I WAS RUNNING THE "GRILL" ON REVIVAL DAY.
I...I PUT THAT GUY IN.

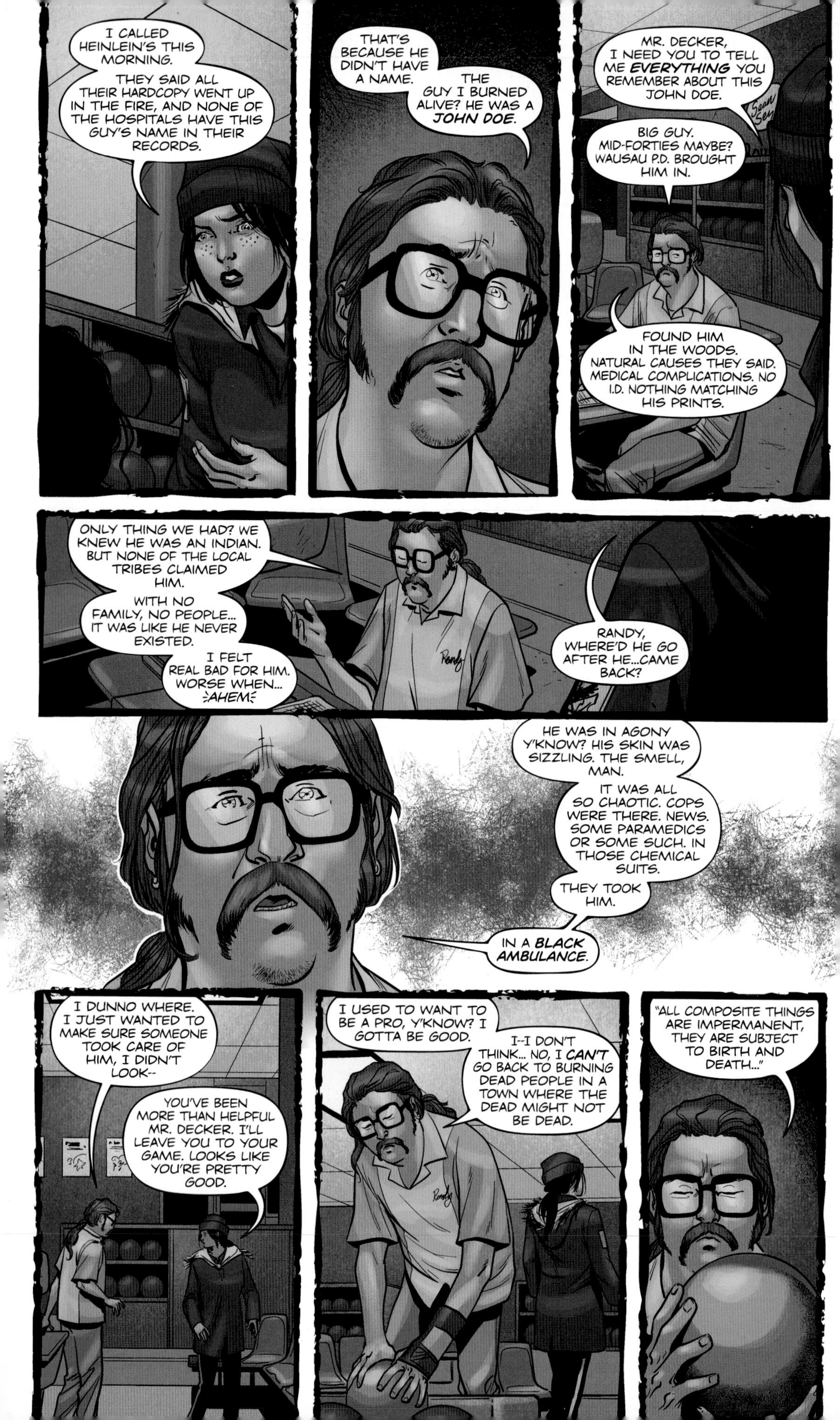
I CALLED HEINLEIN'S THIS MORNING.
THEY SAID ALL THEIR HARDCOPY WENT UP IN THE FIRE, AND NONE OF THE HOSPITALS HAVE THIS GUY'S NAME IN THEIR RECORDS.
THAT'S BECAUSE HE DIDN'T HAVE A NAME.
THE GUY I BURNED ALIVE? HE WAS A JOHN DOE.
MR. DECKER, I NEED YOU TO TELL ME EVERYTHING YOU REMEMBER ABOUT THIS JOHN DOE.
BIG GUY. MID-FORTIES MAYBE? WAUSAU P.D. BROUGHT HIM IN.
FOUND HIM IN THE WOODS. NATURAL CAUSES THEY SAID. MEDICAL COMPLICATIONS. NO I.D. NOTHING MATCHING HIS PRINTS.
ONLY THING WE HAD? WE KNEW HE WAS AN INDIAN. BUT NONE OF THE LOCAL TRIBES CLAIMED HIM.
WITH NO FAMILY, NO PEOPLE... IT WAS LIKE HE NEVER EXISTED.
I FELT REAL BAD FOR HIM. WORSE WHEN... AHEM
RANDY, WHERE'D HE GO AFTER HE...CAME BACK?
HE WAS IN AGONY Y'KNOW? HIS SKIN WAS SIZZLING. THE SMELL, MAN.
IT WAS ALL SO CHAOTIC. COPS WERE THERE. NEWS. SOME PARAMEDICS OR SOME SUCH. IN THOSE CHEMICAL SUITS.
THEY TOOK HIM.
IN A BLACK AMBULANCE.
I DUNNO WHERE. I JUST WANTED TO MAKE SURE SOMEONE TOOK CARE OF HIM, I DIDN'T LOOK--
YOU'VE BEEN MORE THAN HELPFUL MR. DECKER. I'LL LEAVE YOU TO YOUR GAME. LOOKS LIKE YOU'RE PRETTY GOOD.
I USED TO WANT TO BE A PRO, Y'KNOW? I GOTTA BE GOOD.
I--I DON'T THINK... NO, I CAN'T GO BACK TO BURNING DEAD PEOPLE IN A TOWN WHERE THE DEAD MIGHT NOT BE DEAD.
"ALL COMPOSITE THINGS ARE IMPERMANENT, THEY ARE SUBJECT TO BIRTH AND DEATH..."

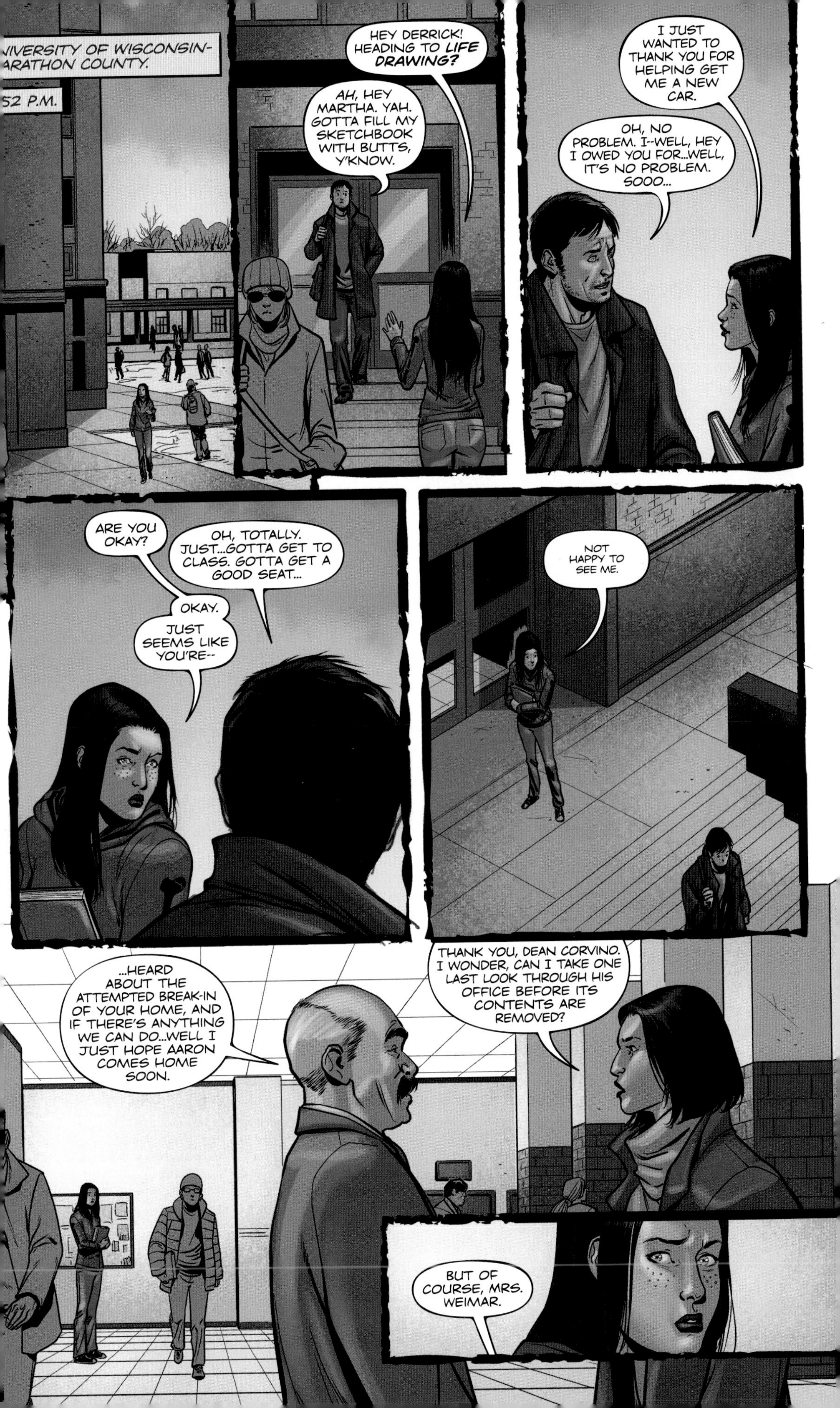

NIVERSITY OF WISCONSIN-
ARATHON COUNTY.
52 P.M.
HEY DERRICK! HEADING TO LIFE DRAWING?
AH, HEY MARTHA. YAH. GOTTA FILL MY SKETCHBOOK WITH BUTTS, Y'KNOW.
I JUST WANTED TO THANK YOU FOR HELPING GET ME A NEW CAR.
OH, NO PROBLEM. I--WELL, HEY I OWED YOU FOR...WELL, IT'S NO PROBLEM. SOOO...
ARE YOU OKAY?
OH, TOTALLY. JUST...GOTTA GET TO CLASS. GOTTA GET A GOOD SEAT...
OKAY.
JUST SEEMS LIKE YOU'RE--
NOT HAPPY TO SEE ME.
...HEARD ABOUT THE ATTEMPTED BREAK-IN OF YOUR HOME, AND IF THERE'S ANYTHING WE CAN DO...WELL I JUST HOPE AARON COMES HOME SOON.
THANK YOU, DEAN CORVINO. I WONDER, CAN I TAKE ONE LAST LOOK THROUGH HIS OFFICE BEFORE ITS CONTENTS ARE REMOVED?
BUT OF COURSE, MRS. WEIMAR.

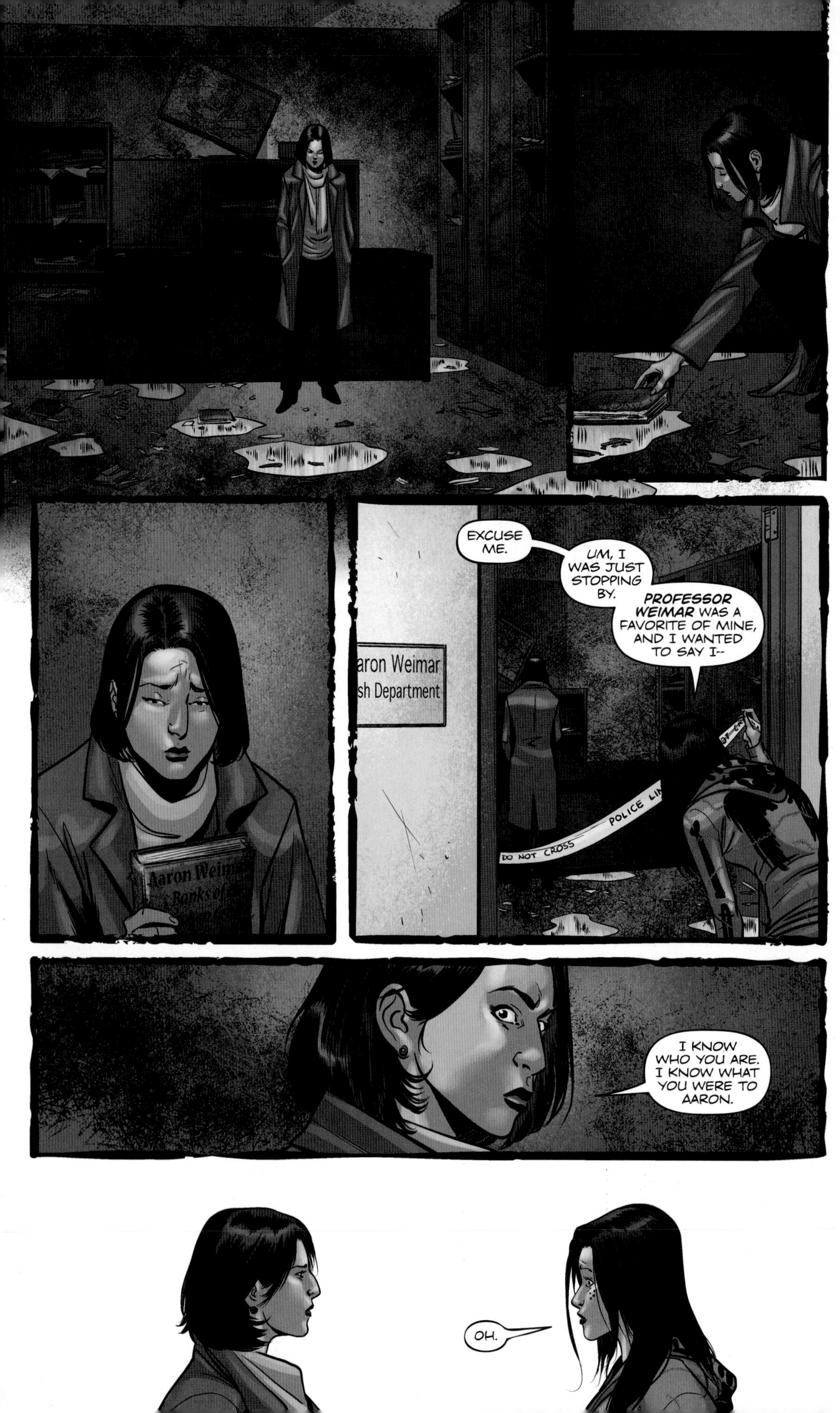
aron Weimar
sh Department
EXCUSE ME.
UM, I WAS JUST STOPPING BY.
PROFESSOR WEIMAR WAS A FAVORITE OF MINE, AND I WANTED TO SAY I--
POLICE LI
DO NOT CROSS
I KNOW WHO YOU ARE. I KNOW WHAT YOU WERE TO AARON.
OH.

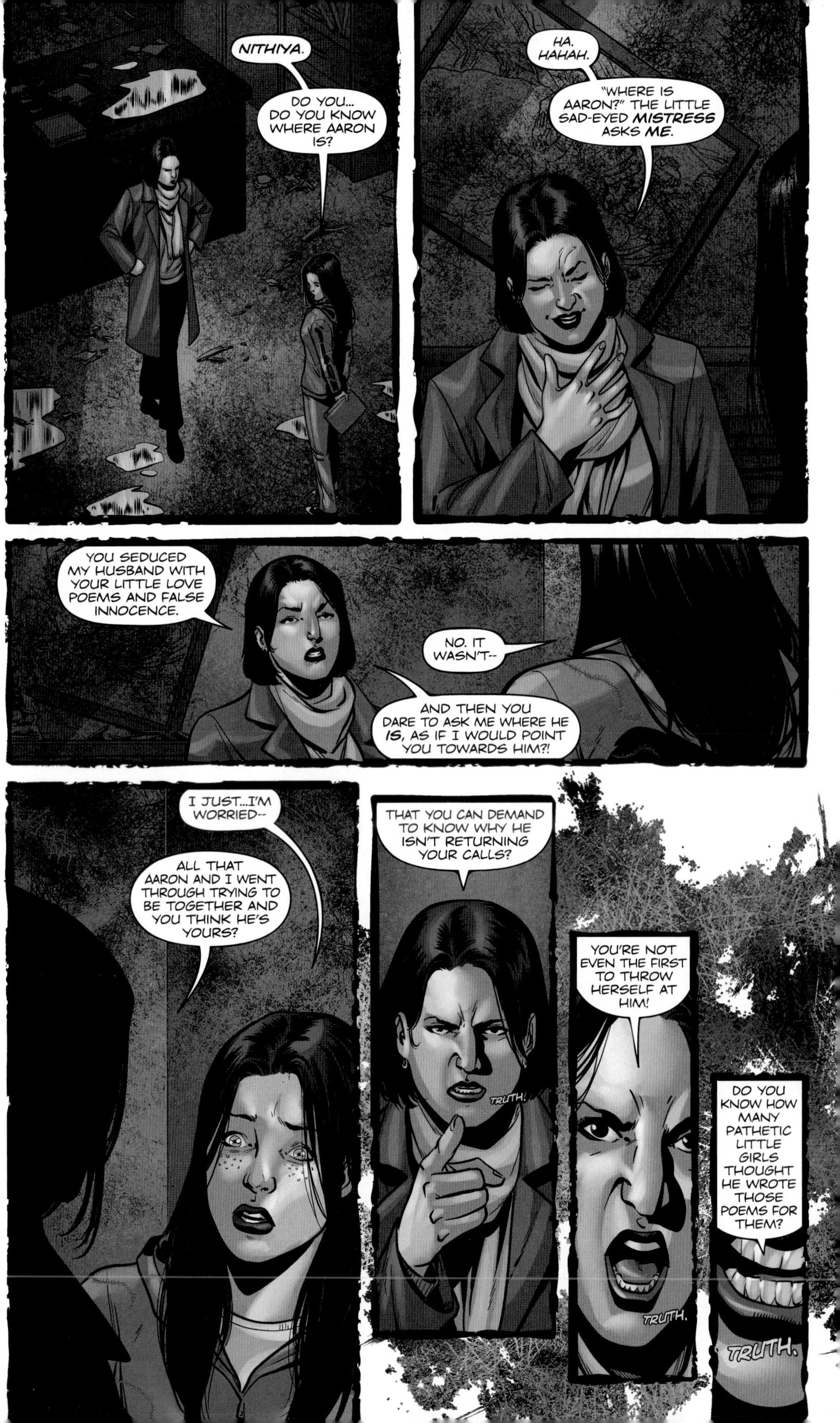
NITHIYA.
DO YOU... DO YOU KNOW WHERE AARON IS?
HA. HAHAH.
"WHERE IS AARON?" THE LITTLE SAD-EYED **MISTRESS** ASKS **ME**.
YOU SEDUCED MY HUSBAND WITH YOUR LITTLE LOVE POEMS AND FALSE INNOCENCE.
NO. IT WASN'T--
AND THEN YOU DARE TO ASK ME WHERE HE **IS**, AS IF I WOULD POINT YOU TOWARDS HIM?!
I JUST...I'M WORRIED--
ALL THAT AARON AND I WENT THROUGH TRYING TO BE TOGETHER AND YOU THINK HE'S YOURS?
THAT YOU CAN DEMAND TO KNOW WHY HE ISN'T RETURNING YOUR CALLS?
TRUTH.
YOU'RE NOT EVEN THE FIRST TO THROW HERSELF AT HIM!
TRUTH.
DO YOU KNOW HOW MANY PATHETIC LITTLE GIRLS THOUGHT HE WROTE THOSE POEMS FOR THEM?
TRUTH.

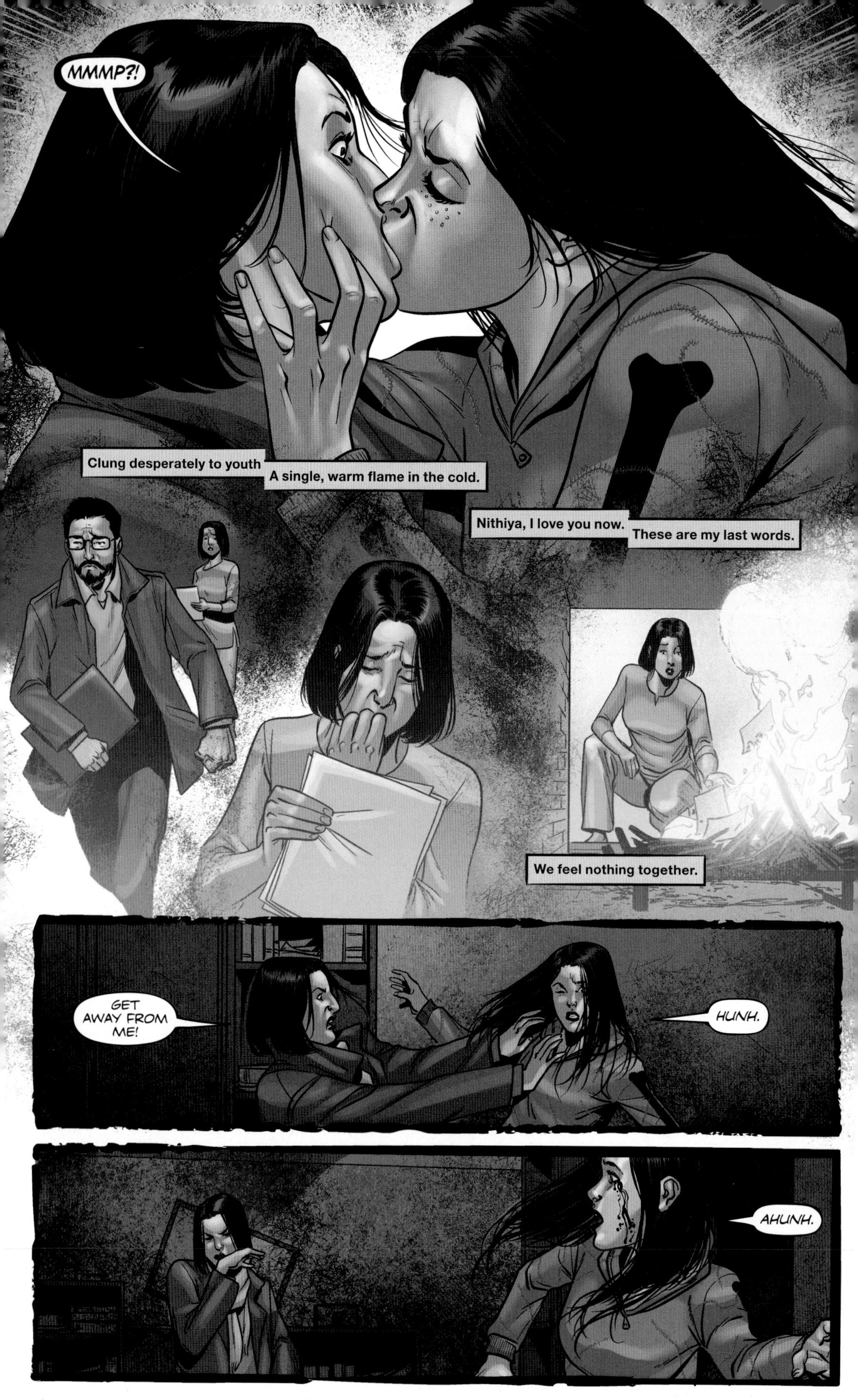
MMMP?!
Clung desperately to youth
A single, warm flame in the cold.
Nithiya, I love you now.
These are my last words.
We feel nothing together.
GET AWAY FROM ME!
HUNH.
AHUNH.

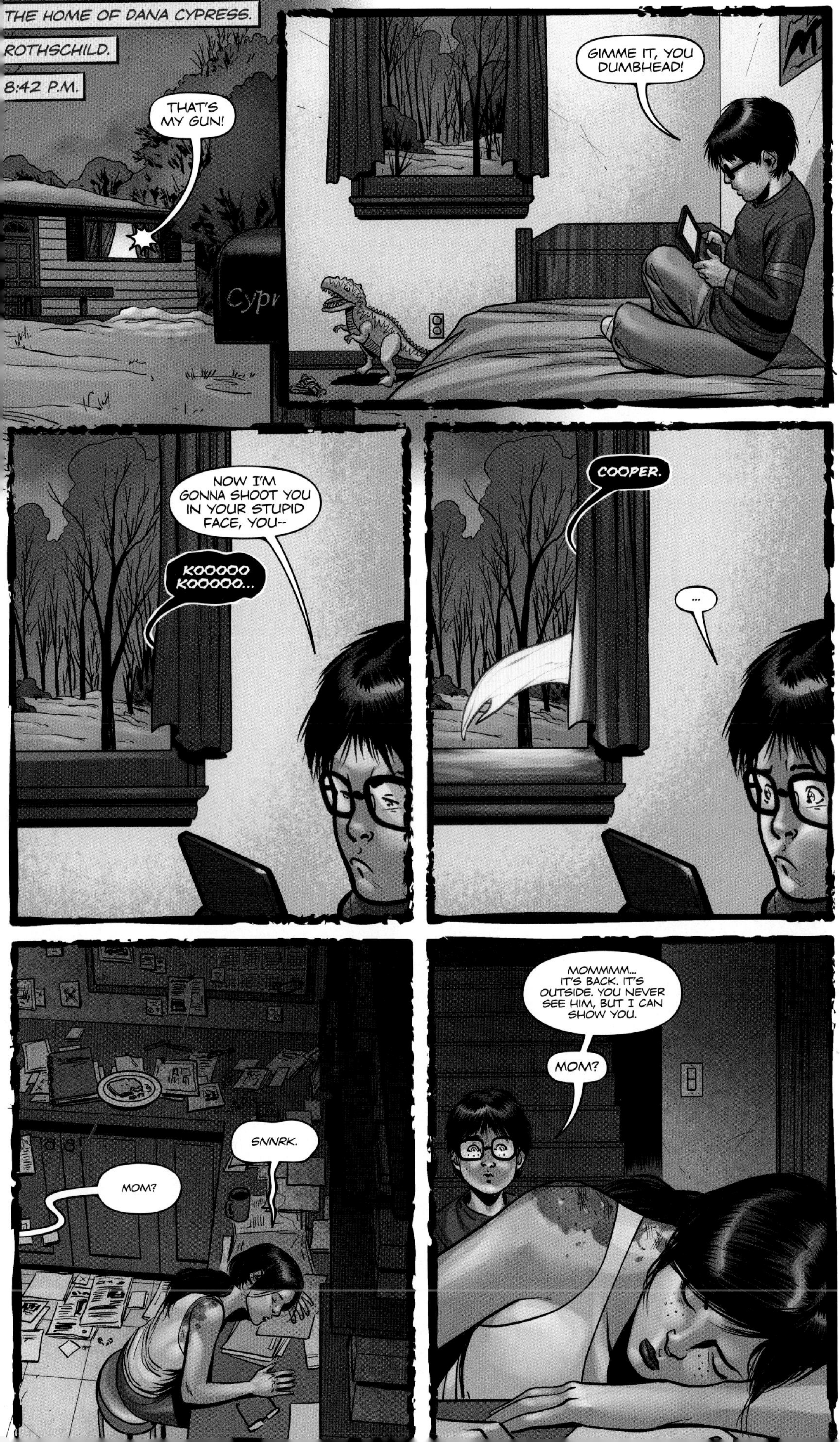
THE HOME OF DANA CYPRESS.
ROTHSCHILD.
8:42 P.M.
THAT'S MY GUN!
Cypr
GIMME IT, YOU DUMBHEAD!
NOW I'M GONNA SHOOT YOU IN YOUR STUPID FACE, YOU--
KOOOOO KOOOOO...
COOPER.
...
MOM?
SNNRK.
MOMMMM... IT'S BACK. IT'S OUTSIDE. YOU NEVER SEE HIM, BUT I CAN SHOW YOU.
MOM?

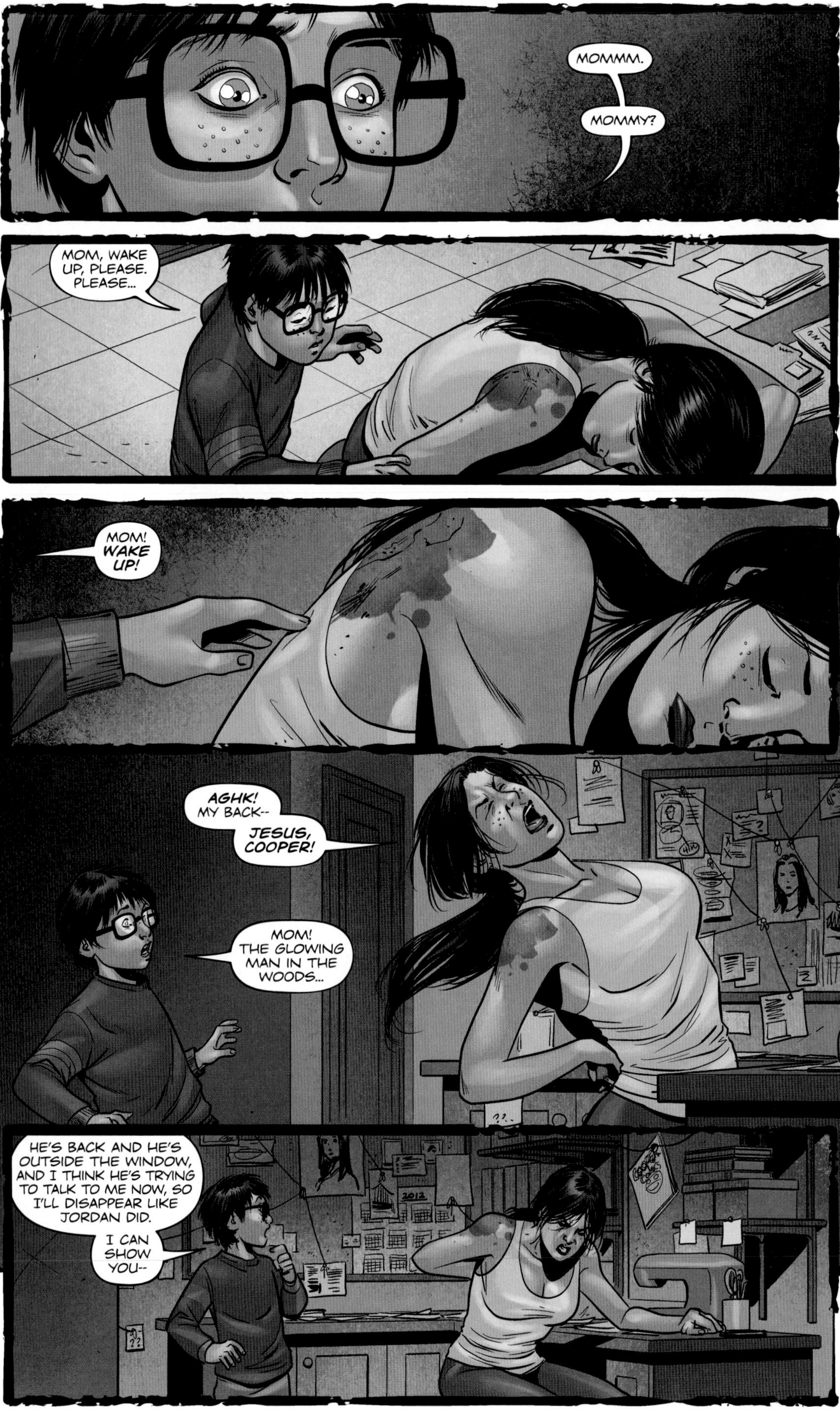
MOMMM.
MOMMY?
MOM, WAKE UP, PLEASE. PLEASE...
MOM! WAKE UP!
AGHK! MY BACK--
JESUS, COOPER!
MOM! THE GLOWING MAN IN THE WOODS...
HE'S BACK AND HE'S OUTSIDE THE WINDOW, AND I THINK HE'S TRYING TO TALK TO ME NOW, SO I'LL DISAPPEAR LIKE JORDAN DID.
I CAN SHOW YOU--

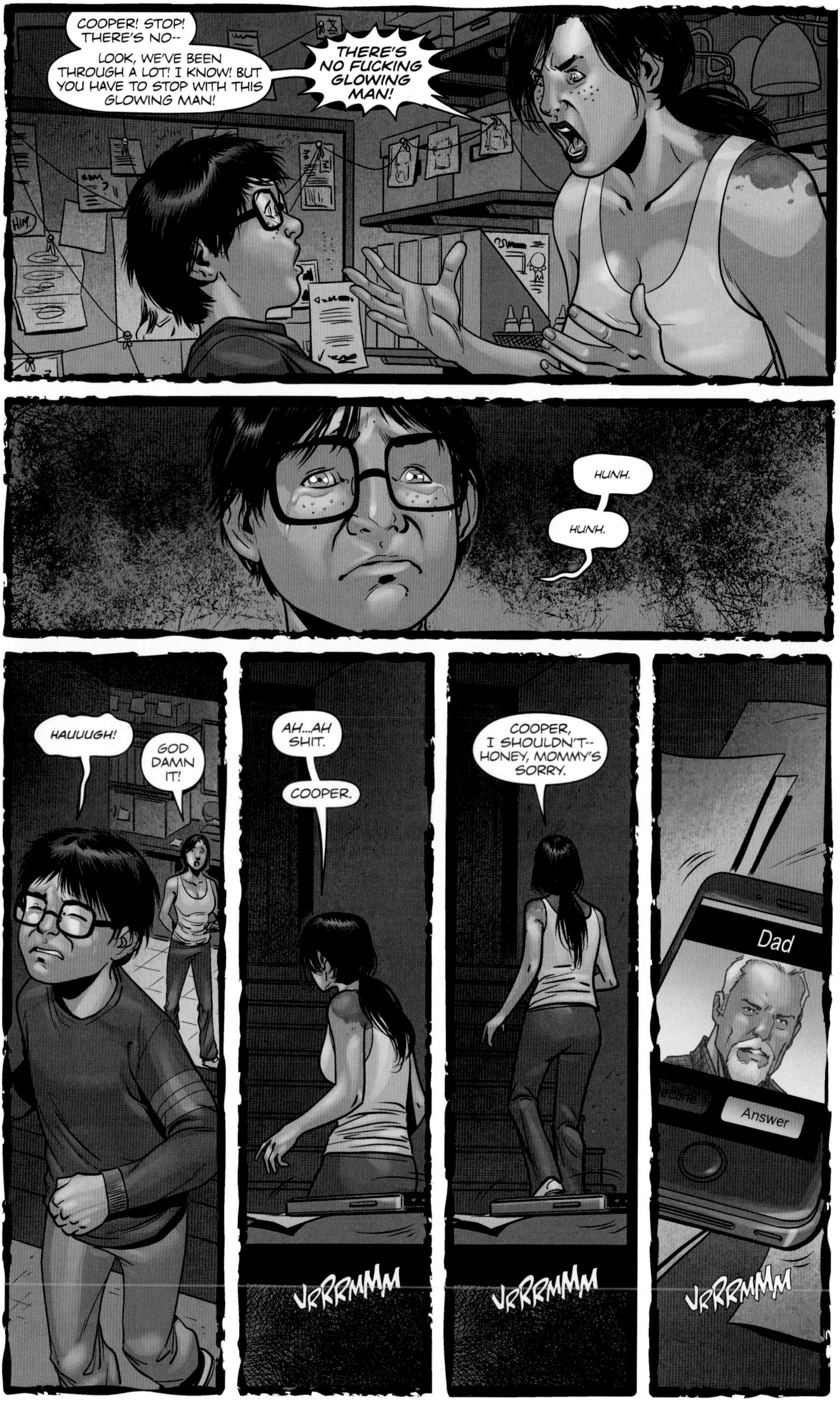

COOPER! STOP! THERE'S NO--
LOOK, WE'VE BEEN THROUGH A LOT! I KNOW! BUT YOU HAVE TO STOP WITH THIS GLOWING MAN!
THERE'S NO FUCKING GLOWING MAN!
HUNH.
HUNH.
HAUUUGH!
GOD DAMN IT!
AH...AH SHIT.
COOPER.
VRRRMMM
COOPER, I SHOULDN'T-- HONEY, MOMMY'S SORRY.
VRRRMMM
Dad
Answer
VRRRMMM

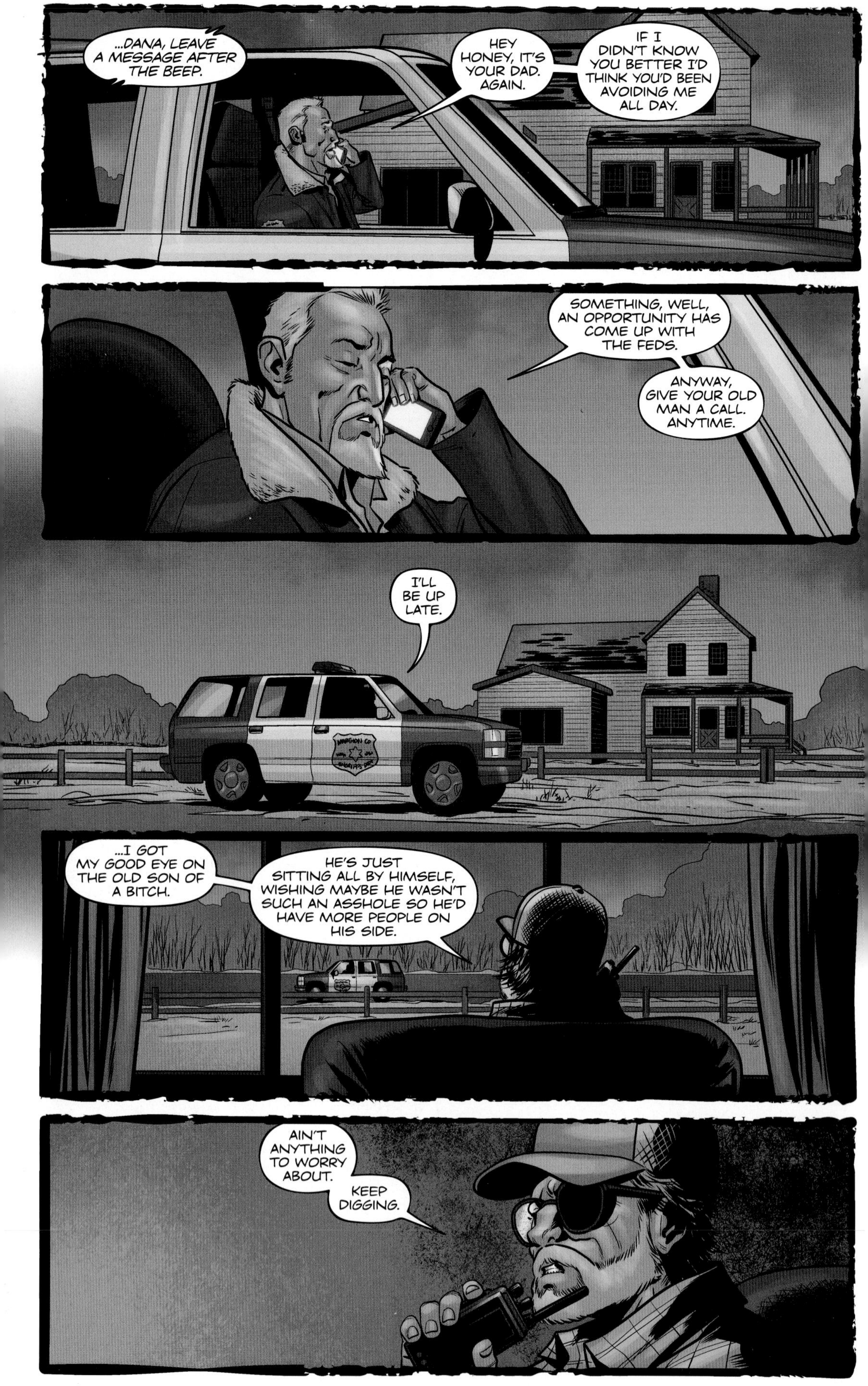
...DANA, LEAVE A MESSAGE AFTER THE BEEP.
HEY HONEY, IT'S YOUR DAD. AGAIN.
IF I DIDN'T KNOW YOU BETTER I'D THINK YOU'D BEEN AVOIDING ME ALL DAY.
SOMETHING, WELL, AN OPPORTUNITY HAS COME UP WITH THE FEDS.
ANYWAY, GIVE YOUR OLD MAN A CALL. ANYTIME.
I'LL BE UP LATE.
...I GOT MY GOOD EYE ON THE OLD SON OF A BITCH.
HE'S JUST SITTING ALL BY HIMSELF, WISHING MAYBE HE WASN'T SUCH AN ASSHOLE SO HE'D HAVE MORE PEOPLE ON HIS SIDE.
AIN'T ANYTHING TO WORRY ABOUT.
KEEP DIGGING.

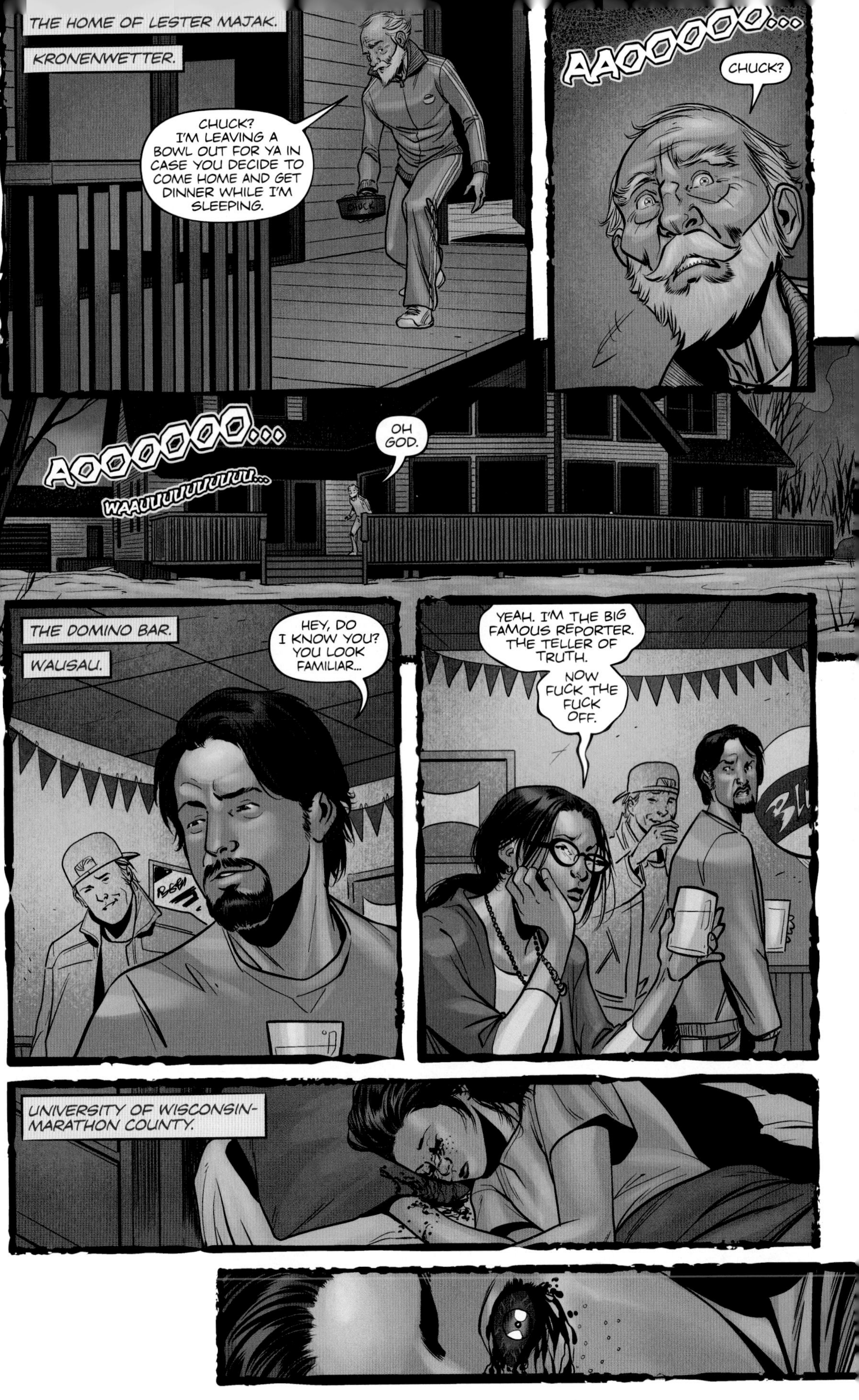
THE HOME OF LESTER MAJAK.
KRONENWETTER.
CHUCK? I'M LEAVING A BOWL OUT FOR YA IN CASE YOU DECIDE TO COME HOME AND GET DINNER WHILE I'M SLEEPING.
CHUCK
AAOOOOOO...
CHUCK?
AOOOOOOO...
WAAUUUUUUUUU...
OH GOD.
THE DOMINO BAR.
WAUSAU.
HEY, DO I KNOW YOU? YOU LOOK FAMILIAR...
YEAH. I'M THE BIG FAMOUS REPORTER. THE TELLER OF TRUTH.
NOW FUCK THE FUCK OFF.
UNIVERSITY OF WISCONSIN-MARATHON COUNTY.

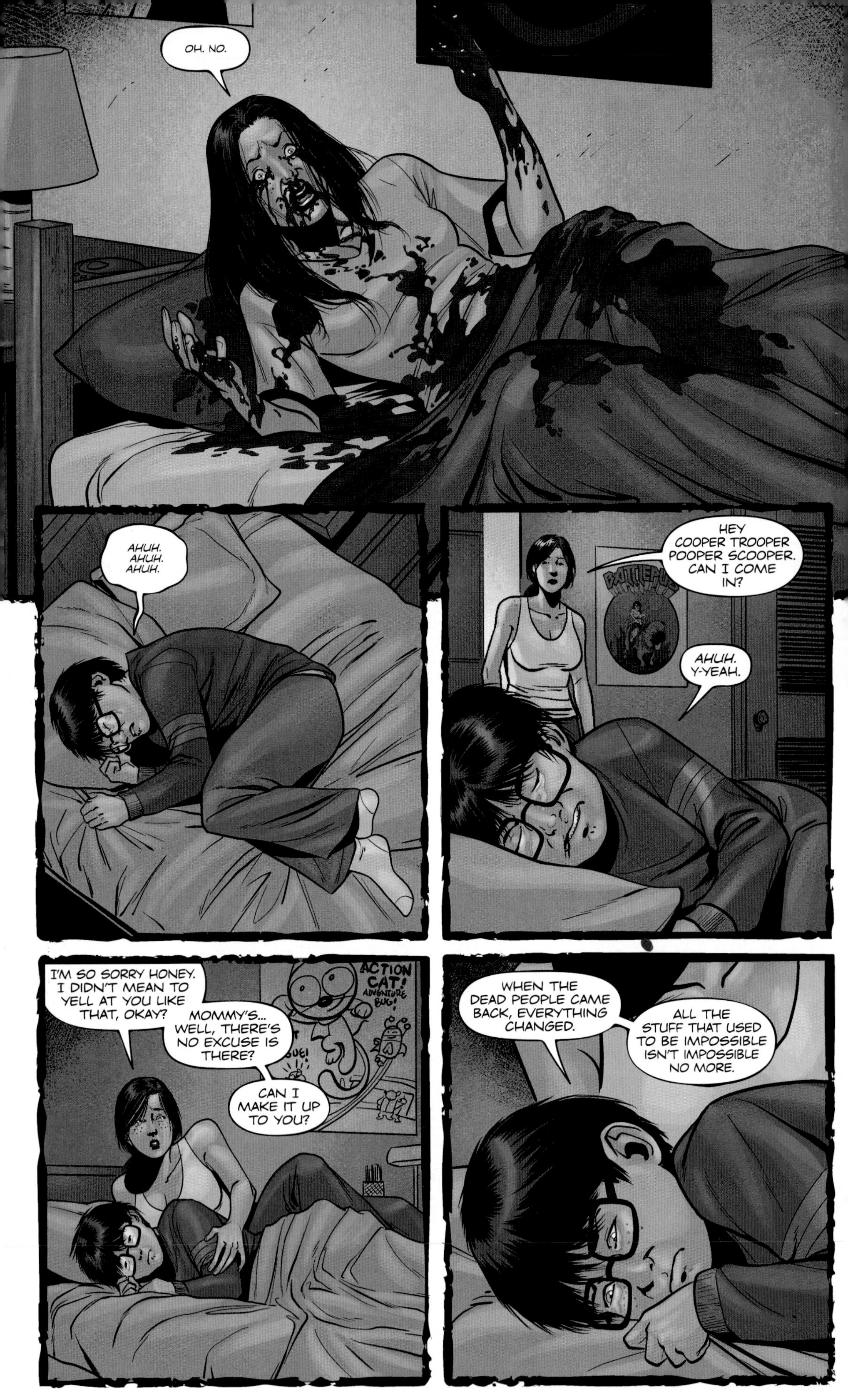
OH. NO.
AHUH. AHUH. AHUH.
HEY COOPER TROOPER POOPER SCOOPER. CAN I COME IN?
AHUH. Y-YEAH.
I'M SO SORRY HONEY. I DIDN'T MEAN TO YELL AT YOU LIKE THAT, OKAY?
MOMMY'S... WELL, THERE'S NO EXCUSE IS THERE?
CAN I MAKE IT UP TO YOU?
ACTION CAT! ADVENTURE BUG!
WHEN THE DEAD PEOPLE CAME BACK, EVERYTHING CHANGED.
ALL THE STUFF THAT USED TO BE IMPOSSIBLE ISN'T IMPOSSIBLE NO MORE.

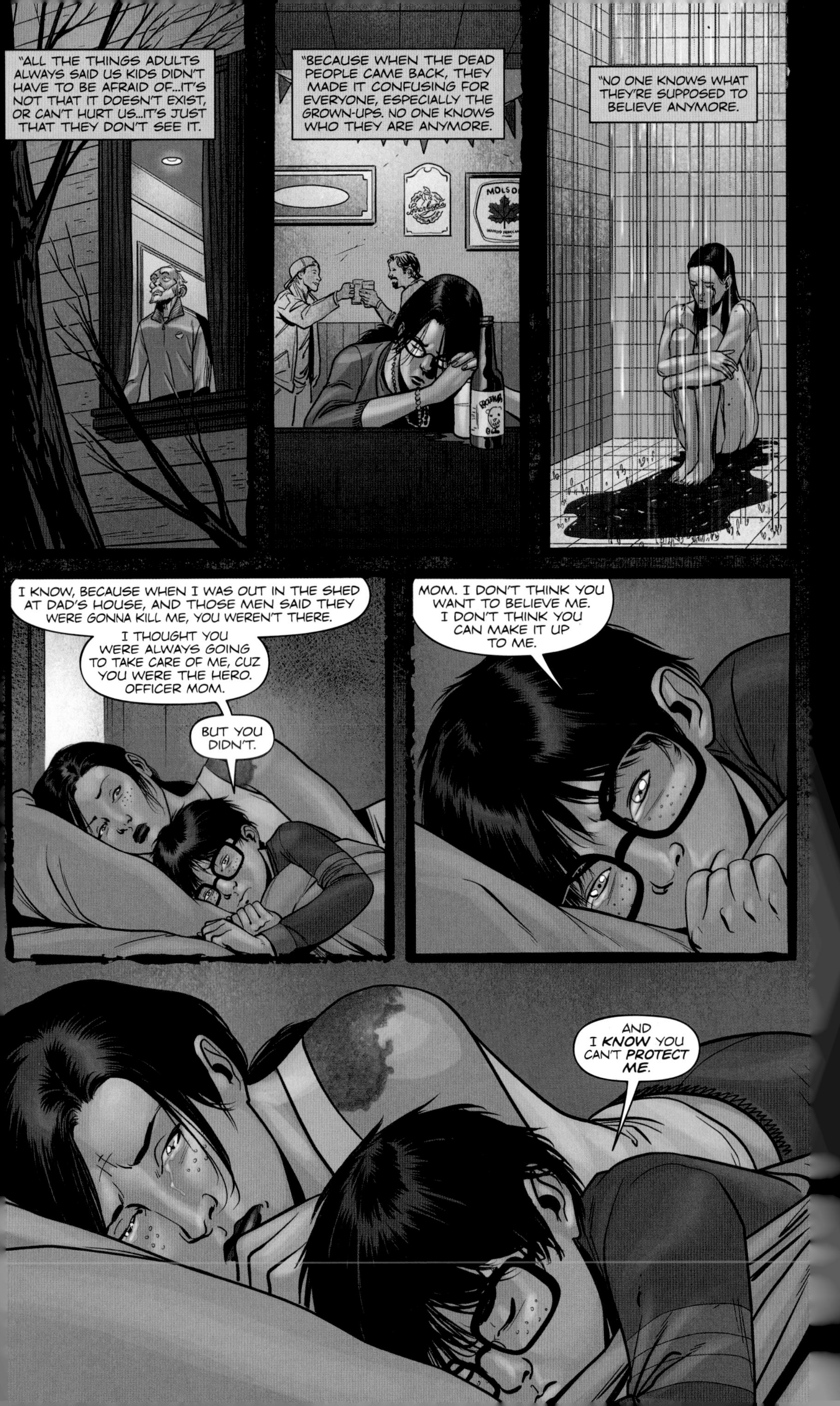

"ALL THE THINGS ADULTS ALWAYS SAID US KIDS DIDN'T HAVE TO BE AFRAID OF...IT'S NOT THAT IT DOESN'T EXIST, OR CAN'T HURT US...IT'S JUST THAT THEY DON'T SEE IT.
"BECAUSE WHEN THE DEAD PEOPLE CAME BACK, THEY MADE IT CONFUSING FOR EVERYONE, ESPECIALLY THE GROWN-UPS. NO ONE KNOWS WHO THEY ARE ANYMORE.
"NO ONE KNOWS WHAT THEY'RE SUPPOSED TO BELIEVE ANYMORE.
I KNOW, BECAUSE WHEN I WAS OUT IN THE SHED AT DAD'S HOUSE, AND THOSE MEN SAID THEY WERE GONNA KILL ME, YOU WEREN'T THERE.
I THOUGHT YOU WERE ALWAYS GOING TO TAKE CARE OF ME, CUZ YOU WERE THE HERO. OFFICER MOM.
BUT YOU DIDN'T.
MOM. I DON'T THINK YOU WANT TO BELIEVE ME. I DON'T THINK YOU CAN MAKE IT UP TO ME.
AND I **KNOW** YOU CAN'T **PROTECT ME**.

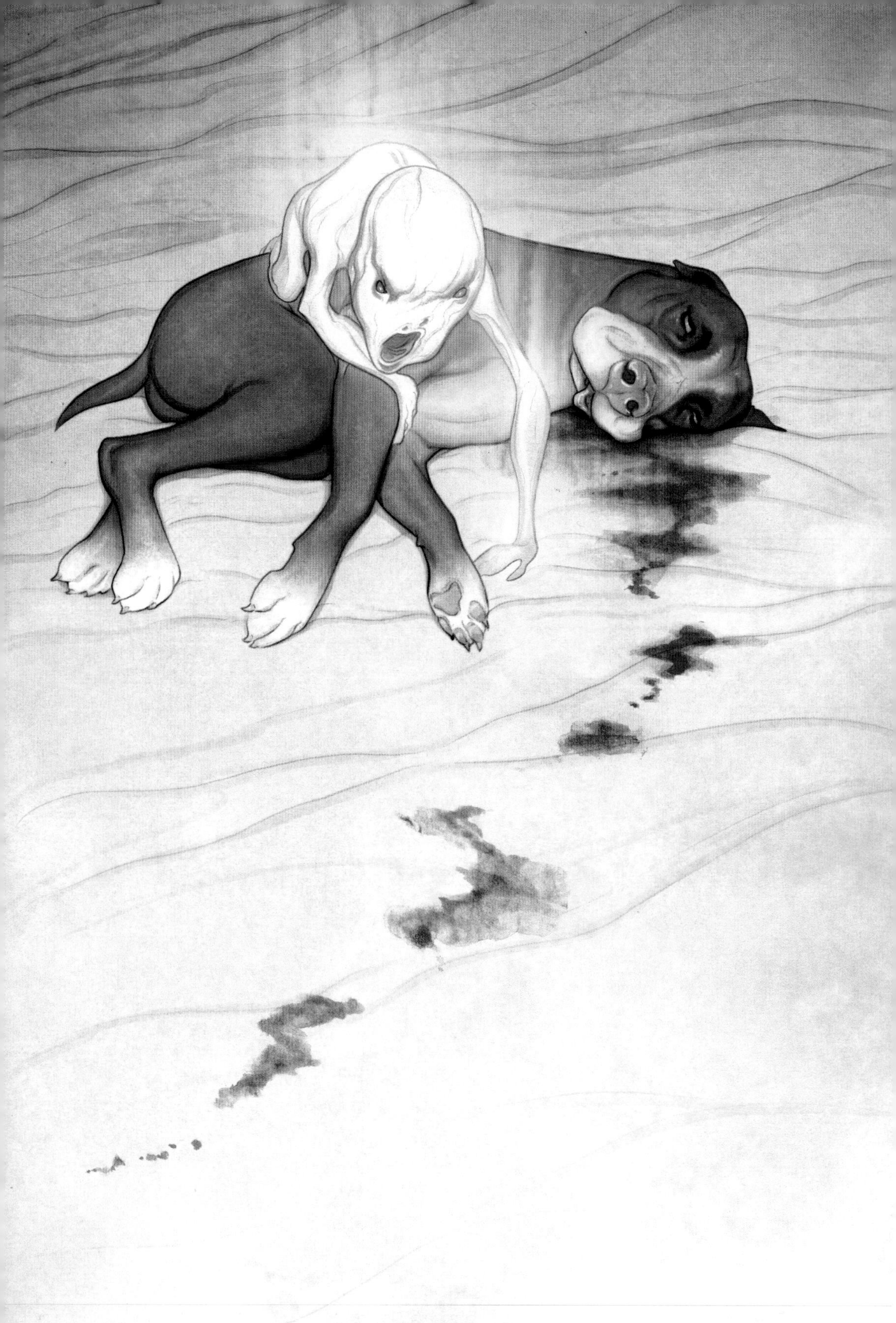

CH. 19

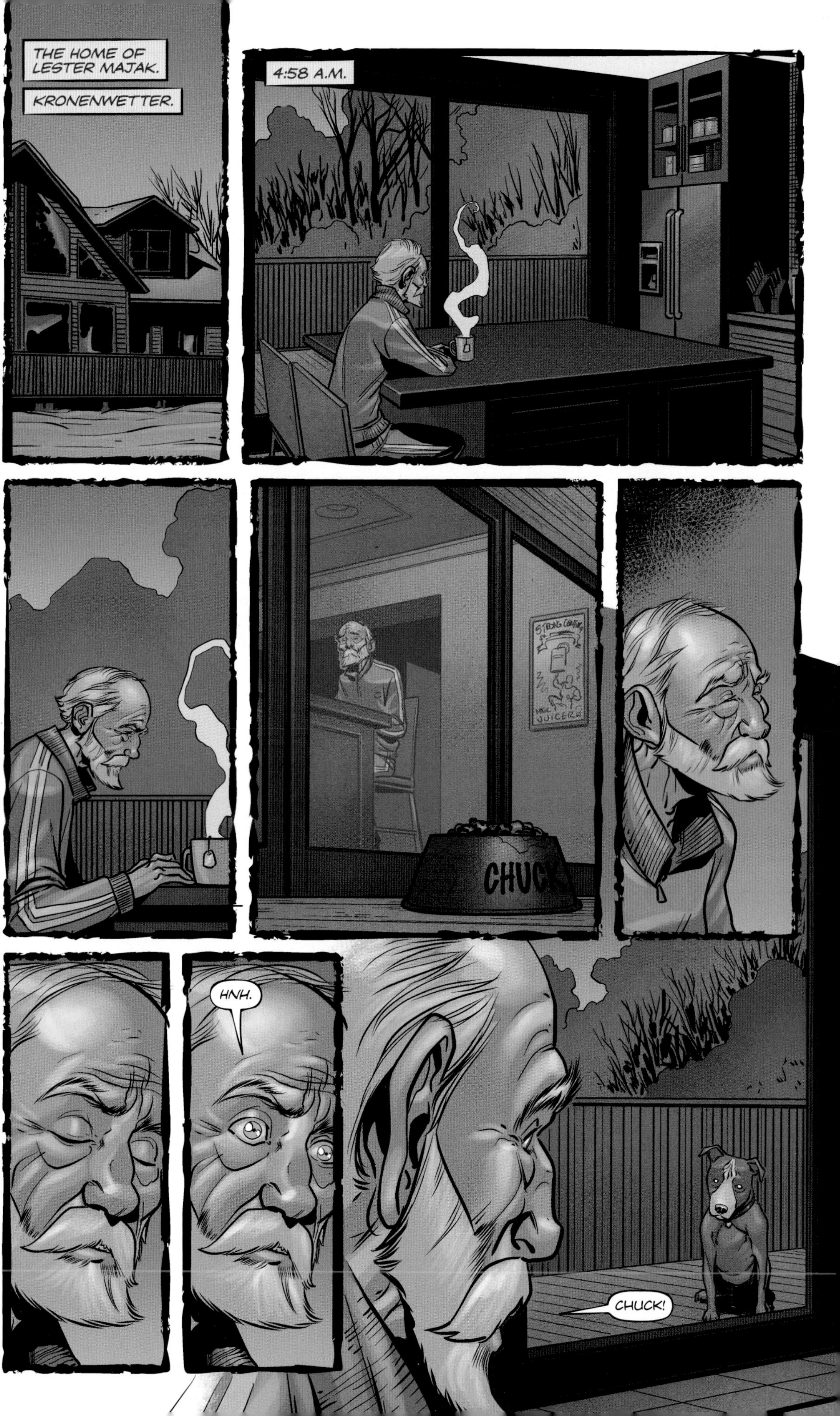

THE HOME OF LESTER MAJAK.
KRONENWETTER.
4:58 A.M.
CHUCK
HNH.
CHUCK!

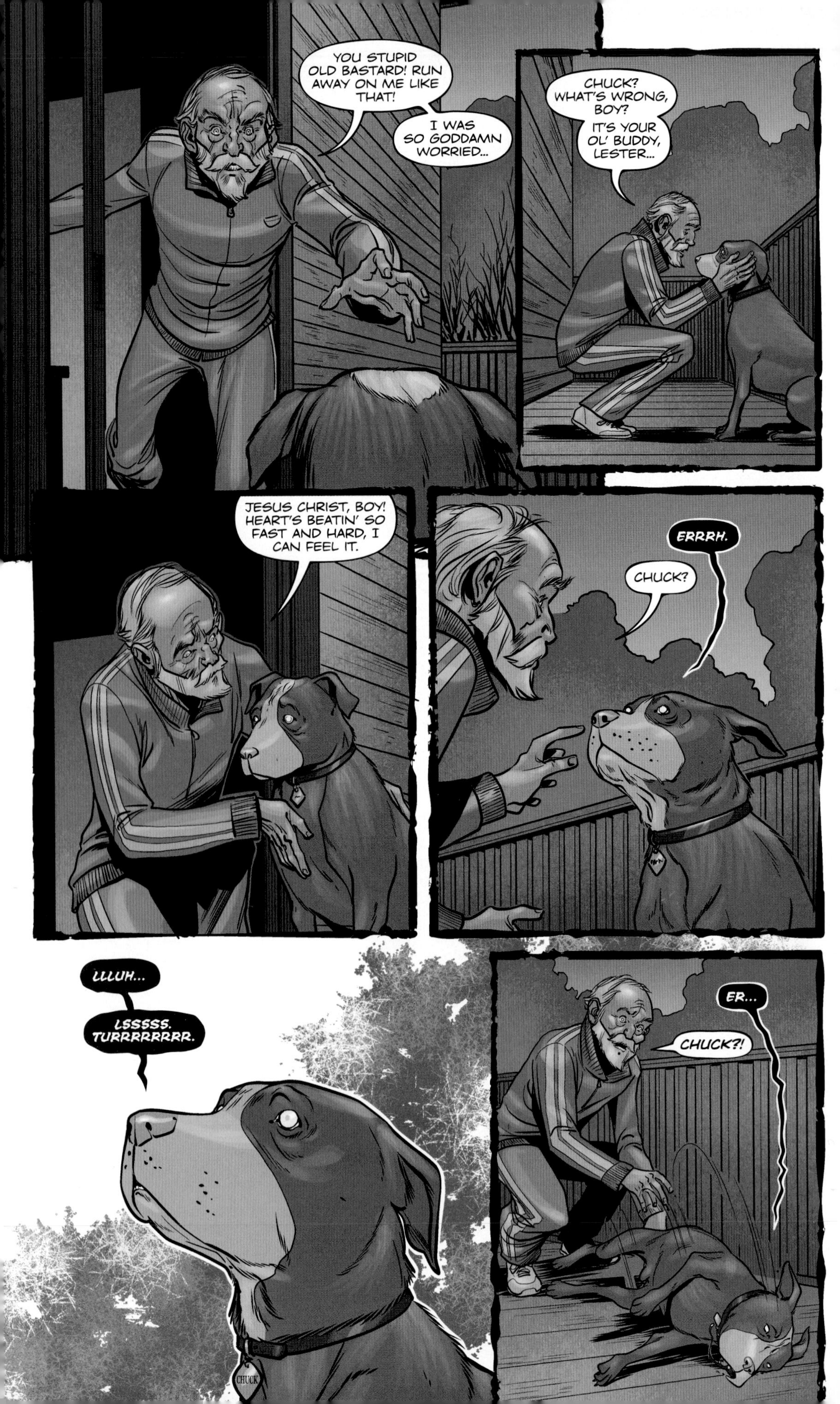
YOU STUPID OLD BASTARD! RUN AWAY ON ME LIKE THAT!
I WAS SO GODDAMN WORRIED...
CHUCK? WHAT'S WRONG, BOY?
IT'S YOUR OL' BUDDY, LESTER...
JESUS CHRIST, BOY! HEART'S BEATIN' SO FAST AND HARD, I CAN FEEL IT.
ERRRH.
CHUCK?
LLLUH...
LSSSSS. TURRRRRRRR.
CHUCK
ER...
CHUCK?!

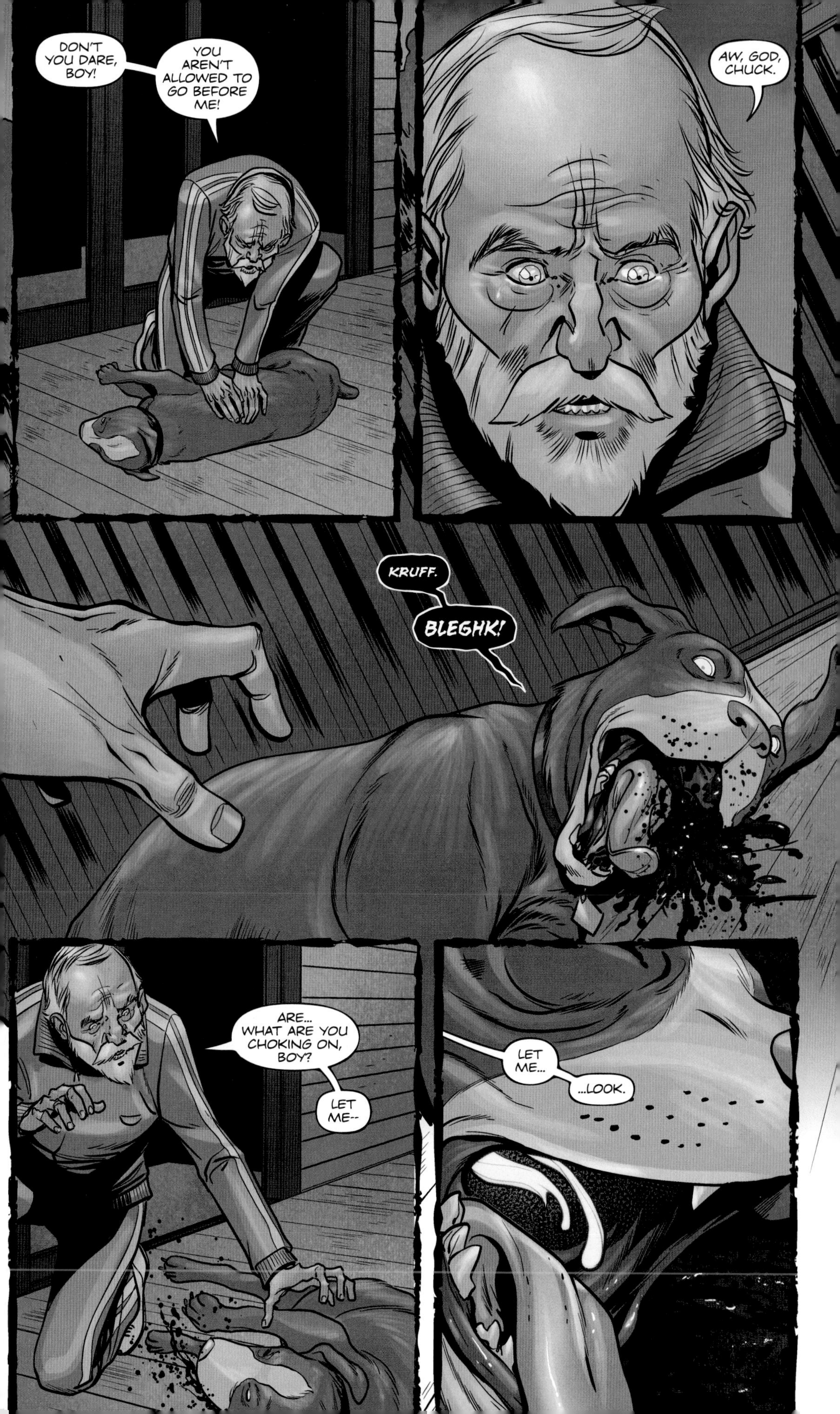
DON'T YOU DARE, BOY!
YOU AREN'T ALLOWED TO GO BEFORE ME!
AW, GOD, CHUCK.
KRUFF.
BLEGHK!
ARE... WHAT ARE YOU CHOKING ON, BOY?
LET ME--
LET ME...
...LOOK.

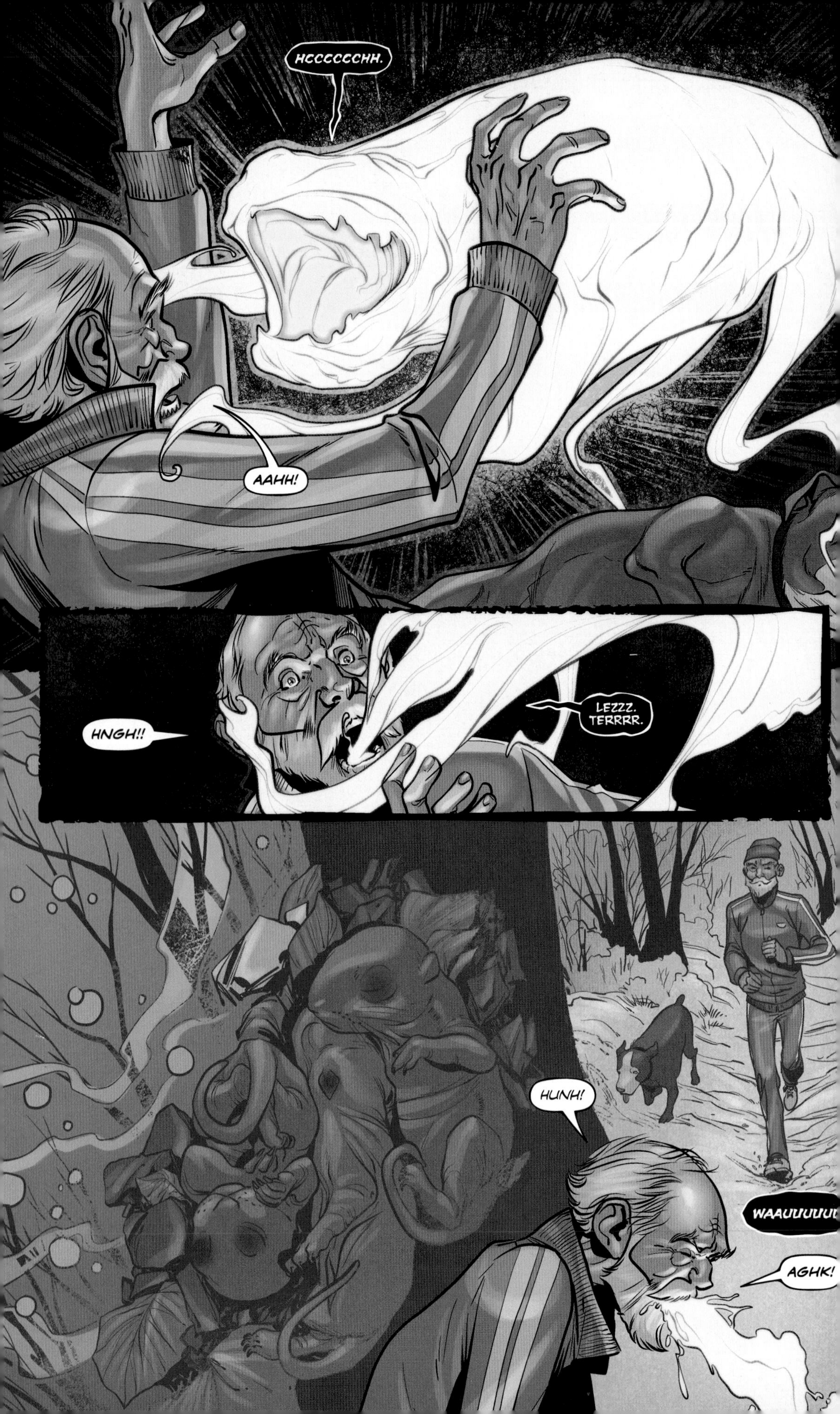
HCCCCCCHH.
AAHH!
HNGH!!
LEZZZ.
TERRRR.
HUNH!
WAAUUUUU
AGHK!

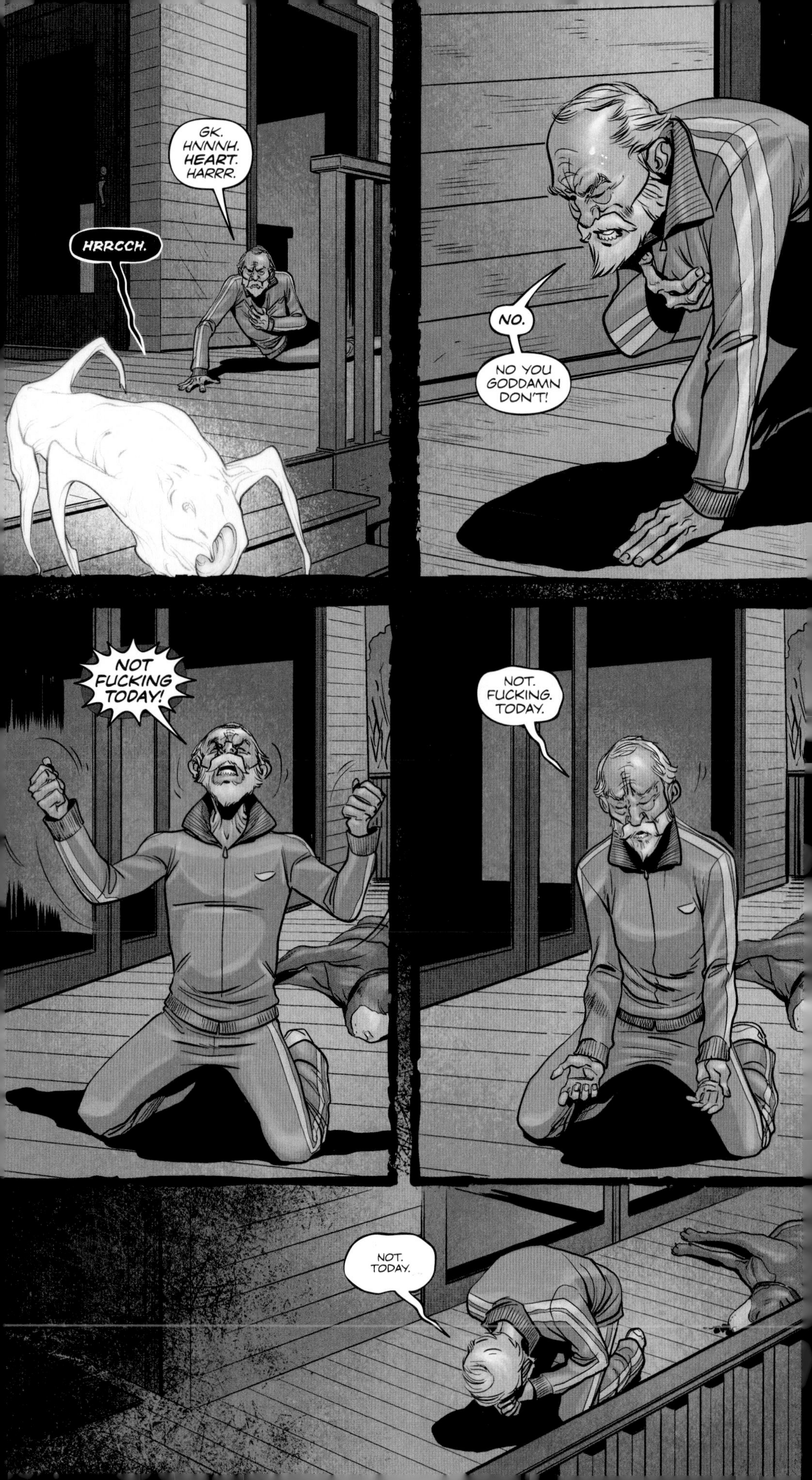
GK. HNNNH. HEART. HARRR.
HRRCCH.
NO.
NO YOU GODDAMN DON'T!
NOT FUCKING TODAY!
NOT. FUCKING. TODAY.
NOT. TODAY.

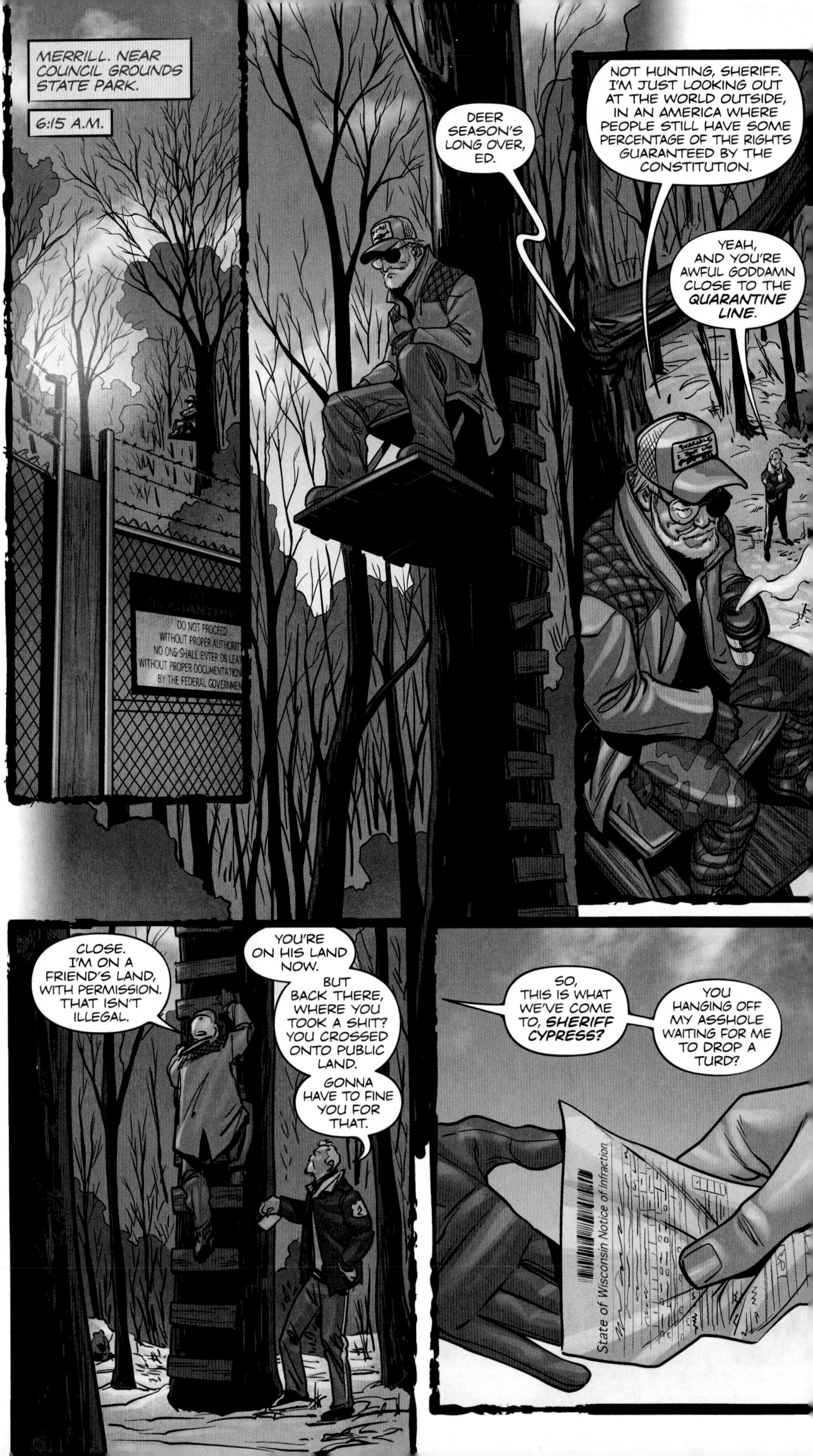
MERRILL. NEAR COUNCIL GROUNDS STATE PARK.
6:15 A.M.
DO NOT PROCEED WITHOUT PROPER AUTHORIT NO ONE SHALL ENTER OR LEAV WITHOUT PROPER DOCUMENTATION BY THE FEDERAL GOVERNMEN
DEER SEASON'S LONG OVER, ED.
NOT HUNTING, SHERIFF. I'M JUST LOOKING OUT AT THE WORLD OUTSIDE, IN AN AMERICA WHERE PEOPLE STILL HAVE SOME PERCENTAGE OF THE RIGHTS GUARANTEED BY THE CONSTITUTION.
YEAH, AND YOU'RE AWFUL GODDAMN CLOSE TO THE QUARANTINE LINE.
CLOSE. I'M ON A FRIEND'S LAND, WITH PERMISSION. THAT ISN'T ILLEGAL.
YOU'RE ON HIS LAND NOW.
BUT BACK THERE, WHERE YOU TOOK A SHIT? YOU CROSSED ONTO PUBLIC LAND.
GONNA HAVE TO FINE YOU FOR THAT.
SO, THIS IS WHAT WE'VE COME TO, SHERIFF CYPRESS?
YOU HANGING OFF MY ASSHOLE WAITING FOR ME TO DROP A TURD?
State of Wisconsin Notice of Infraction

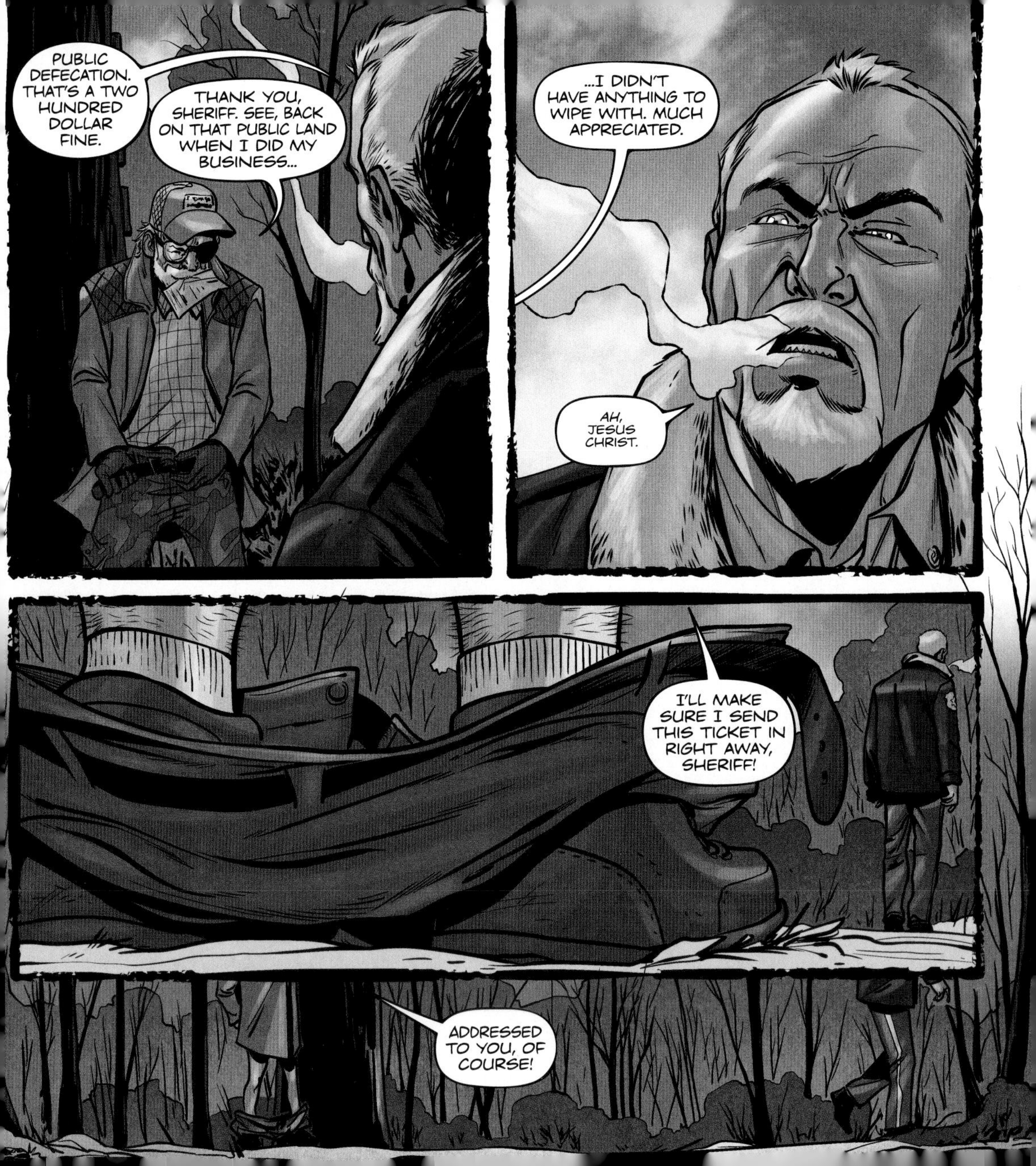
PUBLIC DEFECATION. THAT'S A TWO HUNDRED DOLLAR FINE.
THANK YOU, SHERIFF. SEE, BACK ON THAT PUBLIC LAND WHEN I DID MY BUSINESS...
...I DIDN'T HAVE ANYTHING TO WIPE WITH. MUCH APPRECIATED.
AH, JESUS CHRIST.
I'LL MAKE SURE I SEND THIS TICKET IN RIGHT AWAY, SHERIFF!
ADDRESSED TO YOU, OF COURSE!

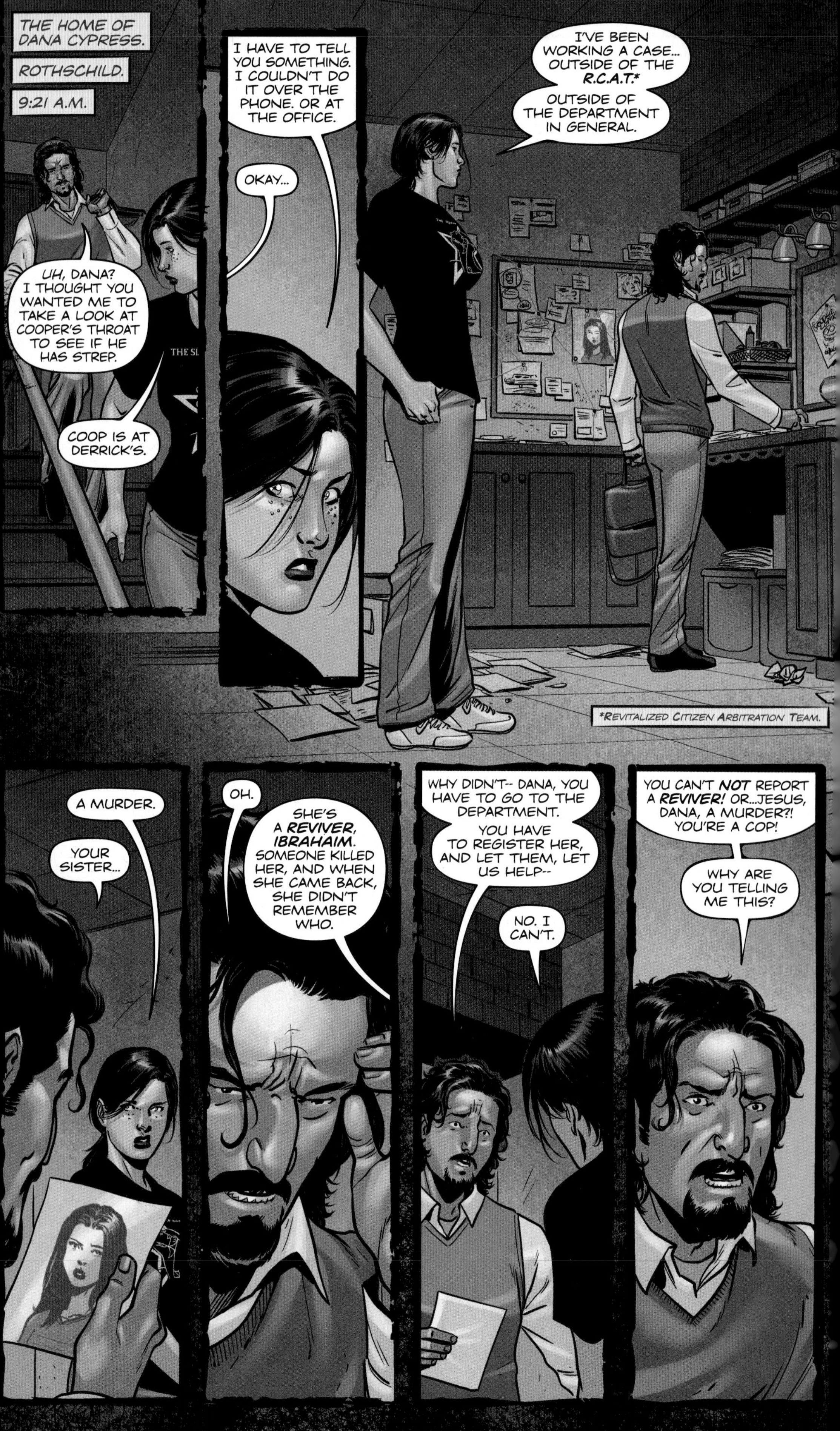
THE HOME OF DANA CYPRESS.
ROTHSCHILD.
9:21 A.M.
UH, DANA? I THOUGHT YOU WANTED ME TO TAKE A LOOK AT COOPER'S THROAT TO SEE IF HE HAS STREP.
COOP IS AT DERRICK'S.
I HAVE TO TELL YOU SOMETHING. I COULDN'T DO IT OVER THE PHONE. OR AT THE OFFICE.
OKAY...
I'VE BEEN WORKING A CASE... OUTSIDE OF THE R.C.A.T.*
OUTSIDE OF THE DEPARTMENT IN GENERAL.
*REVITALIZED CITIZEN ARBITRATION TEAM.
A MURDER.
YOUR SISTER...
OH.
SHE'S A REVIVER, IBRAHAIM. SOMEONE KILLED HER, AND WHEN SHE CAME BACK, SHE DIDN'T REMEMBER WHO.
WHY DIDN'T-- DANA, YOU HAVE TO GO TO THE DEPARTMENT.
YOU HAVE TO REGISTER HER, AND LET THEM, LET US HELP--
NO. I CAN'T.
YOU CAN'T NOT REPORT A REVIVER! OR...JESUS, DANA, A MURDER?! YOU'RE A COP!
WHY ARE YOU TELLING ME THIS?

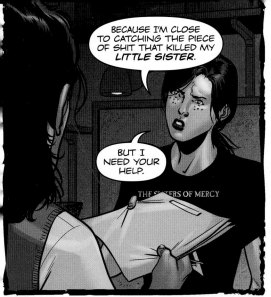

BECAUSE I'M CLOSE TO CATCHING THE PIECE OF SHIT THAT KILLED MY **LITTLE SISTER**.
BUT I NEED YOUR HELP.
THE SISTERS OF MERCY
I NEED TO FIND A MAN CREMATED ON JANUARY SECOND. ***REVIVAL DAY.*** NO NAME.
BUT A REPORT WOULD HAVE BEEN FILED BY THE ***COUNTY MEDICAL EXAMINER***, SO HE COULD REGISTER THE BODY IN THE ***UNCLAIMED PERSON*** DATABASE IN THE ***NAMUS.****
*NATIONAL MISSING AND UNIDENTIFIED PERSONS SYSTEM
YOU'VE WORKED WITH HIM. YOU HAVE ACCESS TO HIS RECORDS. I NEED YOU TO FIND OUT ANYTHING HE KNOWS ABOUT THIS MAN.
RELATIVES WHO MAY HAVE BEEN LOOKING FOR HIM. A NAME. ANYTHING. PLEASE.
GODDAMN IT, DANA! I CAN'T HELP YOU!
LOOK. YOU'RE MY PARTNER. YOU'RE...YOU'RE MY FRIEND.
BUT I'M HERE AS A BIOLOGIST FOR THE C.D.C. I HAVE TO REPORT ***ALL*** INSTANCES OF INFECTION. IT'S MY ***JOB***, DANA!
I'M SORRY.
IBRAHAIM, WAIT--
AGHK!
MERCY

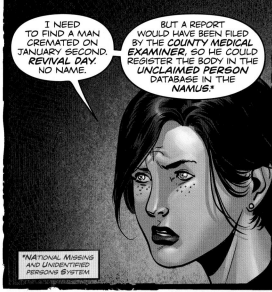

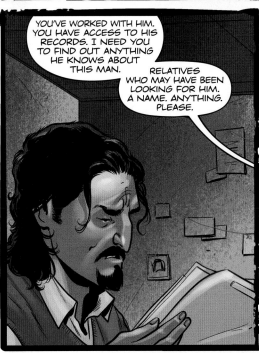

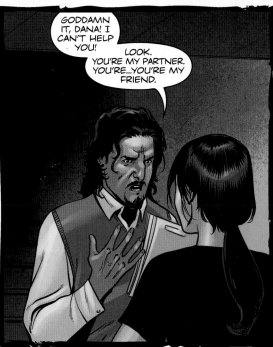

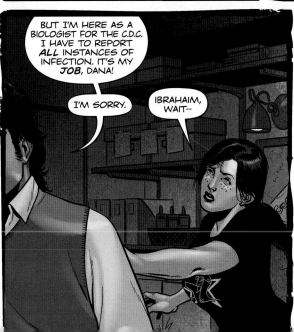

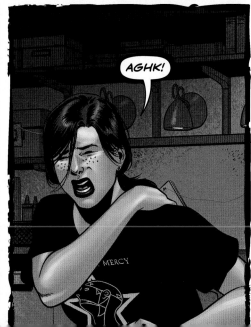

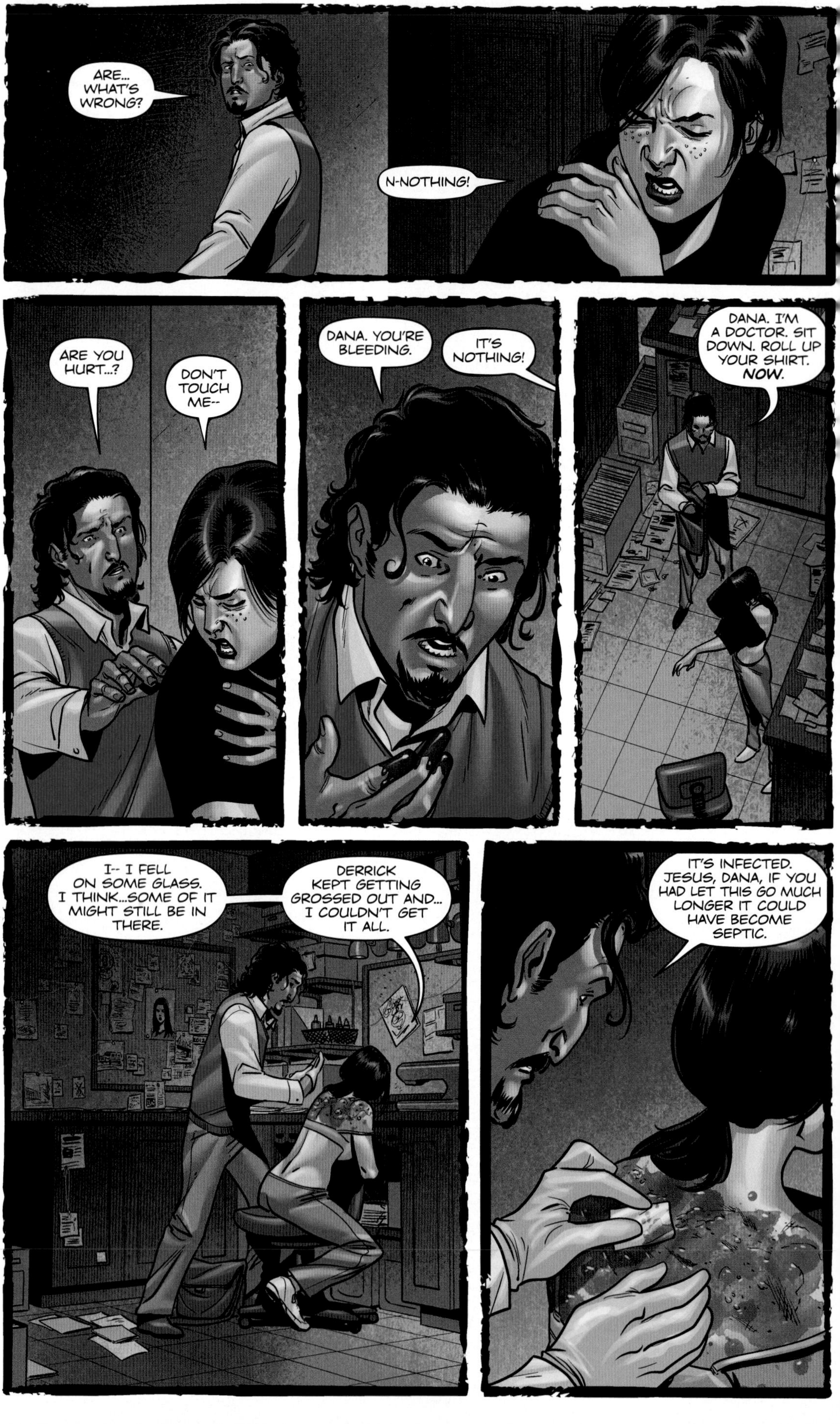

ARE... WHAT'S WRONG?
N-NOTHING!
ARE YOU HURT...?
DON'T TOUCH ME--
DANA. YOU'RE BLEEDING.
IT'S NOTHING!
DANA. I'M A DOCTOR. SIT DOWN. ROLL UP YOUR SHIRT. **NOW.**
I-- I FELL ON SOME GLASS. I THINK...SOME OF IT MIGHT STILL BE IN THERE.
DERRICK KEPT GETTING GROSSED OUT AND... I COULDN'T GET IT ALL.
IT'S INFECTED. JESUS, DANA, IF YOU HAD LET THIS GO MUCH LONGER IT COULD HAVE BECOME SEPTIC.

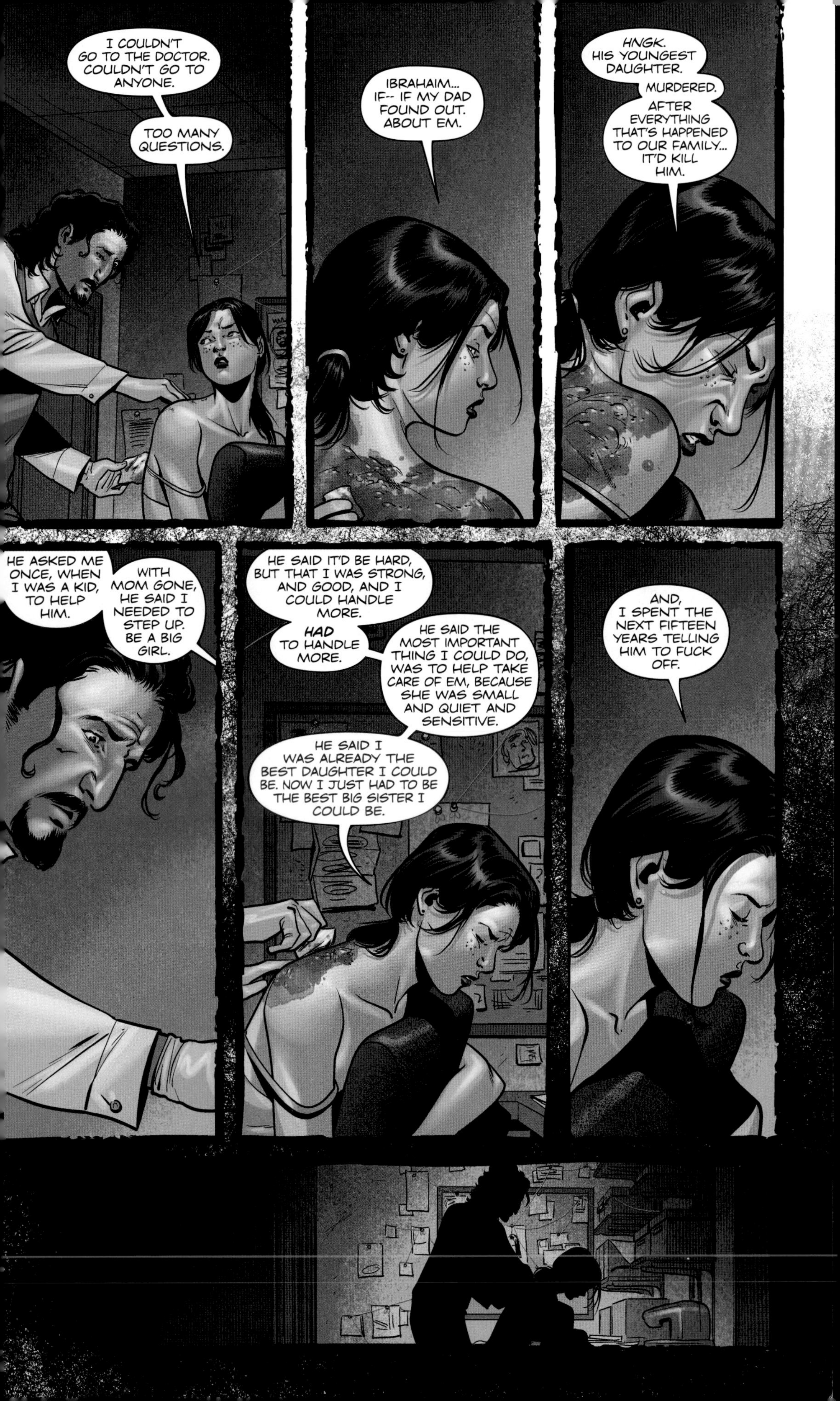

I COULDN'T GO TO THE DOCTOR. COULDN'T GO TO ANYONE.
TOO MANY QUESTIONS.
IBRAHAIM... IF-- IF MY DAD FOUND OUT. ABOUT EM.
HNGK. HIS YOUNGEST DAUGHTER.
MURDERED.
AFTER EVERYTHING THAT'S HAPPENED TO OUR FAMILY... IT'D KILL HIM.
HE ASKED ME ONCE, WHEN I WAS A KID, TO HELP HIM.
WITH MOM GONE, HE SAID I NEEDED TO STEP UP. BE A BIG GIRL.
HE SAID IT'D BE HARD, BUT THAT I WAS STRONG, AND GOOD, AND I COULD HANDLE MORE.
HAD TO HANDLE MORE.
HE SAID THE MOST IMPORTANT THING I COULD DO, WAS TO HELP TAKE CARE OF EM, BECAUSE SHE WAS SMALL AND QUIET AND SENSITIVE.
HE SAID I WAS ALREADY THE BEST DAUGHTER I COULD BE. NOW I JUST HAD TO BE THE BEST BIG SISTER I COULD BE.
AND, I SPENT THE NEXT FIFTEEN YEARS TELLING HIM TO FUCK OFF.

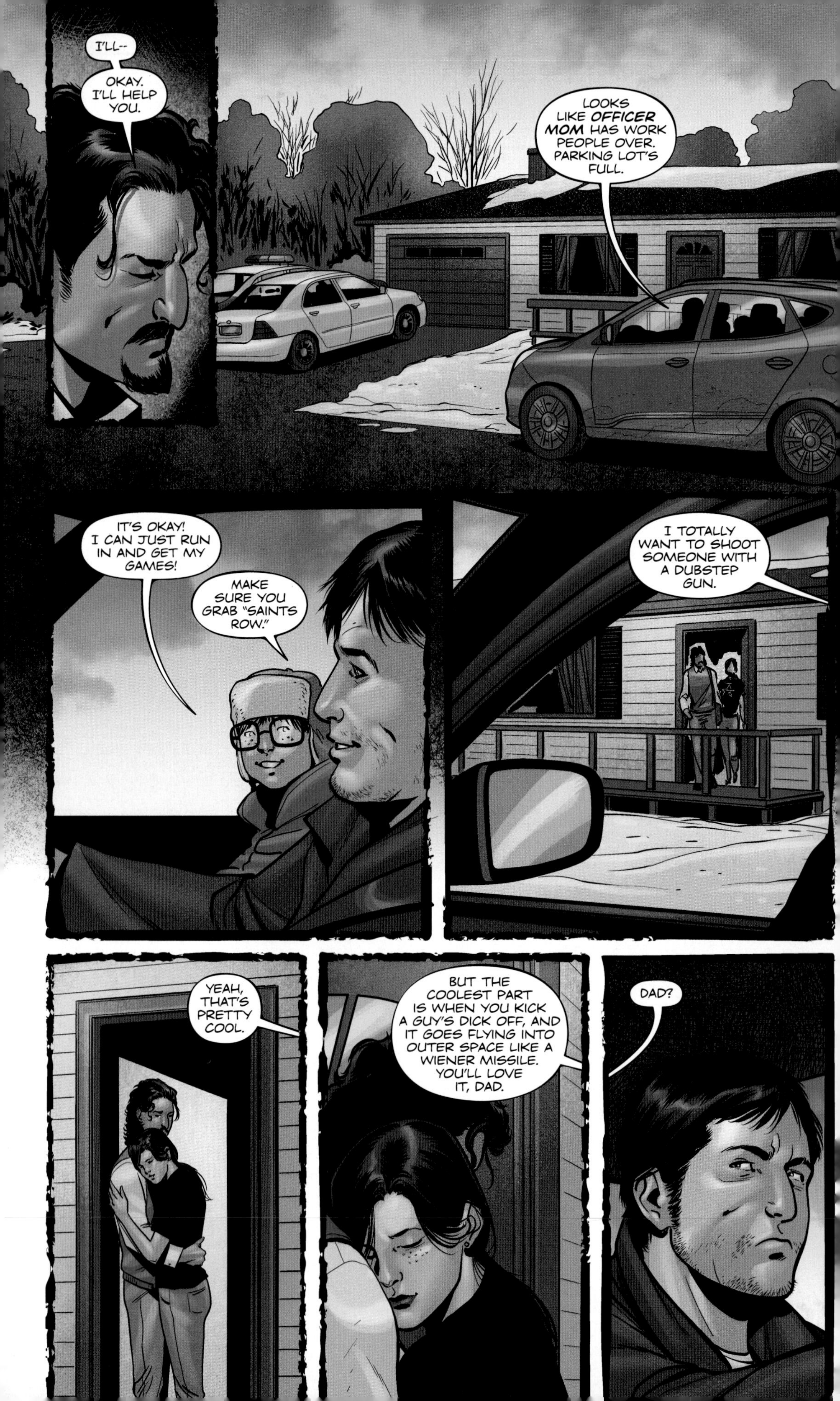
I'LL--
OKAY. I'LL HELP YOU.
LOOKS LIKE **OFFICER MOM** HAS WORK PEOPLE OVER. PARKING LOT'S FULL.
IT'S OKAY! I CAN JUST RUN IN AND GET MY GAMES!
MAKE SURE YOU GRAB "SAINTS ROW."
I TOTALLY WANT TO SHOOT SOMEONE WITH A DUBSTEP GUN.
YEAH, THAT'S PRETTY COOL.
BUT THE COOLEST PART IS WHEN YOU KICK A GUY'S DICK OFF, AND IT GOES FLYING INTO OUTER SPACE LIKE A WIENER MISSILE. YOU'LL LOVE IT, DAD.
DAD?

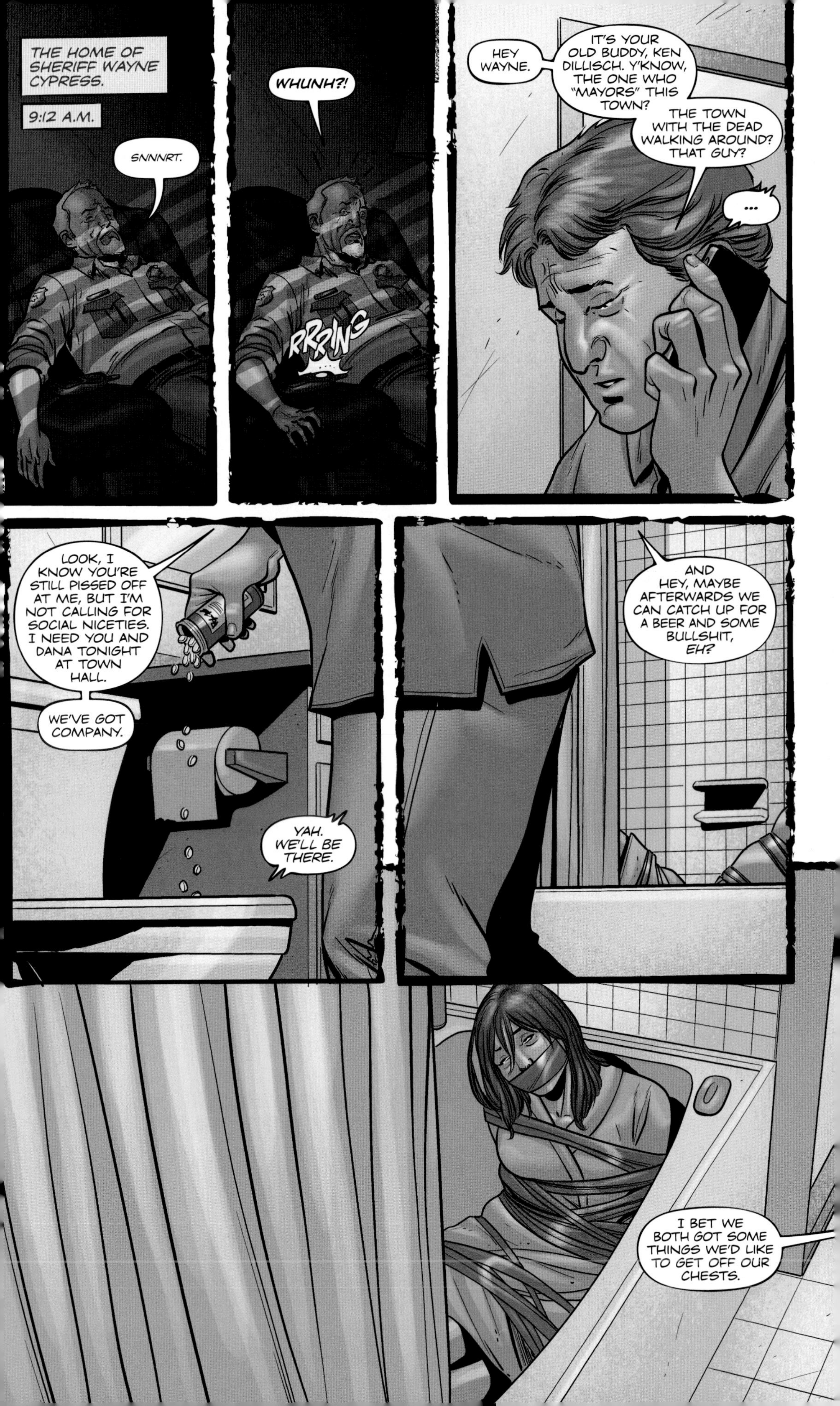
THE HOME OF SHERIFF WAYNE CYPRESS.
9:12 A.M.
SNNNRT.
WHUNH?!
RRRING
HEY WAYNE.
IT'S YOUR OLD BUDDY, KEN DILLISCH. Y'KNOW, THE ONE WHO "MAYORS" THIS TOWN?
THE TOWN WITH THE DEAD WALKING AROUND? THAT GUY?
...
LOOK, I KNOW YOU'RE STILL PISSED OFF AT ME, BUT I'M NOT CALLING FOR SOCIAL NICETIES. I NEED YOU AND DANA TONIGHT AT TOWN HALL.
WE'VE GOT COMPANY.
YAH. WE'LL BE THERE.
AND HEY, MAYBE AFTERWARDS WE CAN CATCH UP FOR A BEER AND SOME BULLSHIT, EH?
I BET WE BOTH GOT SOME THINGS WE'D LIKE TO GET OFF OUR CHESTS.

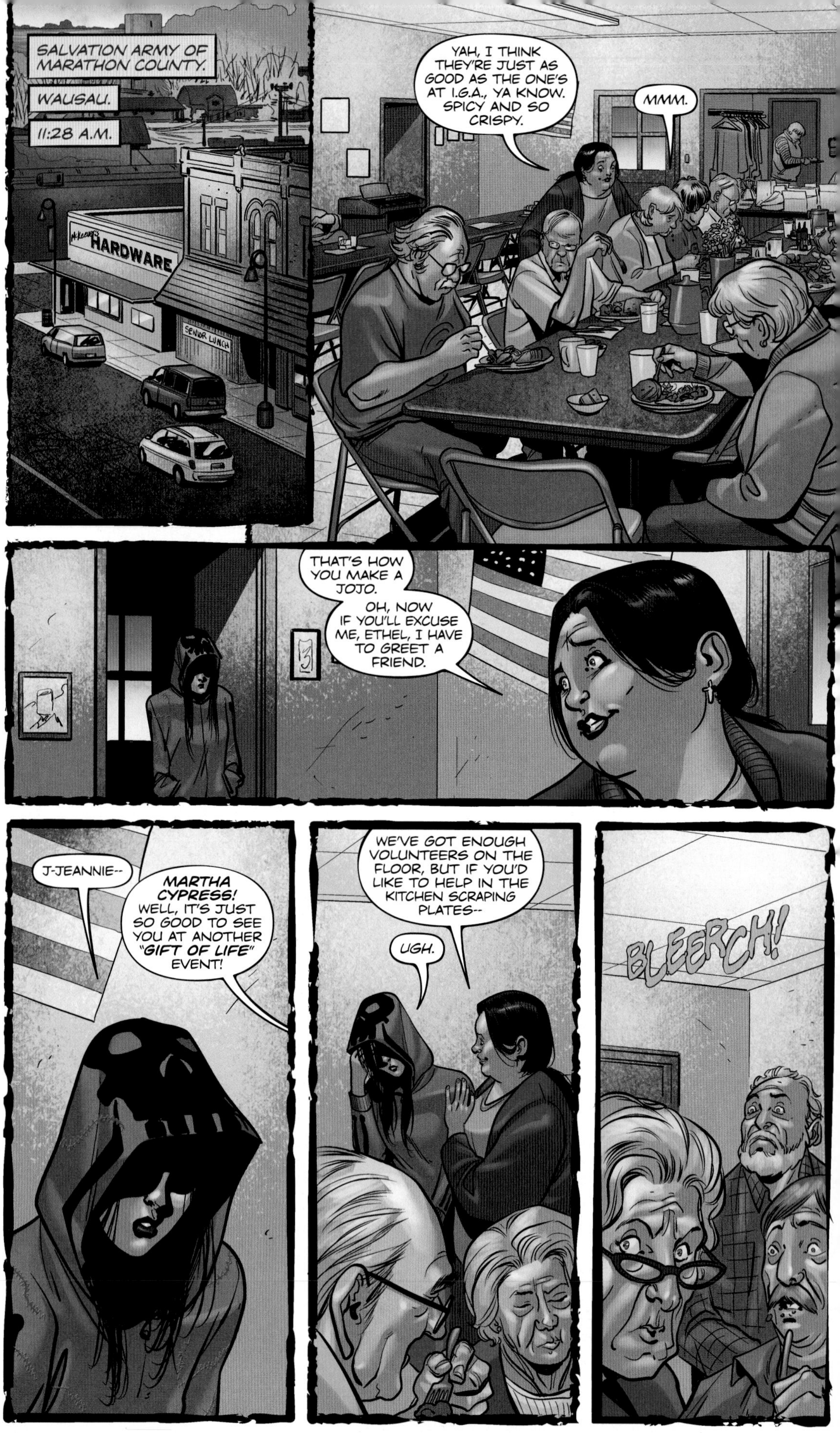
SALVATION ARMY OF MARATHON COUNTY.
WAUSAU.
11:28 A.M.
HARDWARE
SENIOR LUNCH
YAH, I THINK THEY'RE JUST AS GOOD AS THE ONE'S AT I.G.A., YA KNOW. SPICY AND SO CRISPY.
MMM.
THAT'S HOW YOU MAKE A JOJO.
OH, NOW IF YOU'LL EXCUSE ME, ETHEL, I HAVE TO GREET A FRIEND.
J-JEANNIE--
MARTHA CYPRESS! WELL, IT'S JUST SO GOOD TO SEE YOU AT ANOTHER "GIFT OF LIFE" EVENT!
WE'VE GOT ENOUGH VOLUNTEERS ON THE FLOOR, BUT IF YOU'D LIKE TO HELP IN THE KITCHEN SCRAPING PLATES--
UGH.
BLEERCH!

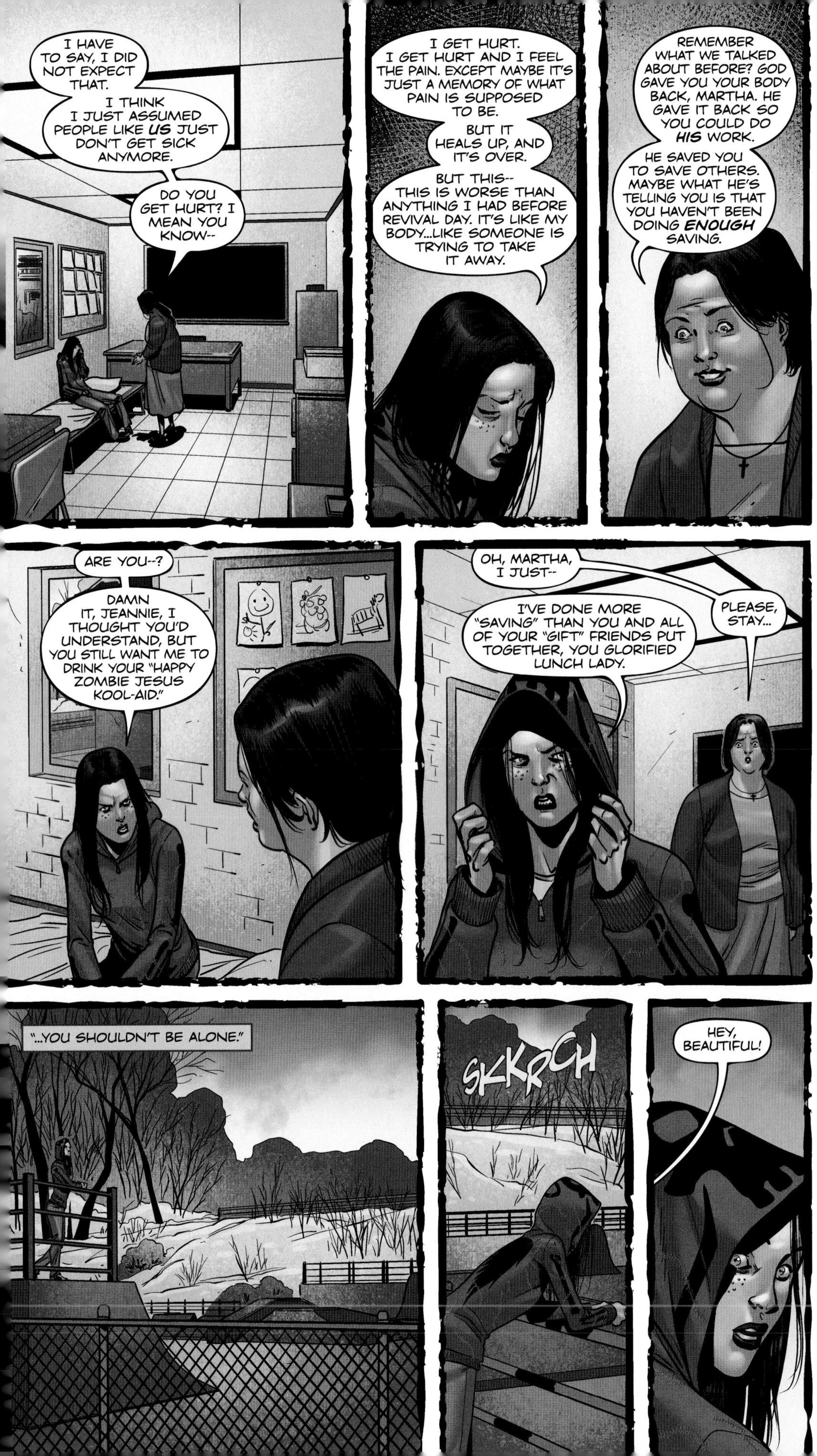
I HAVE TO SAY, I DID NOT EXPECT THAT.
I THINK I JUST ASSUMED PEOPLE LIKE US JUST DON'T GET SICK ANYMORE.
DO YOU GET HURT? I MEAN YOU KNOW--
I GET HURT. I GET HURT AND I FEEL THE PAIN. EXCEPT MAYBE IT'S JUST A MEMORY OF WHAT PAIN IS SUPPOSED TO BE.
BUT IT HEALS UP, AND IT'S OVER.
BUT THIS-- THIS IS WORSE THAN ANYTHING I HAD BEFORE REVIVAL DAY. IT'S LIKE MY BODY...LIKE SOMEONE IS TRYING TO TAKE IT AWAY.
REMEMBER WHAT WE TALKED ABOUT BEFORE? GOD GAVE YOU YOUR BODY BACK, MARTHA. HE GAVE IT BACK SO YOU COULD DO HIS WORK.
HE SAVED YOU TO SAVE OTHERS. MAYBE WHAT HE'S TELLING YOU IS THAT YOU HAVEN'T BEEN DOING ENOUGH SAVING.
ARE YOU--?
DAMN IT, JEANNIE, I THOUGHT YOU'D UNDERSTAND, BUT YOU STILL WANT ME TO DRINK YOUR "HAPPY ZOMBIE JESUS KOOL-AID."
OH, MARTHA, I JUST--
I'VE DONE MORE "SAVING" THAN YOU AND ALL OF YOUR "GIFT" FRIENDS PUT TOGETHER, YOU GLORIFIED LUNCH LADY.
PLEASE, STAY...
"...YOU SHOULDN'T BE ALONE."
SKKRCH
HEY, BEAUTIFUL!

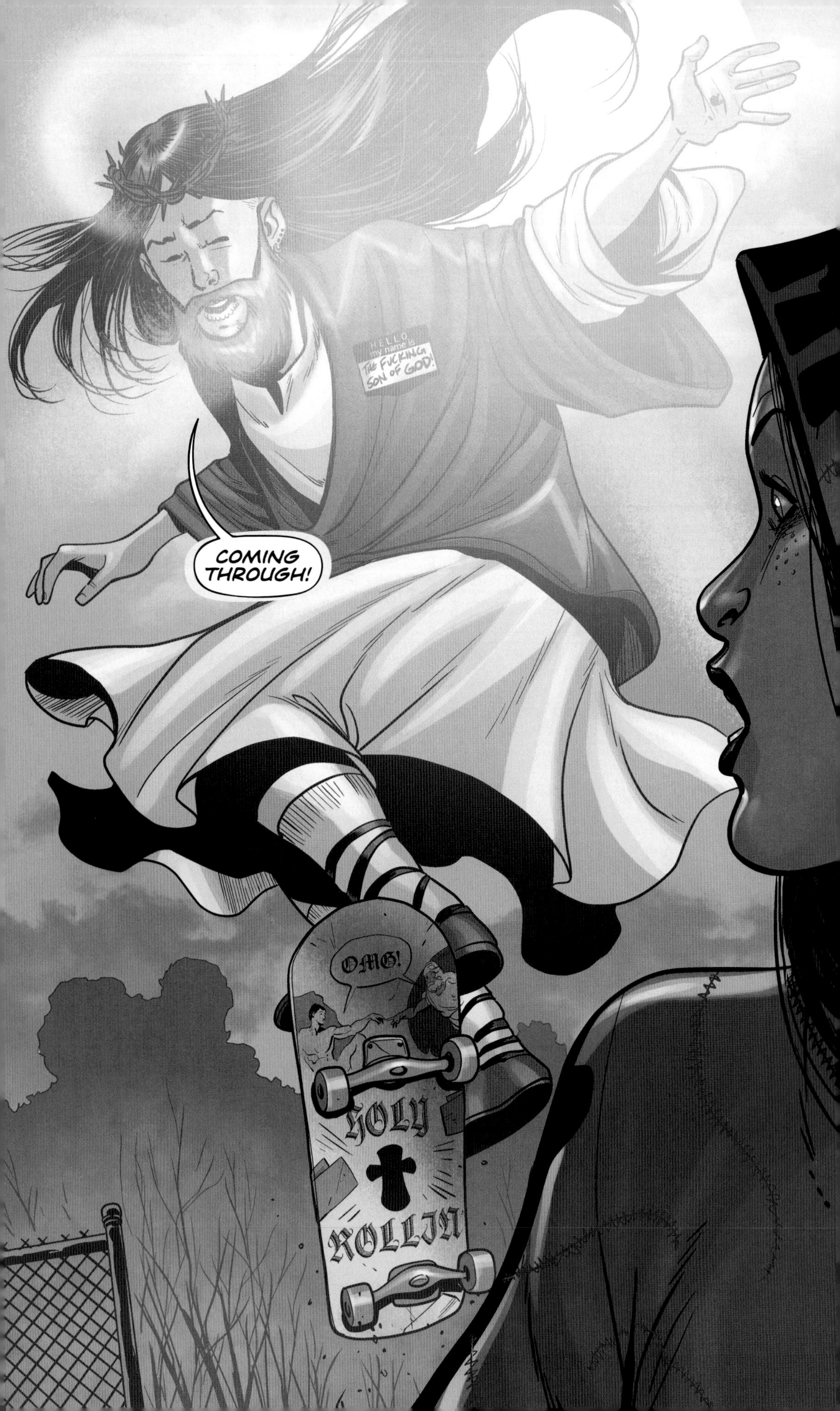
HELLO
my name is
THE FUCKING SON OF GOD!
COMING THROUGH!
OMG!
HOLY
ROLLIN

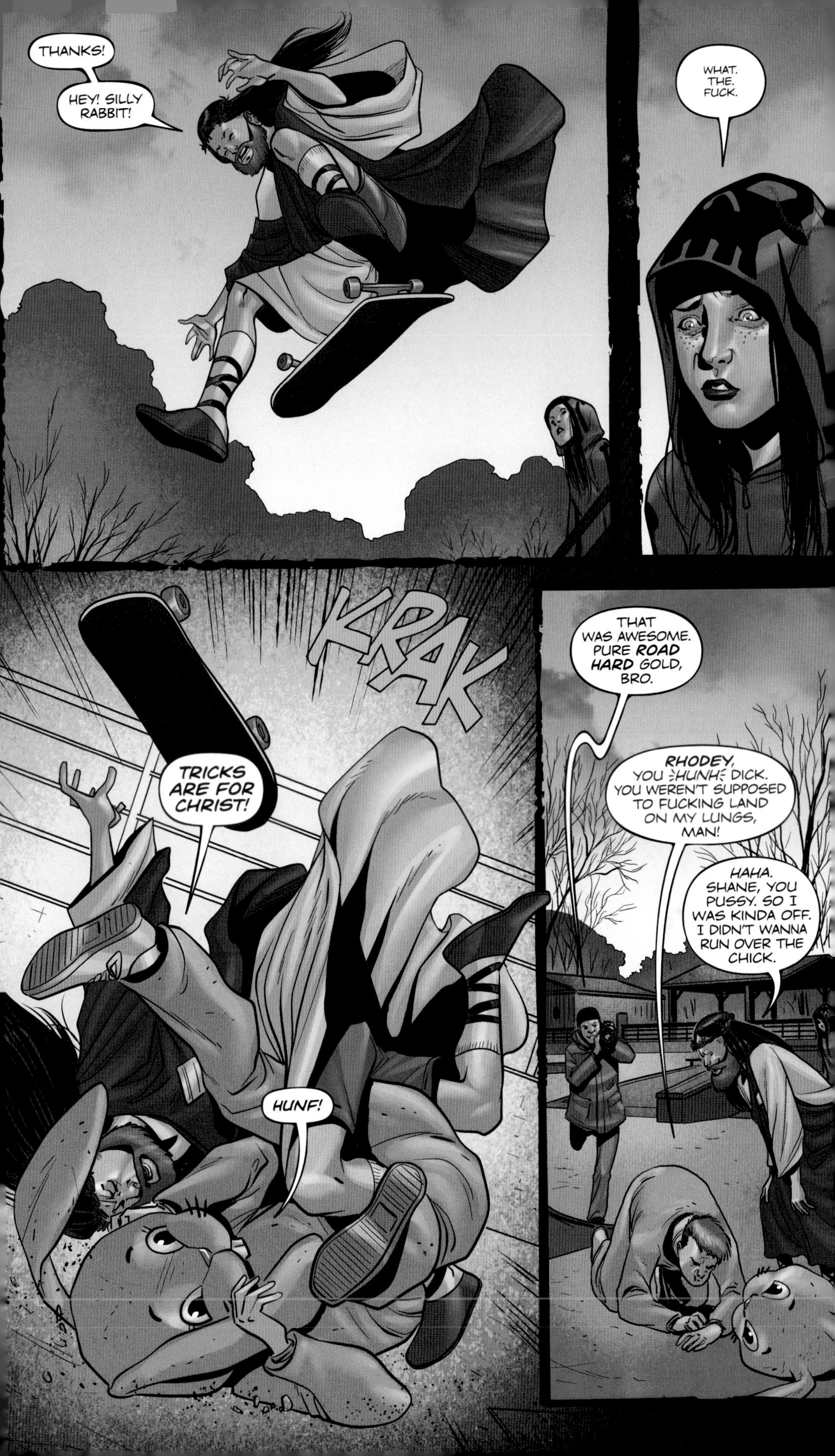
THANKS!
HEY! SILLY RABBIT!
WHAT. THE. FUCK.
KRAK
TRICKS ARE FOR CHRIST!
HUNF!
THAT WAS AWESOME. PURE **ROAD HARD** GOLD, BRO.
RHODEY, YOU ~HUNH~ DICK. YOU WEREN'T SUPPOSED TO FUCKING LAND ON MY LUNGS, MAN!
HAHA. SHANE, YOU PUSSY. SO I WAS KINDA OFF. I DIDN'T WANNA RUN OVER THE CHICK.

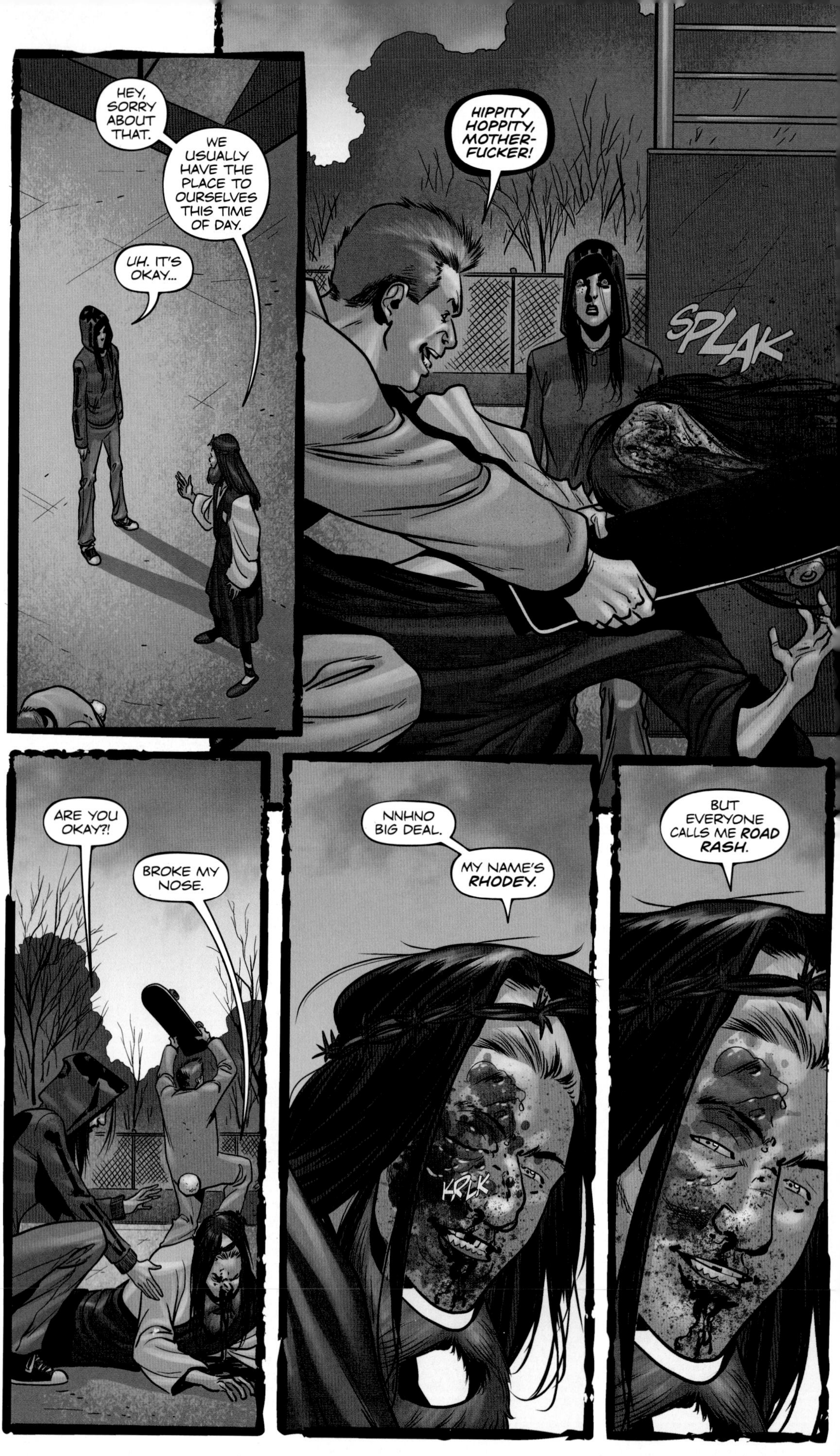
HEY, SORRY ABOUT THAT.
WE USUALLY HAVE THE PLACE TO OURSELVES THIS TIME OF DAY.
UH. IT'S OKAY...
HIPPITY HOPPITY, MOTHER-FUCKER!
SPLAK
ARE YOU OKAY?!
BROKE MY NOSE.
NNHNO BIG DEAL.
MY NAME'S RHODEY.
KRLK
BUT EVERYONE CALLS ME ROAD RASH.

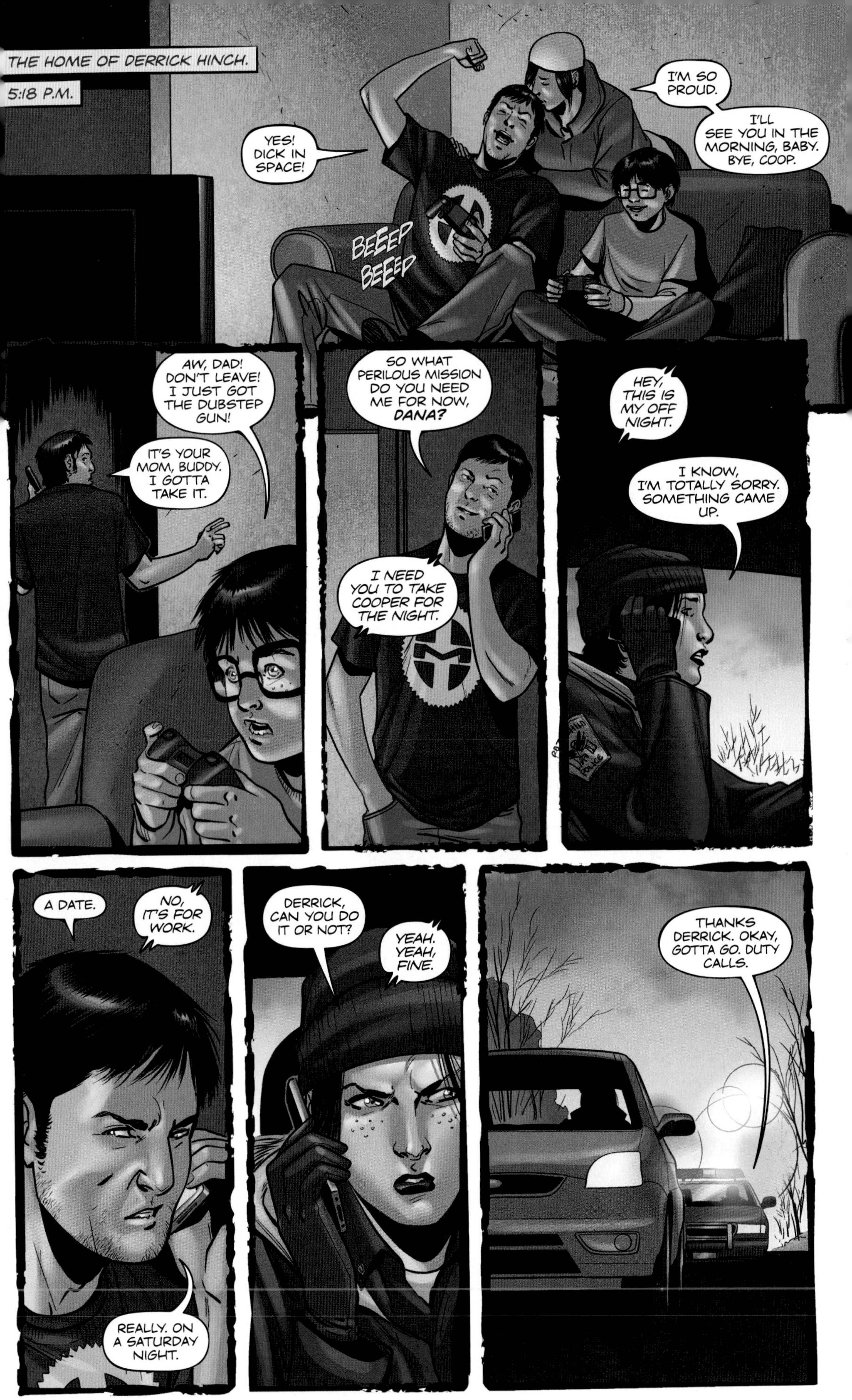
THE HOME OF DERRICK HINCH.
5:18 P.M.
YES! DICK IN SPACE!
I'M SO PROUD.
I'LL SEE YOU IN THE MORNING, BABY. BYE, COOP.
BEEEP BEEEP
AW, DAD! DON'T LEAVE! I JUST GOT THE DUBSTEP GUN!
IT'S YOUR MOM, BUDDY. I GOTTA TAKE IT.
SO WHAT PERILOUS MISSION DO YOU NEED ME FOR NOW, DANA?
I NEED YOU TO TAKE COOPER FOR THE NIGHT.
HEY, THIS IS MY OFF NIGHT.
I KNOW, I'M TOTALLY SORRY. SOMETHING CAME UP.
A DATE.
NO, IT'S FOR WORK.
REALLY. ON A SATURDAY NIGHT.
DERRICK, CAN YOU DO IT OR NOT?
YEAH. YEAH, FINE.
THANKS DERRICK. OKAY, GOTTA GO. DUTY CALLS.

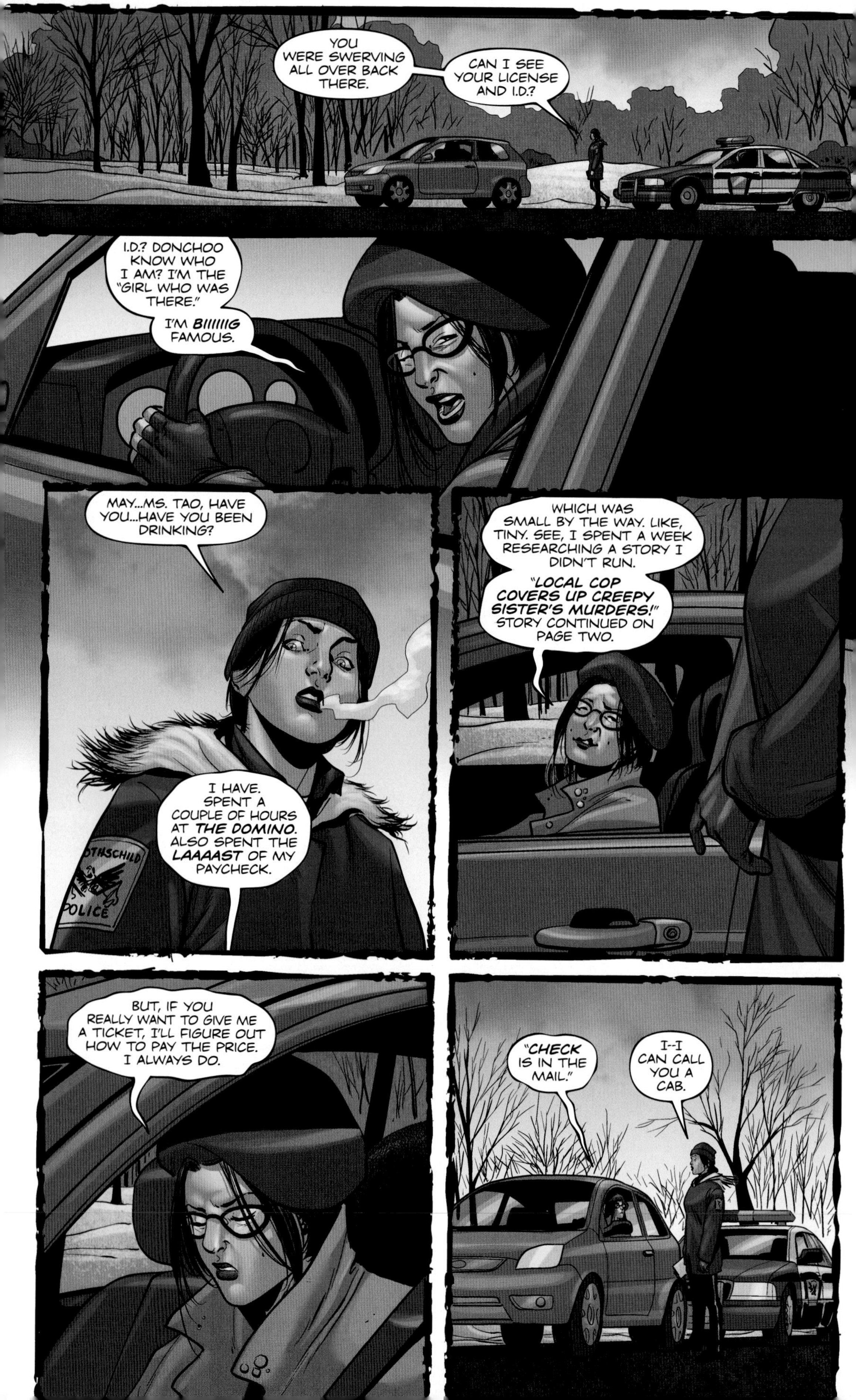
YOU WERE SWERVING ALL OVER BACK THERE.
CAN I SEE YOUR LICENSE AND I.D.?
I.D.? DONCHOO KNOW WHO I AM? I'M THE "GIRL WHO WAS THERE."
I'M **BIIIIIG** FAMOUS.
MAY...MS. TAO, HAVE YOU...HAVE YOU BEEN DRINKING?
I HAVE. SPENT A COUPLE OF HOURS AT **THE DOMINO**. ALSO SPENT THE **LAAAAST** OF MY PAYCHECK.
OTHSCHILD POLICE
WHICH WAS SMALL BY THE WAY. LIKE, TINY. SEE, I SPENT A WEEK RESEARCHING A STORY I DIDN'T RUN.
"***LOCAL COP COVERS UP CREEPY SISTER'S MURDERS!***" STORY CONTINUED ON PAGE TWO.
BUT, IF YOU REALLY WANT TO GIVE ME A TICKET, I'LL FIGURE OUT HOW TO PAY THE PRICE. I ALWAYS DO.
"***CHECK*** IS IN THE MAIL."
I--I CAN CALL YOU A CAB.

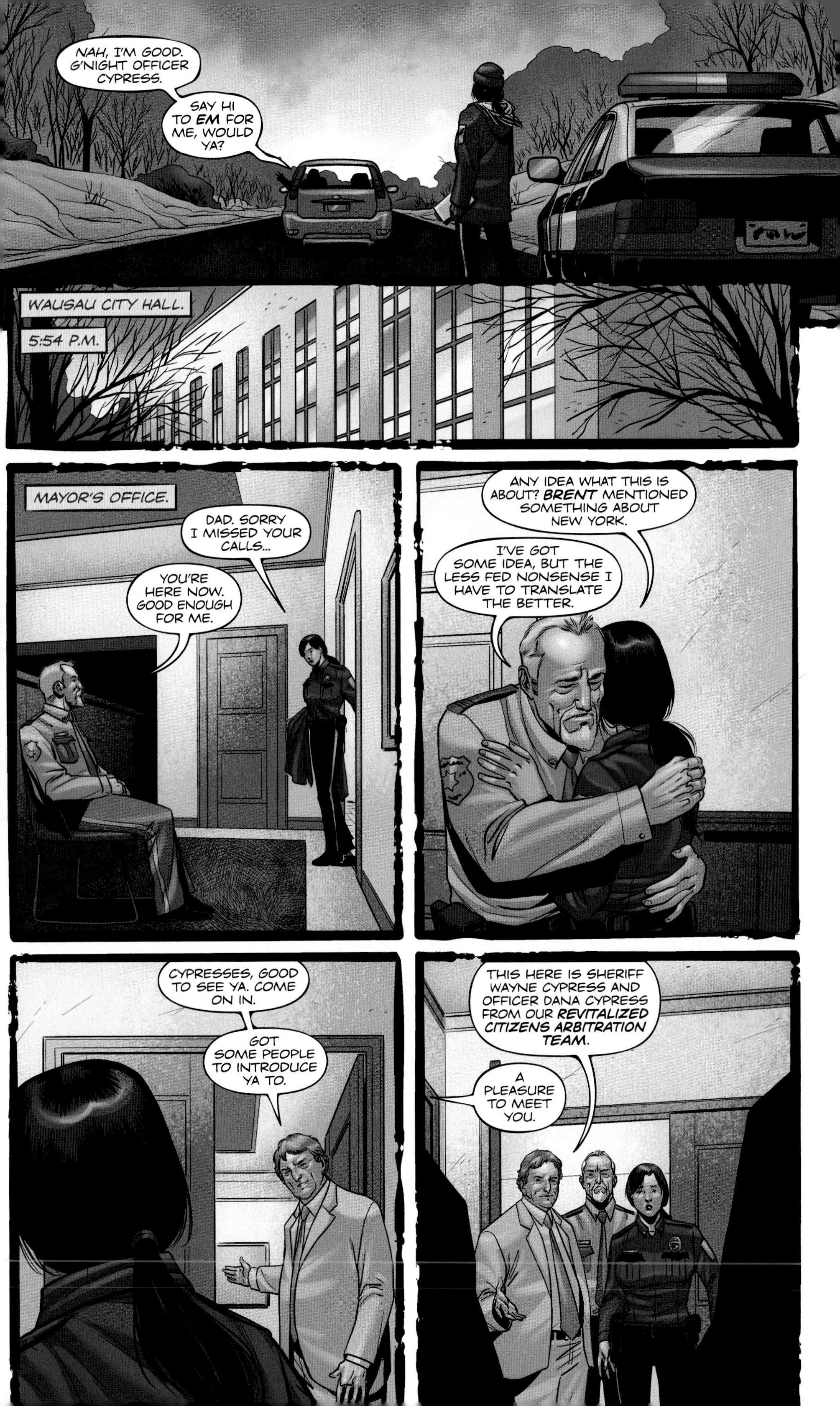
NAH, I'M GOOD. G'NIGHT OFFICER CYPRESS.
SAY HI TO **EM** FOR ME, WOULD YA?
WAUSAU CITY HALL.
5:54 P.M.
MAYOR'S OFFICE.
DAD. SORRY I MISSED YOUR CALLS...
YOU'RE HERE NOW. GOOD ENOUGH FOR ME.
ANY IDEA WHAT THIS IS ABOUT? ***BRENT*** MENTIONED SOMETHING ABOUT NEW YORK.
I'VE GOT SOME IDEA, BUT THE LESS FED NONSENSE I HAVE TO TRANSLATE THE BETTER.
CYPRESSES, GOOD TO SEE YA. COME ON IN.
GOT SOME PEOPLE TO INTRODUCE YA TO.
THIS HERE IS SHERIFF WAYNE CYPRESS AND OFFICER DANA CYPRESS FROM OUR ***REVITALIZED CITIZENS ARBITRATION TEAM***.
A PLEASURE TO MEET YOU.

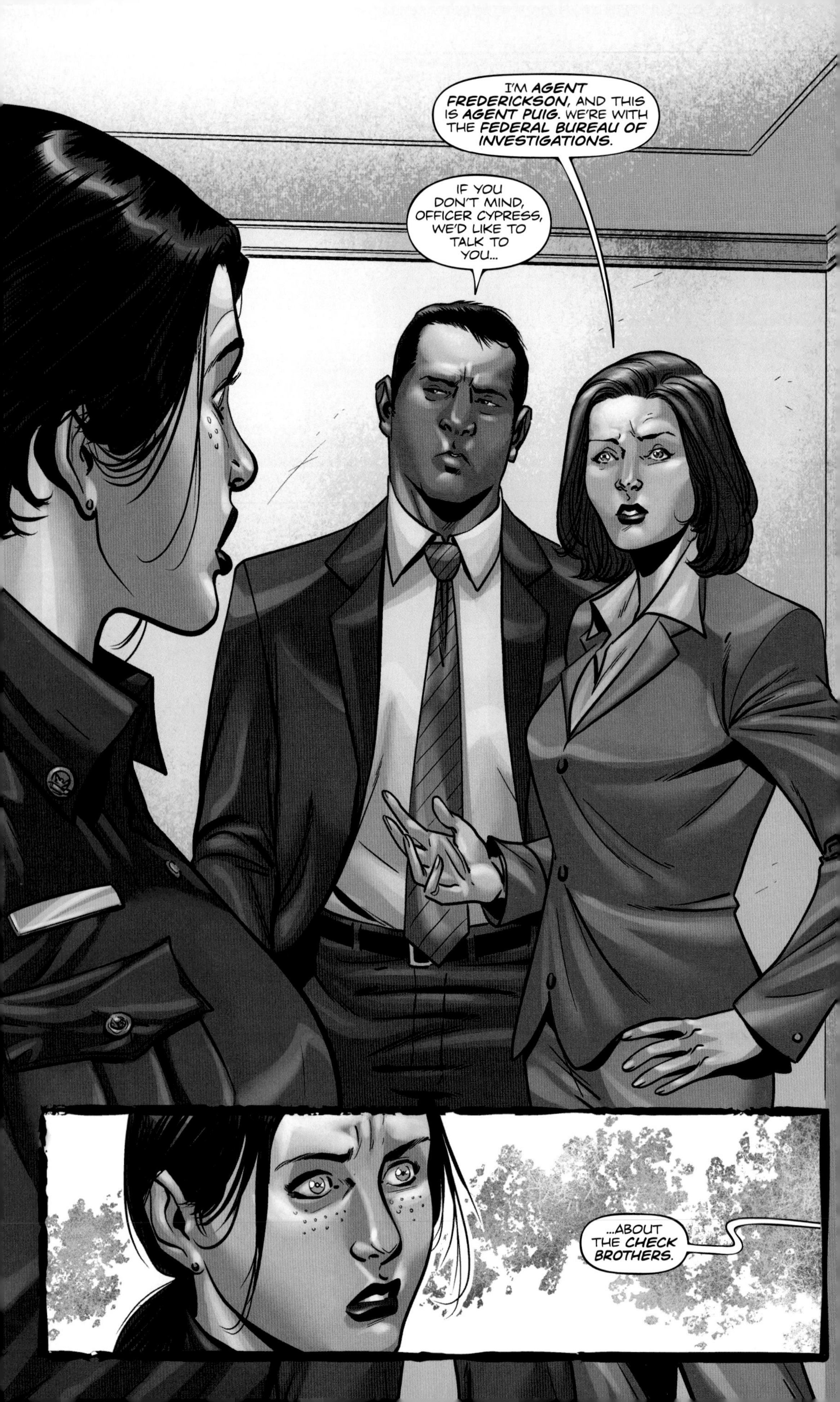
I'M AGENT FREDERICKSON, AND THIS IS AGENT PUIG. WE'RE WITH THE FEDERAL BUREAU OF INVESTIGATIONS.
IF YOU DON'T MIND, OFFICER CYPRESS, WE'D LIKE TO TALK TO YOU...
...ABOUT THE CHECK BROTHERS.

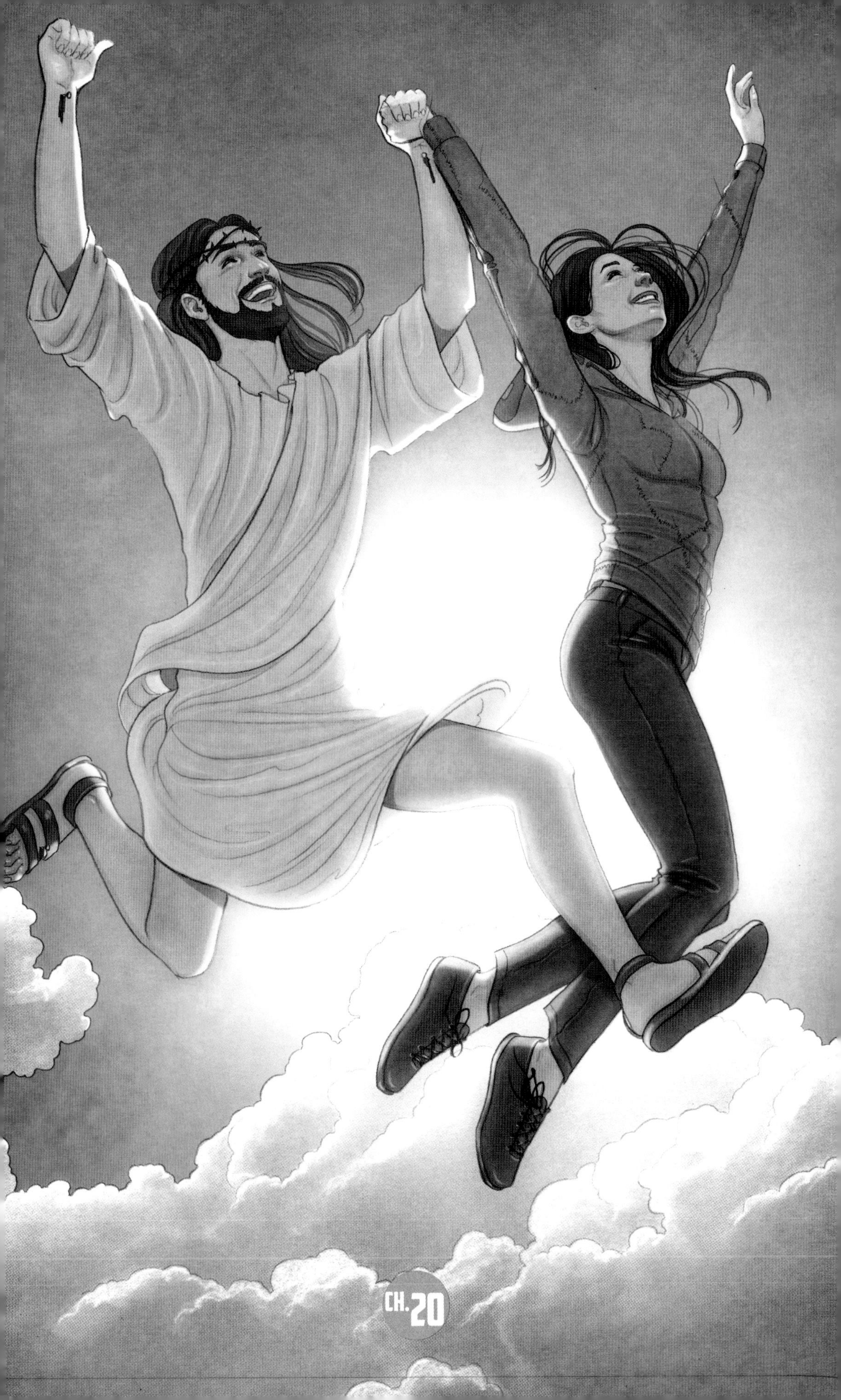
CH. 20

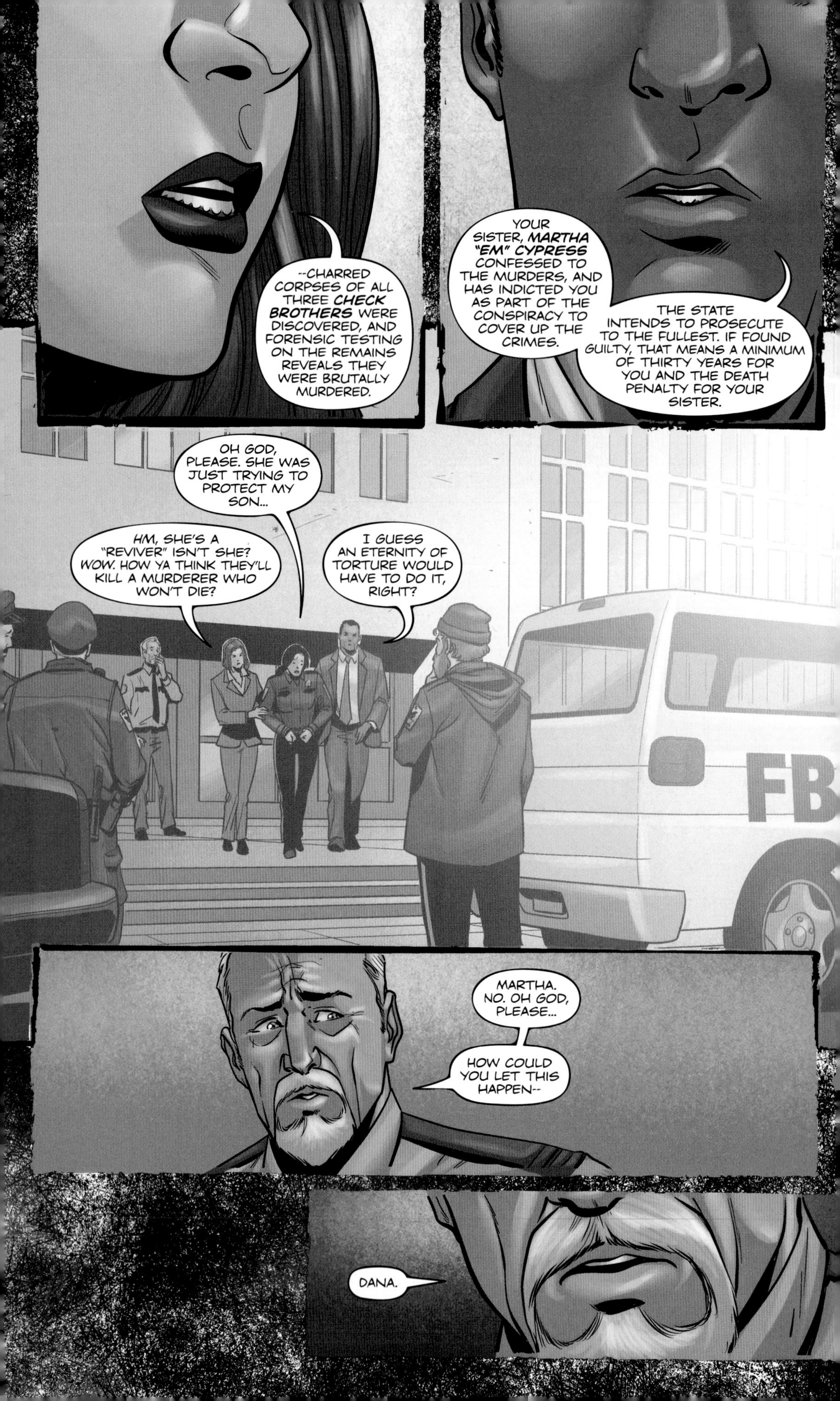
--CHARRED CORPSES OF ALL THREE CHECK BROTHERS WERE DISCOVERED, AND FORENSIC TESTING ON THE REMAINS REVEALS THEY WERE BRUTALLY MURDERED.
YOUR SISTER, MARTHA "EM" CYPRESS CONFESSED TO THE MURDERS, AND HAS INDICTED YOU AS PART OF THE CONSPIRACY TO COVER UP THE CRIMES.
THE STATE INTENDS TO PROSECUTE TO THE FULLEST. IF FOUND GUILTY, THAT MEANS A MINIMUM OF THIRTY YEARS FOR YOU AND THE DEATH PENALTY FOR YOUR SISTER.
OH GOD, PLEASE. SHE WAS JUST TRYING TO PROTECT MY SON...
HM, SHE'S A "REVIVER" ISN'T SHE? WOW. HOW YA THINK THEY'LL KILL A MURDERER WHO WON'T DIE?
I GUESS AN ETERNITY OF TORTURE WOULD HAVE TO DO IT, RIGHT?
FB
MARTHA. NO. OH GOD, PLEASE...
HOW COULD YOU LET THIS HAPPEN--
DANA.

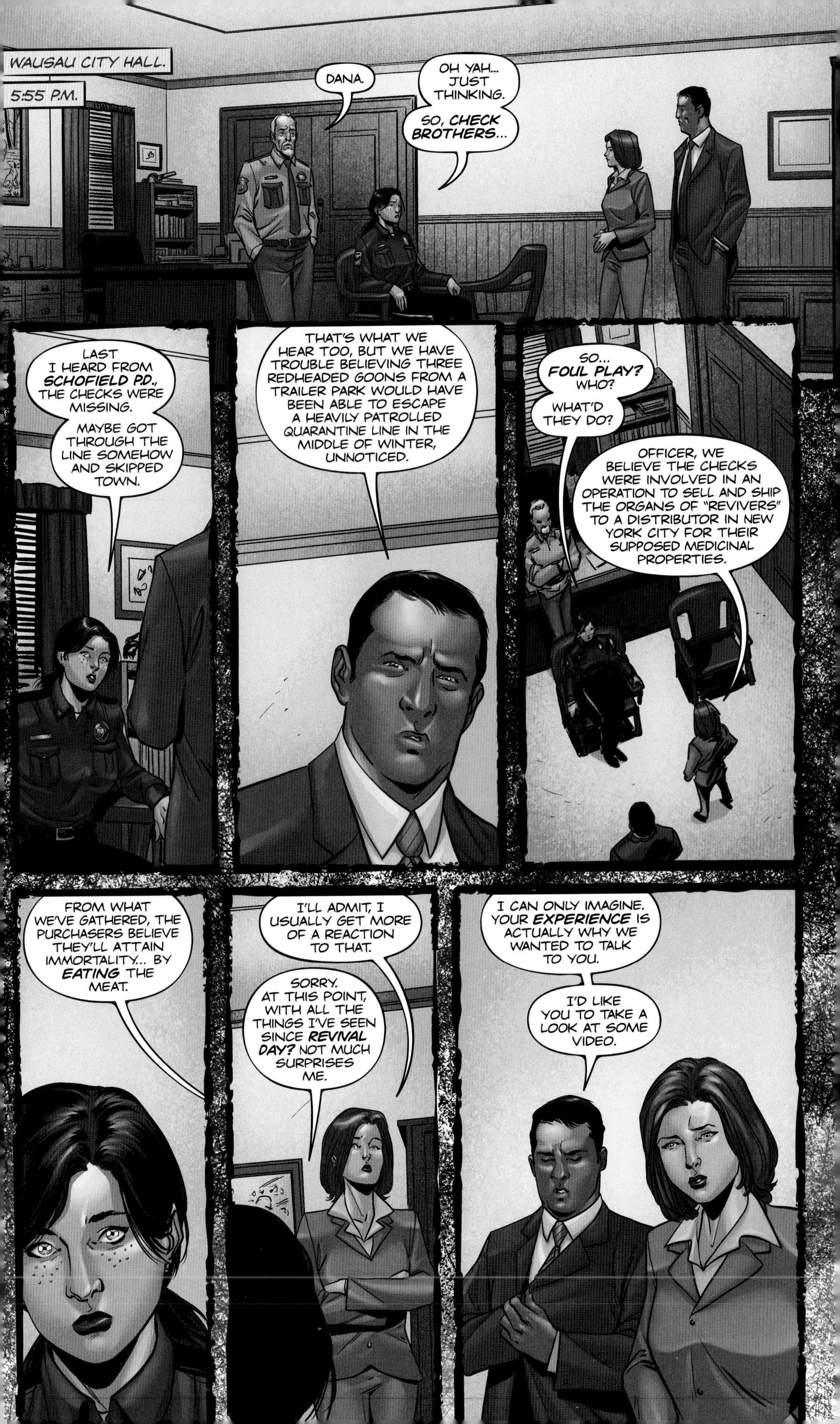
WAUSAU CITY HALL.
5:55 P.M.
DANA.
OH YAH... JUST THINKING.
SO, CHECK BROTHERS...
LAST I HEARD FROM SCHOFIELD P.D., THE CHECKS WERE MISSING.
MAYBE GOT THROUGH THE LINE SOMEHOW AND SKIPPED TOWN.
THAT'S WHAT WE HEAR TOO, BUT WE HAVE TROUBLE BELIEVING THREE REDHEADED GOONS FROM A TRAILER PARK WOULD HAVE BEEN ABLE TO ESCAPE A HEAVILY PATROLLED QUARANTINE LINE IN THE MIDDLE OF WINTER, UNNOTICED.
SO... FOUL PLAY? WHO?
WHAT'D THEY DO?
OFFICER, WE BELIEVE THE CHECKS WERE INVOLVED IN AN OPERATION TO SELL AND SHIP THE ORGANS OF "REVIVERS" TO A DISTRIBUTOR IN NEW YORK CITY FOR THEIR SUPPOSED MEDICINAL PROPERTIES.
FROM WHAT WE'VE GATHERED, THE PURCHASERS BELIEVE THEY'LL ATTAIN IMMORTALITY... BY EATING THE MEAT.
I'LL ADMIT, I USUALLY GET MORE OF A REACTION TO THAT.
SORRY. AT THIS POINT, WITH ALL THE THINGS I'VE SEEN SINCE REVIVAL DAY? NOT MUCH SURPRISES ME.
I CAN ONLY IMAGINE. YOUR EXPERIENCE IS ACTUALLY WHY WE WANTED TO TALK TO YOU.
I'D LIKE YOU TO TAKE A LOOK AT SOME VIDEO.

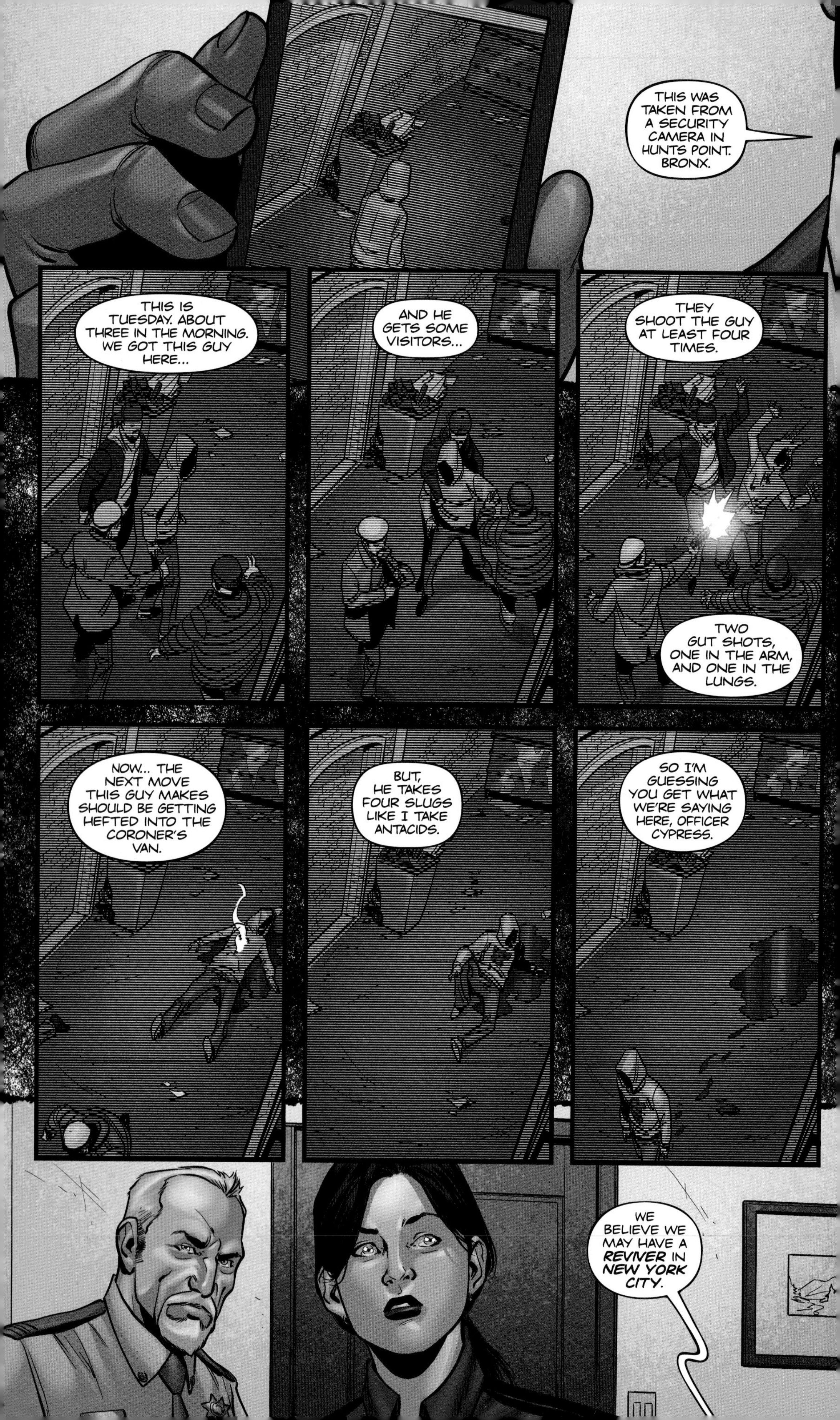
THIS WAS TAKEN FROM A SECURITY CAMERA IN HUNTS POINT. BRONX.
THIS IS TUESDAY. ABOUT THREE IN THE MORNING. WE GOT THIS GUY HERE...
AND HE GETS SOME VISITORS...
THEY SHOOT THE GUY AT LEAST FOUR TIMES.
TWO GUT SHOTS, ONE IN THE ARM, AND ONE IN THE LUNGS.
NOW... THE NEXT MOVE THIS GUY MAKES SHOULD BE GETTING HEFTED INTO THE CORONER'S VAN.
BUT, HE TAKES FOUR SLUGS LIKE I TAKE ANTACIDS.
SO I'M GUESSING YOU GET WHAT WE'RE SAYING HERE, OFFICER CYPRESS.
WE BELIEVE WE MAY HAVE A ***REVIVER*** IN ***NEW YORK CITY***.

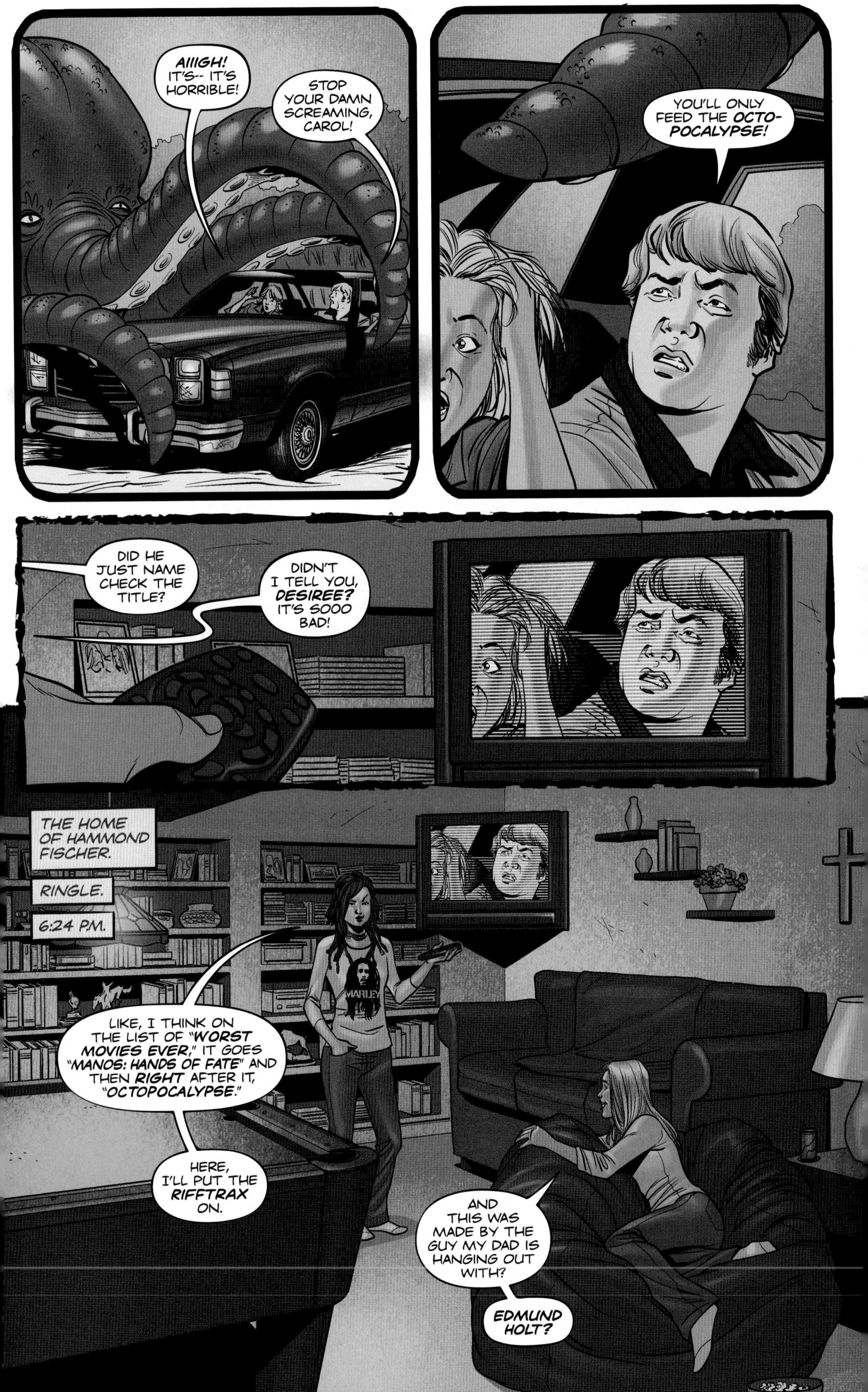
AIIIGH! IT'S-- IT'S HORRIBLE!
STOP YOUR DAMN SCREAMING, CAROL!
YOU'LL ONLY FEED THE OCTO-POCALYPSE!
DID HE JUST NAME CHECK THE TITLE?
DIDN'T I TELL YOU, DESIREE? IT'S SOOO BAD!
THE HOME OF HAMMOND FISCHER.
RINGLE.
6:24 P.M.
LIKE, I THINK ON THE LIST OF "WORST MOVIES EVER," IT GOES "MANOS: HANDS OF FATE" AND THEN RIGHT AFTER IT, "OCTOPOCALYPSE."
HERE, I'LL PUT THE RIFFTRAX ON.
AND THIS WAS MADE BY THE GUY MY DAD IS HANGING OUT WITH?
EDMUND HOLT?
MARLEY

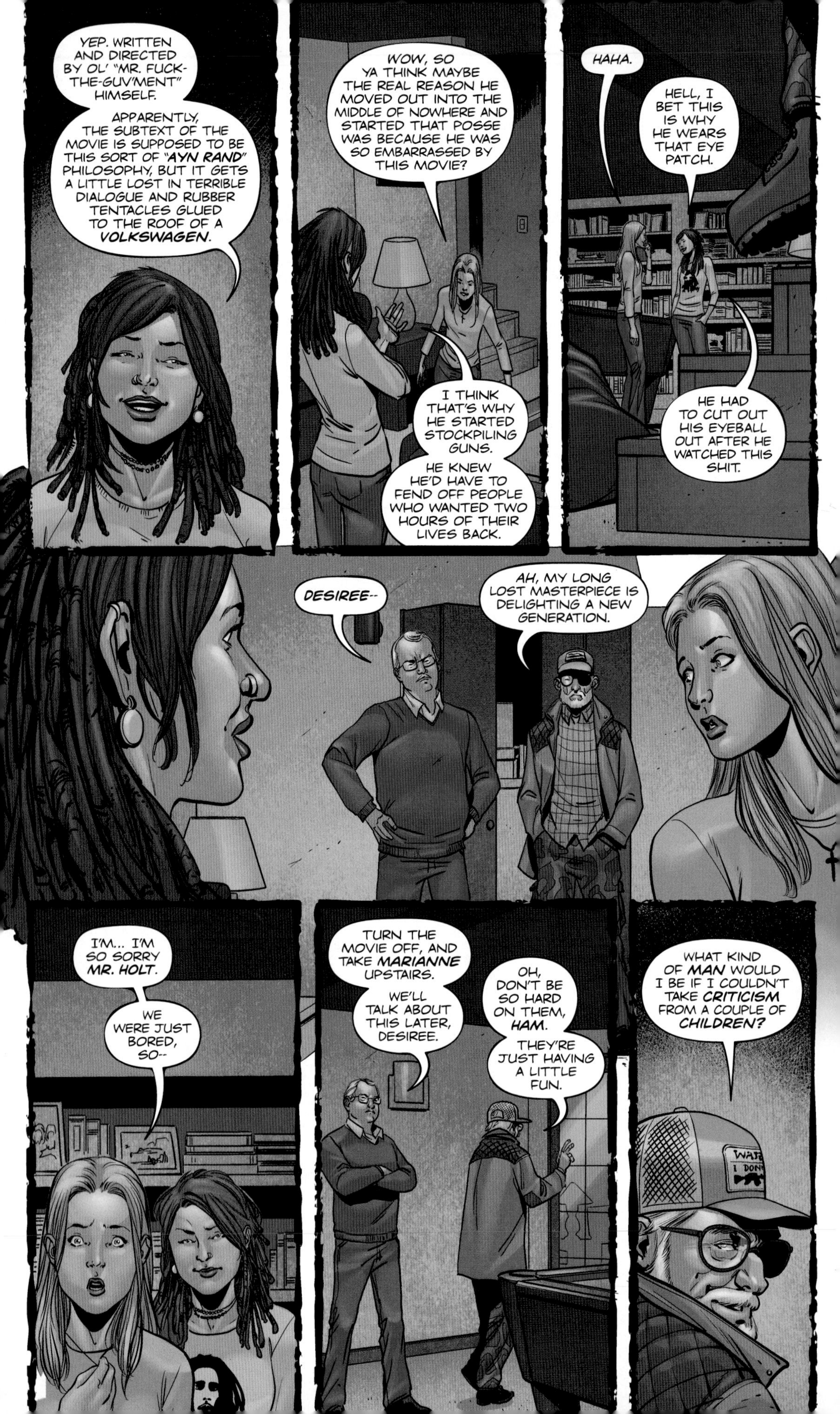
YEP. WRITTEN AND DIRECTED BY OL' "MR. FUCK-THE-GUV'MENT" HIMSELF.
APPARENTLY, THE SUBTEXT OF THE MOVIE IS SUPPOSED TO BE THIS SORT OF "AYN RAND" PHILOSOPHY, BUT IT GETS A LITTLE LOST IN TERRIBLE DIALOGUE AND RUBBER TENTACLES GLUED TO THE ROOF OF A VOLKSWAGEN.
WOW, SO YA THINK MAYBE THE REAL REASON HE MOVED OUT INTO THE MIDDLE OF NOWHERE AND STARTED THAT POSSE WAS BECAUSE HE WAS SO EMBARRASSED BY THIS MOVIE?
I THINK THAT'S WHY HE STARTED STOCKPILING GUNS.
HE KNEW HE'D HAVE TO FEND OFF PEOPLE WHO WANTED TWO HOURS OF THEIR LIVES BACK.
HAHA.
HELL, I BET THIS IS WHY HE WEARS THAT EYE PATCH.
HE HAD TO CUT OUT HIS EYEBALL OUT AFTER HE WATCHED THIS SHIT.
DESIREE--
AH, MY LONG LOST MASTERPIECE IS DELIGHTING A NEW GENERATION.
I'M... I'M SO SORRY MR. HOLT.
WE WERE JUST BORED, SO--
TURN THE MOVIE OFF, AND TAKE MARIANNE UPSTAIRS.
WE'LL TALK ABOUT THIS LATER, DESIREE.
OH, DON'T BE SO HARD ON THEM, HAM.
THEY'RE JUST HAVING A LITTLE FUN.
WHAT KIND OF MAN WOULD I BE IF I COULDN'T TAKE CRITICISM FROM A COUPLE OF CHILDREN?

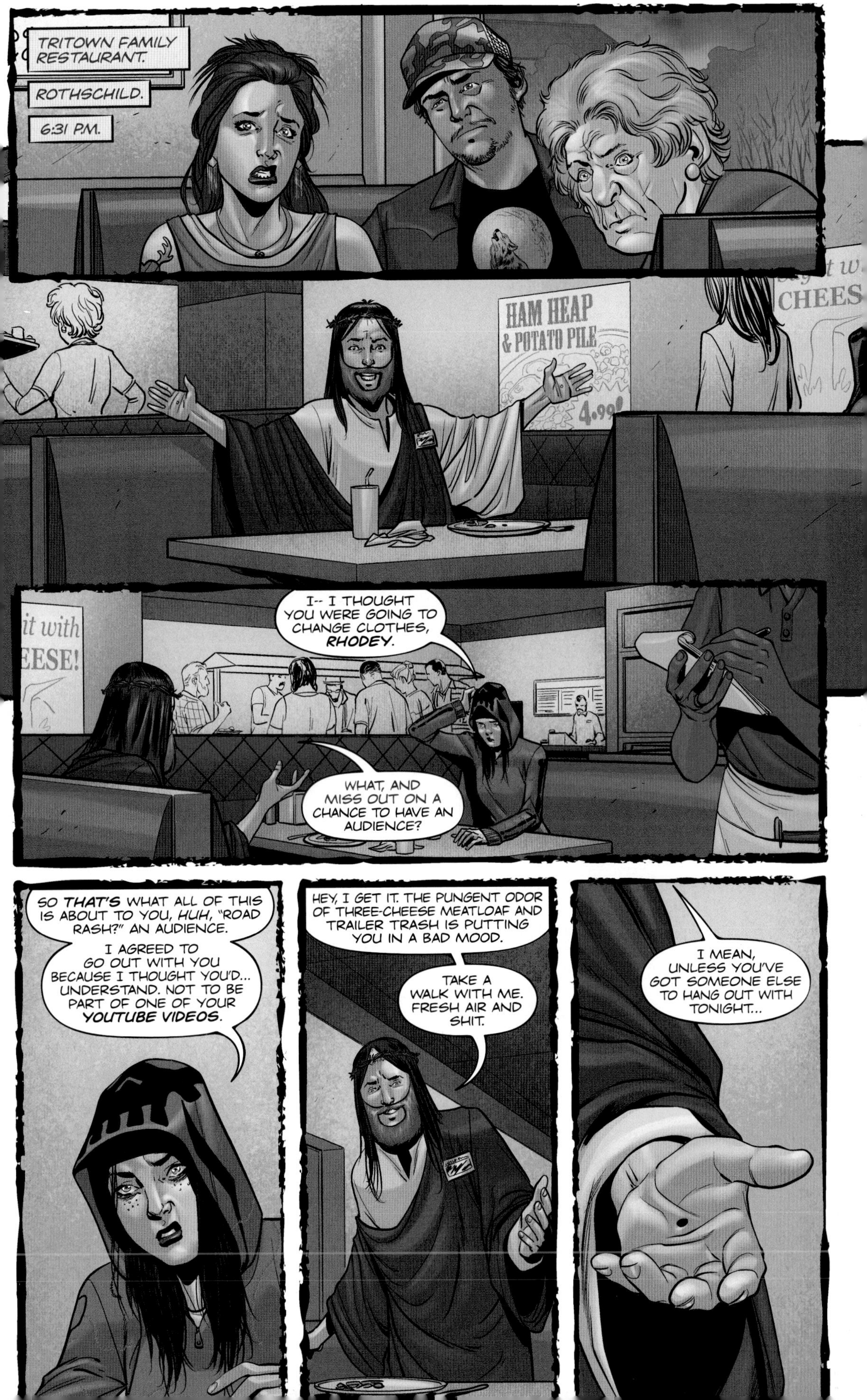

TRITOWN FAMILY RESTAURANT.
ROTHSCHILD.
6:31 P.M.
HAM HEAP & POTATO PILE
4.99
CHEES
I-- I THOUGHT YOU WERE GOING TO CHANGE CLOTHES, RHODEY.
WHAT, AND MISS OUT ON A CHANCE TO HAVE AN AUDIENCE?
SO THAT'S WHAT ALL OF THIS IS ABOUT TO YOU, HUH, "ROAD RASH?" AN AUDIENCE.
I AGREED TO GO OUT WITH YOU BECAUSE I THOUGHT YOU'D... UNDERSTAND. NOT TO BE PART OF ONE OF YOUR YOUTUBE VIDEOS.
HEY, I GET IT. THE PUNGENT ODOR OF THREE-CHEESE MEATLOAF AND TRAILER TRASH IS PUTTING YOU IN A BAD MOOD.
TAKE A WALK WITH ME. FRESH AIR AND SHIT.
I MEAN, UNLESS YOU'VE GOT SOMEONE ELSE TO HANG OUT WITH TONIGHT...

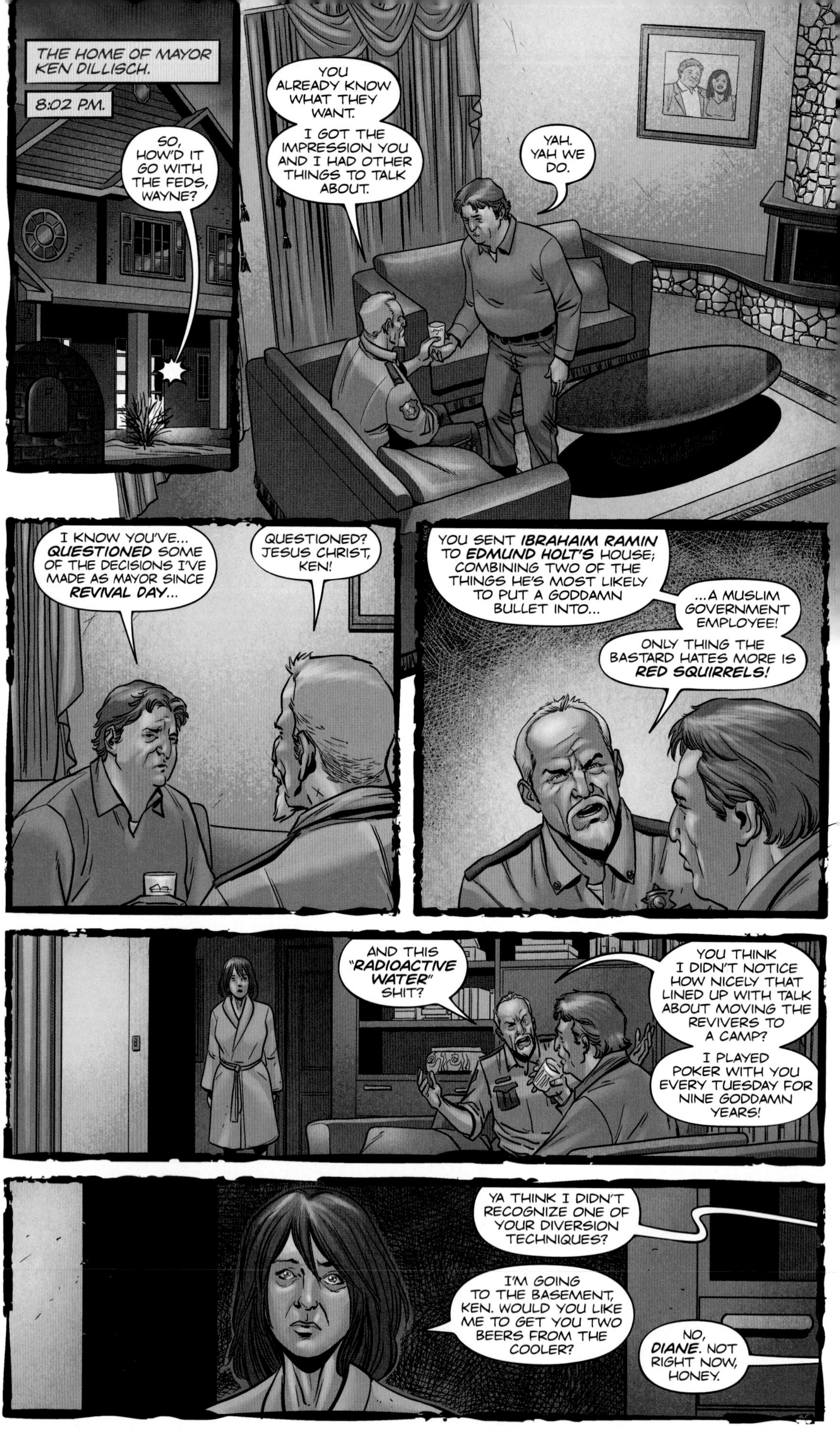
THE HOME OF MAYOR KEN DILLISCH.
8:02 P.M.
SO, HOW'D IT GO WITH THE FEDS, WAYNE?
YOU ALREADY KNOW WHAT THEY WANT.
I GOT THE IMPRESSION YOU AND I HAD OTHER THINGS TO TALK ABOUT.
YAH. YAH WE DO.
I KNOW YOU'VE... QUESTIONED SOME OF THE DECISIONS I'VE MADE AS MAYOR SINCE REVIVAL DAY...
QUESTIONED? JESUS CHRIST, KEN!
YOU SENT IBRAHAIM RAMIN TO EDMUND HOLT'S HOUSE; COMBINING TWO OF THE THINGS HE'S MOST LIKELY TO PUT A GODDAMN BULLET INTO...
...A MUSLIM GOVERNMENT EMPLOYEE!
ONLY THING THE BASTARD HATES MORE IS RED SQUIRRELS!
AND THIS "RADIOACTIVE WATER" SHIT?
YOU THINK I DIDN'T NOTICE HOW NICELY THAT LINED UP WITH TALK ABOUT MOVING THE REVIVERS TO A CAMP?
I PLAYED POKER WITH YOU EVERY TUESDAY FOR NINE GODDAMN YEARS!
YA THINK I DIDN'T RECOGNIZE ONE OF YOUR DIVERSION TECHNIQUES?
I'M GOING TO THE BASEMENT, KEN. WOULD YOU LIKE ME TO GET YOU TWO BEERS FROM THE COOLER?
NO, DIANE. NOT RIGHT NOW, HONEY.

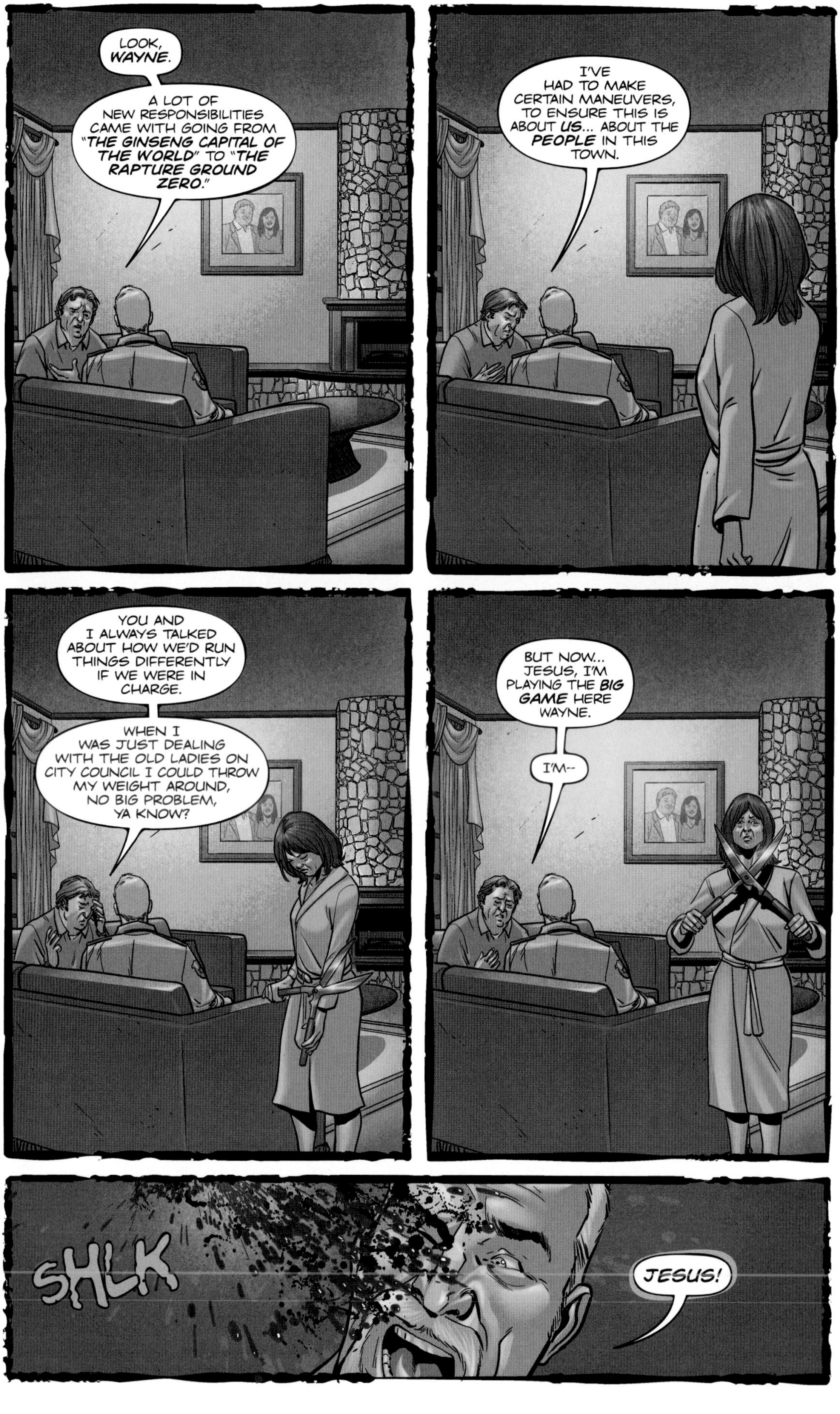
LOOK, WAYNE.
A LOT OF NEW RESPONSIBILITIES CAME WITH GOING FROM "THE GINSENG CAPITAL OF THE WORLD" TO "THE RAPTURE GROUND ZERO."
I'VE HAD TO MAKE CERTAIN MANEUVERS, TO ENSURE THIS IS ABOUT US... ABOUT THE PEOPLE IN THIS TOWN.
YOU AND I ALWAYS TALKED ABOUT HOW WE'D RUN THINGS DIFFERENTLY IF WE WERE IN CHARGE.
WHEN I WAS JUST DEALING WITH THE OLD LADIES ON CITY COUNCIL I COULD THROW MY WEIGHT AROUND, NO BIG PROBLEM, YA KNOW?
BUT NOW... JESUS, I'M PLAYING THE BIG GAME HERE WAYNE.
I'M--
SHLK
JESUS!

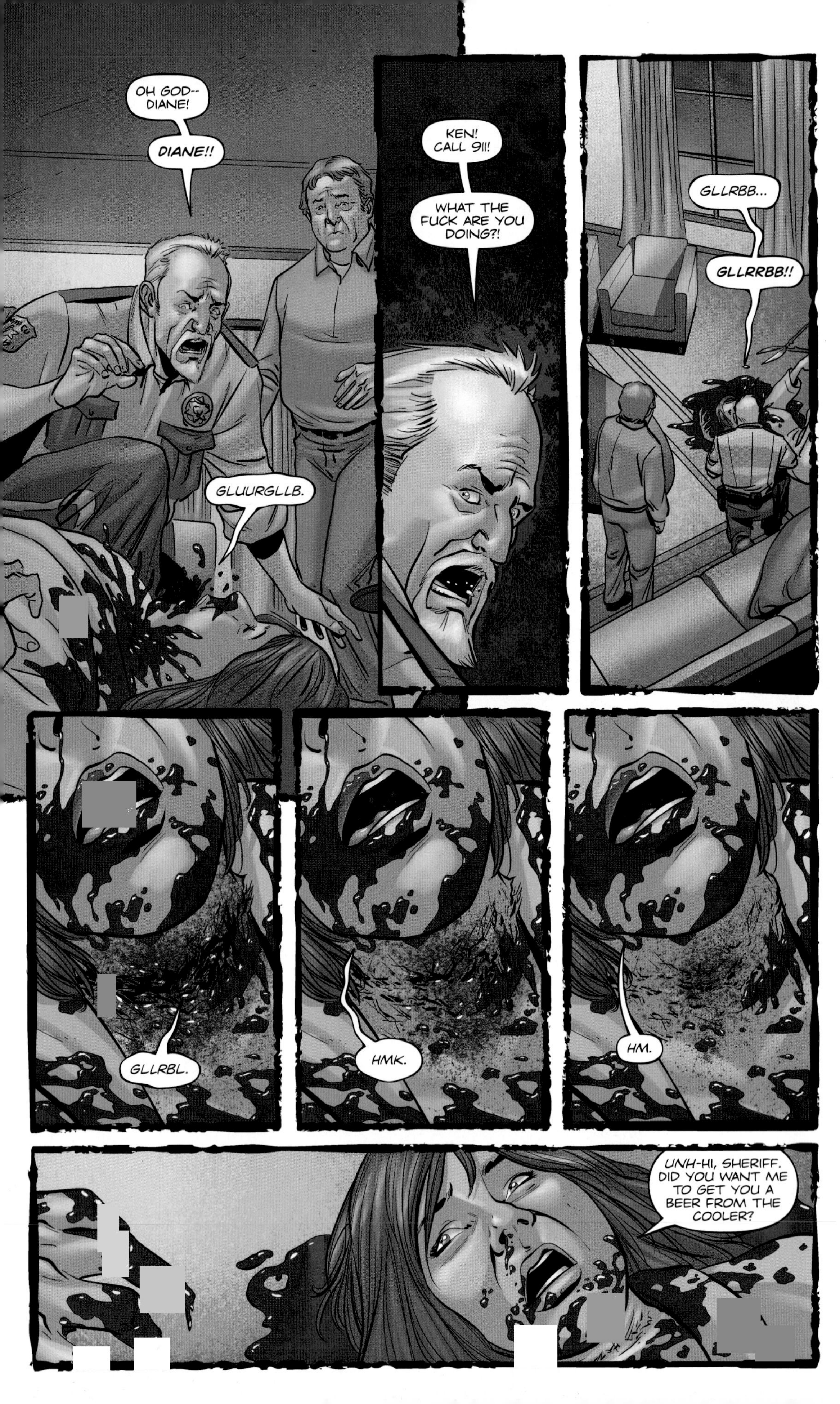
OH GOD--
DIANE!
DIANE!!
GLUURGLLB.
KEN! CALL 911!
WHAT THE FUCK ARE YOU DOING?!
GLLRBB...
GLLRRBB!!
GLLRBL.
HMK.
HM.
UNH-HI, SHERIFF. DID YOU WANT ME TO GET YOU A BEER FROM THE COOLER?

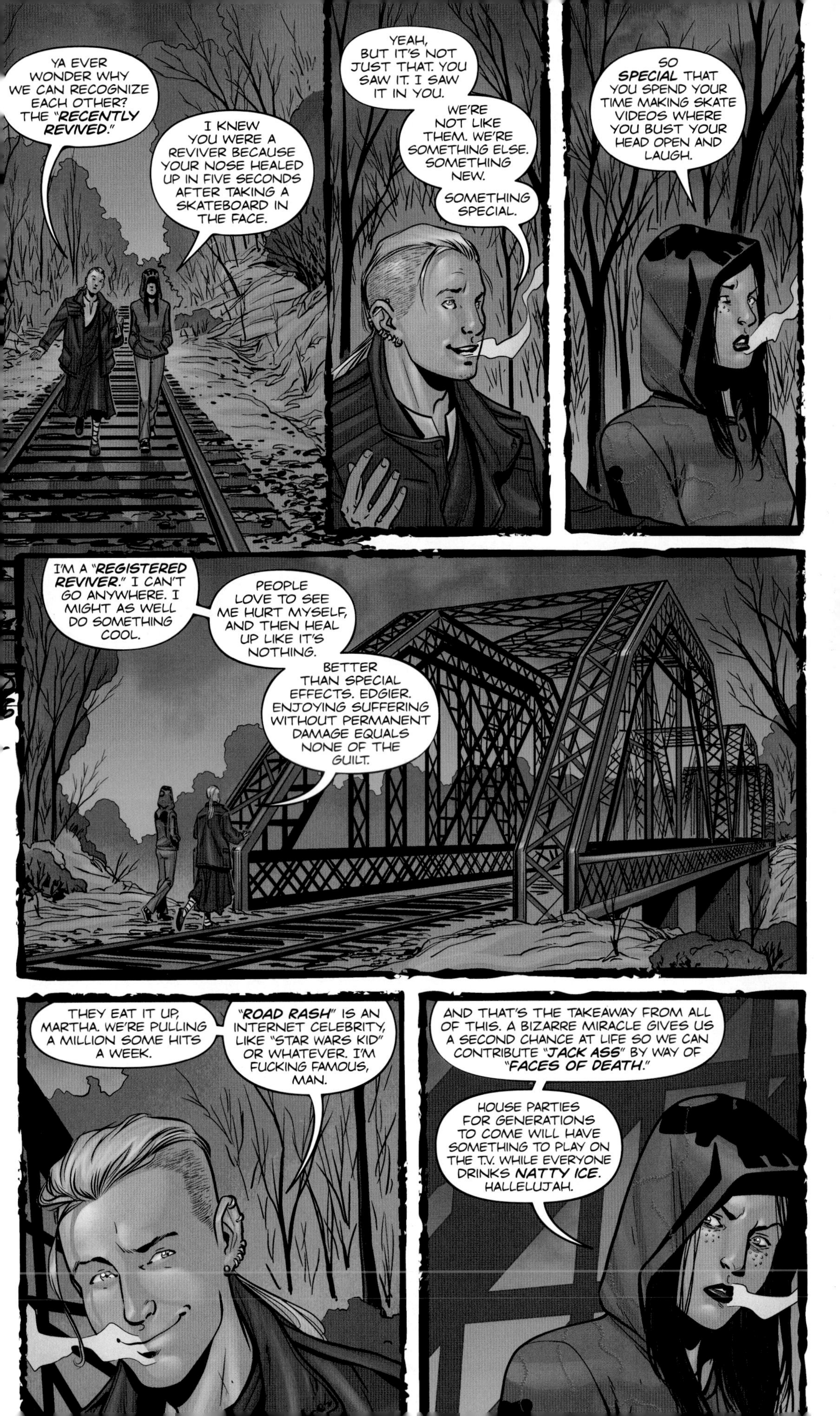
YA EVER WONDER WHY WE CAN RECOGNIZE EACH OTHER? THE "RECENTLY REVIVED."
I KNEW YOU WERE A REVIVER BECAUSE YOUR NOSE HEALED UP IN FIVE SECONDS AFTER TAKING A SKATEBOARD IN THE FACE.
YEAH, BUT IT'S NOT JUST THAT. YOU SAW IT. I SAW IT IN YOU.
WE'RE NOT LIKE THEM. WE'RE SOMETHING ELSE. SOMETHING NEW.
SOMETHING SPECIAL.
SO SPECIAL THAT YOU SPEND YOUR TIME MAKING SKATE VIDEOS WHERE YOU BUST YOUR HEAD OPEN AND LAUGH.
I'M A "REGISTERED REVIVER." I CAN'T GO ANYWHERE. I MIGHT AS WELL DO SOMETHING COOL.
PEOPLE LOVE TO SEE ME HURT MYSELF, AND THEN HEAL UP LIKE IT'S NOTHING.
BETTER THAN SPECIAL EFFECTS. EDGIER. ENJOYING SUFFERING WITHOUT PERMANENT DAMAGE EQUALS NONE OF THE GUILT.
THEY EAT IT UP, MARTHA. WE'RE PULLING A MILLION SOME HITS A WEEK.
"ROAD RASH" IS AN INTERNET CELEBRITY, LIKE "STAR WARS KID" OR WHATEVER. I'M FUCKING FAMOUS, MAN.
AND THAT'S THE TAKEAWAY FROM ALL OF THIS. A BIZARRE MIRACLE GIVES US A SECOND CHANCE AT LIFE SO WE CAN CONTRIBUTE "JACK ASS" BY WAY OF "FACES OF DEATH."
HOUSE PARTIES FOR GENERATIONS TO COME WILL HAVE SOMETHING TO PLAY ON THE T.V. WHILE EVERYONE DRINKS NATTY ICE. HALLELUJAH.

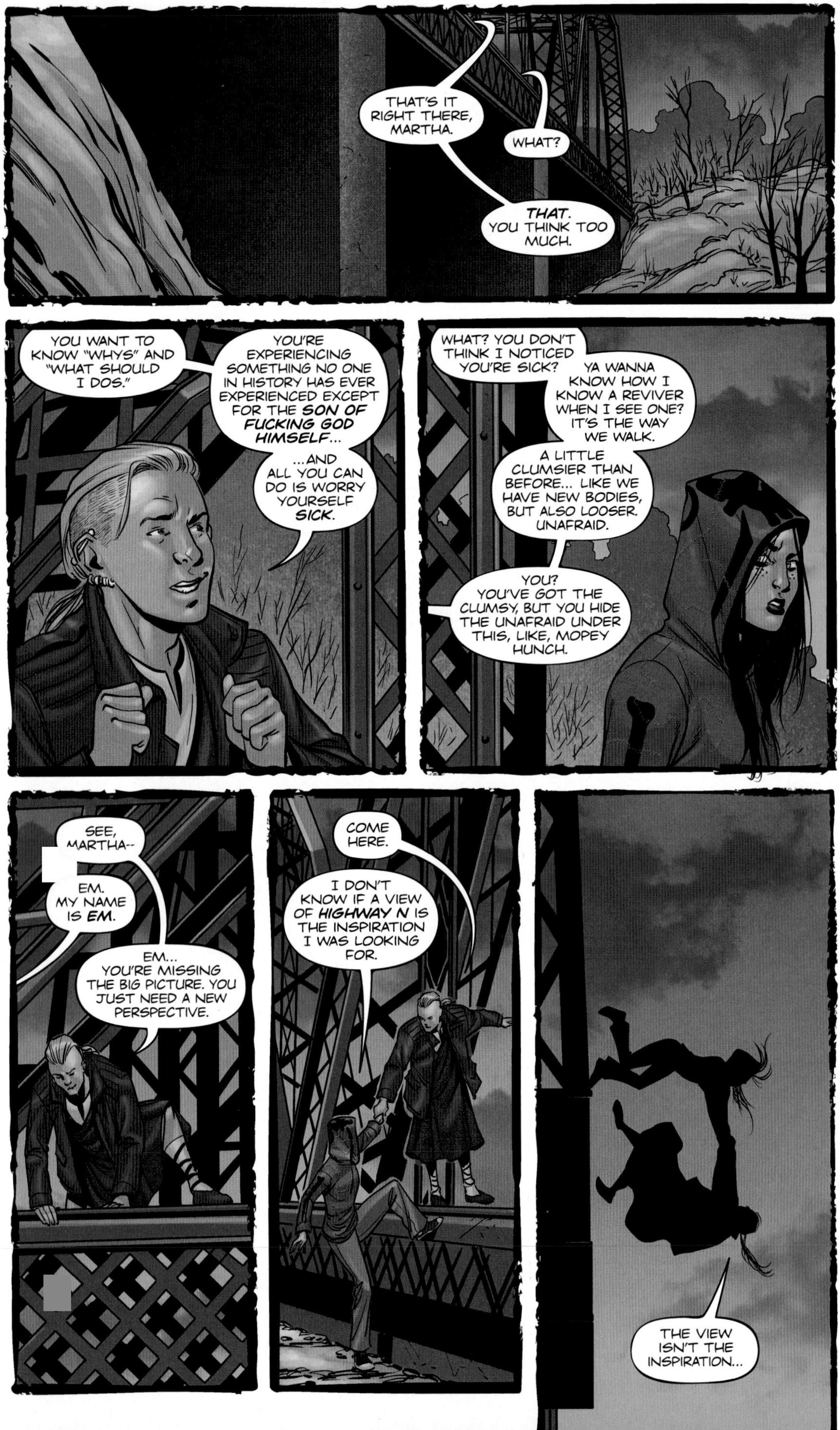
THAT'S IT RIGHT THERE, MARTHA.
WHAT?
THAT. YOU THINK TOO MUCH.
YOU WANT TO KNOW "WHYS" AND "WHAT SHOULD I DOS."
YOU'RE EXPERIENCING SOMETHING NO ONE IN HISTORY HAS EVER EXPERIENCED EXCEPT FOR THE SON OF FUCKING GOD HIMSELF...
...AND ALL YOU CAN DO IS WORRY YOURSELF SICK.
WHAT? YOU DON'T THINK I NOTICED YOU'RE SICK?
YA WANNA KNOW HOW I KNOW A REVIVER WHEN I SEE ONE? IT'S THE WAY WE WALK.
A LITTLE CLUMSIER THAN BEFORE... LIKE WE HAVE NEW BODIES, BUT ALSO LOOSER. UNAFRAID.
YOU? YOU'VE GOT THE CLUMSY, BUT YOU HIDE THE UNAFRAID UNDER THIS, LIKE, MOPEY HUNCH.
SEE, MARTHA--
EM. MY NAME IS EM.
EM... YOU'RE MISSING THE BIG PICTURE. YOU JUST NEED A NEW PERSPECTIVE.
COME HERE.
I DON'T KNOW IF A VIEW OF HIGHWAY N IS THE INSPIRATION I WAS LOOKING FOR.
THE VIEW ISN'T THE INSPIRATION...

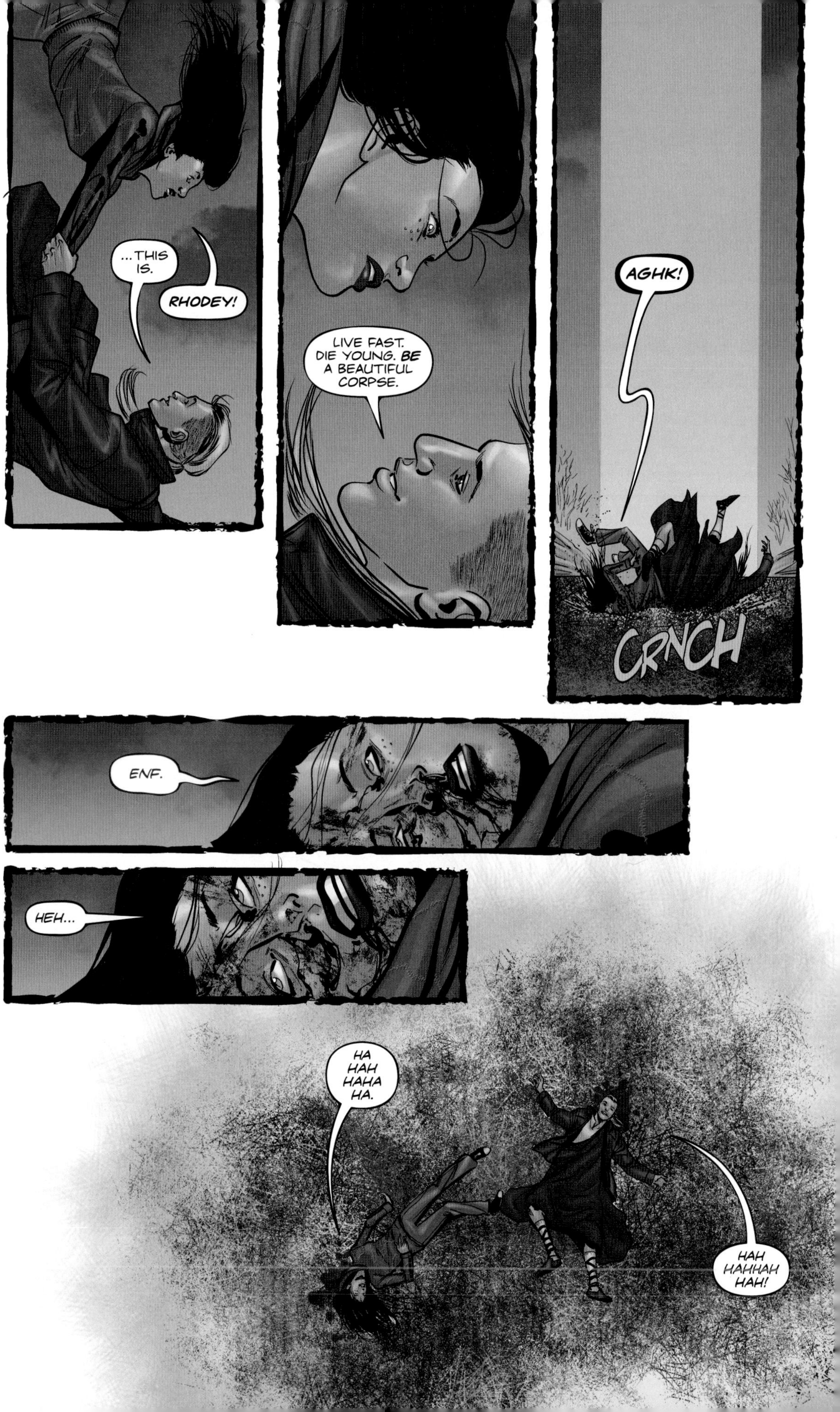
...THIS IS.
RHODEY!
LIVE FAST. DIE YOUNG. BE A BEAUTIFUL CORPSE.
AGHK!
CRNCH
ENF.
HEH...
HA HAH HAHA HA.
HAH HAHHAH HAH!

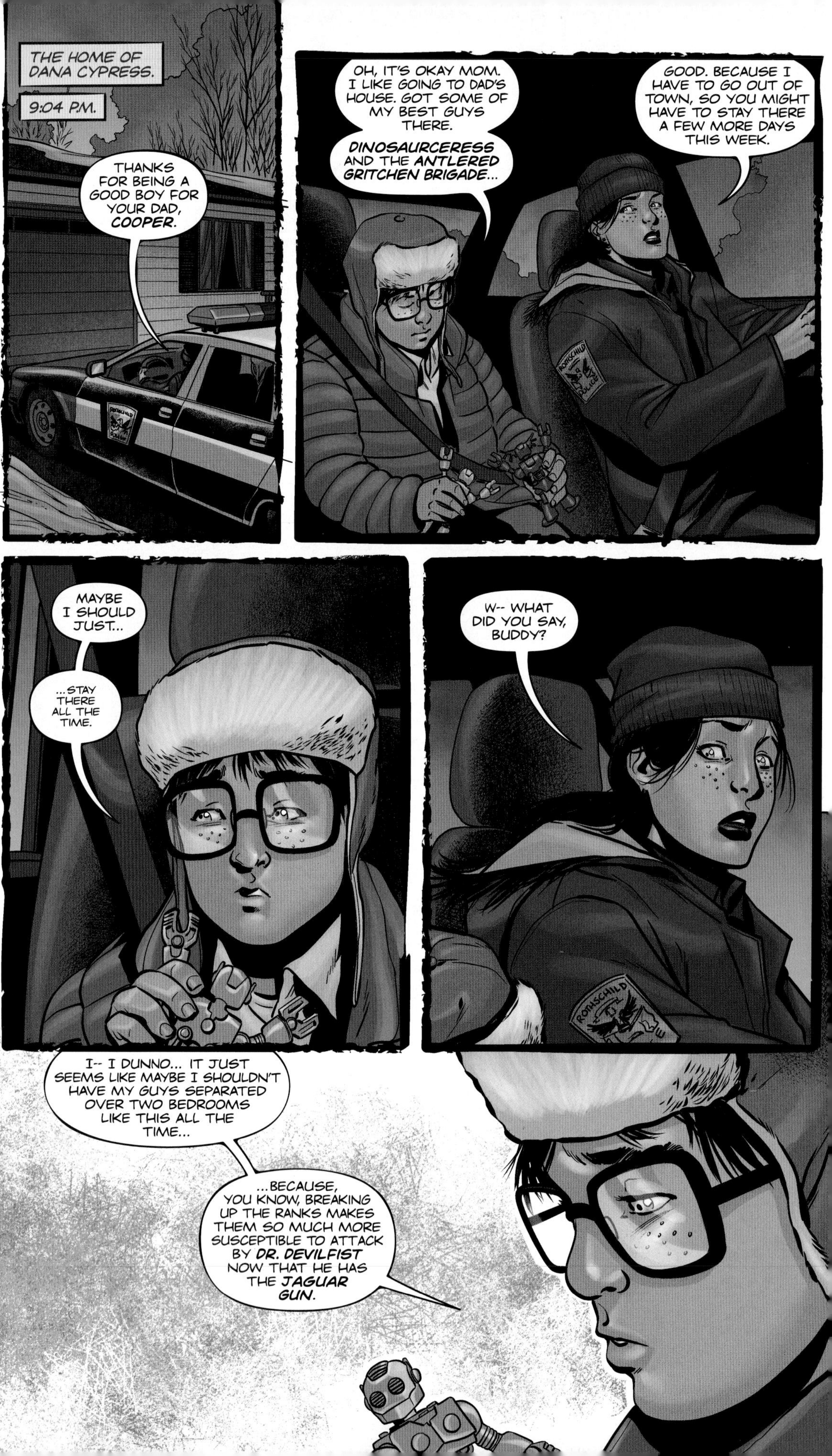

THE HOME OF DANA CYPRESS.
9:04 P.M.
THANKS FOR BEING A GOOD BOY FOR YOUR DAD, COOPER.
OH, IT'S OKAY MOM. I LIKE GOING TO DAD'S HOUSE. GOT SOME OF MY BEST GUYS THERE.
DINOSAURCERESS AND THE ANTLERED GRITCHEN BRIGADE...
GOOD. BECAUSE I HAVE TO GO OUT OF TOWN, SO YOU MIGHT HAVE TO STAY THERE A FEW MORE DAYS THIS WEEK.
MAYBE I SHOULD JUST...
...STAY THERE ALL THE TIME.
W-- WHAT DID YOU SAY, BUDDY?
I-- I DUNNO... IT JUST SEEMS LIKE MAYBE I SHOULDN'T HAVE MY GUYS SEPARATED OVER TWO BEDROOMS LIKE THIS ALL THE TIME...
...BECAUSE, YOU KNOW, BREAKING UP THE RANKS MAKES THEM SO MUCH MORE SUSCEPTIBLE TO ATTACK BY DR. DEVILFIST NOW THAT HE HAS THE JAGUAR GUN.

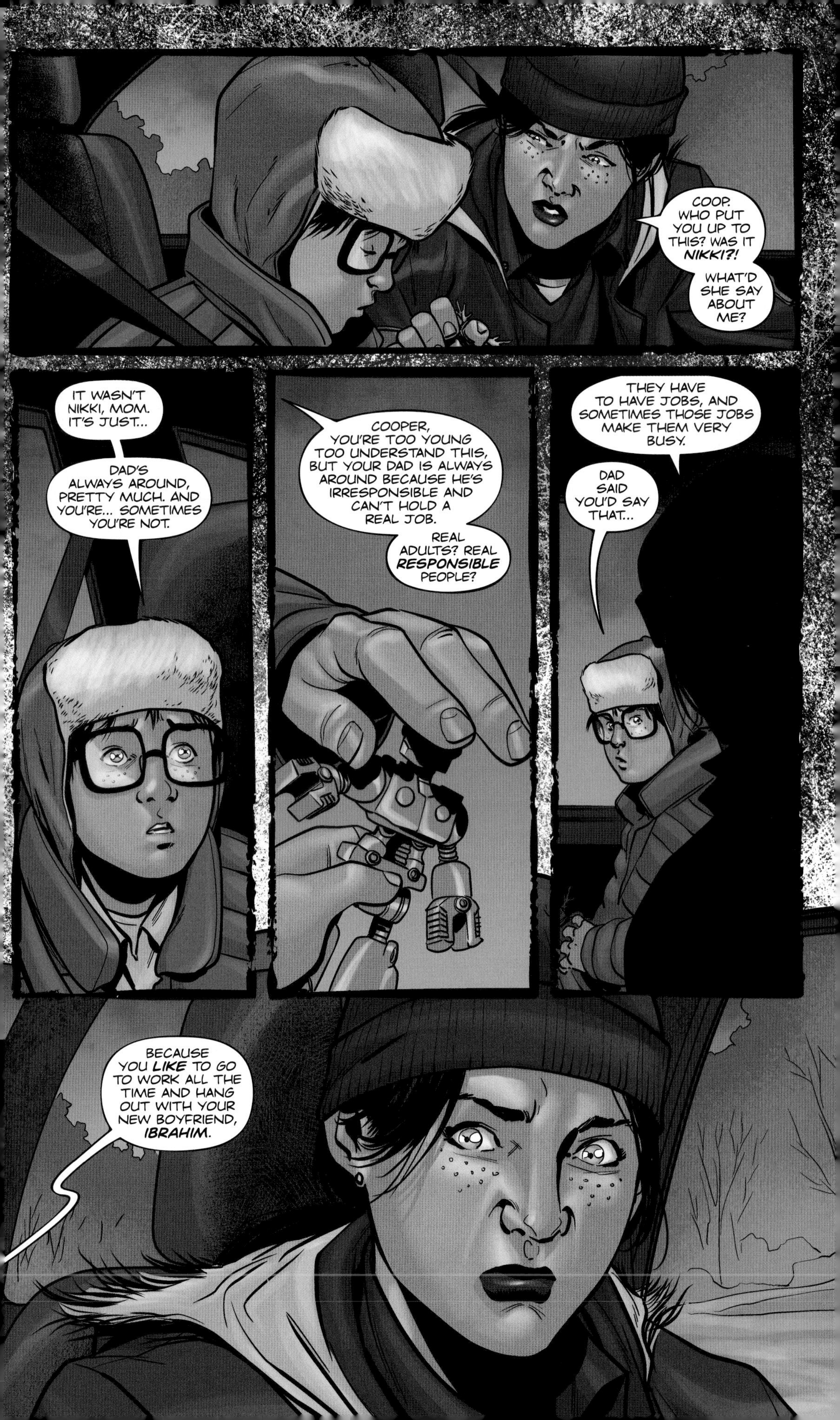
COOP. WHO PUT YOU UP TO THIS? WAS IT NIKKI?!
WHAT'D SHE SAY ABOUT ME?
IT WASN'T NIKKI, MOM. IT'S JUST...
DAD'S ALWAYS AROUND, PRETTY MUCH. AND YOU'RE... SOMETIMES YOU'RE NOT.
COOPER, YOU'RE TOO YOUNG TOO UNDERSTAND THIS, BUT YOUR DAD IS ALWAYS AROUND BECAUSE HE'S IRRESPONSIBLE AND CAN'T HOLD A REAL JOB.
REAL ADULTS? REAL RESPONSIBLE PEOPLE?
THEY HAVE TO HAVE JOBS, AND SOMETIMES THOSE JOBS MAKE THEM VERY BUSY.
DAD SAID YOU'D SAY THAT...
BECAUSE YOU LIKE TO GO TO WORK ALL THE TIME AND HANG OUT WITH YOUR NEW BOYFRIEND, IBRAHIM.

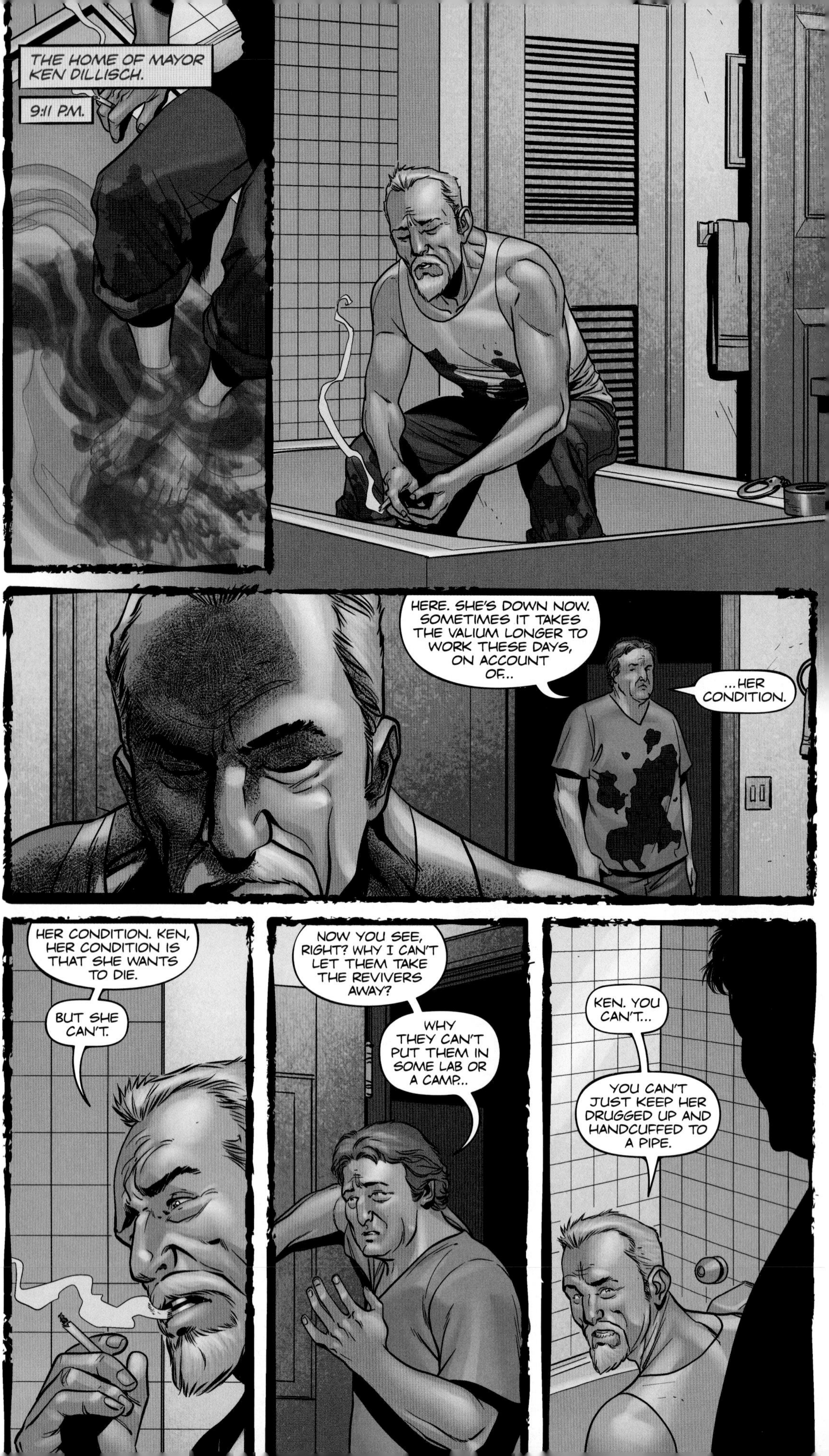
THE HOME OF MAYOR KEN DILLISCH.
9:11 P.M.
HERE. SHE'S DOWN NOW. SOMETIMES IT TAKES THE VALIUM LONGER TO WORK THESE DAYS, ON ACCOUNT OF...
...HER CONDITION.
HER CONDITION. KEN, HER CONDITION IS THAT SHE WANTS TO DIE.
BUT SHE CAN'T.
NOW YOU SEE, RIGHT? WHY I CAN'T LET THEM TAKE THE REVIVERS AWAY?
WHY THEY CAN'T PUT THEM IN SOME LAB OR A CAMP...
KEN. YOU CAN'T...
YOU CAN'T JUST KEEP HER DRUGGED UP AND HANDCUFFED TO A PIPE.

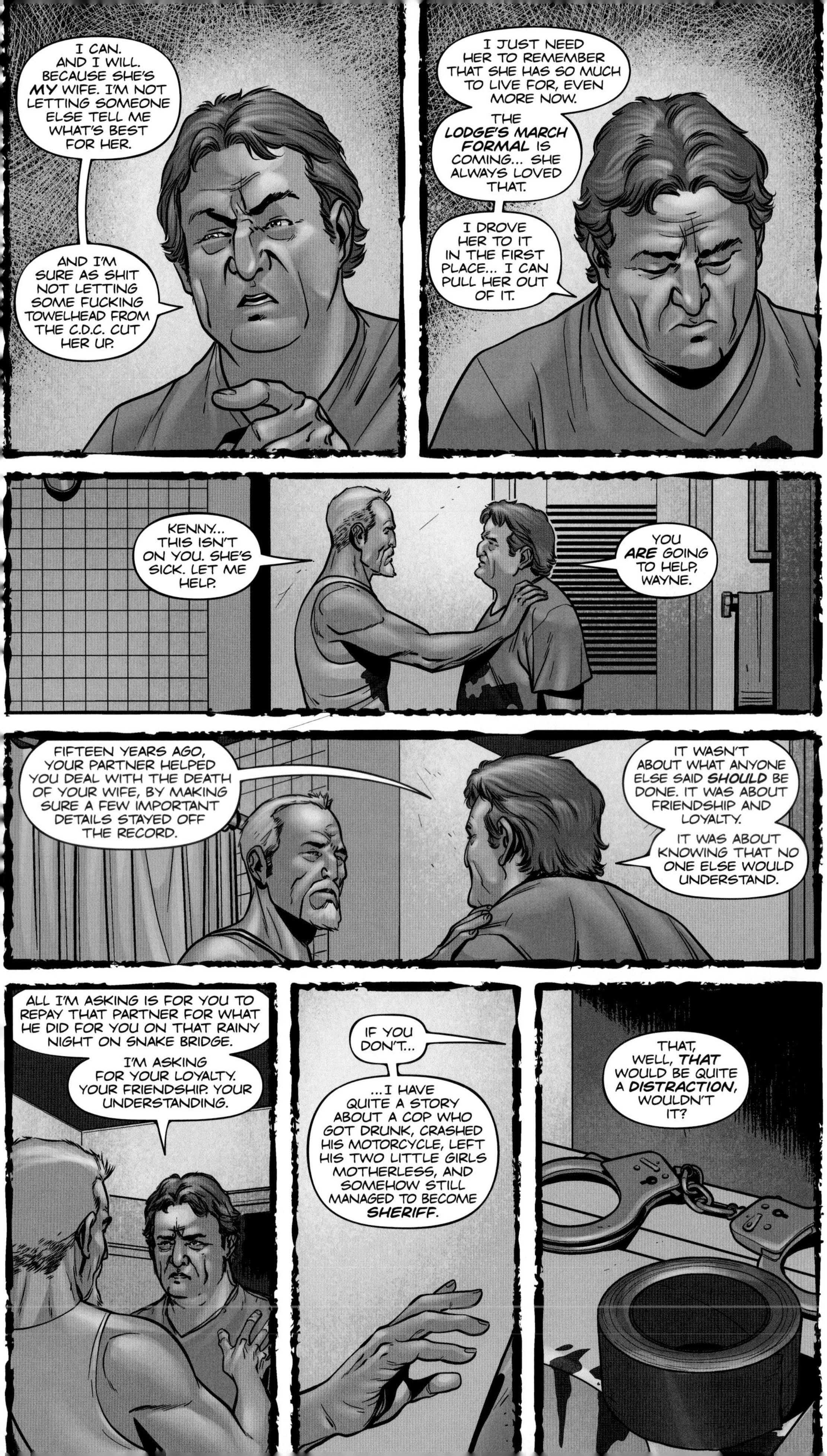
I CAN. AND I WILL. BECAUSE SHE'S **MY** WIFE. I'M NOT LETTING SOMEONE ELSE TELL ME WHAT'S BEST FOR HER.
AND I'M SURE AS SHIT NOT LETTING SOME FUCKING TOWELHEAD FROM THE C.D.C. CUT HER UP.
I JUST NEED HER TO REMEMBER THAT SHE HAS SO MUCH TO LIVE FOR, EVEN MORE NOW.
THE ***LODGE'S MARCH FORMAL*** IS COMING... SHE ALWAYS LOVED THAT.
I DROVE HER TO IT IN THE FIRST PLACE... I CAN PULL HER OUT OF IT.
KENNY... THIS ISN'T ON YOU. SHE'S SICK. LET ME HELP.
YOU ***ARE*** GOING TO HELP, WAYNE.
FIFTEEN YEARS AGO, YOUR PARTNER HELPED YOU DEAL WITH THE DEATH OF YOUR WIFE, BY MAKING SURE A FEW IMPORTANT DETAILS STAYED OFF THE RECORD.
IT WASN'T ABOUT WHAT ANYONE ELSE SAID ***SHOULD*** BE DONE. IT WAS ABOUT FRIENDSHIP AND LOYALTY.
IT WAS ABOUT KNOWING THAT NO ONE ELSE WOULD UNDERSTAND.
ALL I'M ASKING IS FOR YOU TO REPAY THAT PARTNER FOR WHAT HE DID FOR YOU ON THAT RAINY NIGHT ON SNAKE BRIDGE.
I'M ASKING FOR YOUR LOYALTY. YOUR FRIENDSHIP. YOUR UNDERSTANDING.
IF YOU DON'T...
...I HAVE QUITE A STORY ABOUT A COP WHO GOT DRUNK, CRASHED HIS MOTORCYCLE, LEFT HIS TWO LITTLE GIRLS MOTHERLESS, AND SOMEHOW STILL MANAGED TO BECOME ***SHERIFF***.
THAT, WELL, ***THAT*** WOULD BE QUITE A ***DISTRACTION***, WOULDN'T IT?

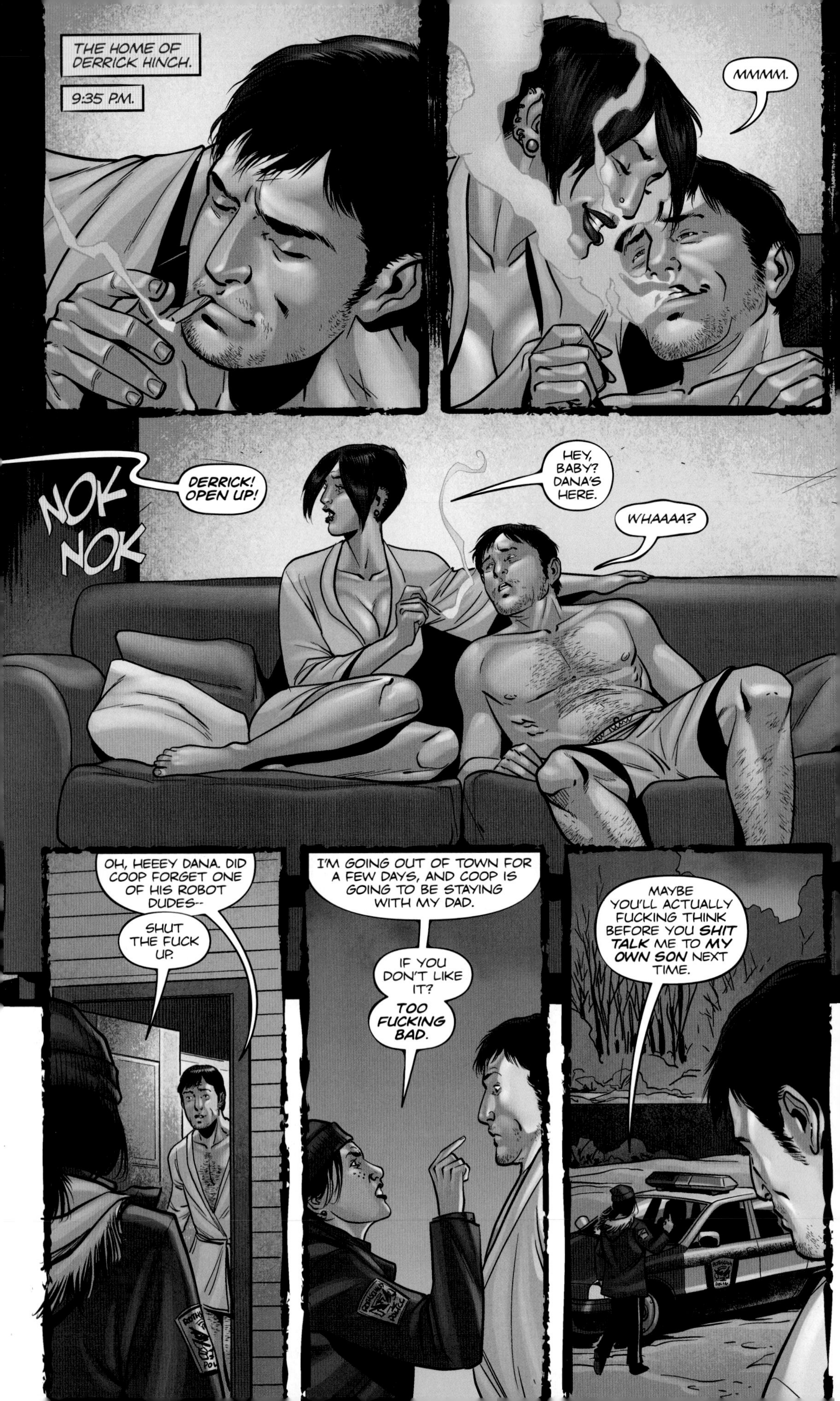

THE HOME OF DERRICK HINCH.
9:35 P.M.
MMMM.
DERRICK! OPEN UP!
NOK NOK
HEY, BABY? DANA'S HERE.
WHAAAA?
OH, HEEEY DANA. DID COOP FORGET ONE OF HIS ROBOT DUDES--
SHUT THE FUCK UP.
I'M GOING OUT OF TOWN FOR A FEW DAYS, AND COOP IS GOING TO BE STAYING WITH MY DAD.
IF YOU DON'T LIKE IT?
TOO FUCKING BAD.
MAYBE YOU'LL ACTUALLY FUCKING THINK BEFORE YOU SHIT TALK ME TO MY OWN SON NEXT TIME.

THE NIGHTLIFE GENTLEMEN'S CLUB.

KRONENWETTER.

10:45 P.M.

TABLE DANCE?

OH, DON'T ACT LIKE YOU'RE SO ASHAMED.

NO. NO DANCE.

USED TO COME HERE ALL THE TIME, BACK IN THE DAY.

CHEAP SKATE MUMMY MUSCLE MAN *LESTER MAJAK.*

YES, WELL, THAT WAS BEFORE I HAD A CERTAIN IMAGE TO MAINTAIN.

HEY, YOU WANNA GET THE *CHIEF* TO COME OFF THE RESERVATION, YOU GOT TO OFFER A LITTLE INCENTIVE.

TITTIES ARE INCENTIVE.

BESIDES I HEAR MOST OF THE STUFF IN THAT BOOK YOU WROTE IS A BUNCH OF BULLSHIT ANYWAY.

OH NO, WAPOOSE. ALL THAT *"INDIAN WISDOM"* GOT TAKEN OUT OF THE BOOK REPRINTS YEARS AGO.

HAHA. REMEMBER THAT TIME I TOLD YOU THAT PEOPLE IN MY TRIBE HAVE USED SEMEN FROM HORSES TO GET RID OF EYE WRINKLES FOR HUNDREDS OF YEARS?

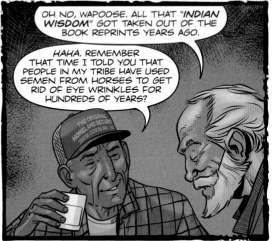

YES. HORSES IN THIS TOWN STILL GET NERVOUS WHEN AN ELDERLY WOMAN GETS ANYWHERE NEAR THEM.

HAH. ONLY THING THAT KEEPS *ME* YOUNG IS LAUGHING AT STUPID WHITE PEOPLE. SO, WHAT'D YOU WANT TO TALK ABOUT, MAJAK?

I-- I'VE HAD AN ENCOUNTER... OF A SPIRITUAL NATURE. A... *GHOST.*

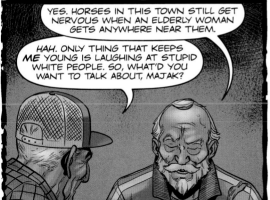

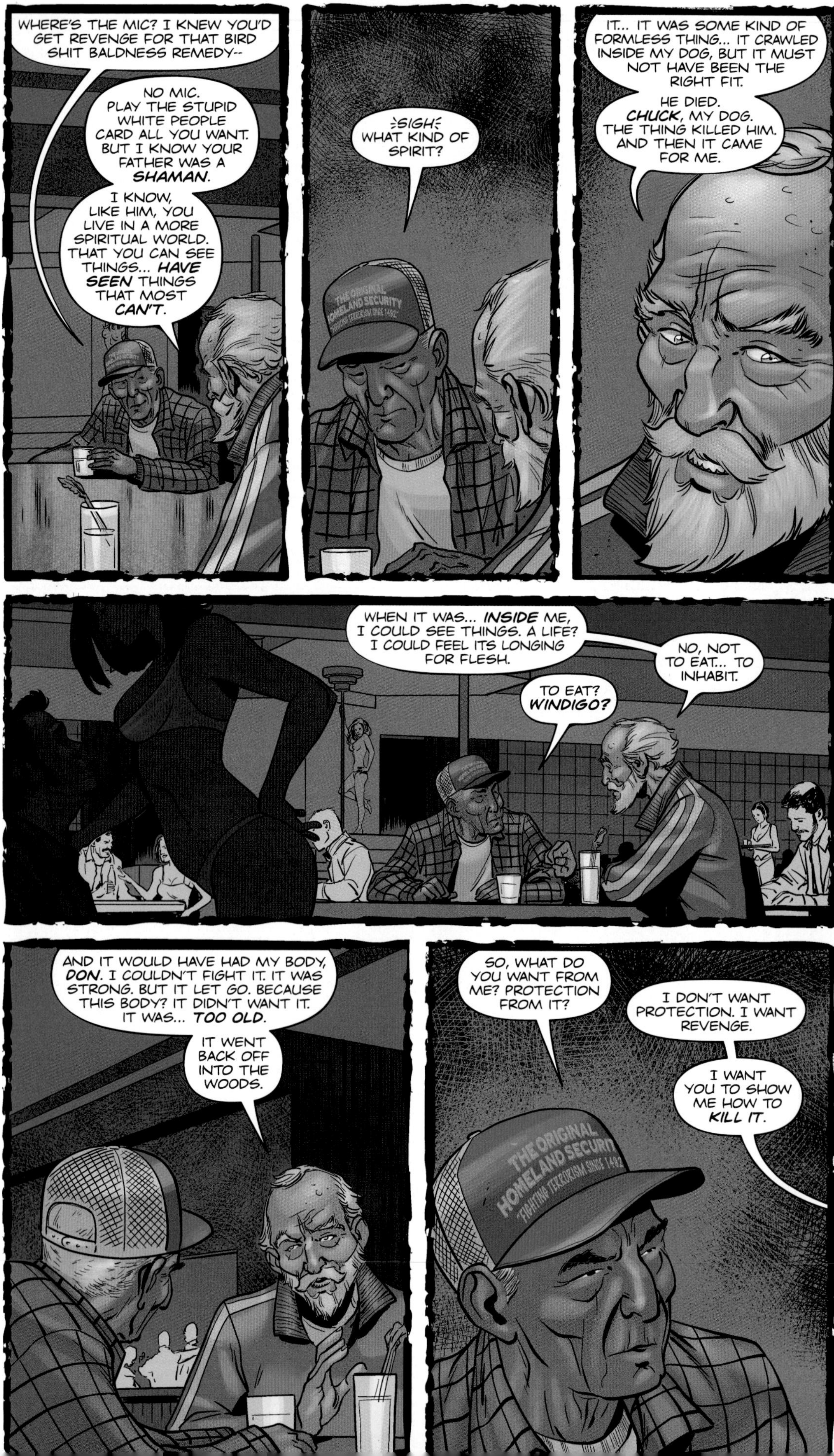
WHERE'S THE MIC? I KNEW YOU'D GET REVENGE FOR THAT BIRD SHIT BALDNESS REMEDY--
NO MIC. PLAY THE STUPID WHITE PEOPLE CARD ALL YOU WANT. BUT I KNOW YOUR FATHER WAS A SHAMAN.
I KNOW, LIKE HIM, YOU LIVE IN A MORE SPIRITUAL WORLD. THAT YOU CAN SEE THINGS... HAVE SEEN THINGS THAT MOST CAN'T.
THE ORIGINAL HOMELAND SECURITY
SIGH WHAT KIND OF SPIRIT?
THE ORIGINAL HOMELAND SECURITY "FIGHTING TERRORISM SINCE 1492"
IT... IT WAS SOME KIND OF FORMLESS THING... IT CRAWLED INSIDE MY DOG, BUT IT MUST NOT HAVE BEEN THE RIGHT FIT.
HE DIED. CHUCK, MY DOG. THE THING KILLED HIM. AND THEN IT CAME FOR ME.
WHEN IT WAS... INSIDE ME, I COULD SEE THINGS. A LIFE? I COULD FEEL ITS LONGING FOR FLESH.
TO EAT? WINDIGO?
NO, NOT TO EAT... TO INHABIT.
AND IT WOULD HAVE HAD MY BODY, DON. I COULDN'T FIGHT IT. IT WAS STRONG. BUT IT LET GO. BECAUSE THIS BODY? IT DIDN'T WANT IT. IT WAS... TOO OLD.
IT WENT BACK OFF INTO THE WOODS.
SO, WHAT DO YOU WANT FROM ME? PROTECTION FROM IT?
I DON'T WANT PROTECTION. I WANT REVENGE.
I WANT YOU TO SHOW ME HOW TO KILL IT.
THE ORIGINAL HOMELAND SECURITY "FIGHTING TERRORISM SINCE 1492"

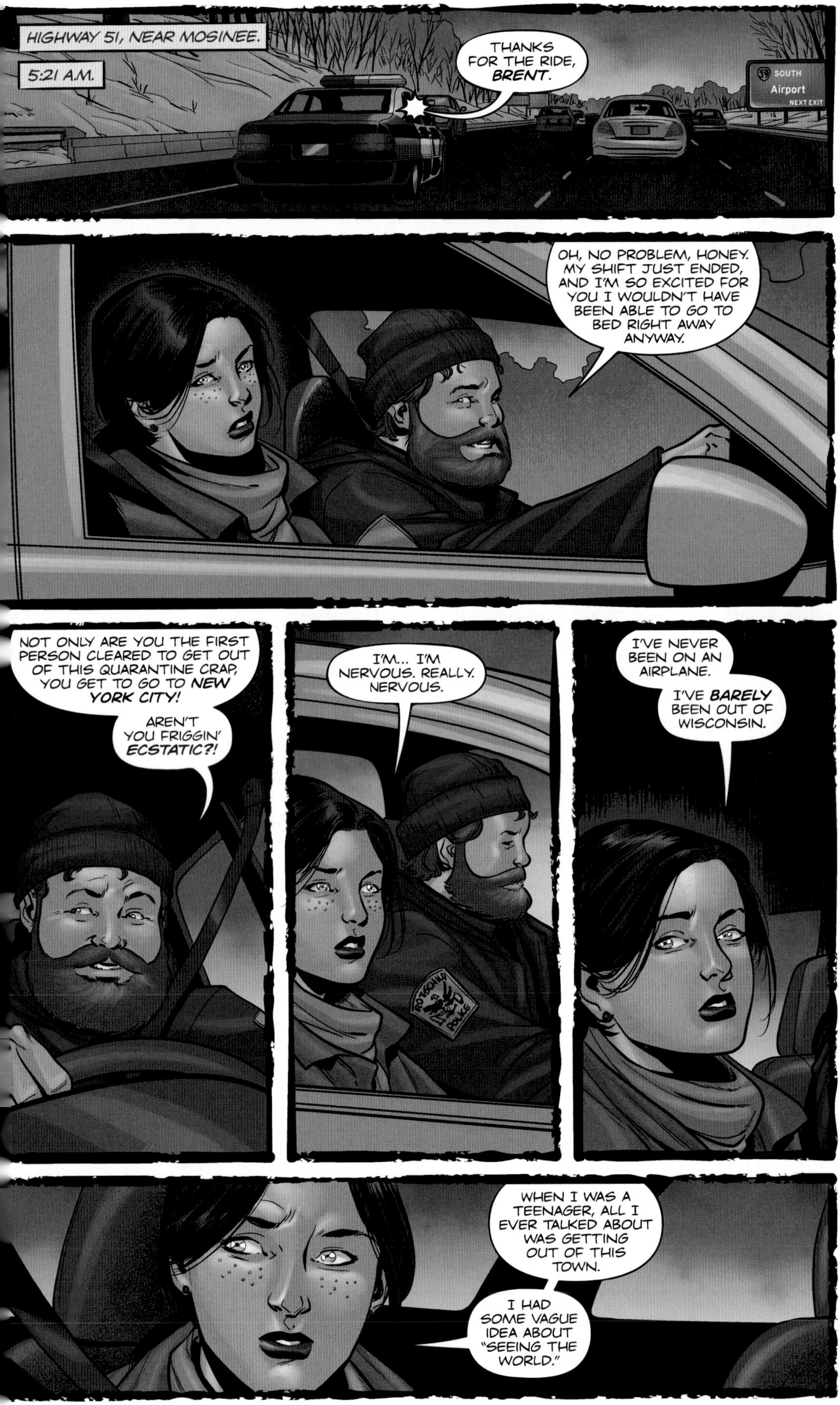
HIGHWAY 51, NEAR MOSINEE.
5:21 A.M.
THANKS FOR THE RIDE, BRENT.
SOUTH Airport NEXT EXIT
OH, NO PROBLEM, HONEY. MY SHIFT JUST ENDED, AND I'M SO EXCITED FOR YOU I WOULDN'T HAVE BEEN ABLE TO GO TO BED RIGHT AWAY ANYWAY.
NOT ONLY ARE YOU THE FIRST PERSON CLEARED TO GET OUT OF THIS QUARANTINE CRAP, YOU GET TO GO TO NEW YORK CITY!
AREN'T YOU FRIGGIN' ECSTATIC?!
I'M... I'M NERVOUS. REALLY. NERVOUS.
I'VE NEVER BEEN ON AN AIRPLANE.
I'VE BARELY BEEN OUT OF WISCONSIN.
WHEN I WAS A TEENAGER, ALL I EVER TALKED ABOUT WAS GETTING OUT OF THIS TOWN.
I HAD SOME VAGUE IDEA ABOUT "SEEING THE WORLD."

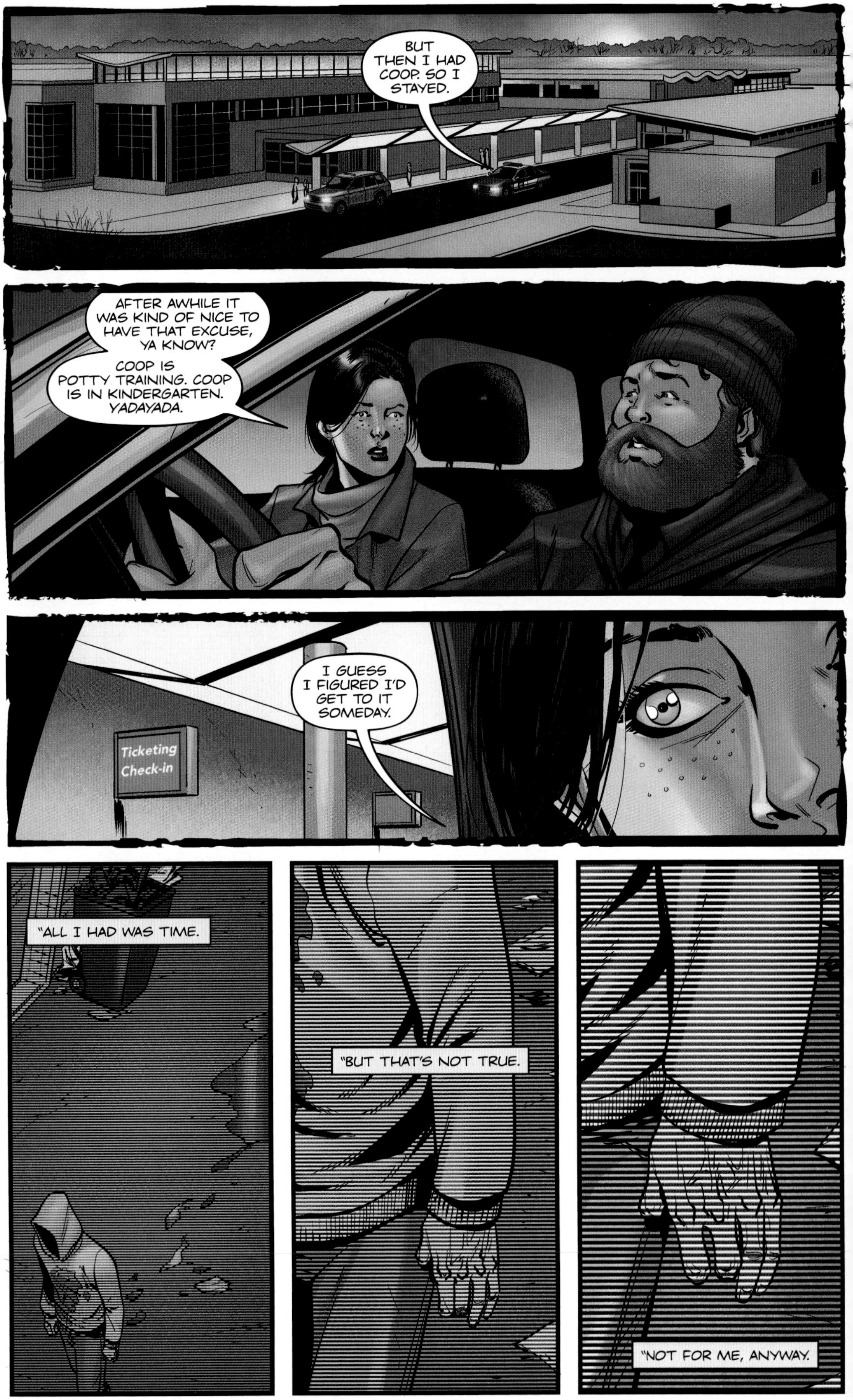
BUT THEN I HAD COOP. SO I STAYED.
AFTER AWHILE IT WAS KIND OF NICE TO HAVE THAT EXCUSE, YA KNOW?
COOP IS POTTY TRAINING. COOP IS IN KINDERGARTEN. YADAYADA.
I GUESS I FIGURED I'D GET TO IT SOMEDAY.
Ticketing Check-in
"ALL I HAD WAS TIME.
"BUT THAT'S NOT TRUE.
"NOT FOR ME, ANYWAY.

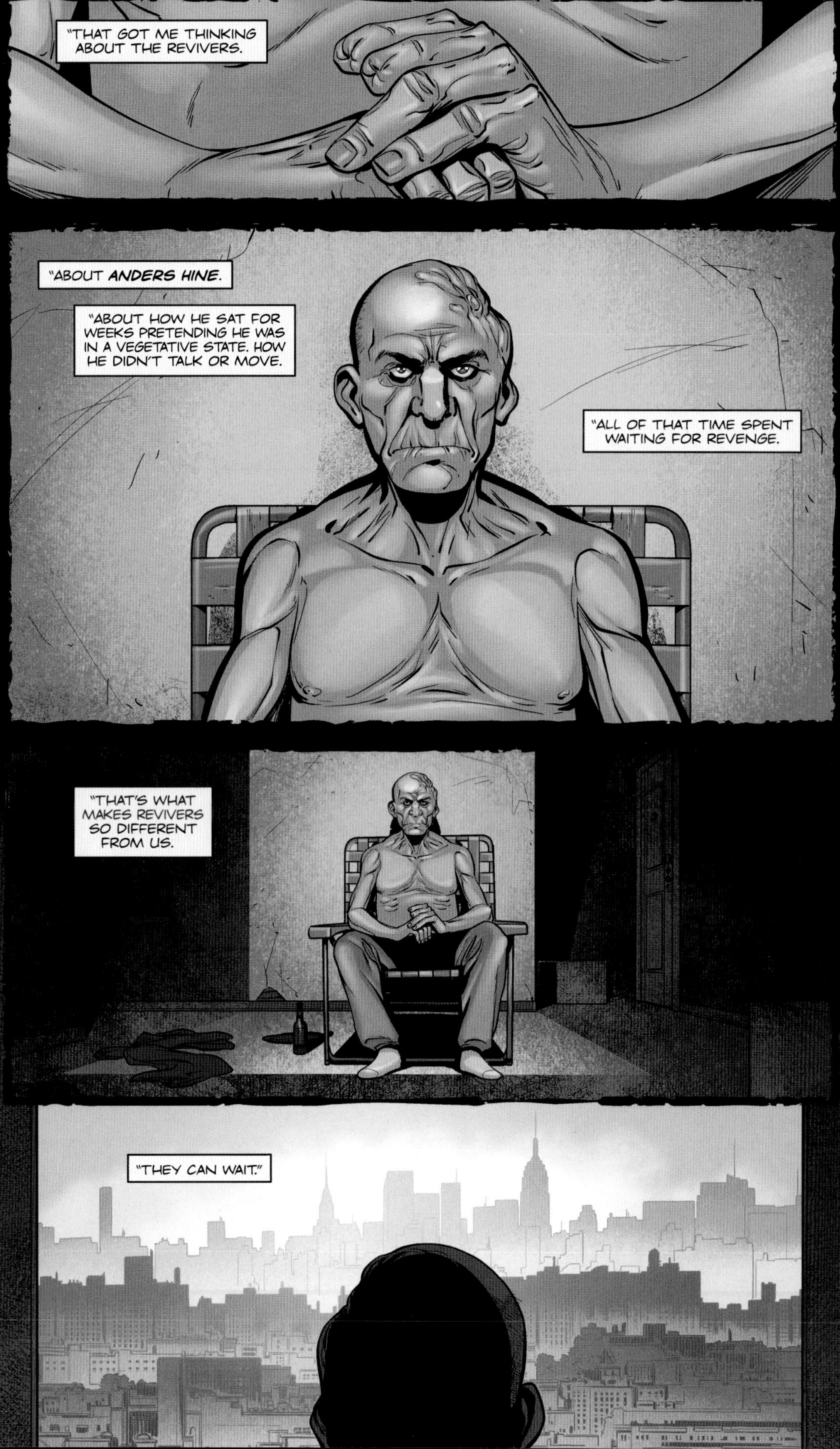
"THAT GOT ME THINKING ABOUT THE REVIVERS.
"ABOUT **ANDERS HINE**.
"ABOUT HOW HE SAT FOR WEEKS PRETENDING HE WAS IN A VEGETATIVE STATE. HOW HE DIDN'T TALK OR MOVE.
"ALL OF THAT TIME SPENT WAITING FOR REVENGE.
"THAT'S WHAT MAKES REVIVERS SO DIFFERENT FROM US.
"THEY CAN WAIT."

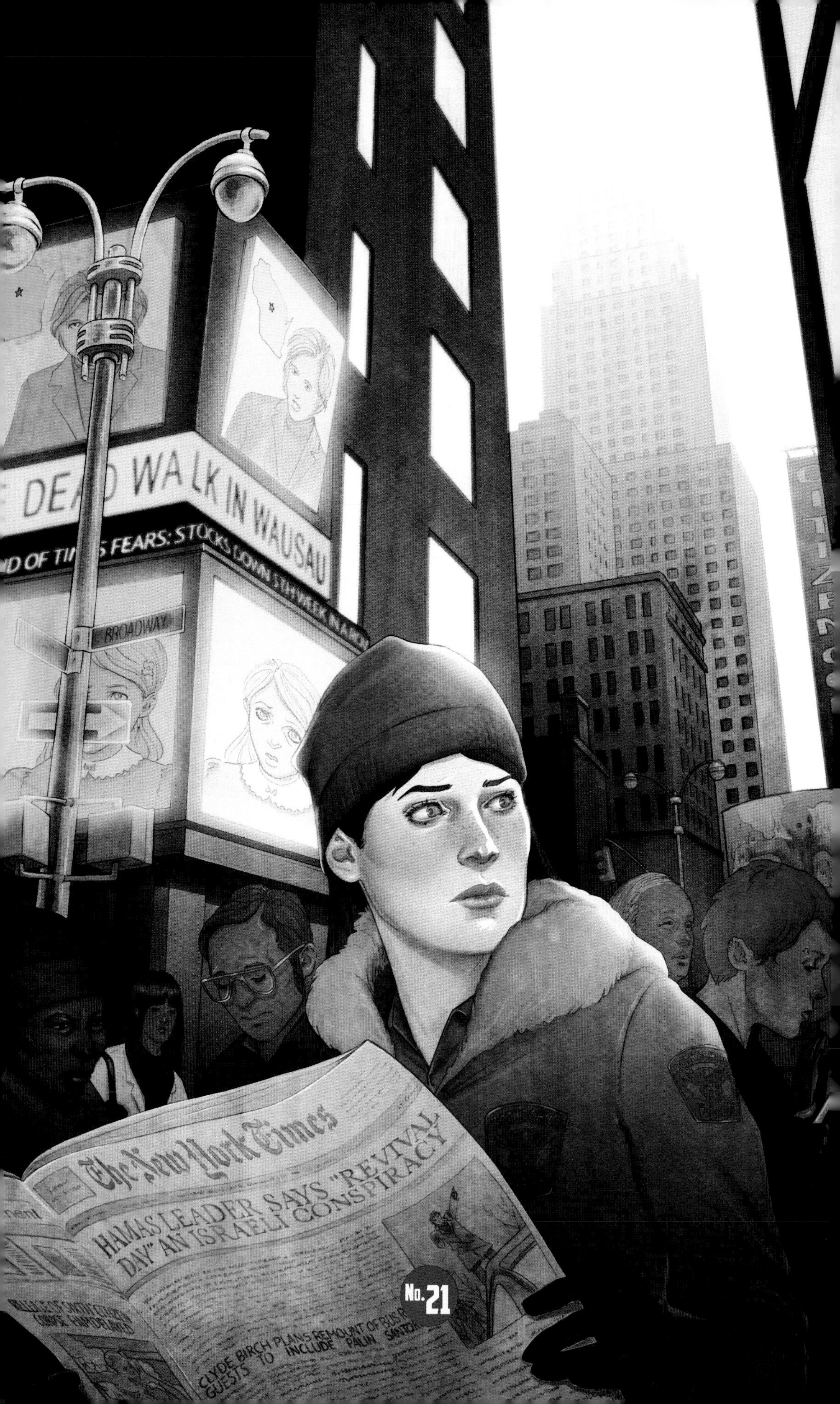
DEA D WALK IN WAUSAU
FEARS: STOCKS DOWN 5TH WEEK
BROADWAY
The New York Times
HAMAS LEADER SAYS "REVIVAL DAY" AN ISRAELI CONSPIRACY
CLYDE BIRCH PLANS REMOUNT OF BUS
GUESTS TO INCLUDE PALIN
No. 21

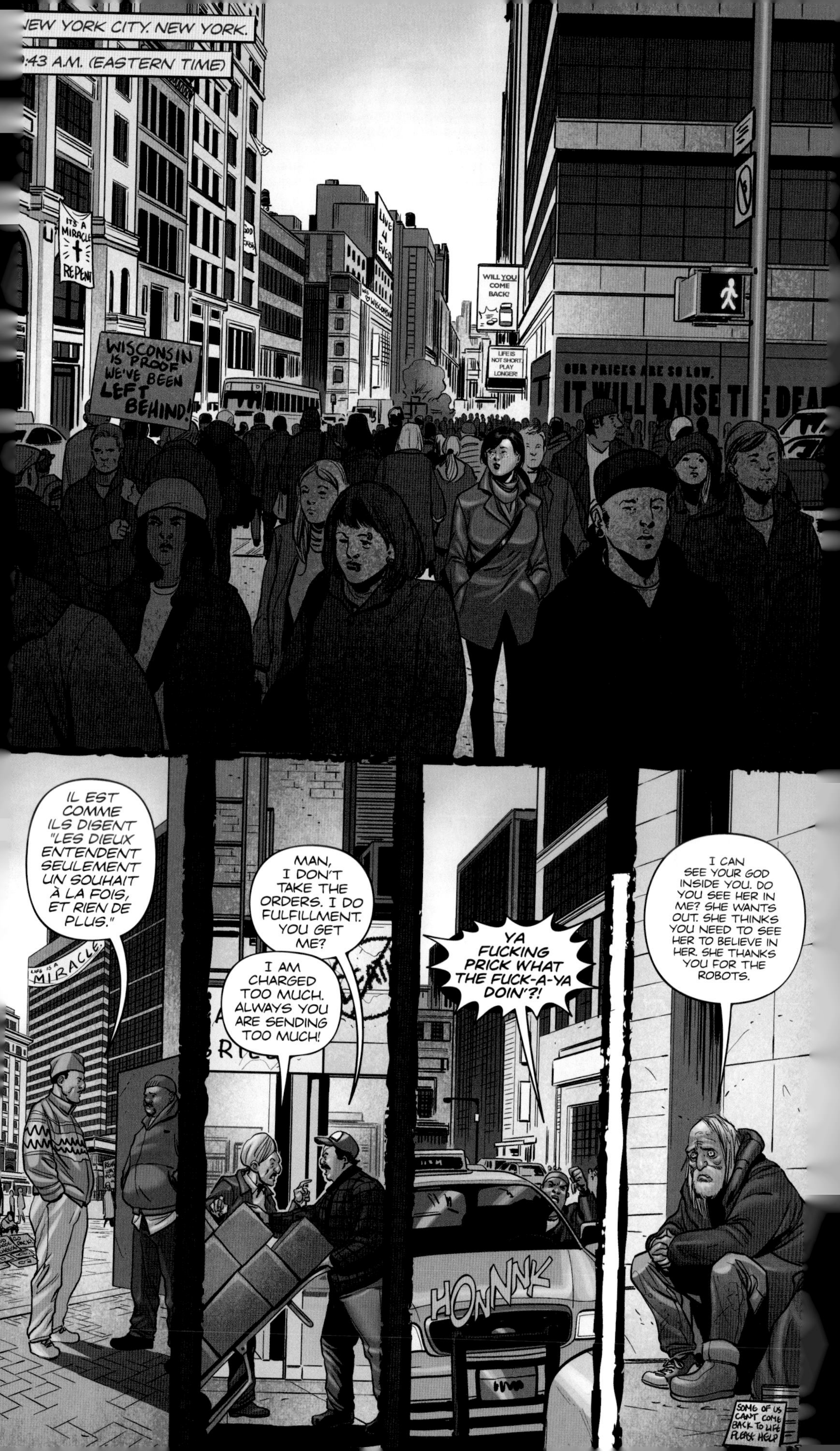

NEW YORK CITY. NEW YORK.
:43 A.M. (EASTERN TIME)
IT'S A MIRACLE REPENT
LIVE 4 EVER
WISCONSIN IS PROOF WE'VE BEEN LEFT BEHIND!
WILL YOU COME BACK!
LIFE IS NOT SHORT. PLAY LONGER!
OUR PRICES ARE SO LOW.
IL EST COMME ILS DISENT "LES DIEUX ENTENDENT SEULEMENT UN SOUHAIT À LA FOIS, ET RIEN DE PLUS."
LIFE IS A MIRACLE.
MAN, I DON'T TAKE THE ORDERS. I DO FULFILLMENT. YOU GET ME?
I AM CHARGED TOO MUCH. ALWAYS YOU ARE SENDING TOO MUCH!
YA FUCKING PRICK WHAT THE FUCK-A-YA DOIN'?!
HONNNK
I CAN SEE YOUR GOD INSIDE YOU. DO YOU SEE HER IN ME? SHE WANTS OUT. SHE THINKS YOU NEED TO SEE HER TO BELIEVE IN HER. SHE THANKS YOU FOR THE ROBOTS.
SOME OF US CANT COME BACK TO LIFE PLEASE HELP

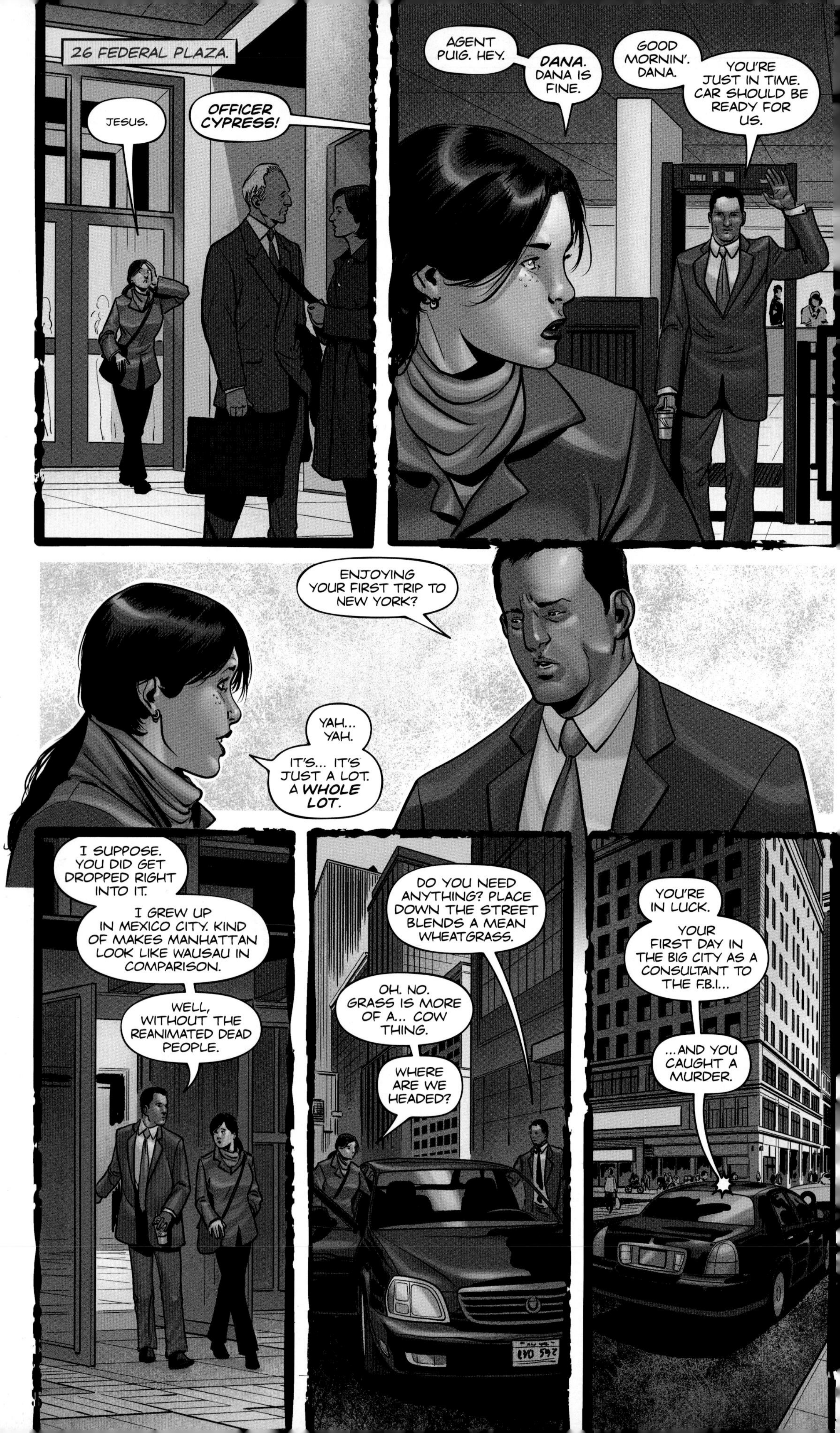
26 FEDERAL PLAZA.
JESUS.
OFFICER CYPRESS!
AGENT PUIG. HEY.
DANA. DANA IS FINE.
GOOD MORNIN'. DANA.
YOU'RE JUST IN TIME. CAR SHOULD BE READY FOR US.
ENJOYING YOUR FIRST TRIP TO NEW YORK?
YAH... YAH.
IT'S... IT'S JUST A LOT. A WHOLE LOT.
I SUPPOSE. YOU DID GET DROPPED RIGHT INTO IT.
I GREW UP IN MEXICO CITY. KIND OF MAKES MANHATTAN LOOK LIKE WAUSAU IN COMPARISON.
WELL, WITHOUT THE REANIMATED DEAD PEOPLE.
DO YOU NEED ANYTHING? PLACE DOWN THE STREET BLENDS A MEAN WHEATGRASS.
OH. NO. GRASS IS MORE OF A... COW THING.
WHERE ARE WE HEADED?
YOU'RE IN LUCK.
YOUR FIRST DAY IN THE BIG CITY AS A CONSULTANT TO THE F.B.I...
...AND YOU CAUGHT A MURDER.

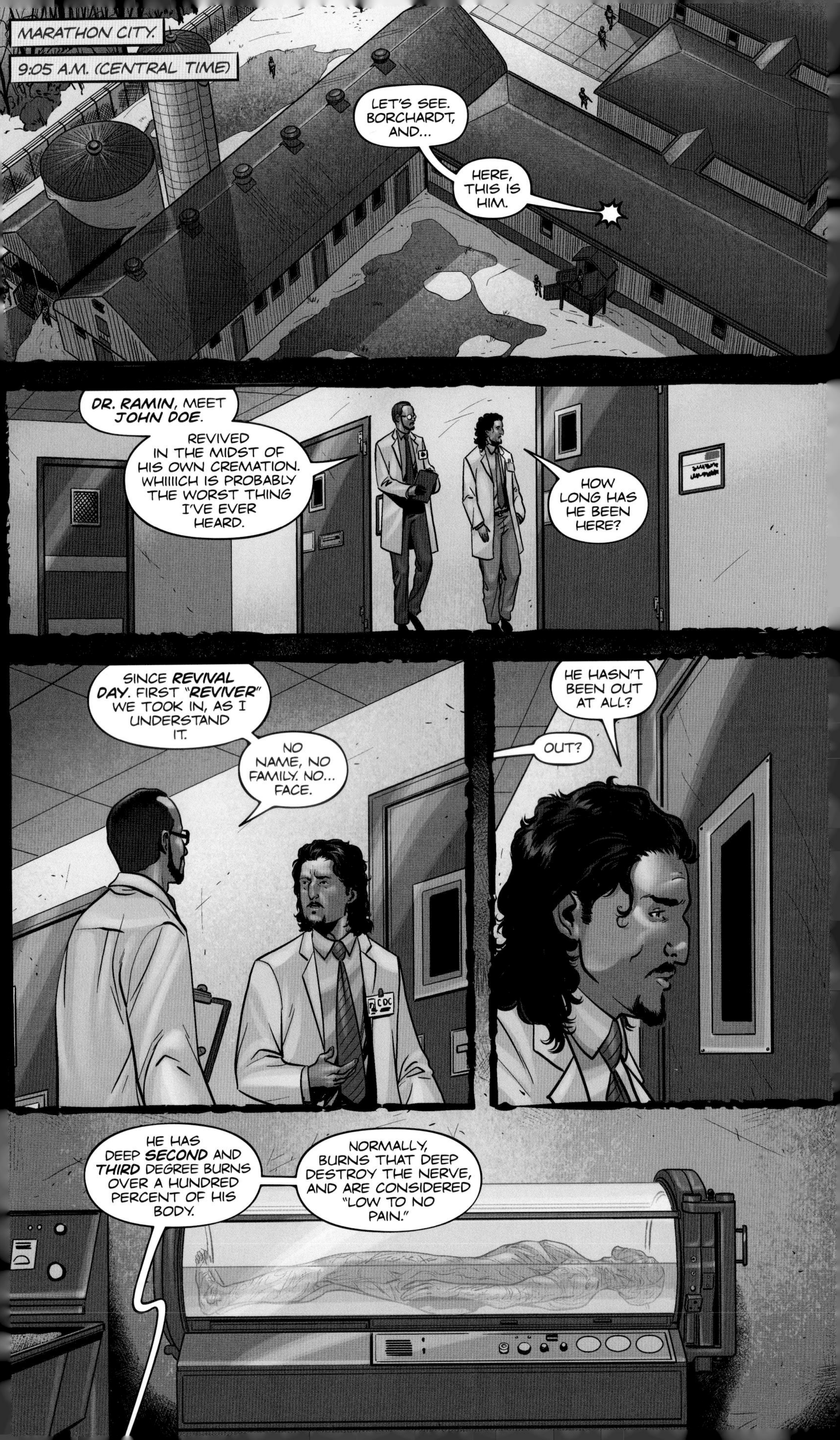
MARATHON CITY.
9:05 A.M. (CENTRAL TIME)
LET'S SEE. BORCHARDT, AND...
HERE, THIS IS HIM.
DR. RAMIN, MEET JOHN DOE.
REVIVED IN THE MIDST OF HIS OWN CREMATION. WHIIIICH IS PROBABLY THE WORST THING I'VE EVER HEARD.
HOW LONG HAS HE BEEN HERE?
SINCE REVIVAL DAY. FIRST "REVIVER" WE TOOK IN, AS I UNDERSTAND IT.
NO NAME, NO FAMILY. NO... FACE.
HE HASN'T BEEN OUT AT ALL?
OUT?
HE HAS DEEP SECOND AND THIRD DEGREE BURNS OVER A HUNDRED PERCENT OF HIS BODY.
NORMALLY, BURNS THAT DEEP DESTROY THE NERVE, AND ARE CONSIDERED "LOW TO NO PAIN."

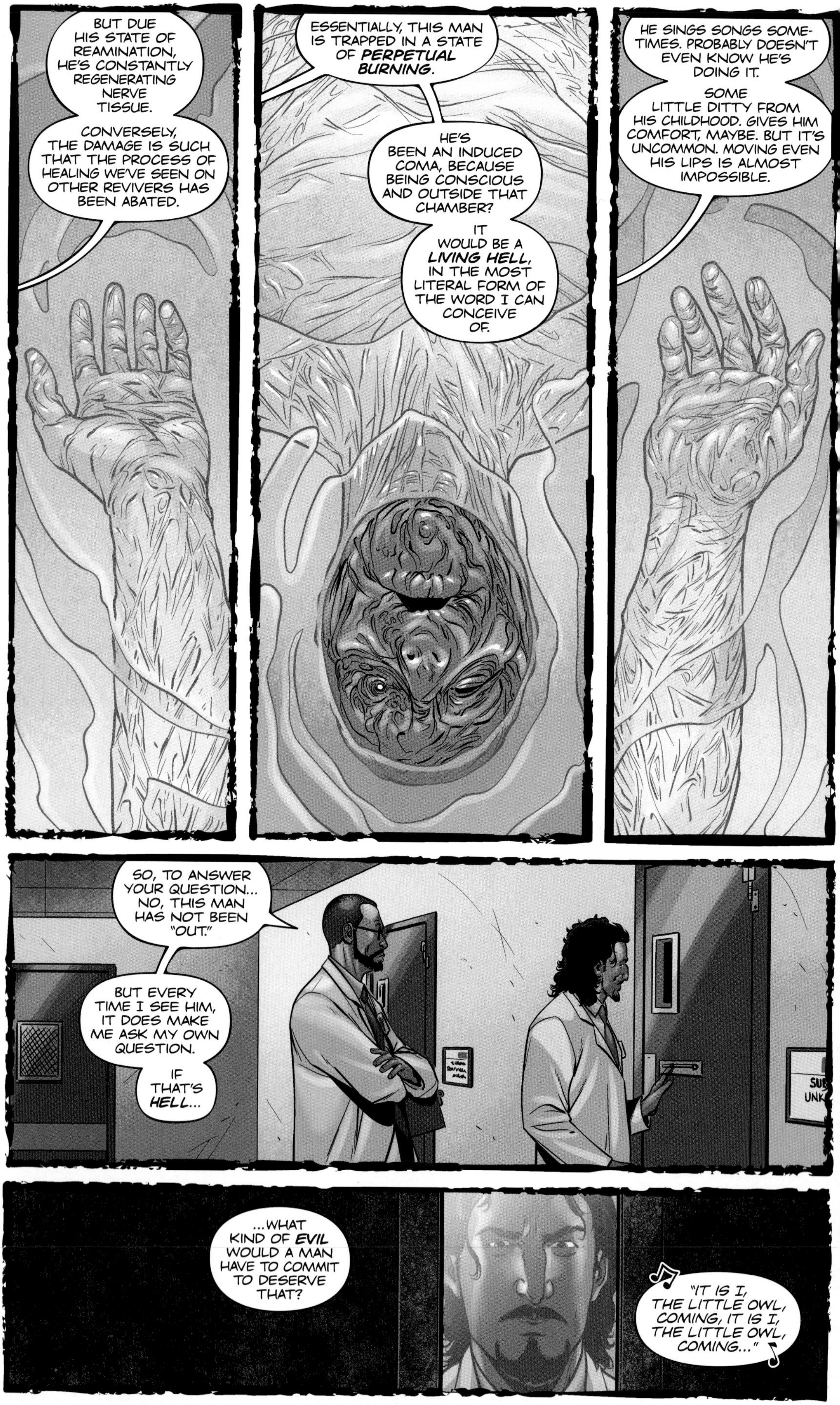
BUT DUE HIS STATE OF REAMINATION, HE'S CONSTANTLY REGENERATING NERVE TISSUE.
CONVERSELY, THE DAMAGE IS SUCH THAT THE PROCESS OF HEALING WE'VE SEEN ON OTHER REVIVERS HAS BEEN ABATED.
ESSENTIALLY, THIS MAN IS TRAPPED IN A STATE OF PERPETUAL BURNING.
HE'S BEEN AN INDUCED COMA, BECAUSE BEING CONSCIOUS AND OUTSIDE THAT CHAMBER?
IT WOULD BE A LIVING HELL, IN THE MOST LITERAL FORM OF THE WORD I CAN CONCEIVE OF.
HE SINGS SONGS SOMETIMES. PROBABLY DOESN'T EVEN KNOW HE'S DOING IT.
SOME LITTLE DITTY FROM HIS CHILDHOOD. GIVES HIM COMFORT, MAYBE. BUT IT'S UNCOMMON. MOVING EVEN HIS LIPS IS ALMOST IMPOSSIBLE.
SO, TO ANSWER YOUR QUESTION... NO, THIS MAN HAS NOT BEEN "OUT."
BUT EVERY TIME I SEE HIM, IT DOES MAKE ME ASK MY OWN QUESTION.
IF THAT'S HELL...
...WHAT KIND OF EVIL WOULD A MAN HAVE TO COMMIT TO DESERVE THAT?
"IT IS I, THE LITTLE OWL, COMING, IT IS I, THE LITTLE OWL, COMING..."

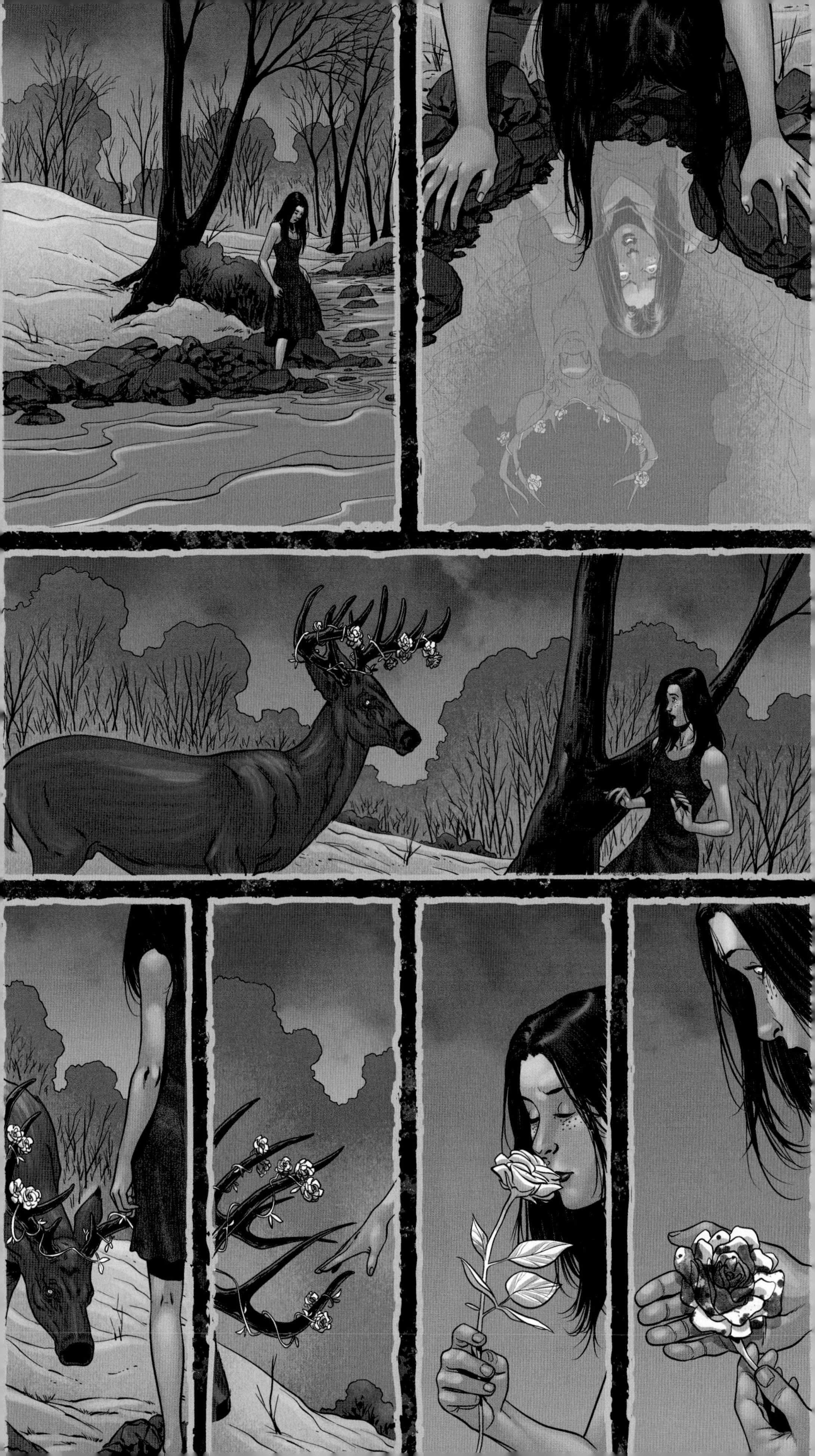

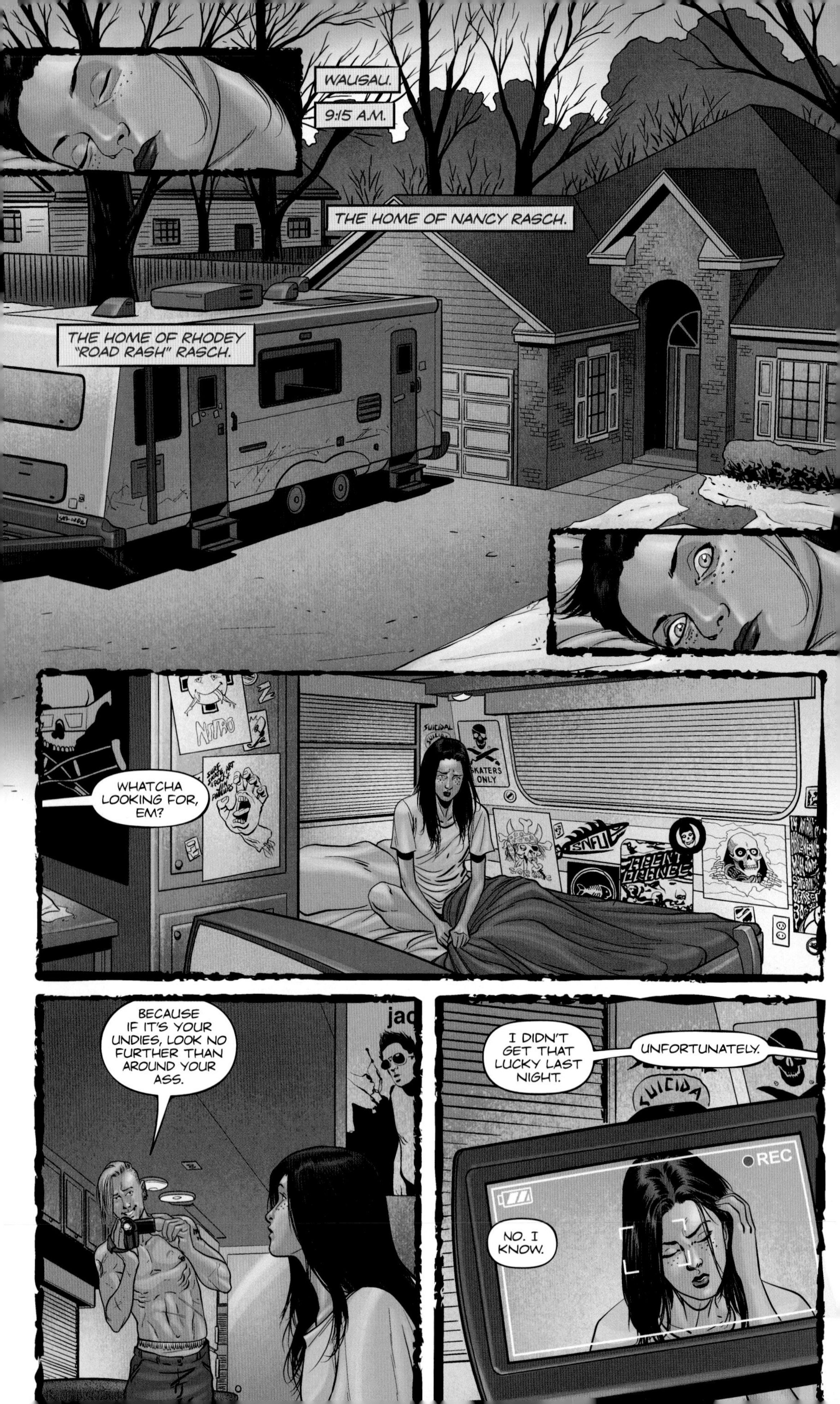
WAUSAU.
9:15 A.M.
THE HOME OF NANCY RASCH.
THE HOME OF RHODEY "ROAD RASH" RASCH.
WHATCHA LOOKING FOR, EM?
BECAUSE IF IT'S YOUR UNDIES, LOOK NO FURTHER THAN AROUND YOUR ASS.
I DIDN'T GET THAT LUCKY LAST NIGHT.
UNFORTUNATELY.
NO. I KNOW.
REC

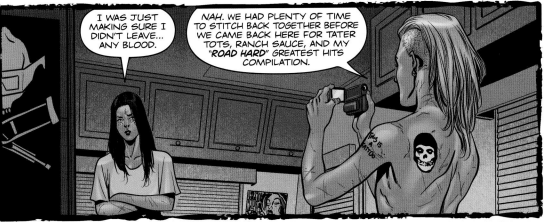

I WAS JUST MAKING SURE I DIDN'T LEAVE... ANY BLOOD.

NAH. WE HAD PLENTY OF TIME TO STITCH BACK TOGETHER BEFORE WE CAME BACK HERE FOR TATER TOTS, RANCH SAUCE, AND MY *"ROAD HARD"* GREATEST HITS COMPILATION.

I SHOULD GO, *RHODEY.* I HAVE A CLASS.

IT'S COOL. I DO HAVE TO GET TO WORK.

BEING A FAMOUS INTERNET DAREDEVIL MEANS CONSTANTLY COMING UP WITH NEW WAYS TO COMBINE PAIN AND FARTING.

HM. SOMETHING DIFFERENT ABOUT YOU TODAY, EM. LESS HUNCH. LESS MOPEY.

Y'KNOW WHAT?

YOU SHOULD PROBABLY CALL ME.

I THINK I'M GOOD FOR YOU.

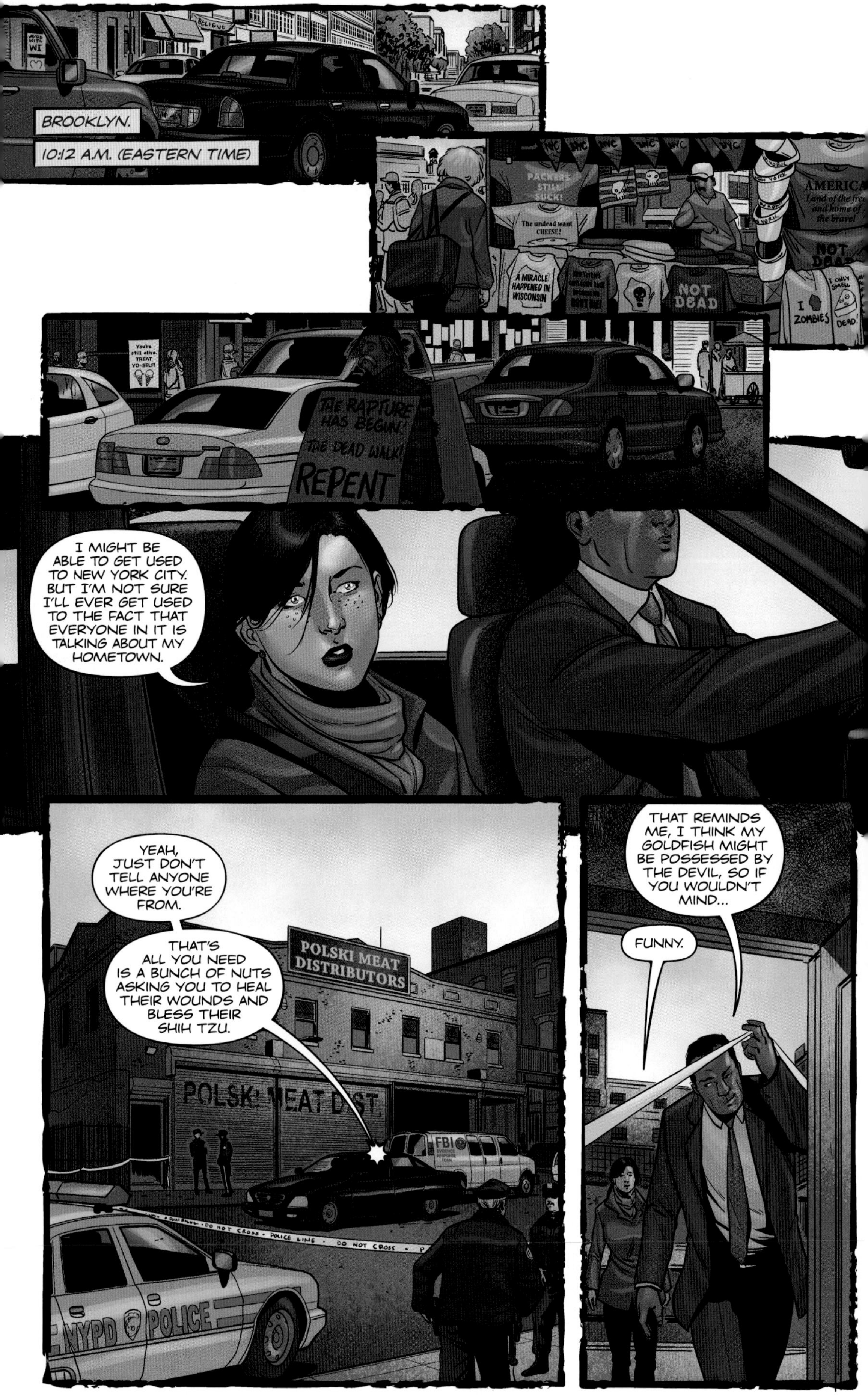
BROOKLYN.
10:12 A.M. (EASTERN TIME)
PACKERS STILL SUCK!
The undead want CHEESE!
A MIRACLE! HAPPENED IN WISCONSIN
NOT DEAD
AMERICA Land of the free and home of the brave!
I ONLY SMELL DEAD!
ZOMBIES
You're still alive. TREAT YO-SELF!
THE RAPTURE HAS BEGUN! THE DEAD WALK! REPENT
I MIGHT BE ABLE TO GET USED TO NEW YORK CITY. BUT I'M NOT SURE I'LL EVER GET USED TO THE FACT THAT EVERYONE IN IT IS TALKING ABOUT MY HOMETOWN.
YEAH, JUST DON'T TELL ANYONE WHERE YOU'RE FROM.
THAT'S ALL YOU NEED IS A BUNCH OF NUTS ASKING YOU TO HEAL THEIR WOUNDS AND BLESS THEIR SHIH TZU.
POLSKI MEAT DISTRIBUTORS
POLSKI MEAT DIST.
FBI
DO NOT CROSS • POLICE LINE • DO NOT CROSS
NYPD POLICE
THAT REMINDS ME, I THINK MY GOLDFISH MIGHT BE POSSESSED BY THE DEVIL, SO IF YOU WOULDN'T MIND...
FUNNY.

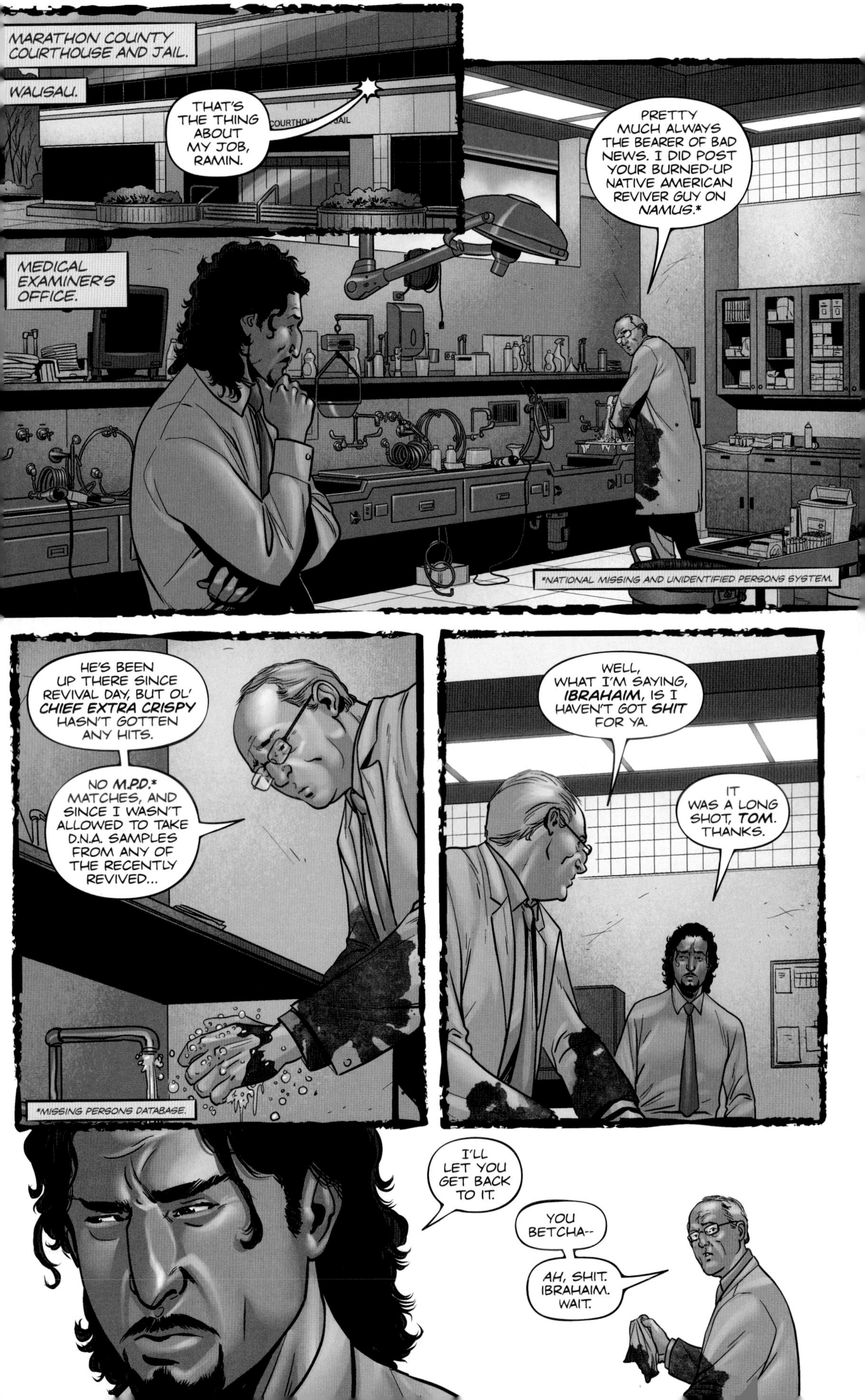
MARATHON COUNTY COURTHOUSE AND JAIL.
WAUSAU.
THAT'S THE THING ABOUT MY JOB, RAMIN.
COURTHOUSE JAIL
MEDICAL EXAMINER'S OFFICE.
PRETTY MUCH ALWAYS THE BEARER OF BAD NEWS. I DID POST YOUR BURNED-UP NATIVE AMERICAN REVIVER GUY ON NAMUS.*
*NATIONAL MISSING AND UNIDENTIFIED PERSONS SYSTEM.
HE'S BEEN UP THERE SINCE REVIVAL DAY, BUT OL' CHIEF EXTRA CRISPY HASN'T GOTTEN ANY HITS.
NO M.P.D.* MATCHES, AND SINCE I WASN'T ALLOWED TO TAKE D.N.A. SAMPLES FROM ANY OF THE RECENTLY REVIVED...
*MISSING PERSONS DATABASE.
WELL, WHAT I'M SAYING, IBRAHAIM, IS I HAVEN'T GOT SHIT FOR YA.
IT WAS A LONG SHOT, TOM. THANKS.
I'LL LET YOU GET BACK TO IT.
YOU BETCHA--
AH, SHIT. IBRAHAIM. WAIT.

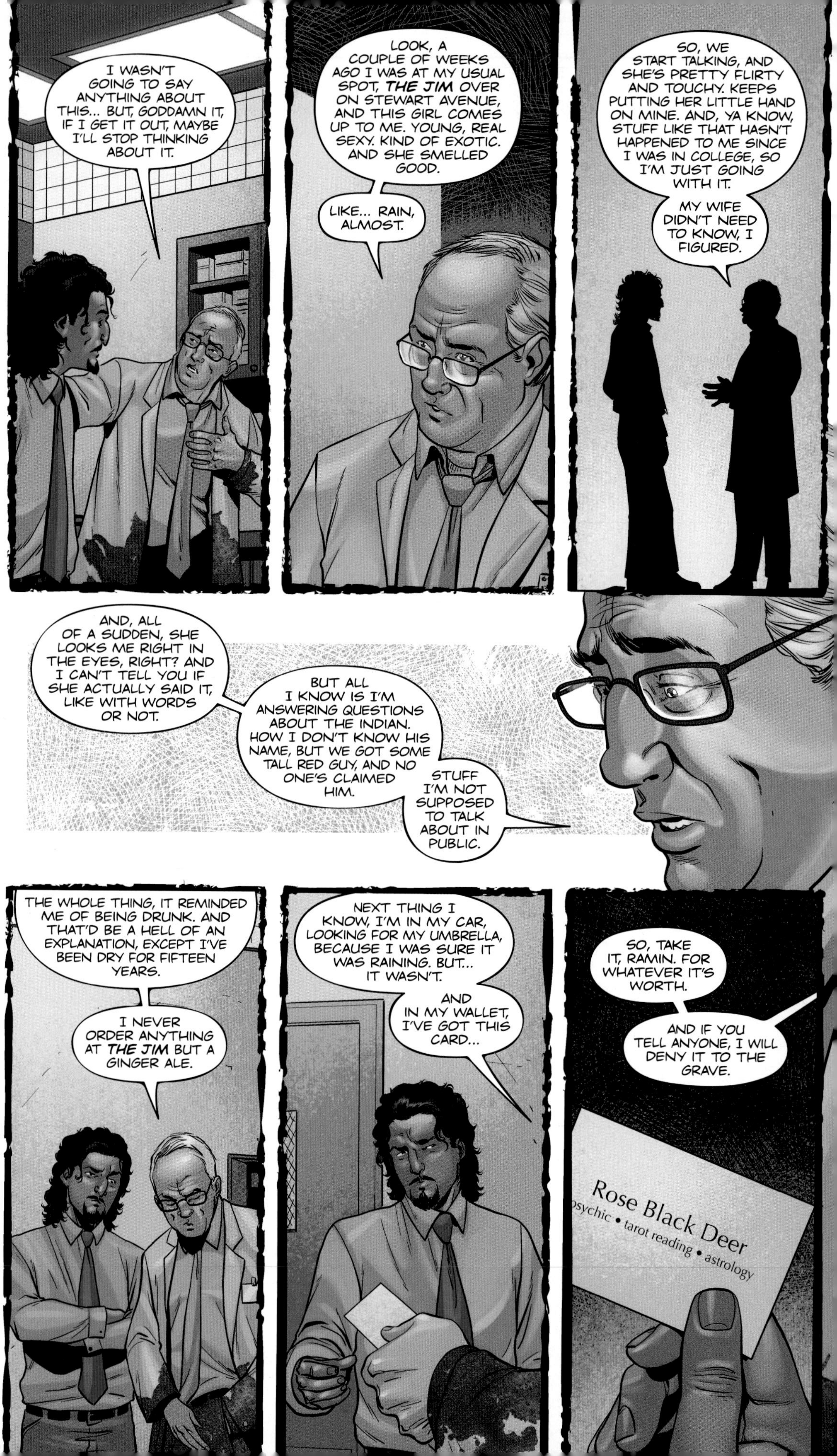
I WASN'T GOING TO SAY ANYTHING ABOUT THIS... BUT, GODDAMN IT, IF I GET IT OUT, MAYBE I'LL STOP THINKING ABOUT IT.
LOOK, A COUPLE OF WEEKS AGO I WAS AT MY USUAL SPOT, THE JIM OVER ON STEWART AVENUE, AND THIS GIRL COMES UP TO ME. YOUNG, REAL SEXY. KIND OF EXOTIC. AND SHE SMELLED GOOD.
LIKE... RAIN, ALMOST.
SO, WE START TALKING, AND SHE'S PRETTY FLIRTY AND TOUCHY. KEEPS PUTTING HER LITTLE HAND ON MINE. AND, YA KNOW, STUFF LIKE THAT HASN'T HAPPENED TO ME SINCE I WAS IN COLLEGE, SO I'M JUST GOING WITH IT.
MY WIFE DIDN'T NEED TO KNOW, I FIGURED.
AND, ALL OF A SUDDEN, SHE LOOKS ME RIGHT IN THE EYES, RIGHT? AND I CAN'T TELL YOU IF SHE ACTUALLY SAID IT, LIKE WITH WORDS OR NOT.
BUT ALL I KNOW IS I'M ANSWERING QUESTIONS ABOUT THE INDIAN. HOW I DON'T KNOW HIS NAME, BUT WE GOT SOME TALL RED GUY, AND NO ONE'S CLAIMED HIM.
STUFF I'M NOT SUPPOSED TO TALK ABOUT IN PUBLIC.
THE WHOLE THING, IT REMINDED ME OF BEING DRUNK. AND THAT'D BE A HELL OF AN EXPLANATION, EXCEPT I'VE BEEN DRY FOR FIFTEEN YEARS.
I NEVER ORDER ANYTHING AT THE JIM BUT A GINGER ALE.
NEXT THING I KNOW, I'M IN MY CAR, LOOKING FOR MY UMBRELLA, BECAUSE I WAS SURE IT WAS RAINING. BUT... IT WASN'T.
AND IN MY WALLET, I'VE GOT THIS CARD...
SO, TAKE IT, RAMIN. FOR WHATEVER IT'S WORTH.
AND IF YOU TELL ANYONE, I WILL DENY IT TO THE GRAVE.
Rose Black Deer
psychic • tarot reading • astrology

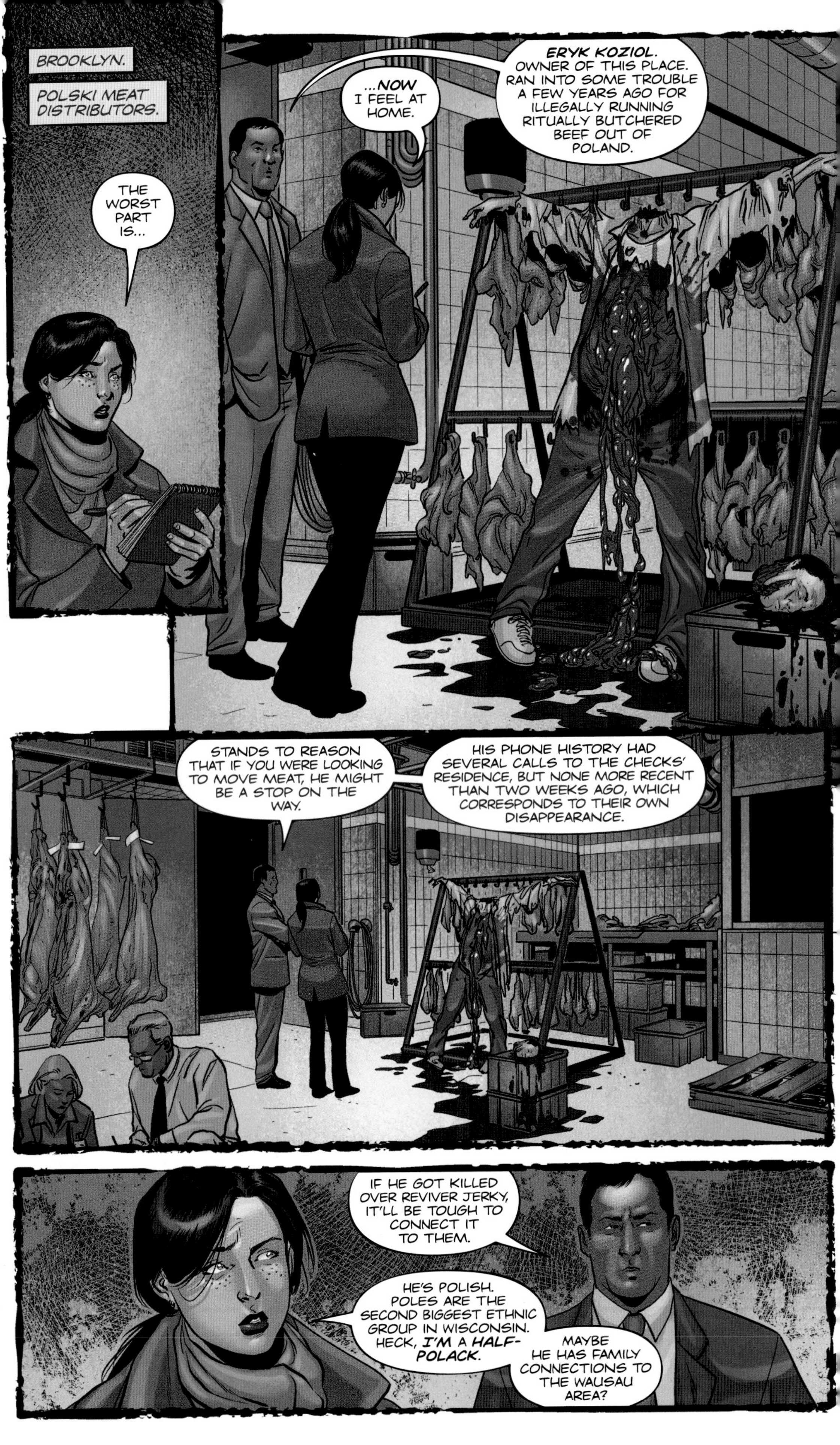
BROOKLYN.
POLSKI MEAT DISTRIBUTORS.
THE WORST PART IS...
...NOW I FEEL AT HOME.
ERYK KOZIOL. OWNER OF THIS PLACE. RAN INTO SOME TROUBLE A FEW YEARS AGO FOR ILLEGALLY RUNNING RITUALLY BUTCHERED BEEF OUT OF POLAND.
STANDS TO REASON THAT IF YOU WERE LOOKING TO MOVE MEAT, HE MIGHT BE A STOP ON THE WAY.
HIS PHONE HISTORY HAD SEVERAL CALLS TO THE CHECKS' RESIDENCE, BUT NONE MORE RECENT THAN TWO WEEKS AGO, WHICH CORRESPONDS TO THEIR OWN DISAPPEARANCE.
IF HE GOT KILLED OVER REVIVER JERKY, IT'LL BE TOUGH TO CONNECT IT TO THEM.
HE'S POLISH. POLES ARE THE SECOND BIGGEST ETHNIC GROUP IN WISCONSIN. HECK, I'M A HALF-POLACK.
MAYBE HE HAS FAMILY CONNECTIONS TO THE WAUSAU AREA?

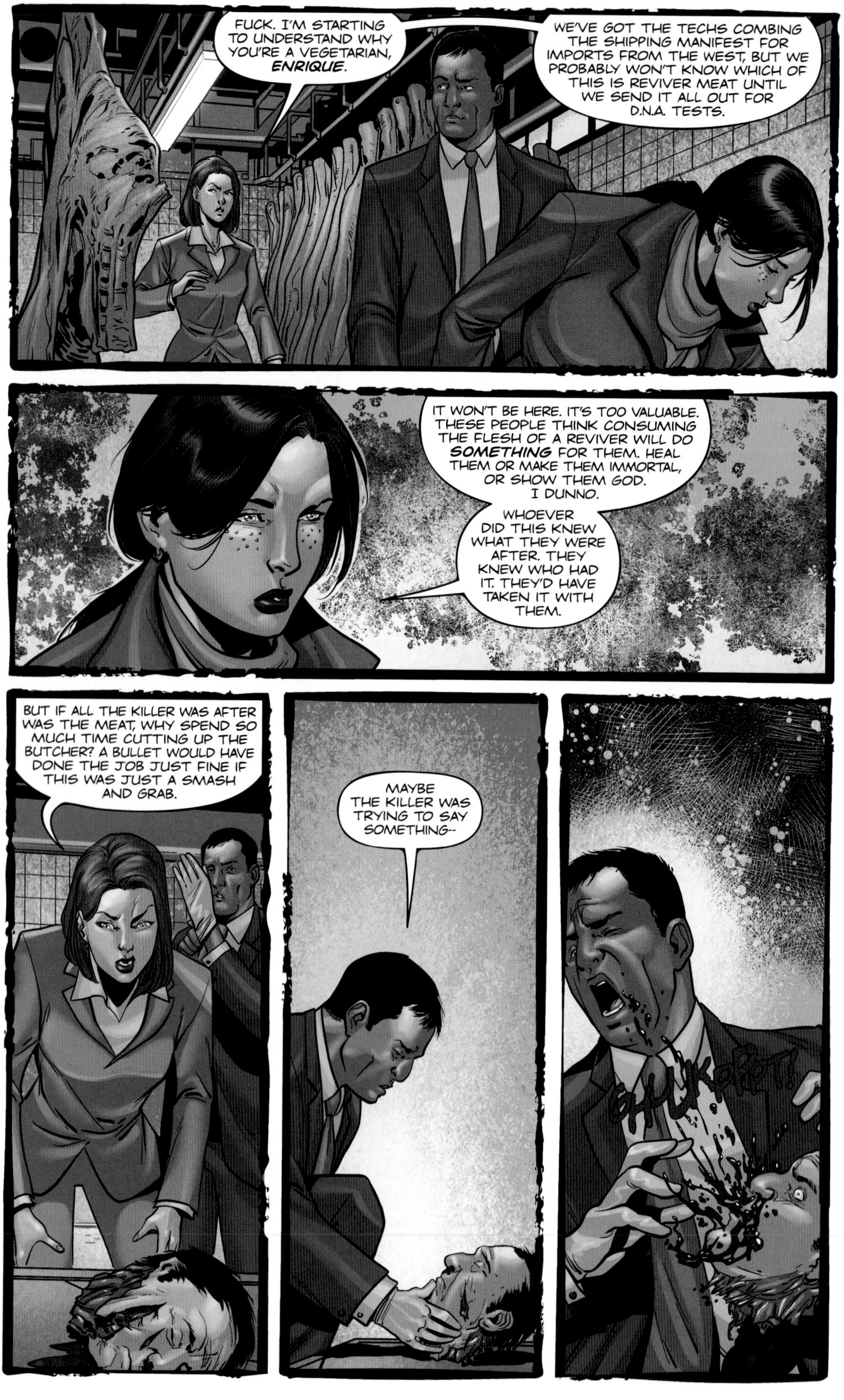
FUCK. I'M STARTING TO UNDERSTAND WHY YOU'RE A VEGETARIAN, ENRIQUE.
WE'VE GOT THE TECHS COMBING THE SHIPPING MANIFEST FOR IMPORTS FROM THE WEST, BUT WE PROBABLY WON'T KNOW WHICH OF THIS IS REVIVER MEAT UNTIL WE SEND IT ALL OUT FOR D.N.A. TESTS.
IT WON'T BE HERE. IT'S TOO VALUABLE. THESE PEOPLE THINK CONSUMING THE FLESH OF A REVIVER WILL DO SOMETHING FOR THEM. HEAL THEM OR MAKE THEM IMMORTAL, OR SHOW THEM GOD. I DUNNO.
WHOEVER DID THIS KNEW WHAT THEY WERE AFTER. THEY KNEW WHO HAD IT. THEY'D HAVE TAKEN IT WITH THEM.
BUT IF ALL THE KILLER WAS AFTER WAS THE MEAT, WHY SPEND SO MUCH TIME CUTTING UP THE BUTCHER? A BULLET WOULD HAVE DONE THE JOB JUST FINE IF THIS WAS JUST A SMASH AND GRAB.
MAYBE THE KILLER WAS TRYING TO SAY SOMETHING--

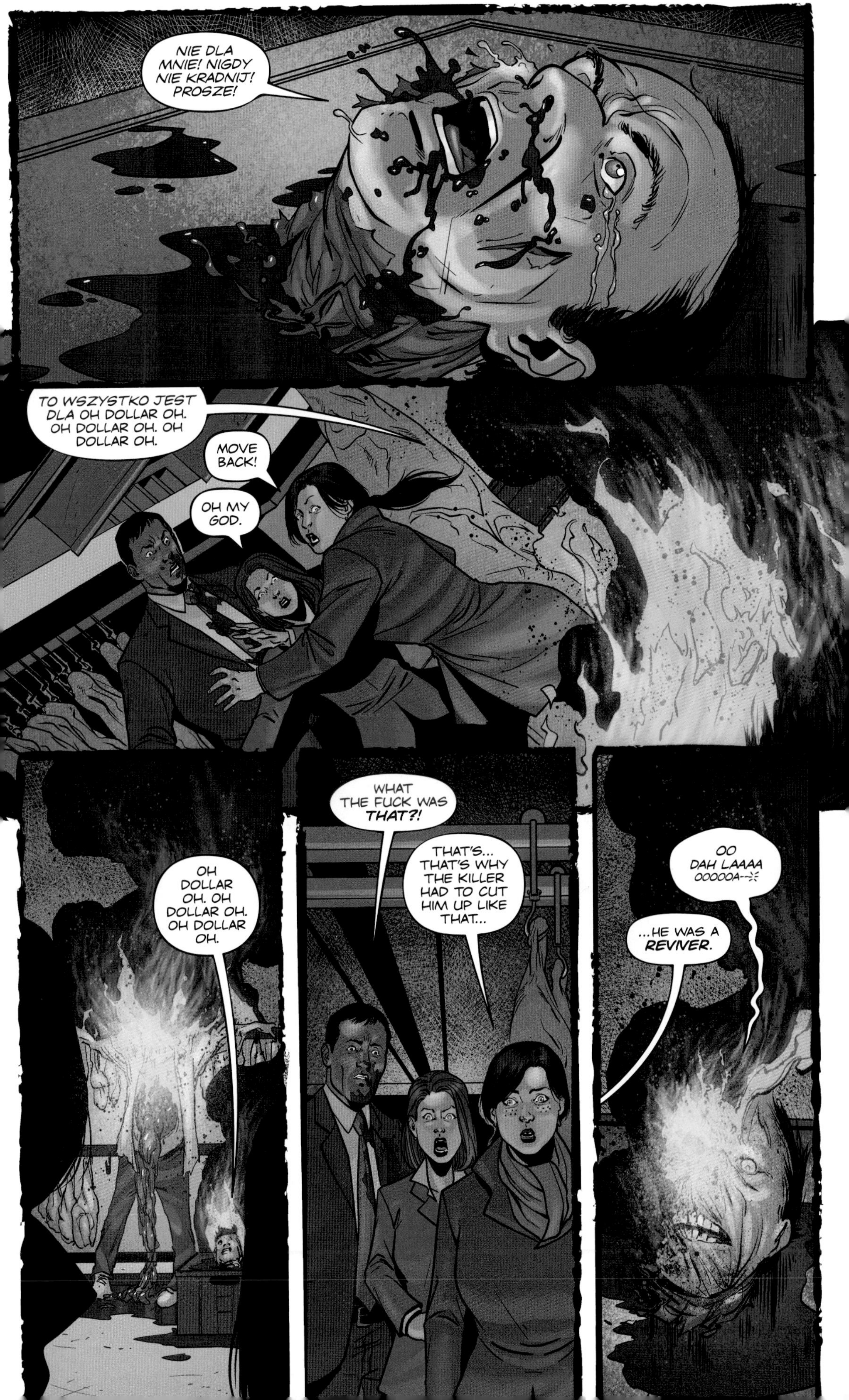
NIE DLA MNIE! NIGDY NIE KRADNIJ! PROSZE!
TO WSZYSTKO JEST DLA OH DOLLAR OH. OH DOLLAR OH. OH DOLLAR OH.
MOVE BACK!
OH MY GOD.
OH DOLLAR OH. OH DOLLAR OH. OH DOLLAR OH.
WHAT THE FUCK WAS *THAT?!*
THAT'S... THAT'S WHY THE KILLER HAD TO CUT HIM UP LIKE THAT...
...HE WAS A ***REVIVER***.
OO DAH LAAAA OOOOOA--

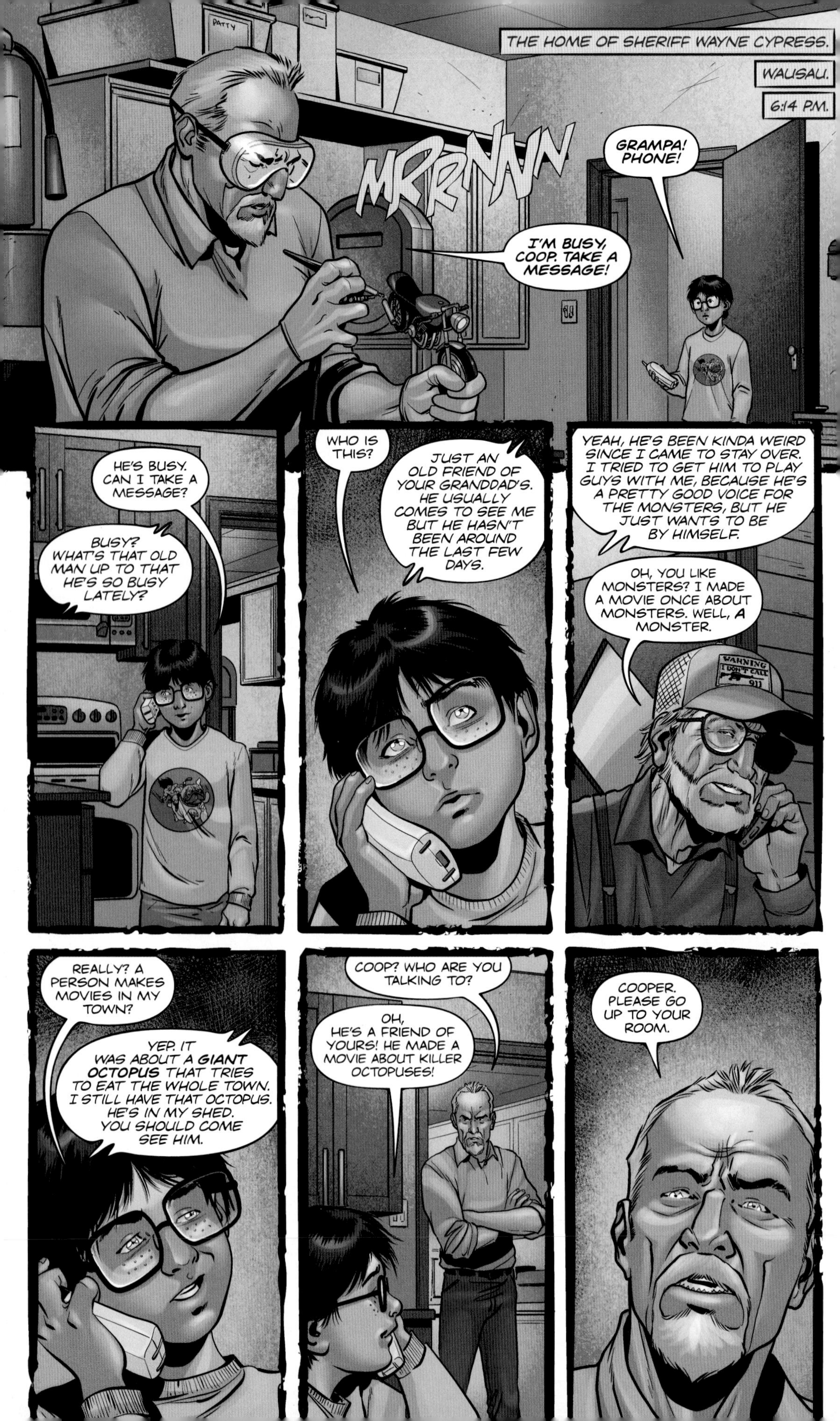
THE HOME OF SHERIFF WAYNE CYPRESS.
WAUSAU.
6:14 P.M.
MRRNNN
GRAMPA! PHONE!
I'M BUSY, COOP. TAKE A MESSAGE!
HE'S BUSY. CAN I TAKE A MESSAGE?
BUSY? WHAT'S THAT OLD MAN UP TO THAT HE'S SO BUSY LATELY?
WHO IS THIS?
JUST AN OLD FRIEND OF YOUR GRANDDAD'S. HE USUALLY COMES TO SEE ME BUT HE HASN'T BEEN AROUND THE LAST FEW DAYS.
YEAH, HE'S BEEN KINDA WEIRD SINCE I CAME TO STAY OVER. I TRIED TO GET HIM TO PLAY GUYS WITH ME, BECAUSE HE'S A PRETTY GOOD VOICE FOR THE MONSTERS, BUT HE JUST WANTS TO BE BY HIMSELF.
OH, YOU LIKE MONSTERS? I MADE A MOVIE ONCE ABOUT MONSTERS. WELL, **A** MONSTER.
WARNING I DON'T CALL 911
REALLY? A PERSON MAKES MOVIES IN MY TOWN?
YEP. IT WAS ABOUT A **GIANT OCTOPUS** THAT TRIES TO EAT THE WHOLE TOWN. I STILL HAVE THAT OCTOPUS. HE'S IN MY SHED. YOU SHOULD COME SEE HIM.
COOP? WHO ARE YOU TALKING TO?
OH, HE'S A FRIEND OF YOURS! HE MADE A MOVIE ABOUT KILLER OCTOPUSES!
COOPER. PLEASE GO UP TO YOUR ROOM.

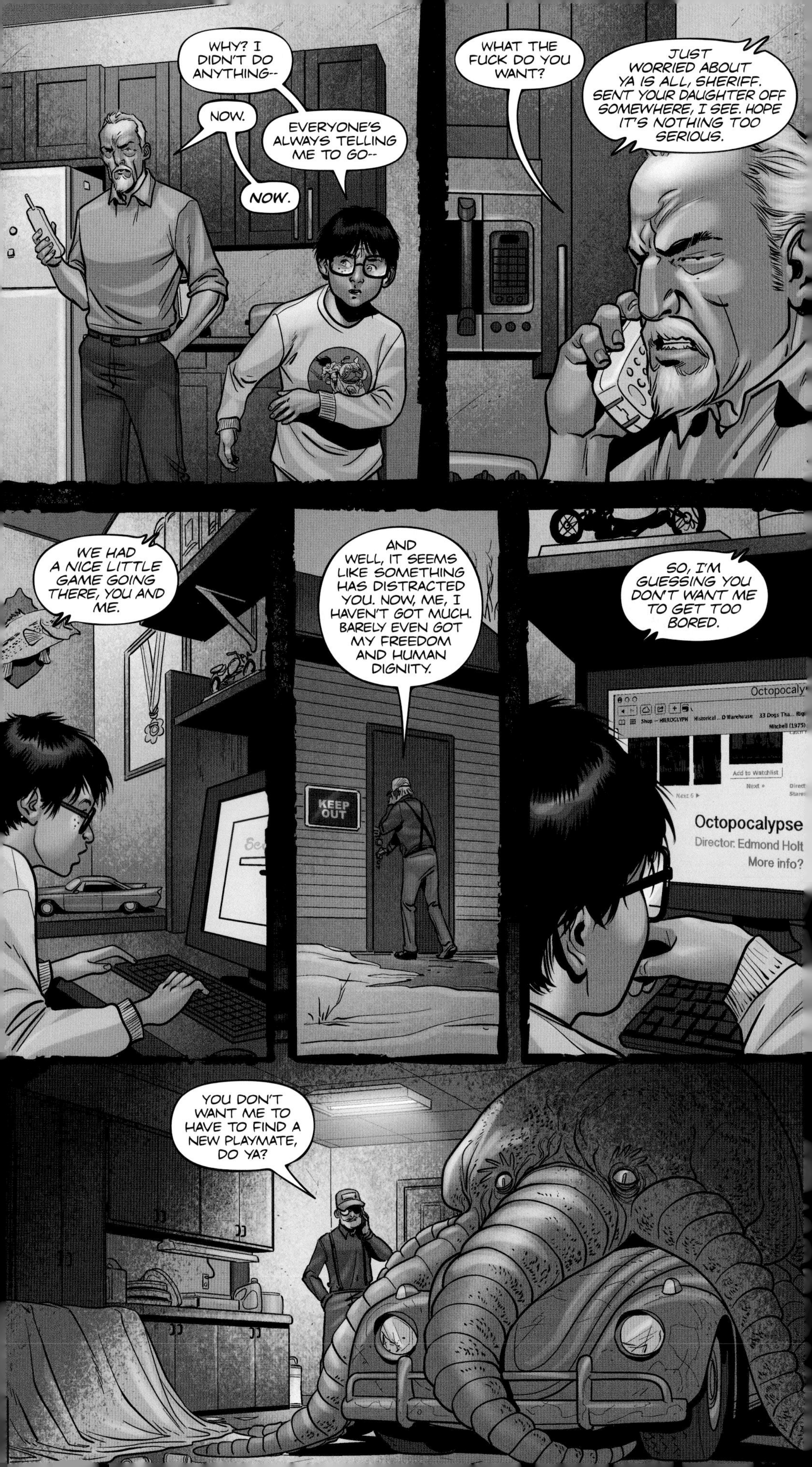
WHY? I DIDN'T DO ANYTHING--
NOW.
EVERYONE'S ALWAYS TELLING ME TO GO--
NOW.
WHAT THE FUCK DO YOU WANT?
JUST WORRIED ABOUT YA IS ALL, SHERIFF. SENT YOUR DAUGHTER OFF SOMEWHERE, I SEE. HOPE IT'S NOTHING TOO SERIOUS.
WE HAD A NICE LITTLE GAME GOING THERE, YOU AND ME.
AND WELL, IT SEEMS LIKE SOMETHING HAS DISTRACTED YOU. NOW, ME, I HAVEN'T GOT MUCH. BARELY EVEN GOT MY FREEDOM AND HUMAN DIGNITY.
KEEP OUT
SO, I'M GUESSING YOU DON'T WANT ME TO GET TOO BORED.
Octopocalypse
Director: Edmond Holt
More info?
YOU DON'T WANT ME TO HAVE TO FIND A NEW PLAYMATE, DO YA?

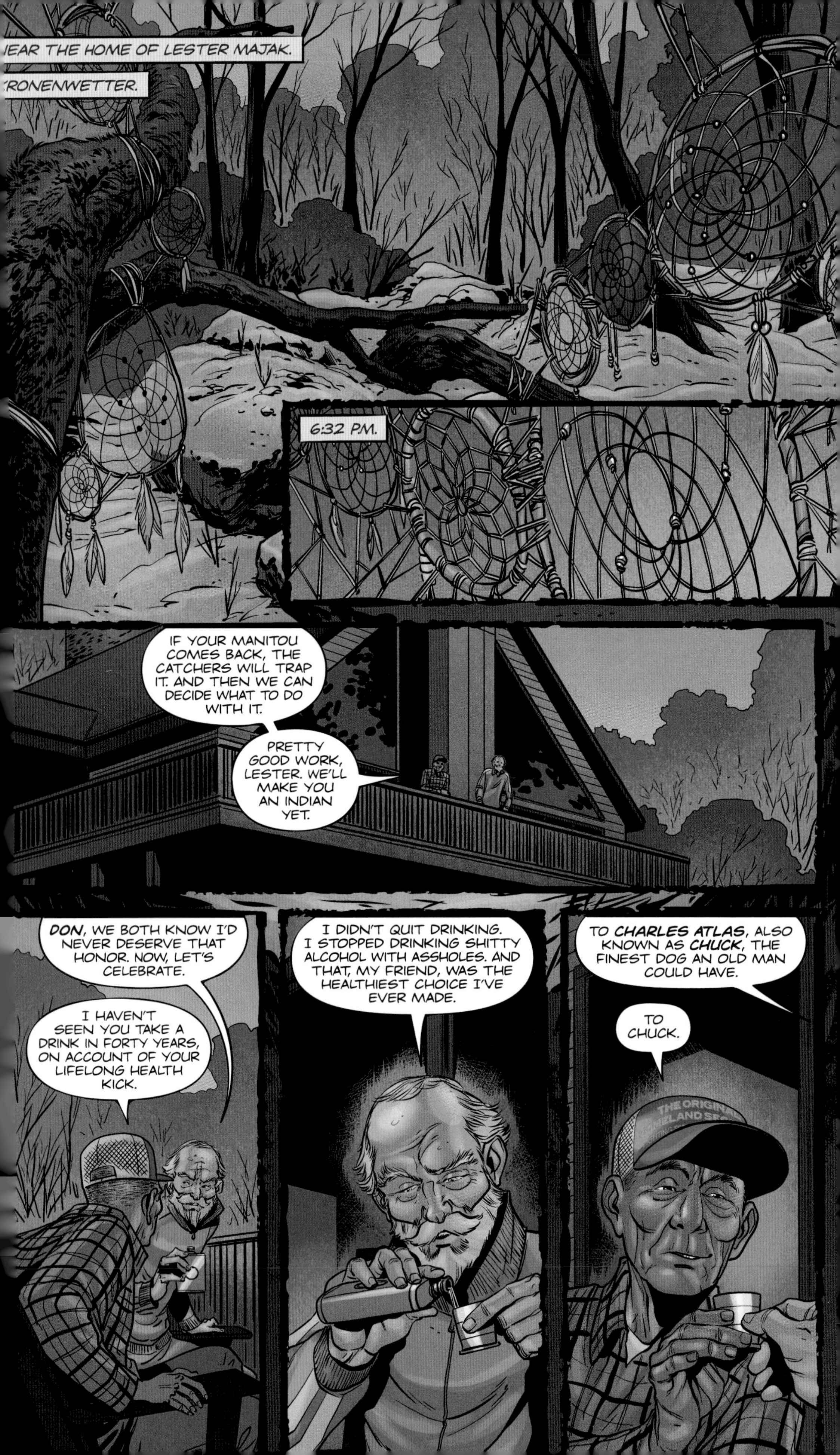

NEAR THE HOME OF LESTER MAJAK.
KRONENWETTER.
6:32 P.M.
IF YOUR MANITOU COMES BACK, THE CATCHERS WILL TRAP IT. AND THEN WE CAN DECIDE WHAT TO DO WITH IT.
PRETTY GOOD WORK, LESTER. WE'LL MAKE YOU AN INDIAN YET.
DON, WE BOTH KNOW I'D NEVER DESERVE THAT HONOR. NOW, LET'S CELEBRATE.
I HAVEN'T SEEN YOU TAKE A DRINK IN FORTY YEARS, ON ACCOUNT OF YOUR LIFELONG HEALTH KICK.
I DIDN'T QUIT DRINKING. I STOPPED DRINKING SHITTY ALCOHOL WITH ASSHOLES. AND THAT, MY FRIEND, WAS THE HEALTHIEST CHOICE I'VE EVER MADE.
TO CHARLES ATLAS, ALSO KNOWN AS CHUCK, THE FINEST DOG AN OLD MAN COULD HAVE.
TO CHUCK.

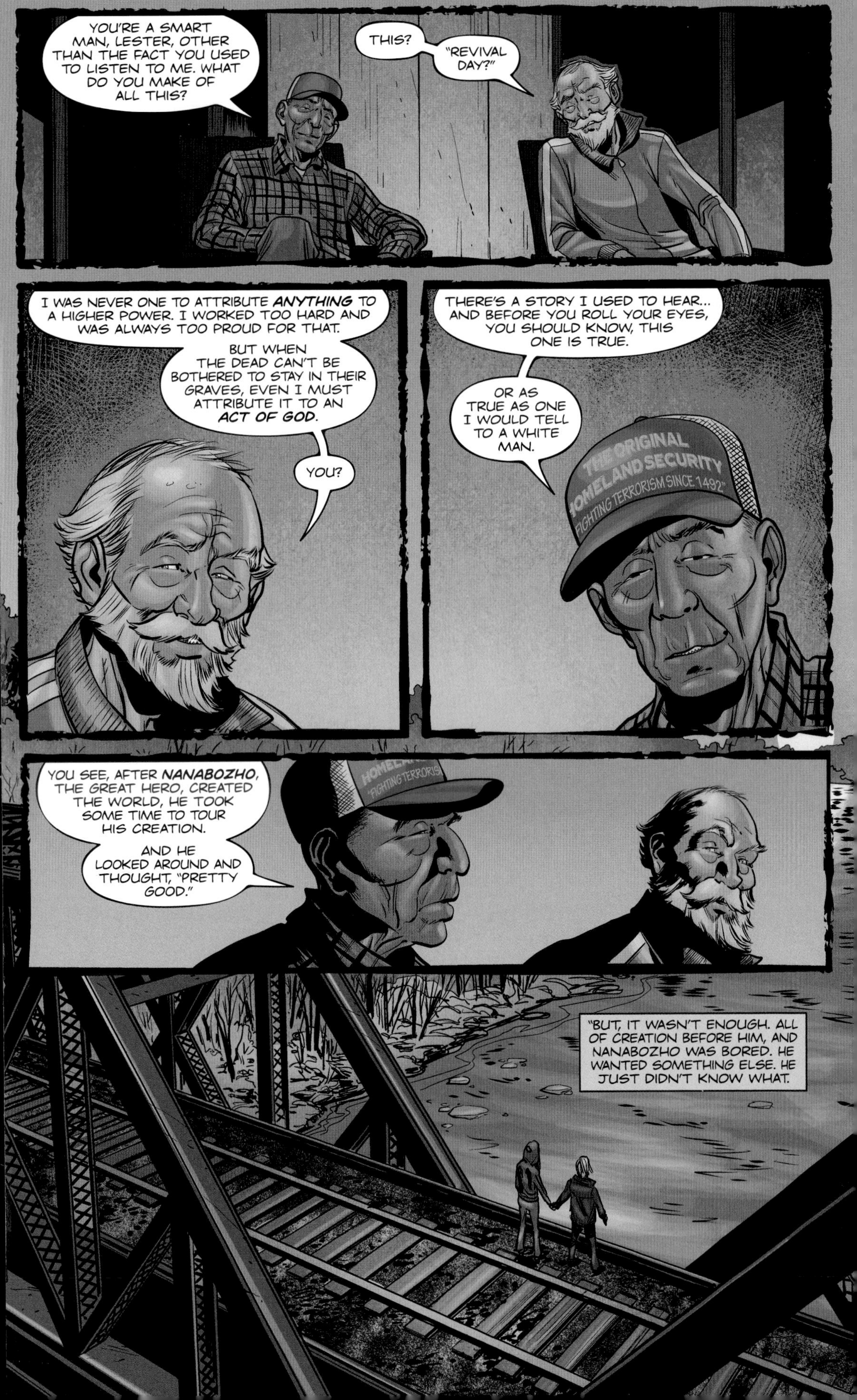

YOU'RE A SMART MAN, LESTER, OTHER THAN THE FACT YOU USED TO LISTEN TO ME. WHAT DO YOU MAKE OF ALL THIS?
THIS?
"REVIVAL DAY?"
I WAS NEVER ONE TO ATTRIBUTE ANYTHING TO A HIGHER POWER. I WORKED TOO HARD AND WAS ALWAYS TOO PROUD FOR THAT.
BUT WHEN THE DEAD CAN'T BE BOTHERED TO STAY IN THEIR GRAVES, EVEN I MUST ATTRIBUTE IT TO AN ACT OF GOD.
YOU?
THERE'S A STORY I USED TO HEAR... AND BEFORE YOU ROLL YOUR EYES, YOU SHOULD KNOW, THIS ONE IS TRUE.
OR AS TRUE AS ONE I WOULD TELL TO A WHITE MAN.
THE ORIGINAL HOMELAND SECURITY "FIGHTING TERRORISM SINCE 1492"
YOU SEE, AFTER NANABOZHO, THE GREAT HERO, CREATED THE WORLD, HE TOOK SOME TIME TO TOUR HIS CREATION.
AND HE LOOKED AROUND AND THOUGHT, "PRETTY GOOD."
"BUT, IT WASN'T ENOUGH. ALL OF CREATION BEFORE HIM, AND NANABOZHO WAS BORED. HE WANTED SOMETHING ELSE. HE JUST DIDN'T KNOW WHAT.

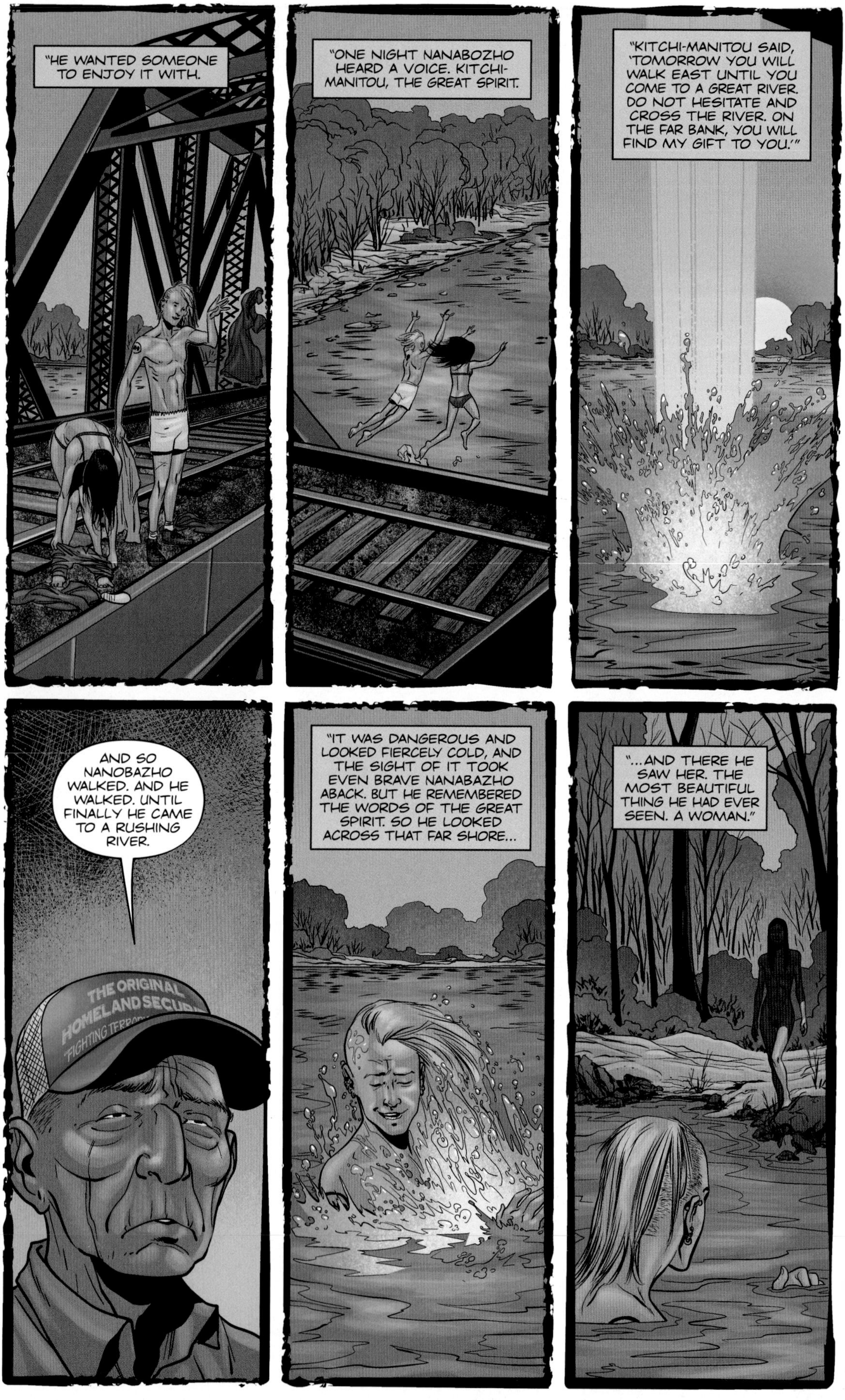
"HE WANTED SOMEONE TO ENJOY IT WITH.
"ONE NIGHT NANABOZHO HEARD A VOICE. KITCHI-MANITOU, THE GREAT SPIRIT.
"KITCHI-MANITOU SAID, 'TOMORROW YOU WILL WALK EAST UNTIL YOU COME TO A GREAT RIVER. DO NOT HESITATE AND CROSS THE RIVER. ON THE FAR BANK, YOU WILL FIND MY GIFT TO YOU.'"
AND SO NANOBAZHO WALKED. AND HE WALKED. UNTIL FINALLY HE CAME TO A RUSHING RIVER.
THE ORIGINAL HOMELAND SECURI
"FIGHTING TERROR
"IT WAS DANGEROUS AND LOOKED FIERCELY COLD, AND THE SIGHT OF IT TOOK EVEN BRAVE NANABAZHO ABACK. BUT HE REMEMBERED THE WORDS OF THE GREAT SPIRIT. SO HE LOOKED ACROSS THAT FAR SHORE...
"...AND THERE HE SAW HER. THE MOST BEAUTIFUL THING HE HAD EVER SEEN. A WOMAN."

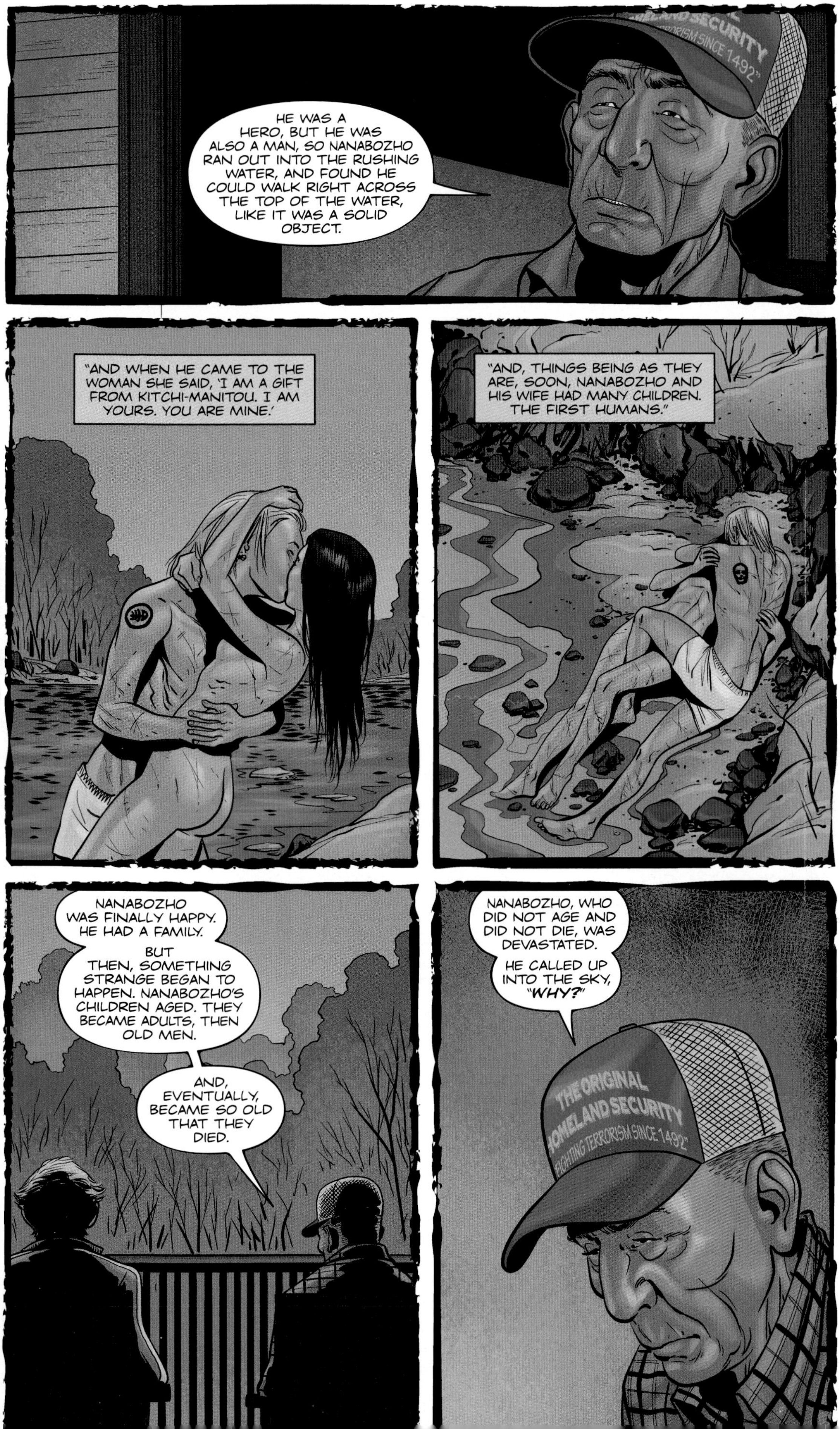

HE WAS A HERO, BUT HE WAS ALSO A MAN, SO NANABOZHO RAN OUT INTO THE RUSHING WATER, AND FOUND HE COULD WALK RIGHT ACROSS THE TOP OF THE WATER, LIKE IT WAS A SOLID OBJECT.
"AND WHEN HE CAME TO THE WOMAN SHE SAID, 'I AM A GIFT FROM KITCHI-MANITOU. I AM YOURS. YOU ARE MINE.'
"AND, THINGS BEING AS THEY ARE, SOON, NANABOZHO AND HIS WIFE HAD MANY CHILDREN. THE FIRST HUMANS."
NANABOZHO WAS FINALLY HAPPY. HE HAD A FAMILY.
BUT THEN, SOMETHING STRANGE BEGAN TO HAPPEN. NANABOZHO'S CHILDREN AGED. THEY BECAME ADULTS, THEN OLD MEN.
AND, EVENTUALLY, BECAME SO OLD THAT THEY DIED.
NANABOZHO, WHO DID NOT AGE AND DID NOT DIE, WAS DEVASTATED.
HE CALLED UP INTO THE SKY, "*WHY?*"
THE ORIGINAL
HOMELAND SECURITY
FIGHTING TERRORISM SINCE "1492"

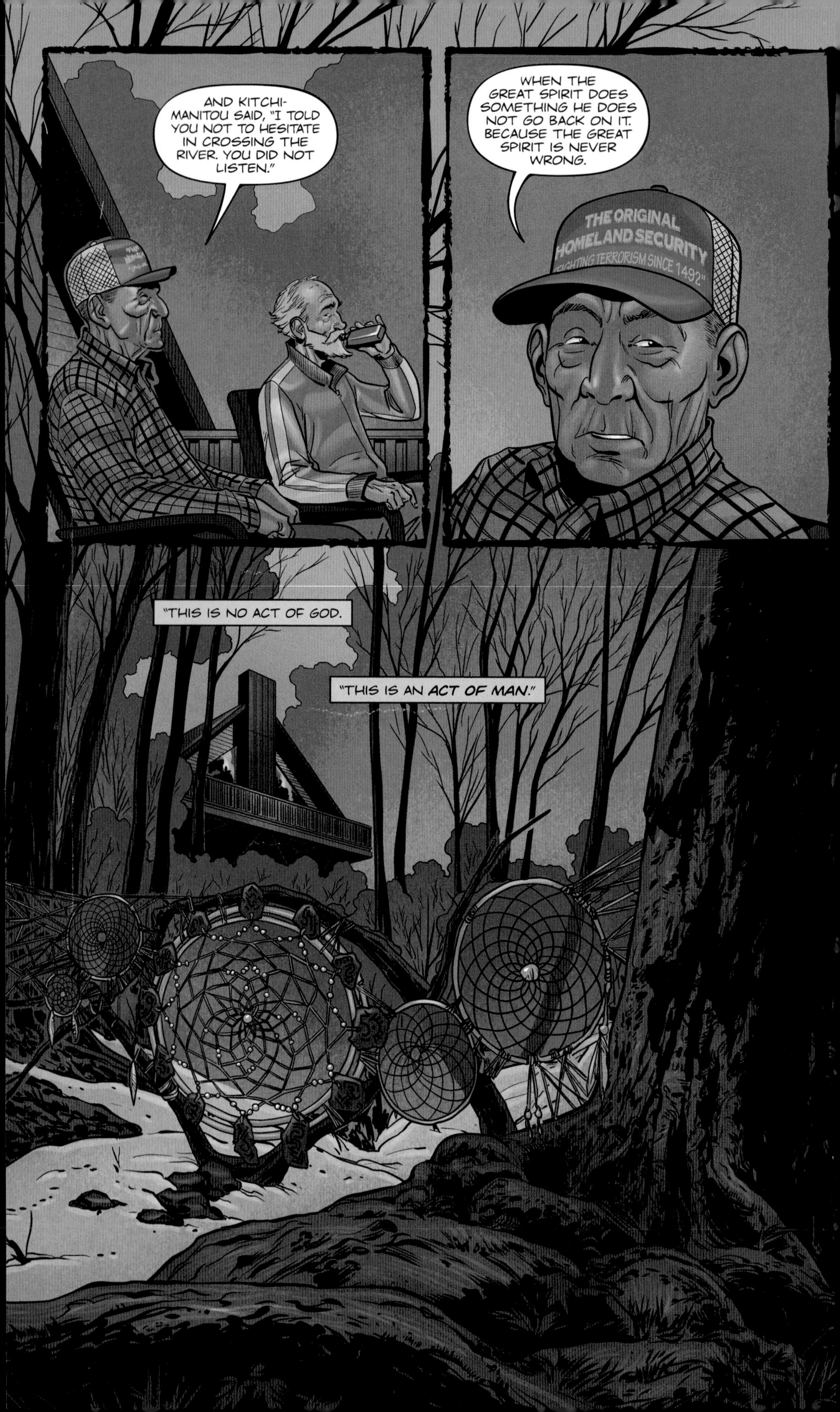
AND KITCHI-MANITOU SAID, "I TOLD YOU NOT TO HESITATE IN CROSSING THE RIVER. YOU DID NOT LISTEN."
WHEN THE GREAT SPIRIT DOES SOMETHING HE DOES NOT GO BACK ON IT. BECAUSE THE GREAT SPIRIT IS NEVER WRONG.
THE ORIGINAL HOMELAND SECURITY FIGHTING TERRORISM SINCE 1492"
"THIS IS NO ACT OF GOD.
"THIS IS AN ACT OF MAN."

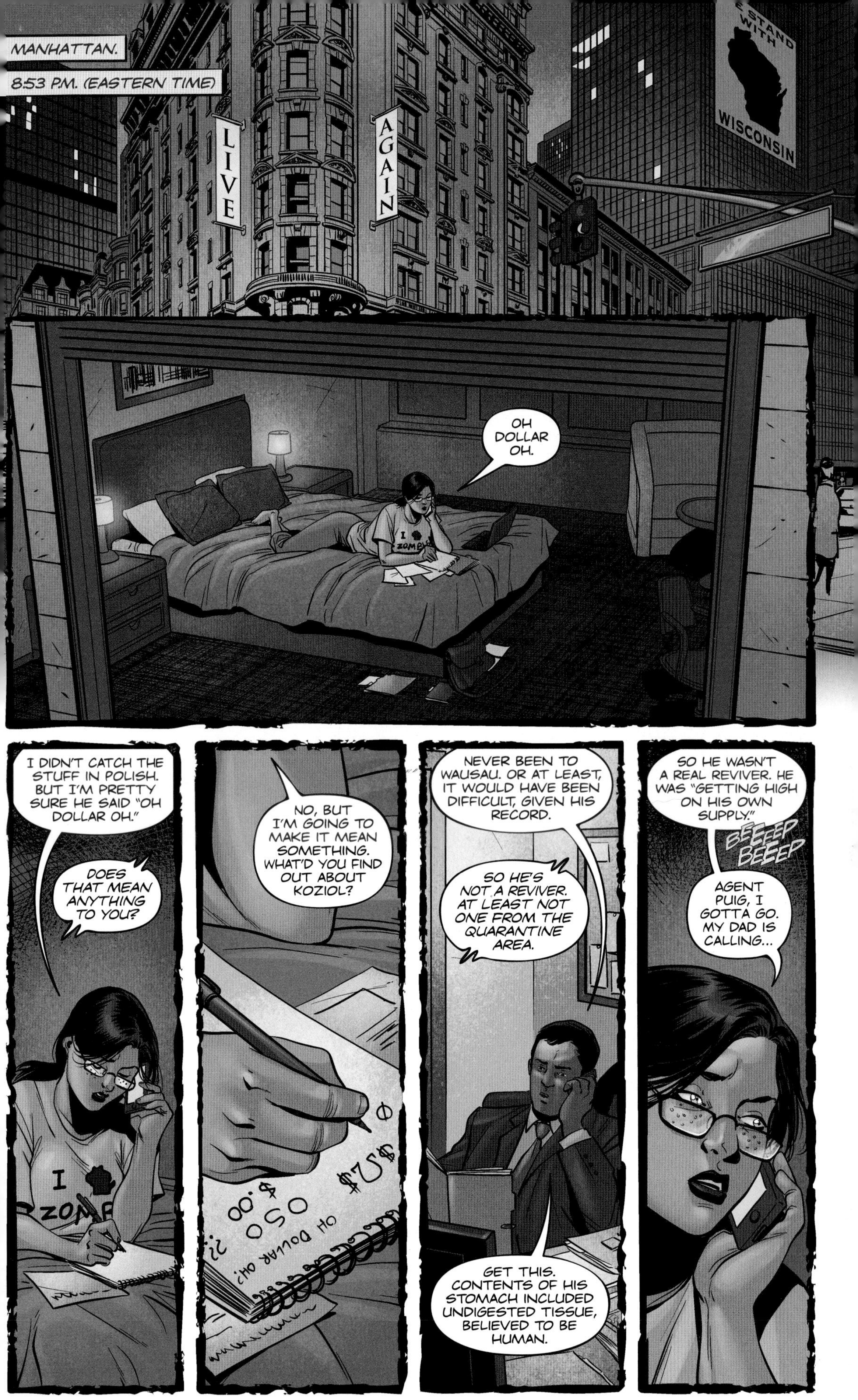

MANHATTAN.
8:53 P.M. (EASTERN TIME)
LIVE
AGAIN
WE STAND WITH WISCONSIN
OH DOLLAR OH.
I DIDN'T CATCH THE STUFF IN POLISH. BUT I'M PRETTY SURE HE SAID "OH DOLLAR OH."
DOES THAT MEAN ANYTHING TO YOU?
NO, BUT I'M GOING TO MAKE IT MEAN SOMETHING. WHAT'D YOU FIND OUT ABOUT KOZIOL?
OH DOLLAR OH??
NEVER BEEN TO WAUSAU. OR AT LEAST, IT WOULD HAVE BEEN DIFFICULT, GIVEN HIS RECORD.
SO HE'S NOT A REVIVER. AT LEAST NOT ONE FROM THE QUARANTINE AREA.
GET THIS. CONTENTS OF HIS STOMACH INCLUDED UNDIGESTED TISSUE, BELIEVED TO BE HUMAN.
SO HE WASN'T A REAL REVIVER. HE WAS "GETTING HIGH ON HIS OWN SUPPLY."
BEEEEP BEEEP
AGENT PUIG, I GOTTA GO. MY DAD IS CALLING...

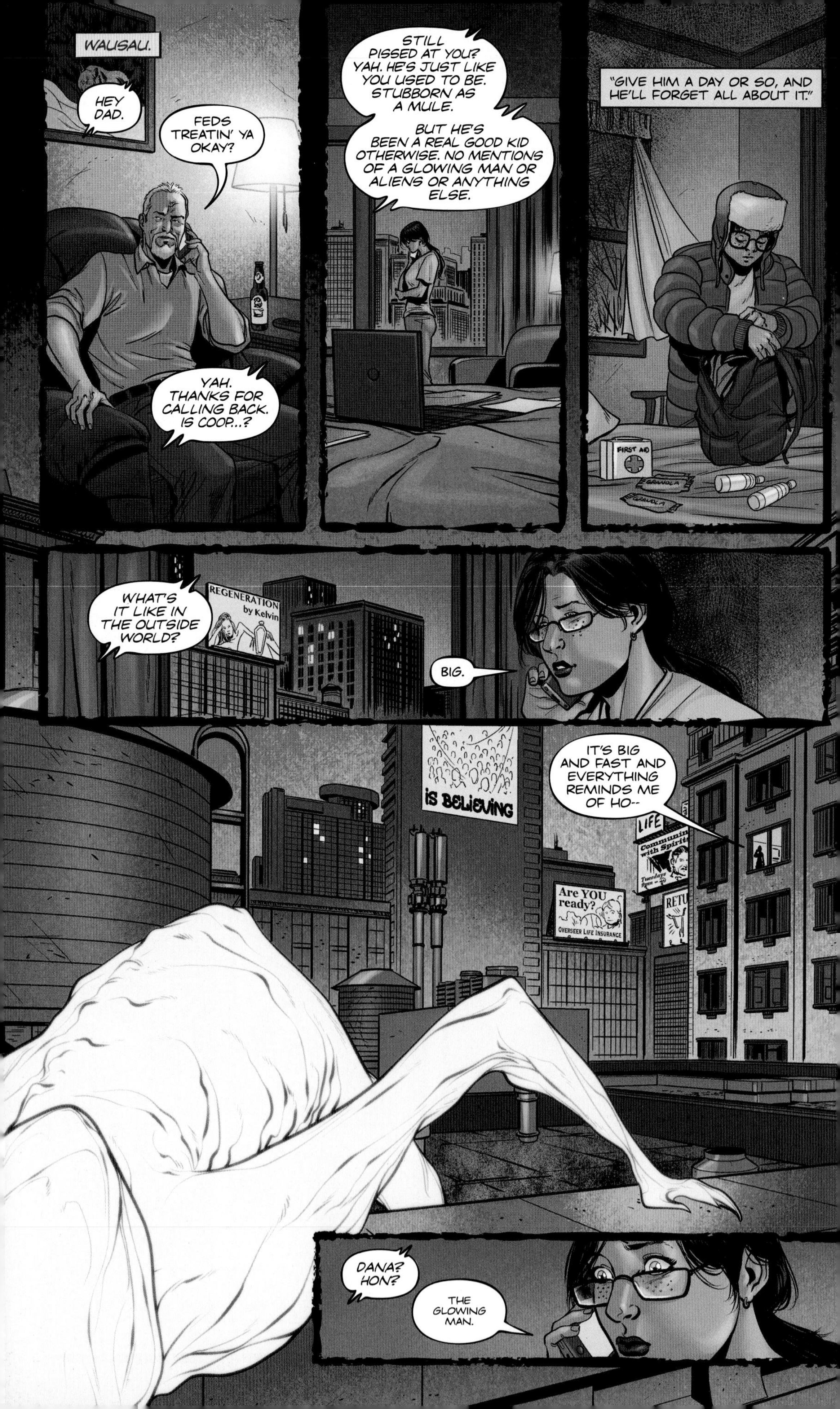

WAUSAU.
HEY DAD.
FEDS TREATIN' YA OKAY?
YAH. THANKS FOR CALLING BACK. IS COOP...?
STILL PISSED AT YOU? YAH. HE'S JUST LIKE YOU USED TO BE. STUBBORN AS A MULE.
BUT HE'S BEEN A REAL GOOD KID OTHERWISE. NO MENTIONS OF A GLOWING MAN OR ALIENS OR ANYTHING ELSE.
"GIVE HIM A DAY OR SO, AND HE'LL FORGET ALL ABOUT IT."
FIRST AID
GRANOLA
GRANOLA
REGENERATION by Kelvin
WHAT'S IT LIKE IN THE OUTSIDE WORLD?
BIG.
IS BELIEVING
IT'S BIG AND FAST AND EVERYTHING REMINDS ME OF HO--
LIFE
Communin with Spirits
Are YOU ready?
OVERSEER LIFE INSURANCE
DANA? HON?
THE GLOWING MAN.

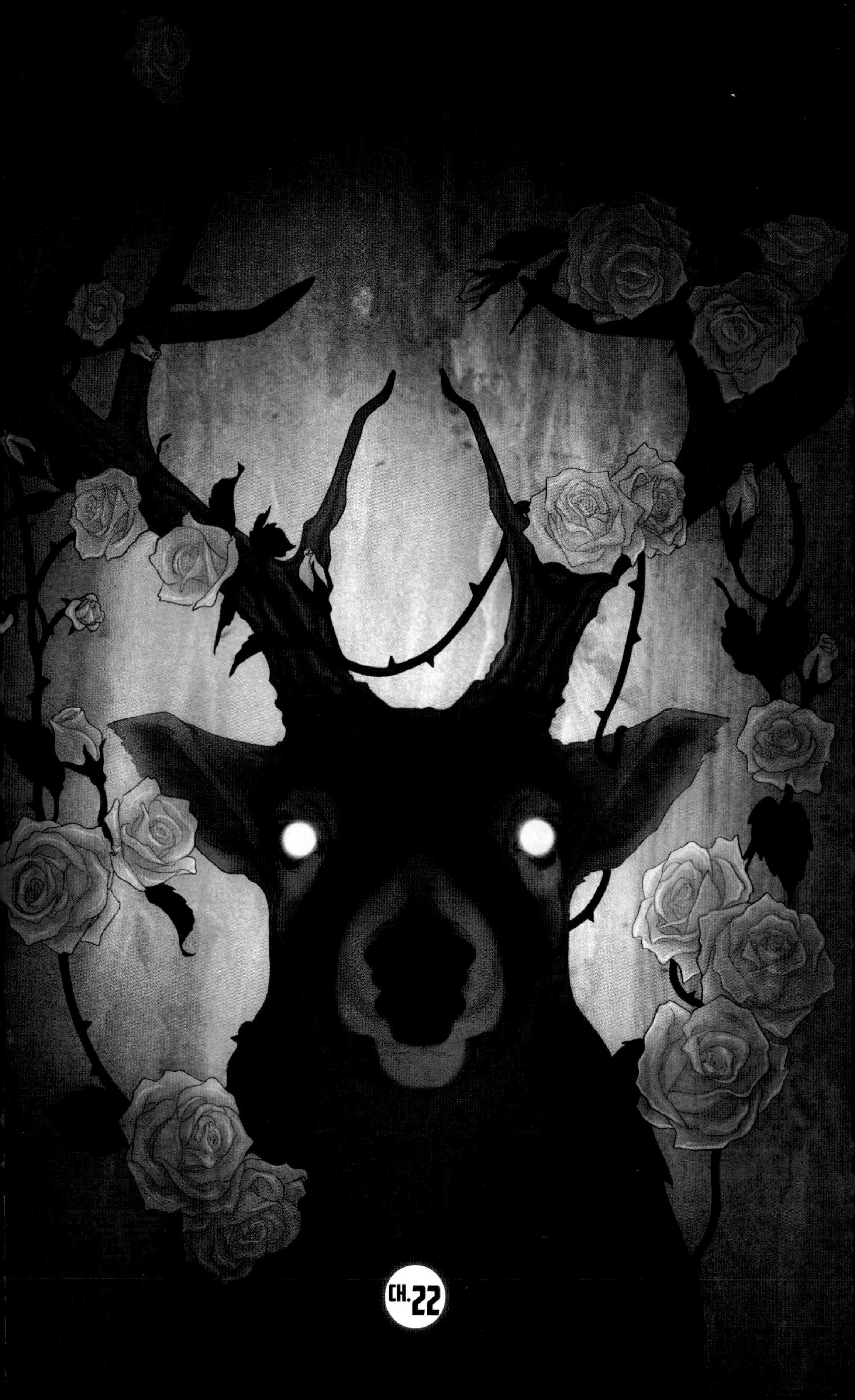
CH. 22

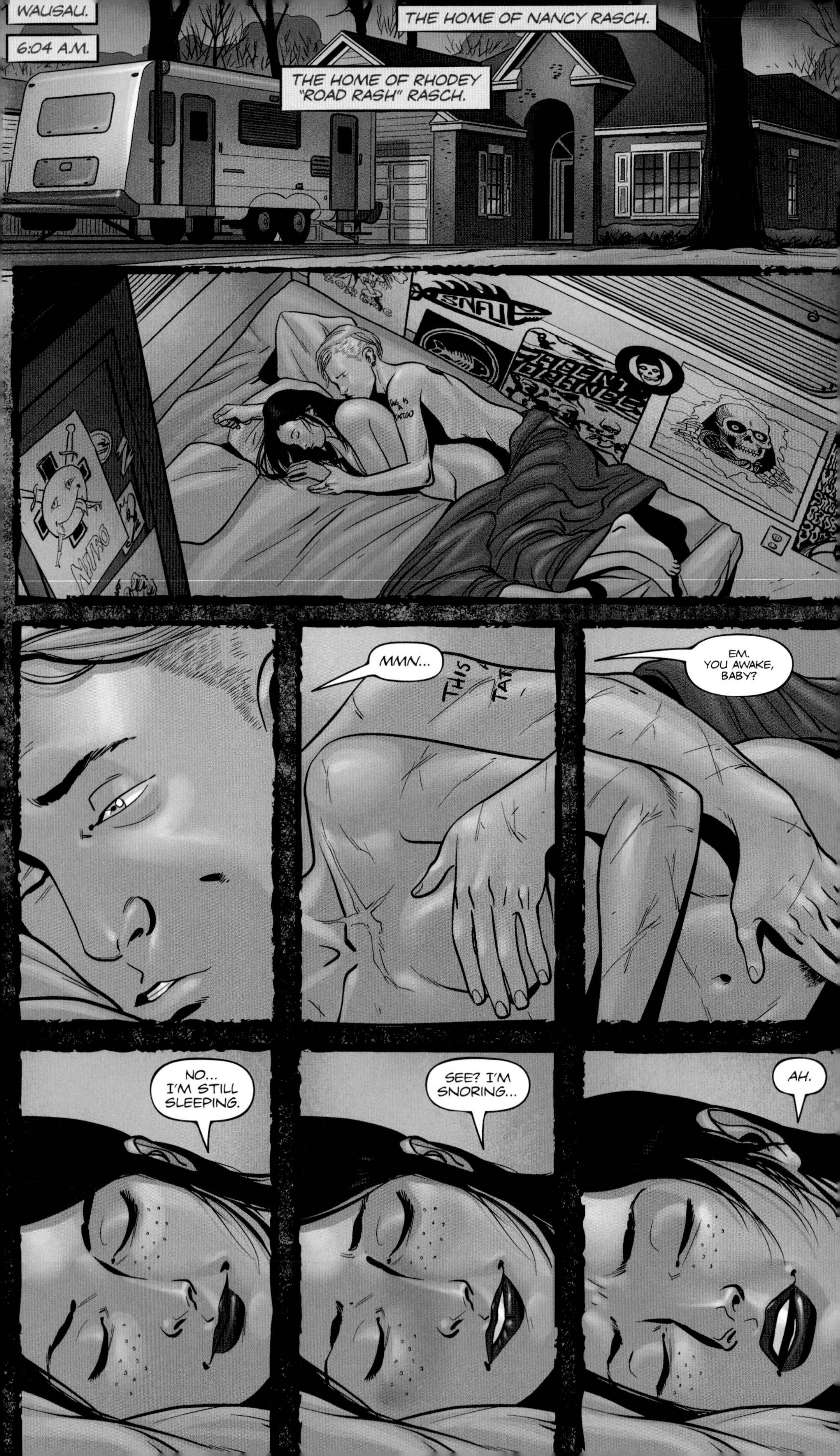
WAUSAU.
6:04 A.M.
THE HOME OF NANCY RASCH.
THE HOME OF RHODEY "ROAD RASH" RASCH.
MMN...
EM. YOU AWAKE, BABY?
NO... I'M STILL SLEEPING.
SEE? I'M SNORING...
AH.

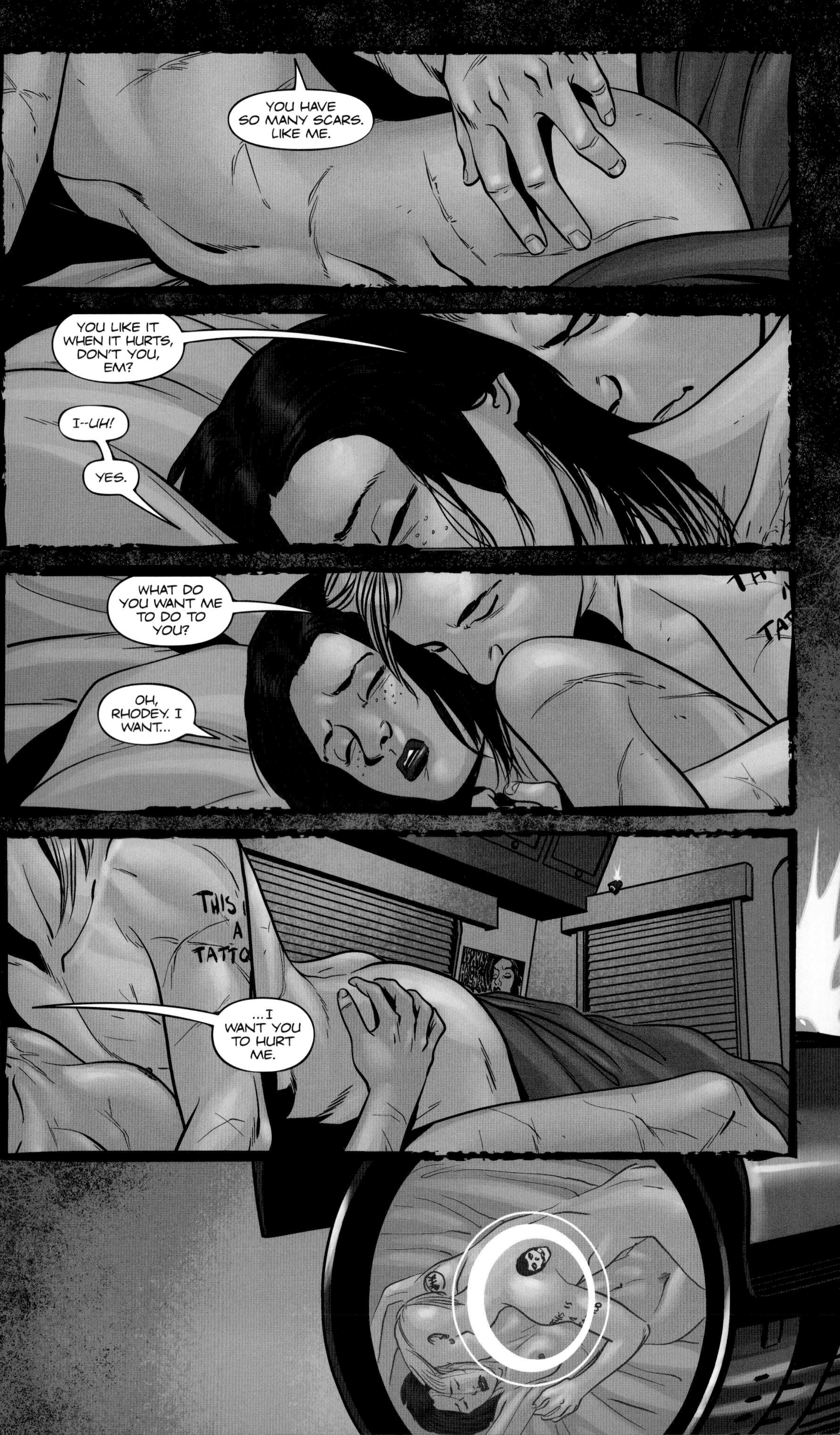
YOU HAVE SO MANY SCARS. LIKE ME.
YOU LIKE IT WHEN IT HURTS, DON'T YOU, EM?
I--UH!
YES.
WHAT DO YOU WANT ME TO DO TO YOU?
OH, RHODEY. I WANT...
...I WANT YOU TO HURT ME.

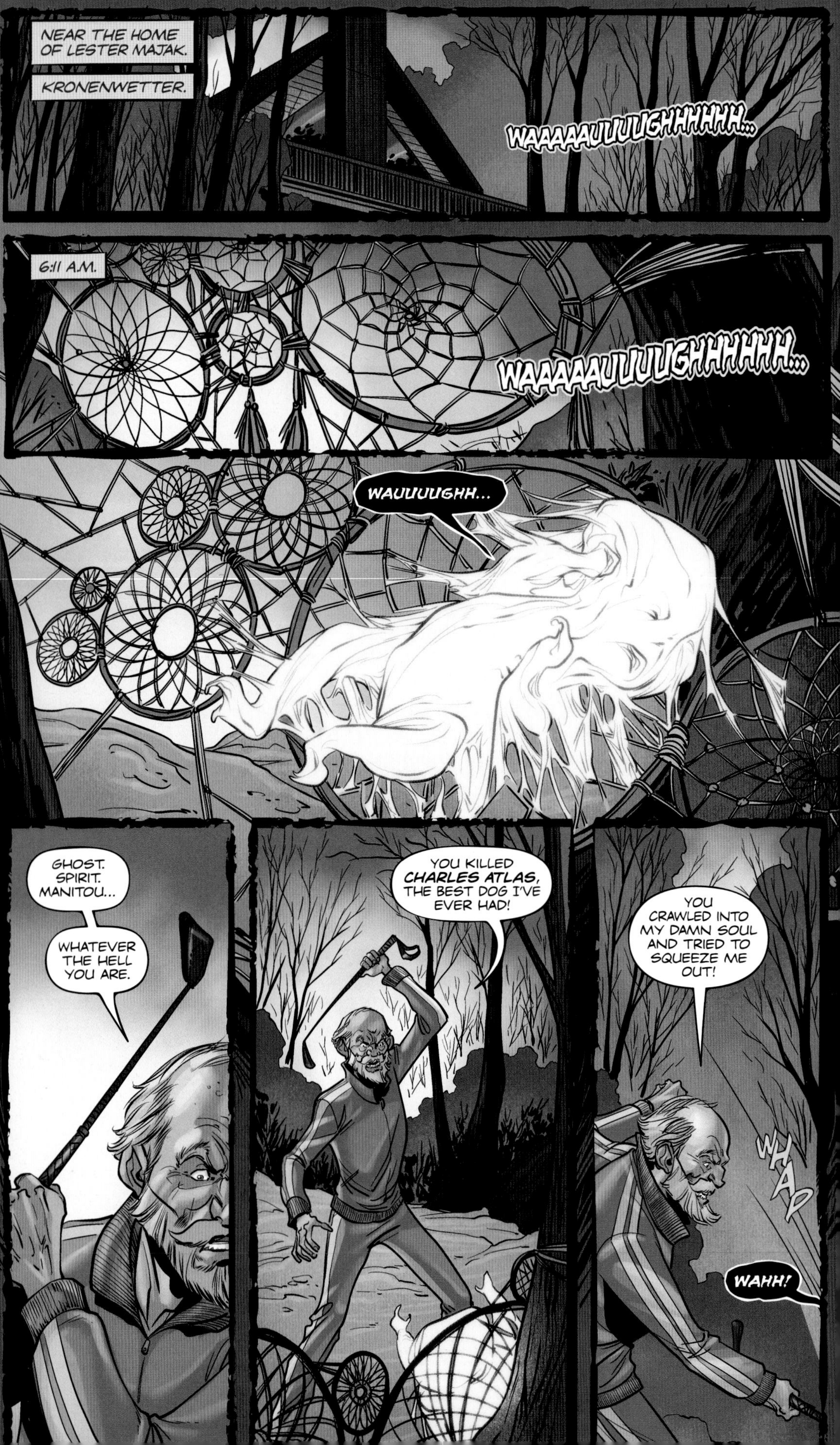
NEAR THE HOME OF LESTER MAJAK.
KRONENWETTER.
WAAAAAUUUUGHHHHH...
6:11 A.M.
WAAAAAUUUUGHHHHHH...
WAUUUUGHH...
GHOST. SPIRIT. MANITOU...
WHATEVER THE HELL YOU ARE.
YOU KILLED CHARLES ATLAS, THE BEST DOG I'VE EVER HAD!
YOU CRAWLED INTO MY DAMN SOUL AND TRIED TO SQUEEZE ME OUT!
WHAP
WAHH!

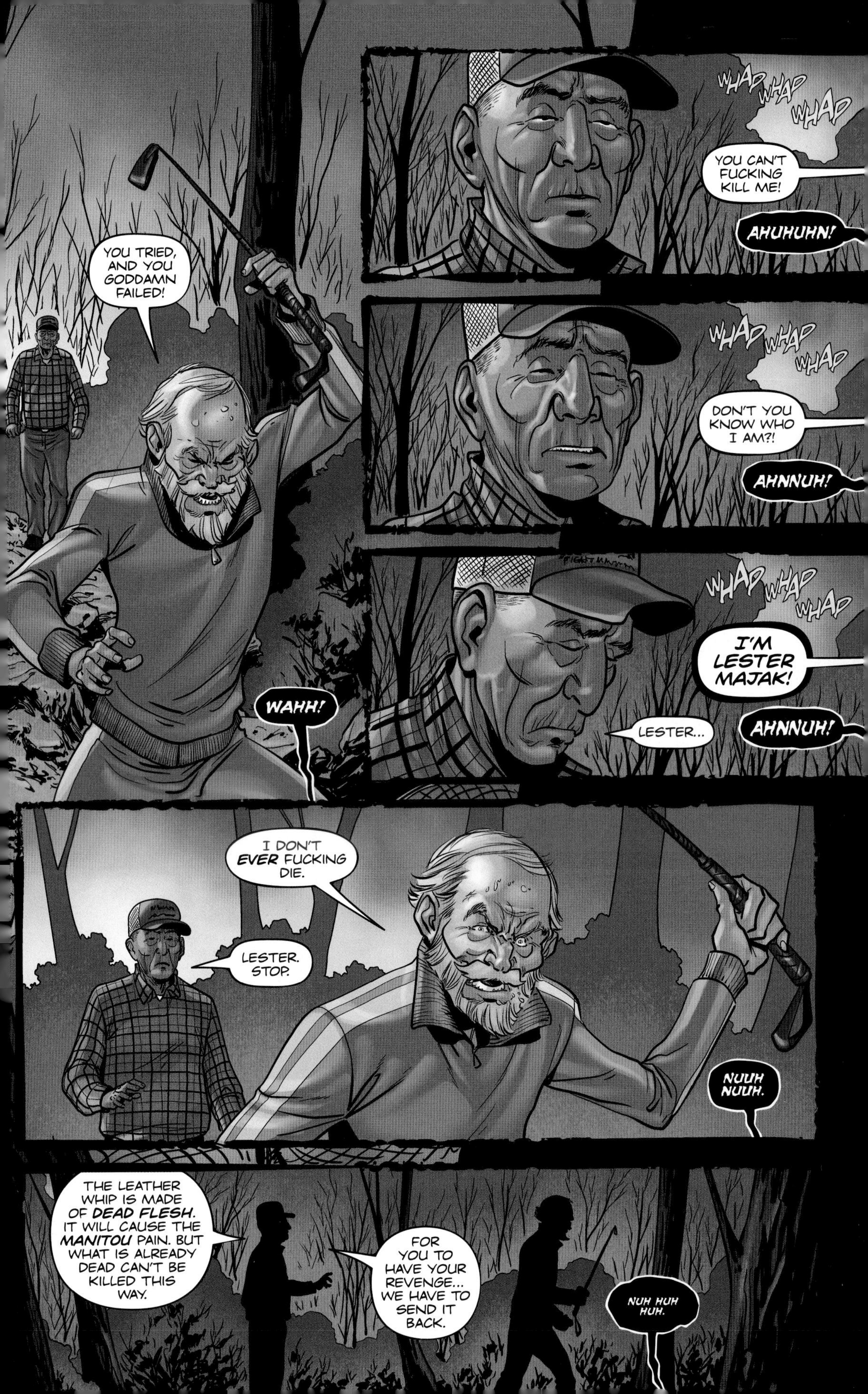

YOU TRIED, AND YOU GODDAMN FAILED!
WHAP WHAP WHAP
YOU CAN'T FUCKING KILL ME!
AHUHUHN!
WHAP WHAP WHAP
DON'T YOU KNOW WHO I AM?!
AHNNUH!
WHAP WHAP WHAP
I'M LESTER MAJAK!
AHNNUH!
LESTER...
WAHH!
I DON'T EVER FUCKING DIE.
LESTER. STOP.
NUUH NUUH.
THE LEATHER WHIP IS MADE OF DEAD FLESH. IT WILL CAUSE THE MANITOU PAIN. BUT WHAT IS ALREADY DEAD CAN'T BE KILLED THIS WAY.
FOR YOU TO HAVE YOUR REVENGE... WE HAVE TO SEND IT BACK.
NUH HUH HUH.

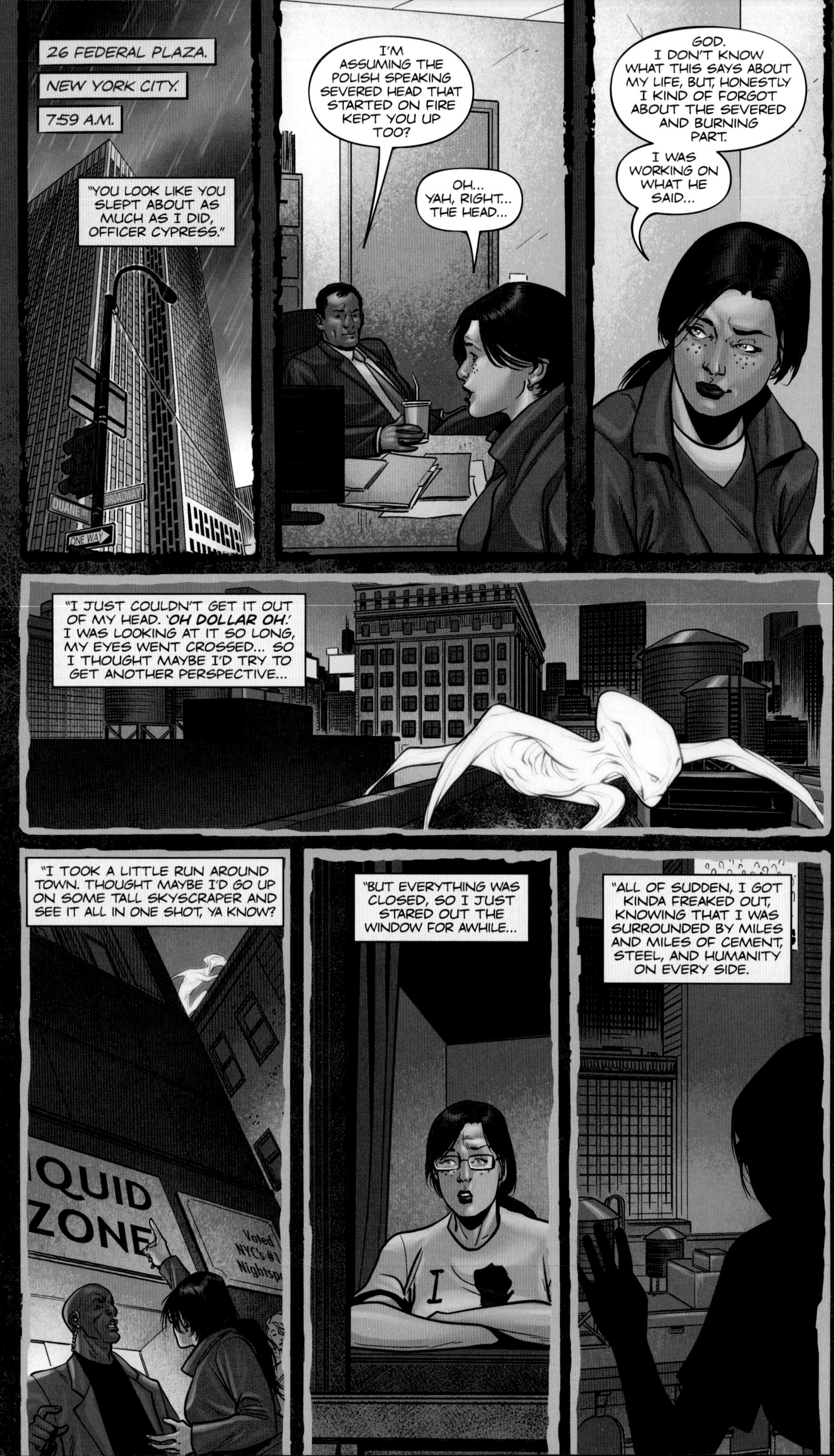

26 FEDERAL PLAZA.
NEW YORK CITY.
7:59 A.M.
"YOU LOOK LIKE YOU SLEPT ABOUT AS MUCH AS I DID, OFFICER CYPRESS."
BROADWAY
DUANE ST
ONE WAY
I'M ASSUMING THE POLISH SPEAKING SEVERED HEAD THAT STARTED ON FIRE KEPT YOU UP TOO?
OH... YAH, RIGHT... THE HEAD...
GOD. I DON'T KNOW WHAT THIS SAYS ABOUT MY LIFE, BUT, HONESTLY I KIND OF FORGOT ABOUT THE SEVERED AND BURNING PART.
I WAS WORKING ON WHAT HE SAID...
"I JUST COULDN'T GET IT OUT OF MY HEAD. 'OH DOLLAR OH.' I WAS LOOKING AT IT SO LONG, MY EYES WENT CROSSED... SO I THOUGHT MAYBE I'D TRY TO GET ANOTHER PERSPECTIVE...
"I TOOK A LITTLE RUN AROUND TOWN. THOUGHT MAYBE I'D GO UP ON SOME TALL SKYSCRAPER AND SEE IT ALL IN ONE SHOT, YA KNOW?
IQUID ZONE
Voted NYC's #1 Nightsp
"BUT EVERYTHING WAS CLOSED, SO I JUST STARED OUT THE WINDOW FOR AWHILE...
I
"ALL OF SUDDEN, I GOT KINDA FREAKED OUT, KNOWING THAT I WAS SURROUNDED BY MILES AND MILES OF CEMENT, STEEL, AND HUMANITY ON EVERY SIDE.

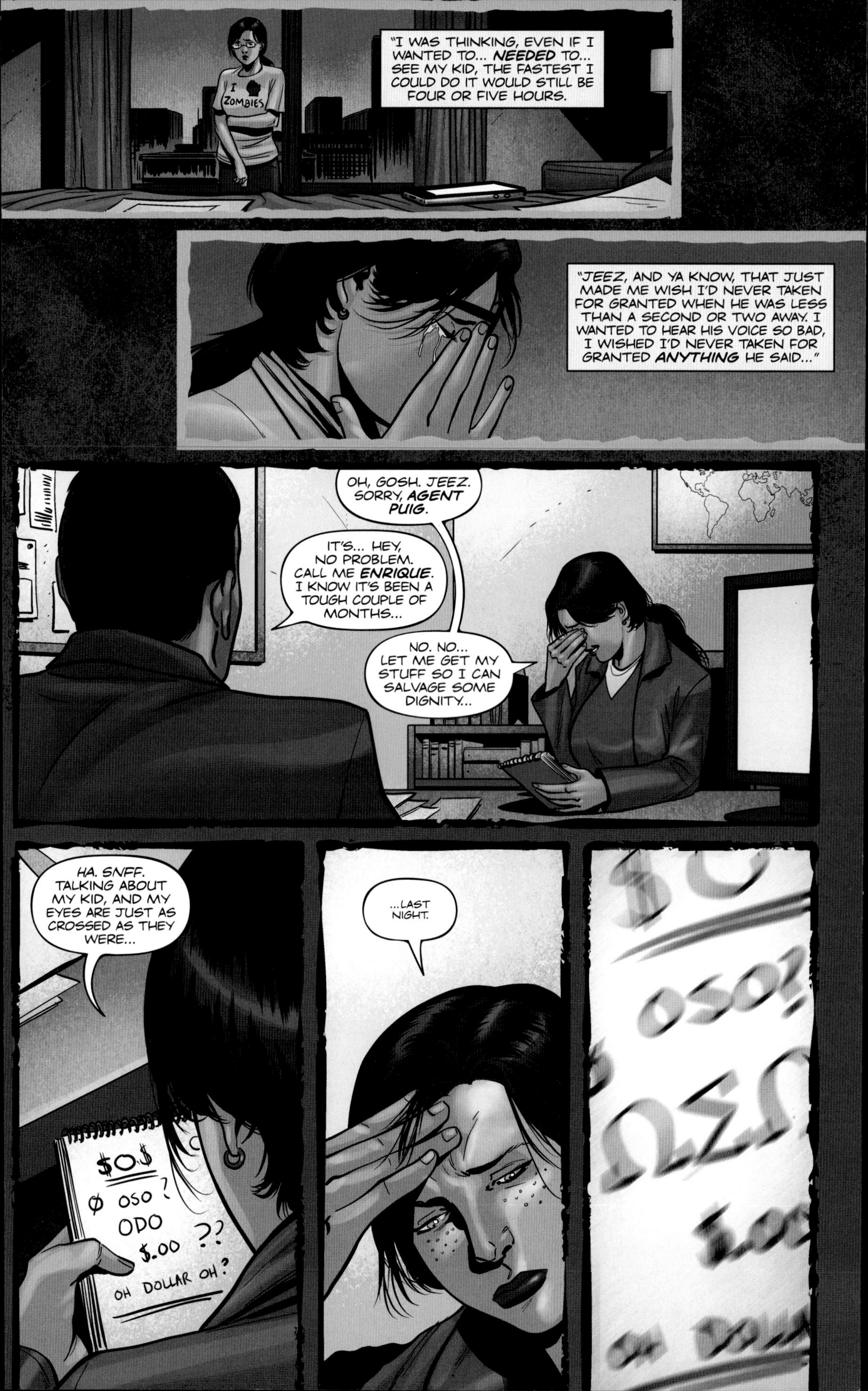
"I WAS THINKING, EVEN IF I WANTED TO... NEEDED TO... SEE MY KID, THE FASTEST I COULD DO IT WOULD STILL BE FOUR OR FIVE HOURS.
I ♥ ZOMBIES
"JEEZ, AND YA KNOW, THAT JUST MADE ME WISH I'D NEVER TAKEN FOR GRANTED WHEN HE WAS LESS THAN A SECOND OR TWO AWAY. I WANTED TO HEAR HIS VOICE SO BAD, I WISHED I'D NEVER TAKEN FOR GRANTED ANYTHING HE SAID..."
OH, GOSH. JEEZ. SORRY, AGENT PUIG.
IT'S... HEY, NO PROBLEM. CALL ME ENRIQUE. I KNOW IT'S BEEN A TOUGH COUPLE OF MONTHS...
NO. NO... LET ME GET MY STUFF SO I CAN SALVAGE SOME DIGNITY...
HA. SNFF. TALKING ABOUT MY KID, AND MY EYES ARE JUST AS CROSSED AS THEY WERE...
$O.$
Ø OSO ?
ODO
$.00 ??
OH DOLLAR OH ?
...LAST NIGHT.

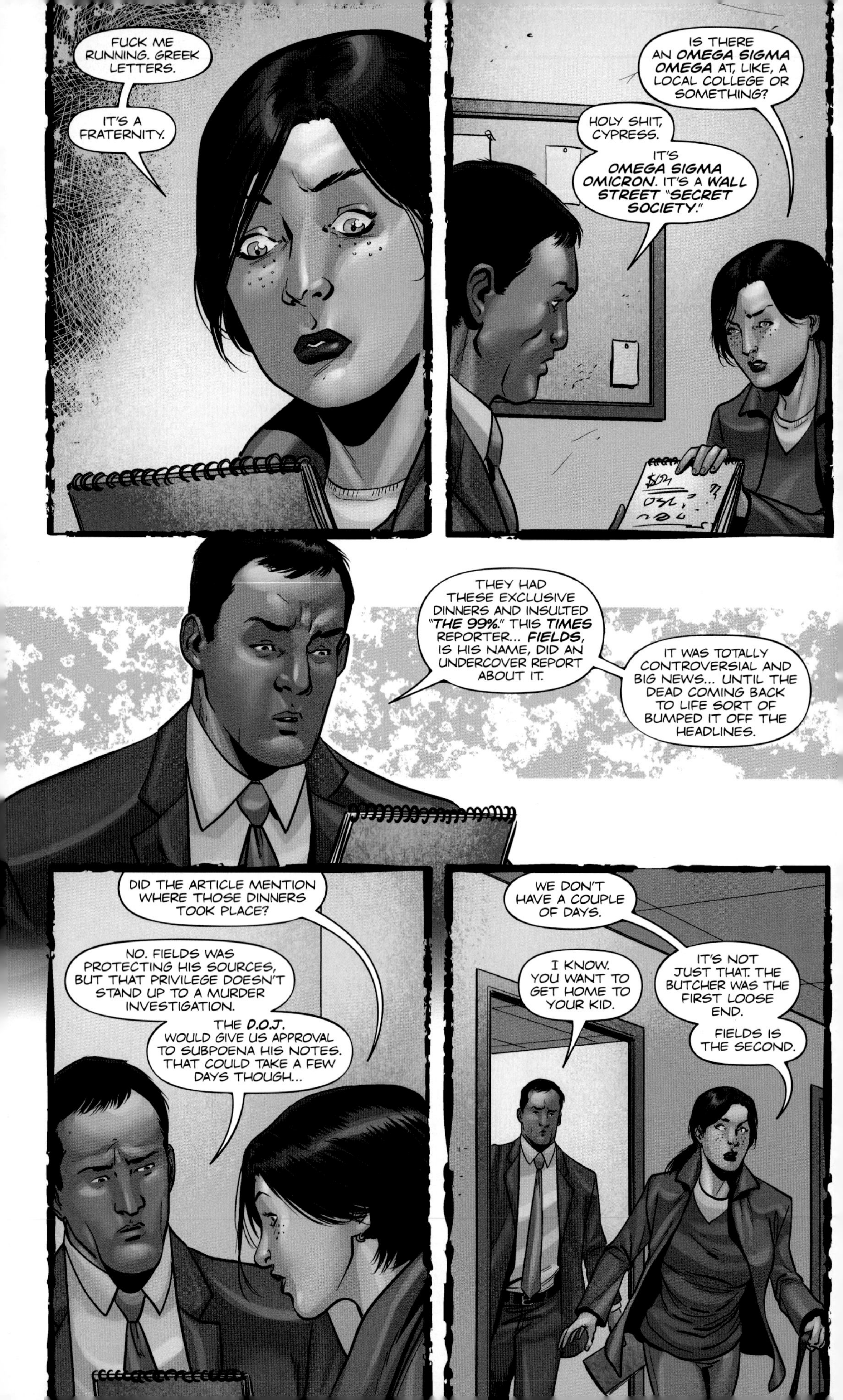
FUCK ME RUNNING. GREEK LETTERS.
IT'S A FRATERNITY.
IS THERE AN OMEGA SIGMA OMEGA AT, LIKE, A LOCAL COLLEGE OR SOMETHING?
HOLY SHIT, CYPRESS.
IT'S OMEGA SIGMA OMICRON. IT'S A WALL STREET "SECRET SOCIETY."
THEY HAD THESE EXCLUSIVE DINNERS AND INSULTED "THE 99%." THIS TIMES REPORTER... FIELDS, IS HIS NAME, DID AN UNDERCOVER REPORT ABOUT IT.
IT WAS TOTALLY CONTROVERSIAL AND BIG NEWS... UNTIL THE DEAD COMING BACK TO LIFE SORT OF BUMPED IT OFF THE HEADLINES.
DID THE ARTICLE MENTION WHERE THOSE DINNERS TOOK PLACE?
NO. FIELDS WAS PROTECTING HIS SOURCES, BUT THAT PRIVILEGE DOESN'T STAND UP TO A MURDER INVESTIGATION.
THE D.O.J. WOULD GIVE US APPROVAL TO SUBPOENA HIS NOTES. THAT COULD TAKE A FEW DAYS THOUGH...
WE DON'T HAVE A COUPLE OF DAYS.
I KNOW. YOU WANT TO GET HOME TO YOUR KID.
IT'S NOT JUST THAT. THE BUTCHER WAS THE FIRST LOOSE END.
FIELDS IS THE SECOND.

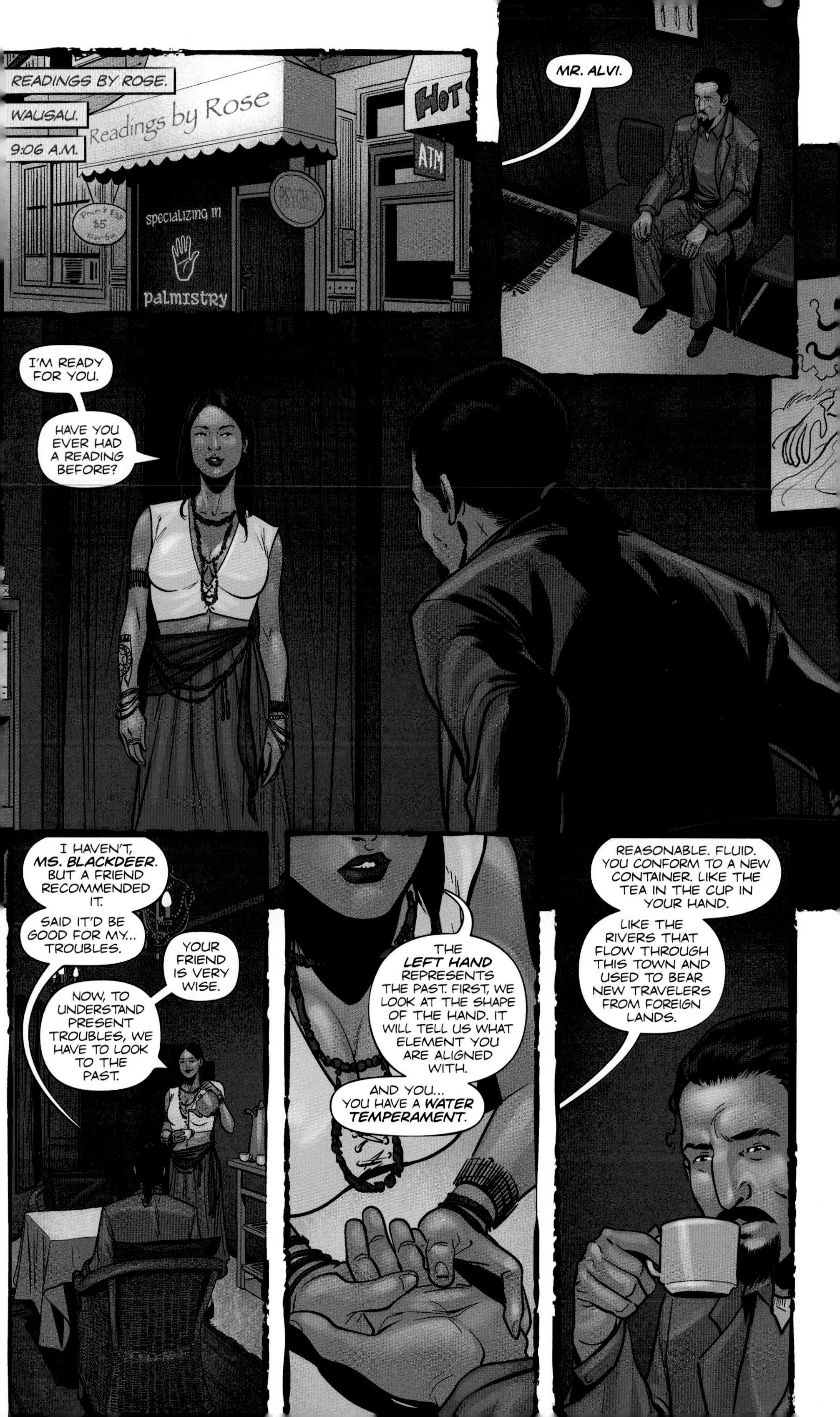

READINGS BY ROSE.
WAUSAU.
9:06 A.M.
Readings by Rose
specializing in
palmistry
PSYCHIC
HOT
ATM
MR. ALVI.
I'M READY FOR YOU.
HAVE YOU EVER HAD A READING BEFORE?
I HAVEN'T, MS. BLACKDEER. BUT A FRIEND RECOMMENDED IT.
SAID IT'D BE GOOD FOR MY... TROUBLES.
YOUR FRIEND IS VERY WISE.
NOW, TO UNDERSTAND PRESENT TROUBLES, WE HAVE TO LOOK TO THE PAST.
THE LEFT HAND REPRESENTS THE PAST. FIRST, WE LOOK AT THE SHAPE OF THE HAND. IT WILL TELL US WHAT ELEMENT YOU ARE ALIGNED WITH.
AND YOU... YOU HAVE A WATER TEMPERAMENT.
REASONABLE. FLUID. YOU CONFORM TO A NEW CONTAINER. LIKE THE TEA IN THE CUP IN YOUR HAND.
LIKE THE RIVERS THAT FLOW THROUGH THIS TOWN AND USED TO BEAR NEW TRAVELERS FROM FOREIGN LANDS.

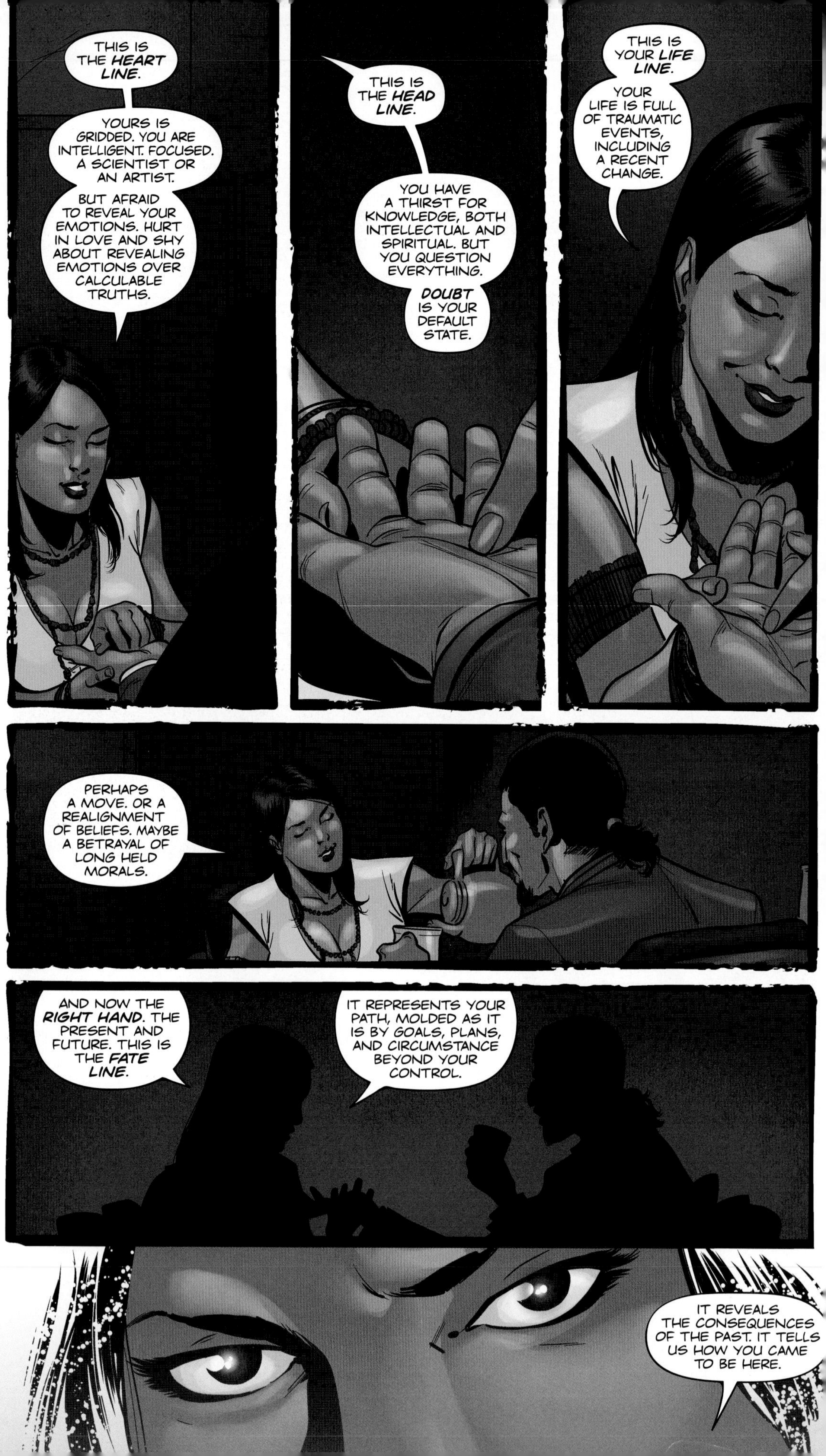
THIS IS THE HEART LINE.
YOURS IS GRIDDED. YOU ARE INTELLIGENT. FOCUSED. A SCIENTIST OR AN ARTIST.
BUT AFRAID TO REVEAL YOUR EMOTIONS. HURT IN LOVE AND SHY ABOUT REVEALING EMOTIONS OVER CALCULABLE TRUTHS.
THIS IS THE HEAD LINE.
YOU HAVE A THIRST FOR KNOWLEDGE, BOTH INTELLECTUAL AND SPIRITUAL. BUT YOU QUESTION EVERYTHING.
DOUBT IS YOUR DEFAULT STATE.
THIS IS YOUR LIFE LINE.
YOUR LIFE IS FULL OF TRAUMATIC EVENTS, INCLUDING A RECENT CHANGE.
PERHAPS A MOVE. OR A REALIGNMENT OF BELIEFS. MAYBE A BETRAYAL OF LONG HELD MORALS.
AND NOW THE RIGHT HAND. THE PRESENT AND FUTURE. THIS IS THE FATE LINE.
IT REPRESENTS YOUR PATH, MOLDED AS IT IS BY GOALS, PLANS, AND CIRCUMSTANCE BEYOND YOUR CONTROL.
IT REVEALS THE CONSEQUENCES OF THE PAST. IT TELLS US HOW YOU CAME TO BE HERE.

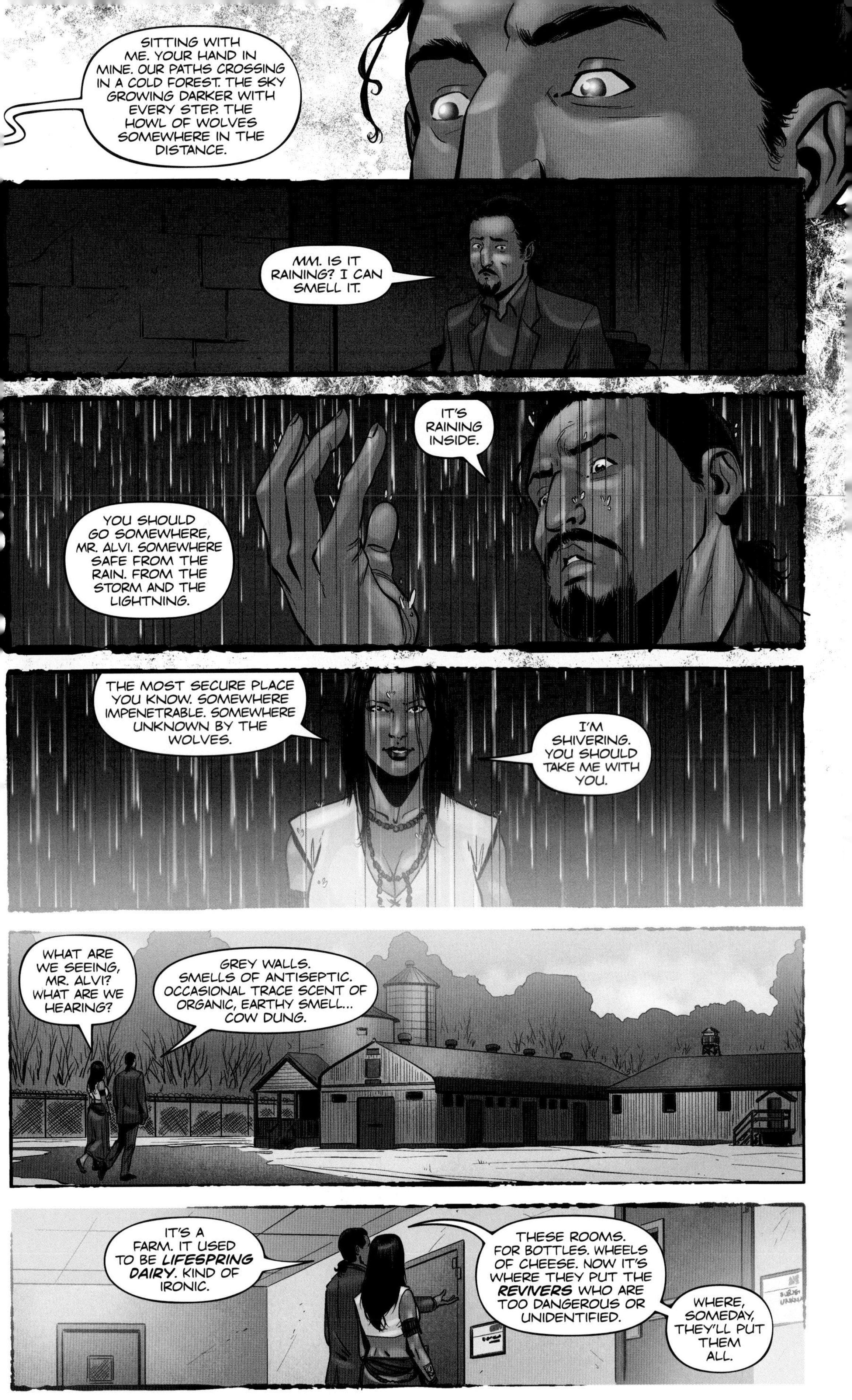
SITTING WITH ME. YOUR HAND IN MINE. OUR PATHS CROSSING IN A COLD FOREST. THE SKY GROWING DARKER WITH EVERY STEP. THE HOWL OF WOLVES SOMEWHERE IN THE DISTANCE.
MM. IS IT RAINING? I CAN SMELL IT.
IT'S RAINING INSIDE.
YOU SHOULD GO SOMEWHERE, MR. ALVI. SOMEWHERE SAFE FROM THE RAIN. FROM THE STORM AND THE LIGHTNING.
THE MOST SECURE PLACE YOU KNOW. SOMEWHERE IMPENETRABLE. SOMEWHERE UNKNOWN BY THE WOLVES.
I'M SHIVERING. YOU SHOULD TAKE ME WITH YOU.
WHAT ARE WE SEEING, MR. ALVI? WHAT ARE WE HEARING?
GREY WALLS. SMELLS OF ANTISEPTIC. OCCASIONAL TRACE SCENT OF ORGANIC, EARTHY SMELL... COW DUNG.
IT'S A FARM. IT USED TO BE ***LIFESPRING DAIRY***. KIND OF IRONIC.
THESE ROOMS. FOR BOTTLES. WHEELS OF CHEESE. NOW IT'S WHERE THEY PUT THE ***REVIVERS*** WHO ARE TOO DANGEROUS OR UNIDENTIFIED.
WHERE, SOMEDAY, THEY'LL PUT THEM ALL.

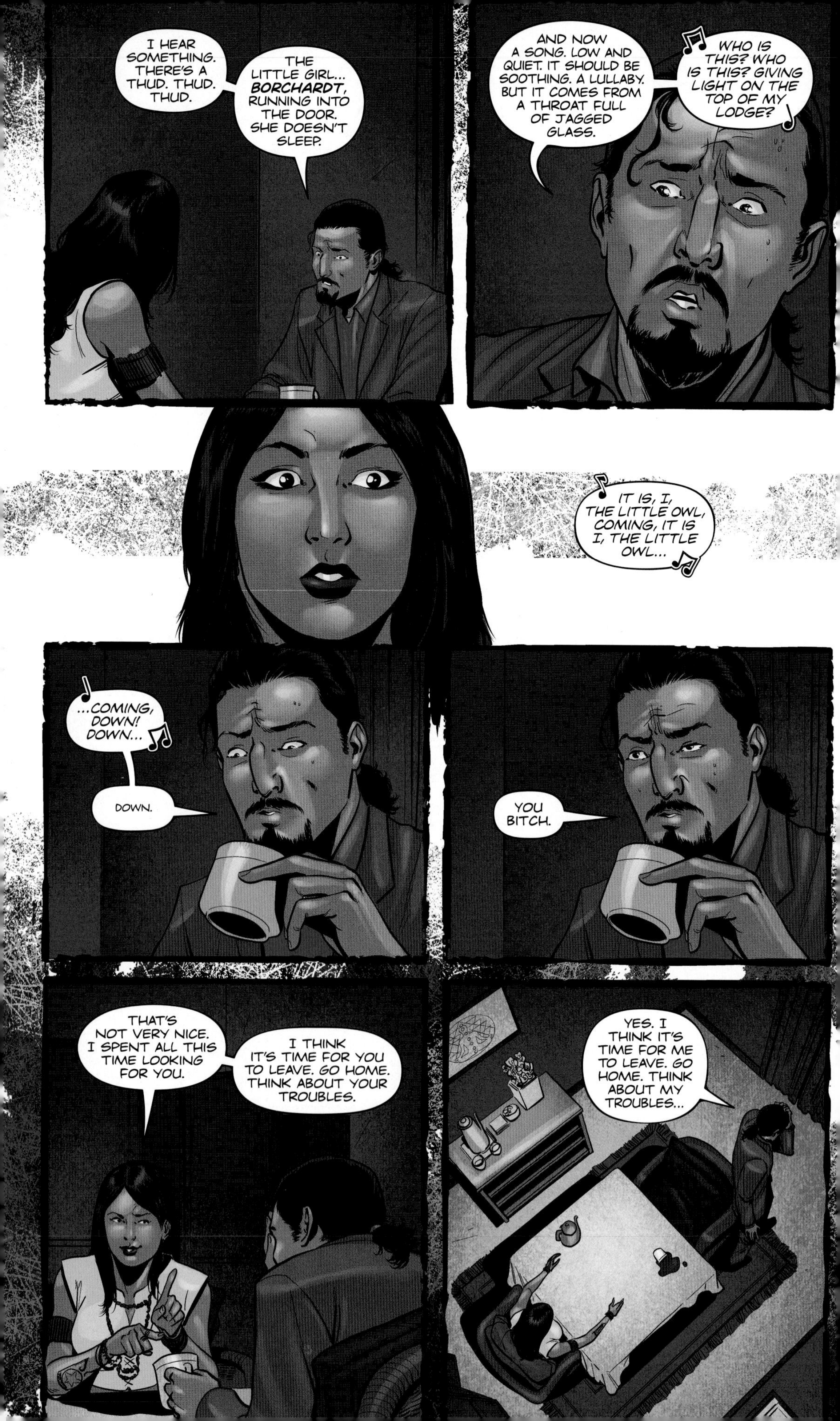
I HEAR SOMETHING. THERE'S A THUD. THUD. THUD.
THE LITTLE GIRL... BORCHARDT, RUNNING INTO THE DOOR. SHE DOESN'T SLEEP.
AND NOW A SONG. LOW AND QUIET. IT SHOULD BE SOOTHING. A LULLABY. BUT IT COMES FROM A THROAT FULL OF JAGGED GLASS.
WHO IS THIS? WHO IS THIS? GIVING LIGHT ON THE TOP OF MY LODGE?
IT IS, I, THE LITTLE OWL, COMING, IT IS I, THE LITTLE OWL...
...COMING, DOWN! DOWN...
DOWN.
YOU BITCH.
THAT'S NOT VERY NICE. I SPENT ALL THIS TIME LOOKING FOR YOU.
I THINK IT'S TIME FOR YOU TO LEAVE. GO HOME. THINK ABOUT YOUR TROUBLES.
YES. I THINK IT'S TIME FOR ME TO LEAVE. GO HOME. THINK ABOUT MY TROUBLES...

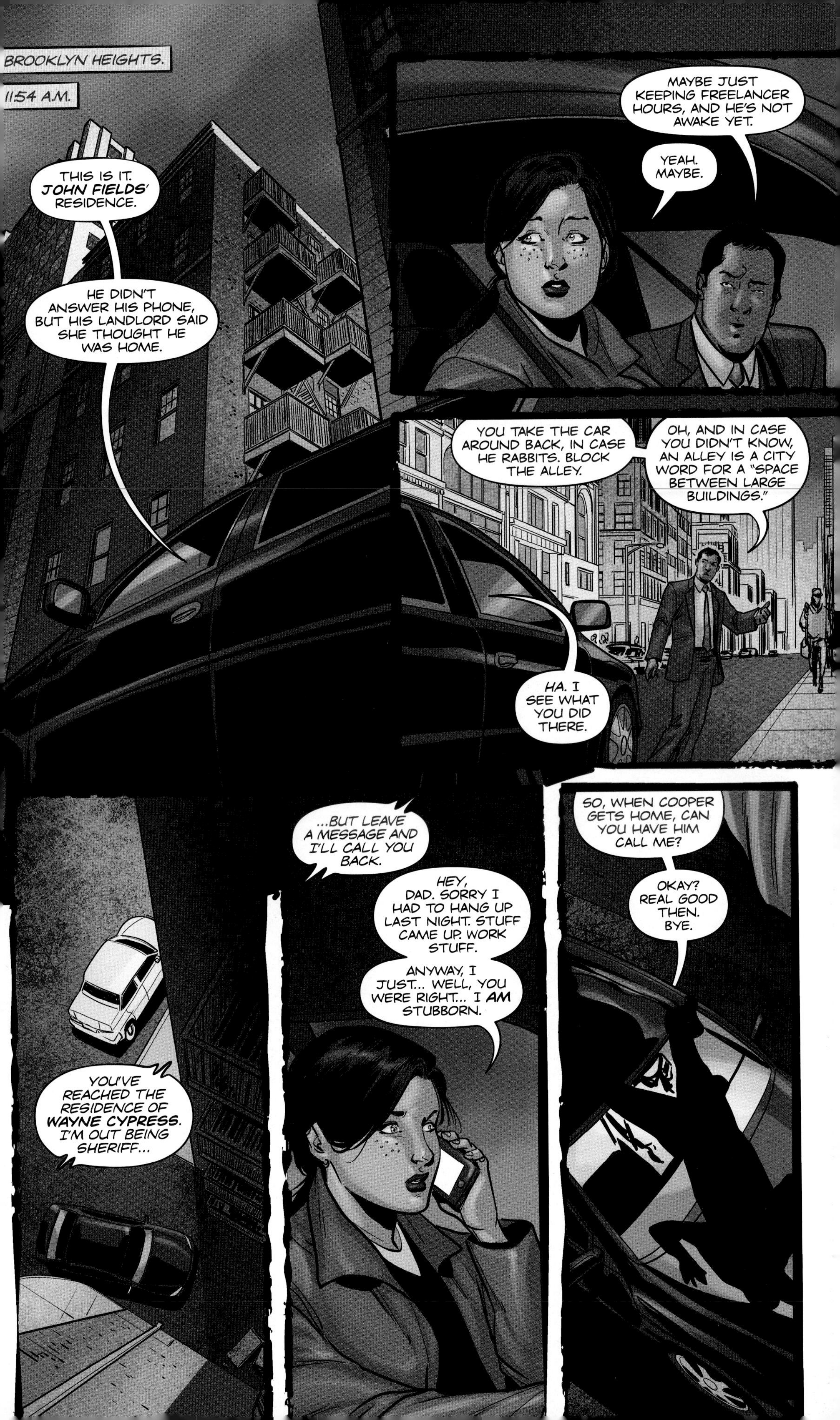
BROOKLYN HEIGHTS.
11:54 A.M.
THIS IS IT. JOHN FIELDS' RESIDENCE.
HE DIDN'T ANSWER HIS PHONE, BUT HIS LANDLORD SAID SHE THOUGHT HE WAS HOME.
MAYBE JUST KEEPING FREELANCER HOURS, AND HE'S NOT AWAKE YET.
YEAH. MAYBE.
YOU TAKE THE CAR AROUND BACK, IN CASE HE RABBITS. BLOCK THE ALLEY.
OH, AND IN CASE YOU DIDN'T KNOW, AN ALLEY IS A CITY WORD FOR A "SPACE BETWEEN LARGE BUILDINGS."
HA. I SEE WHAT YOU DID THERE.
YOU'VE REACHED THE RESIDENCE OF WAYNE CYPRESS. I'M OUT BEING SHERIFF...
...BUT LEAVE A MESSAGE AND I'LL CALL YOU BACK.
HEY, DAD. SORRY I HAD TO HANG UP LAST NIGHT. STUFF CAME UP. WORK STUFF.
ANYWAY, I JUST... WELL, YOU WERE RIGHT... I AM STUBBORN.
SO, WHEN COOPER GETS HOME, CAN YOU HAVE HIM CALL ME?
OKAY? REAL GOOD THEN. BYE.

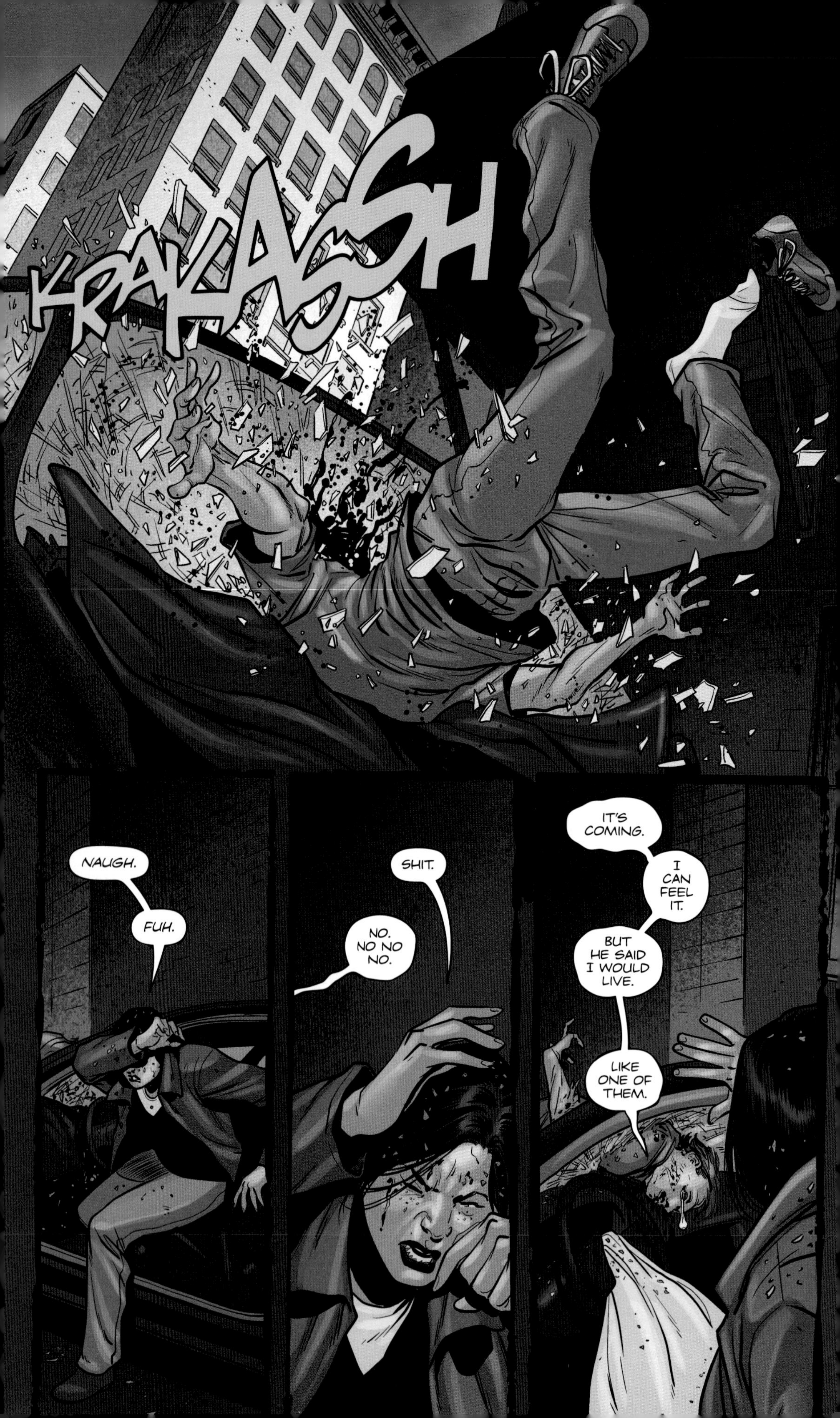
KRAKASH
NAUGH.
FUH.
SHIT.
NO. NO NO NO.
IT'S COMING.
I CAN FEEL IT.
BUT HE SAID I WOULD LIVE.
LIKE ONE OF THEM.

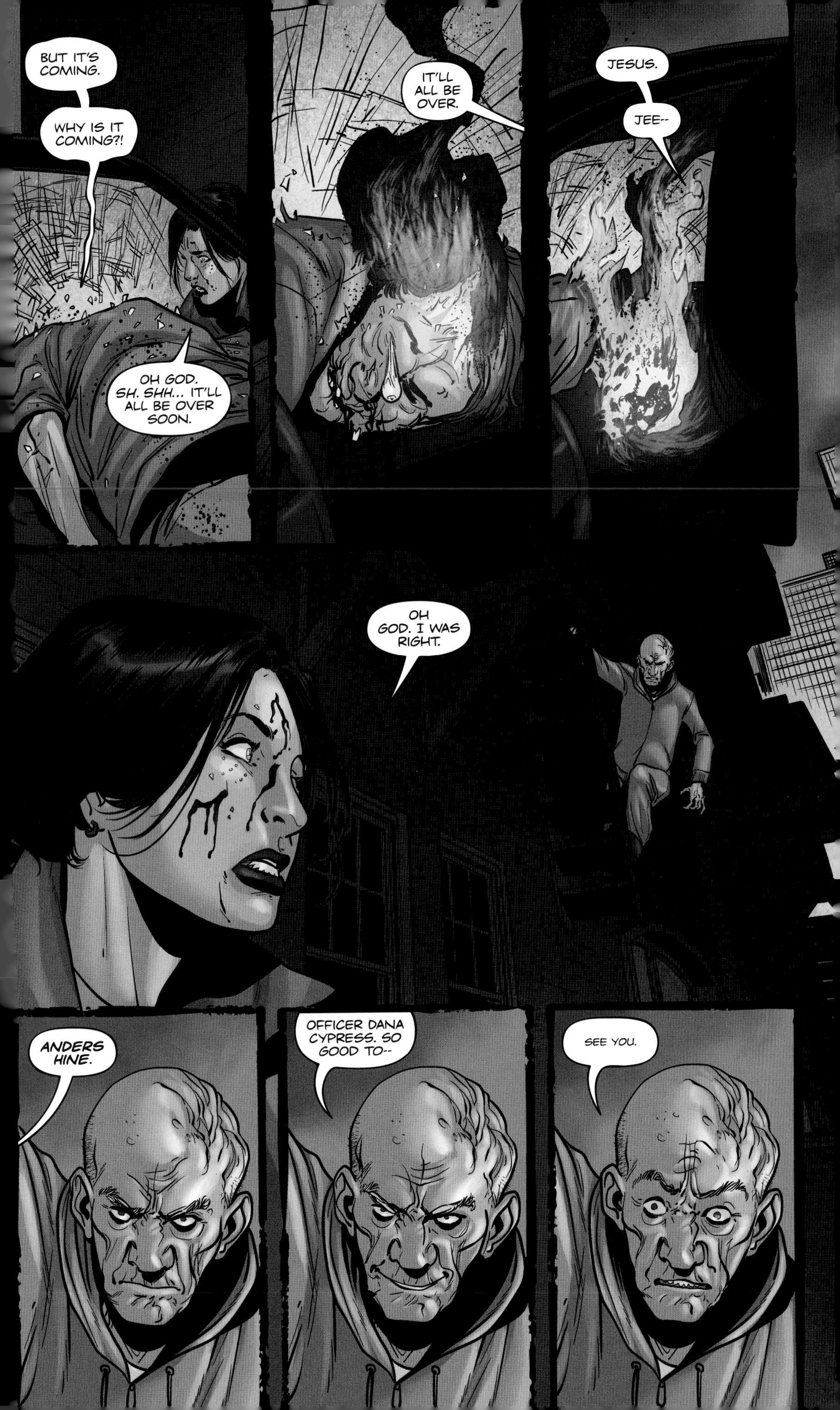
BUT IT'S COMING.
WHY IS IT COMING?!
OH GOD. SH. SHH... IT'LL ALL BE OVER SOON.
IT'LL ALL BE OVER.
JESUS.
JEE--
OH GOD. I WAS RIGHT.
ANDERS HINE.
OFFICER DANA CYPRESS. SO GOOD TO--
SEE YOU.

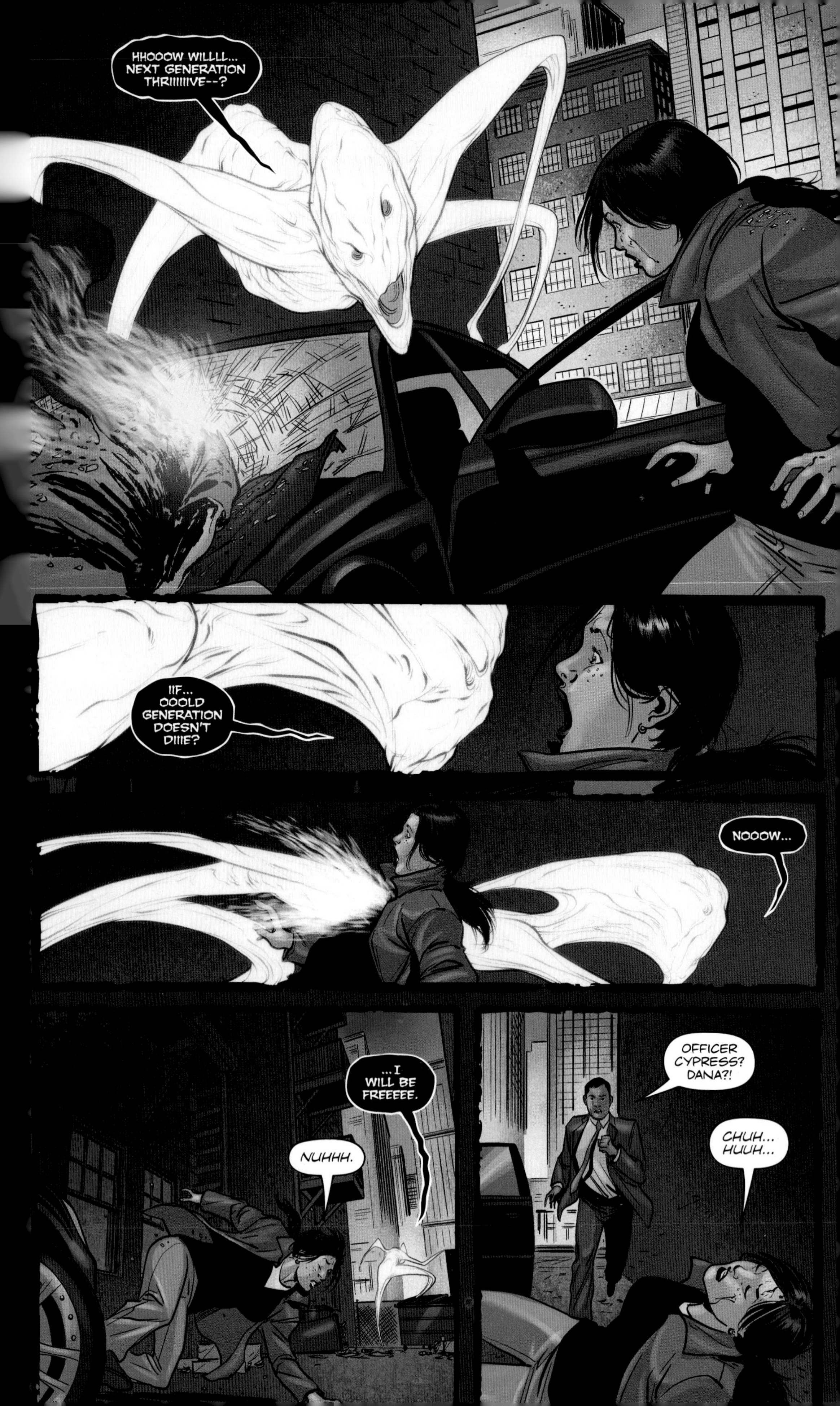
HHOOOW WILLLL... NEXT GENERATION THRIIIIIIVE--?
IIF... OOOLD GENERATION DOESN'T DIIIE?
NOOOW...
NUHHH.
...I WILL BE FREEEEE.
OFFICER CYPRESS? DANA?!
CHUH... HUUH...

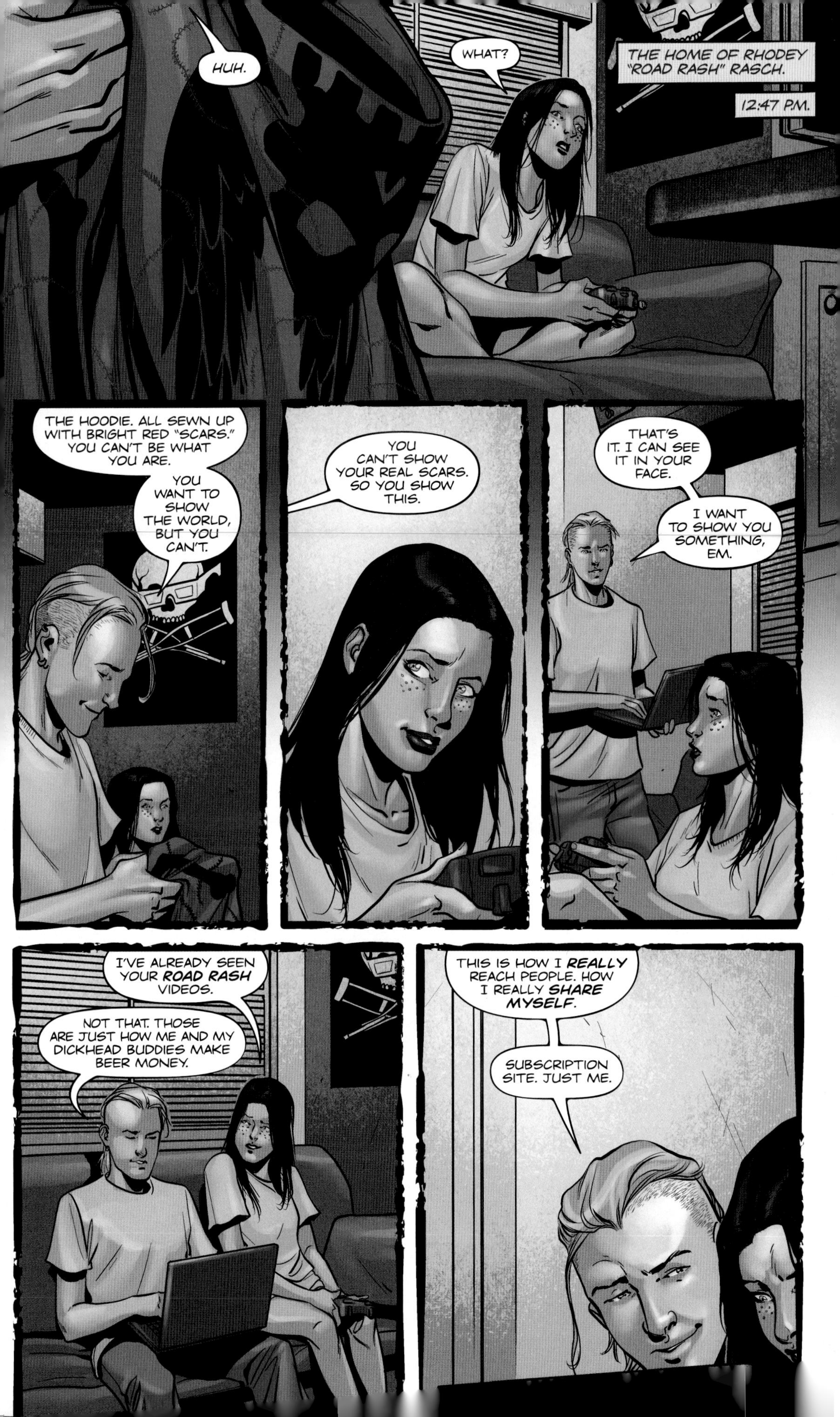
THE HOME OF RHODEY "ROAD RASH" RASCH.
12:47 P.M.
HUH.
WHAT?
THE HOODIE. ALL SEWN UP WITH BRIGHT RED "SCARS." YOU CAN'T BE WHAT YOU ARE.
YOU WANT TO SHOW THE WORLD, BUT YOU CAN'T.
YOU CAN'T SHOW YOUR REAL SCARS. SO YOU SHOW THIS.
THAT'S IT. I CAN SEE IT IN YOUR FACE.
I WANT TO SHOW YOU SOMETHING, EM.
I'VE ALREADY SEEN YOUR ROAD RASH VIDEOS.
NOT THAT. THOSE ARE JUST HOW ME AND MY DICKHEAD BUDDIES MAKE BEER MONEY.
THIS IS HOW I REALLY REACH PEOPLE. HOW I REALLY SHARE MYSELF.
SUBSCRIPTION SITE. JUST ME.

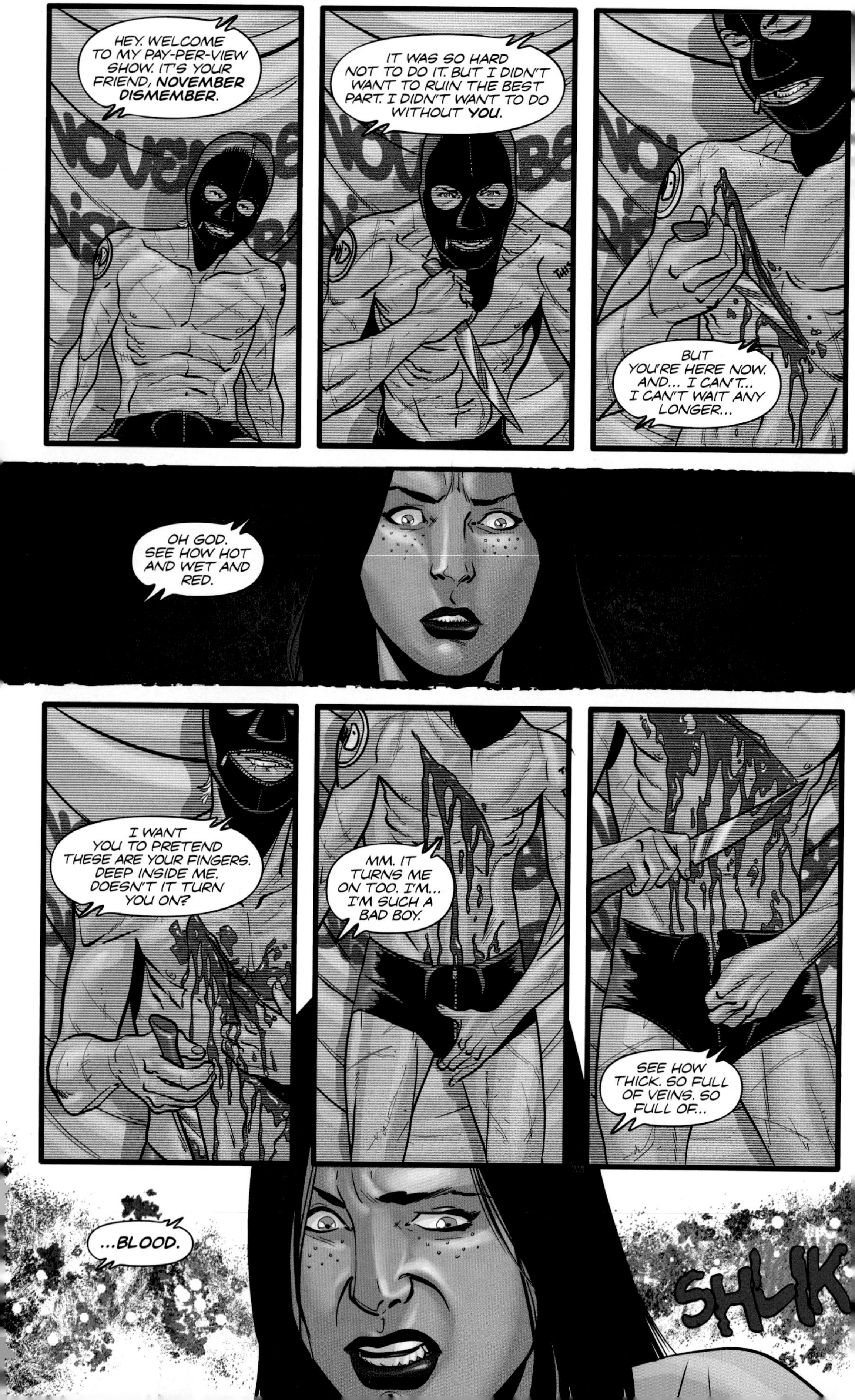
HEY. WELCOME TO MY PAY-PER-VIEW SHOW. IT'S YOUR FRIEND, NOVEMBER DISMEMBER.
IT WAS SO HARD NOT TO DO IT. BUT I DIDN'T WANT TO RUIN THE BEST PART. I DIDN'T WANT TO DO WITHOUT YOU.
BUT YOU'RE HERE NOW. AND... I CAN'T... I CAN'T WAIT ANY LONGER...
OH GOD. SEE HOW HOT AND WET AND RED.
I WANT YOU TO PRETEND THESE ARE YOUR FINGERS. DEEP INSIDE ME. DOESN'T IT TURN YOU ON?
MM. IT TURNS ME ON TOO. I'M... I'M SUCH A BAD BOY.
SEE HOW THICK. SO FULL OF VEINS. SO FULL OF...
...BLOOD.
SHLIK

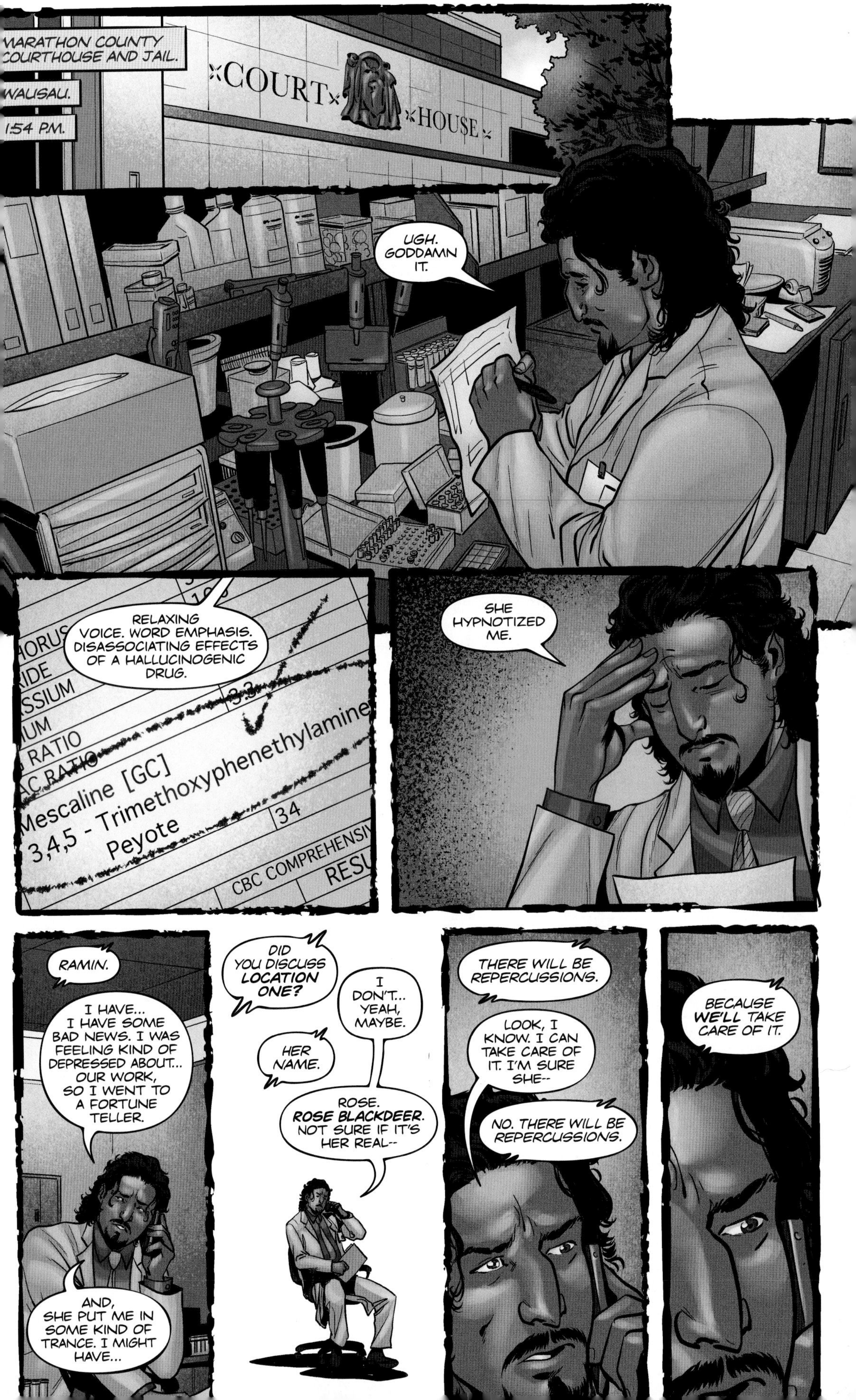
MARATHON COUNTY COURTHOUSE AND JAIL.
WAUSAU.
1:54 P.M.
COURT HOUSE
UGH. GODDAMN IT.
RELAXING VOICE. WORD EMPHASIS. DISASSOCIATING EFFECTS OF A HALLUCINOGENIC DRUG.
Mescaline [GC]
3,4,5 - Trimethoxyphenethylamine
Peyote
CBC COMPREHENSIV
SHE HYPNOTIZED ME.
RAMIN.
I HAVE... I HAVE SOME BAD NEWS. I WAS FEELING KIND OF DEPRESSED ABOUT... OUR WORK, SO I WENT TO A FORTUNE TELLER.
AND, SHE PUT ME IN SOME KIND OF TRANCE. I MIGHT HAVE...
DID YOU DISCUSS **LOCATION ONE?**
I DON'T... YEAH, MAYBE.
HER NAME.
ROSE. **ROSE BLACKDEER.** NOT SURE IF IT'S HER REAL--
THERE WILL BE REPERCUSSIONS.
LOOK, I KNOW. I CAN TAKE CARE OF IT. I'M SURE SHE--
NO. THERE WILL BE REPERCUSSIONS.
BECAUSE **WE'LL** TAKE CARE OF IT.

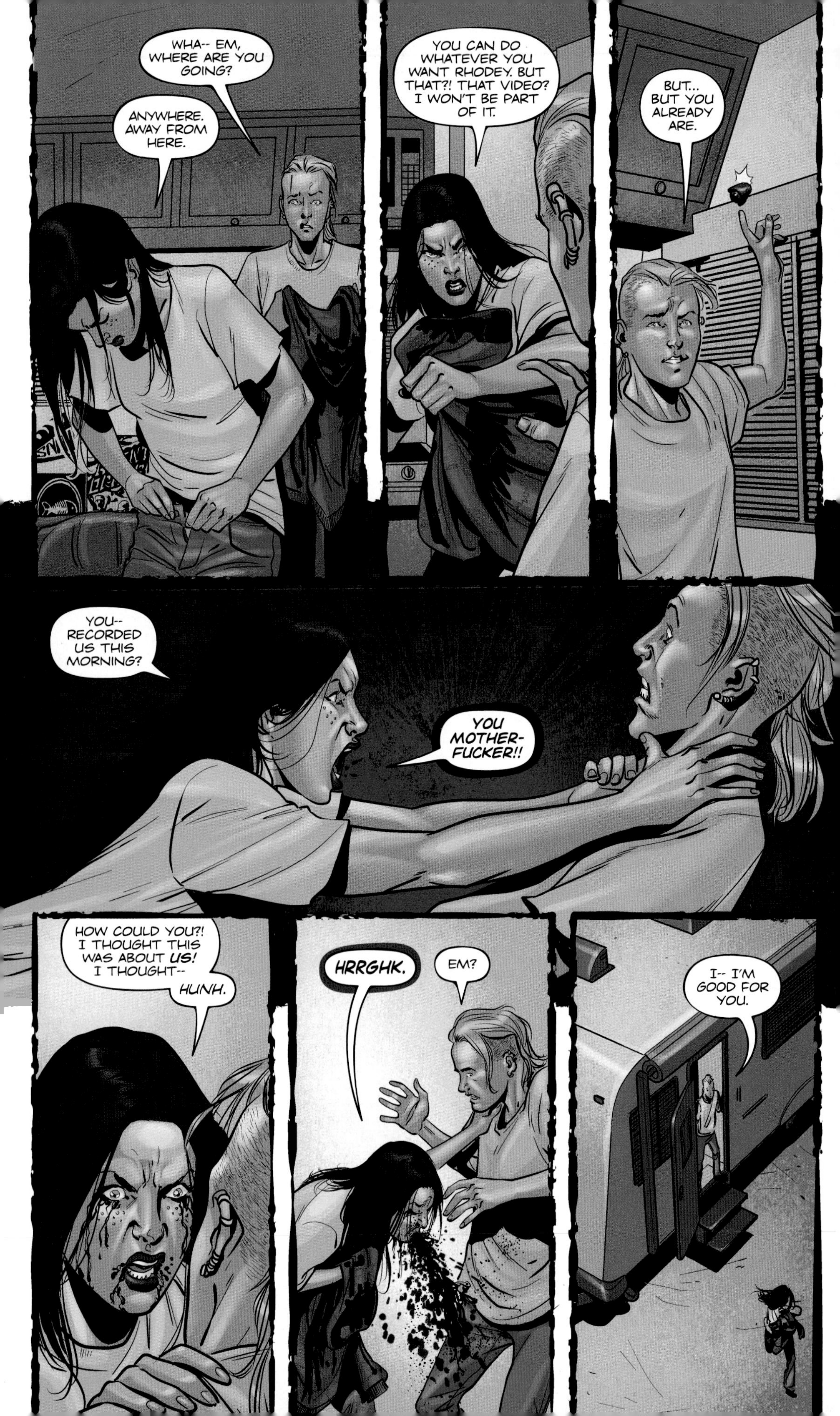
WHA-- EM, WHERE ARE YOU GOING?
ANYWHERE. AWAY FROM HERE.
YOU CAN DO WHATEVER YOU WANT RHODEY. BUT THAT?! THAT VIDEO? I WON'T BE PART OF IT.
BUT... BUT YOU ALREADY ARE.
YOU-- RECORDED US THIS MORNING?
YOU MOTHER-FUCKER!!
HOW COULD YOU?! I THOUGHT THIS WAS ABOUT US! I THOUGHT--
HUNH.
HRRGHK.
EM?
I-- I'M GOOD FOR YOU.

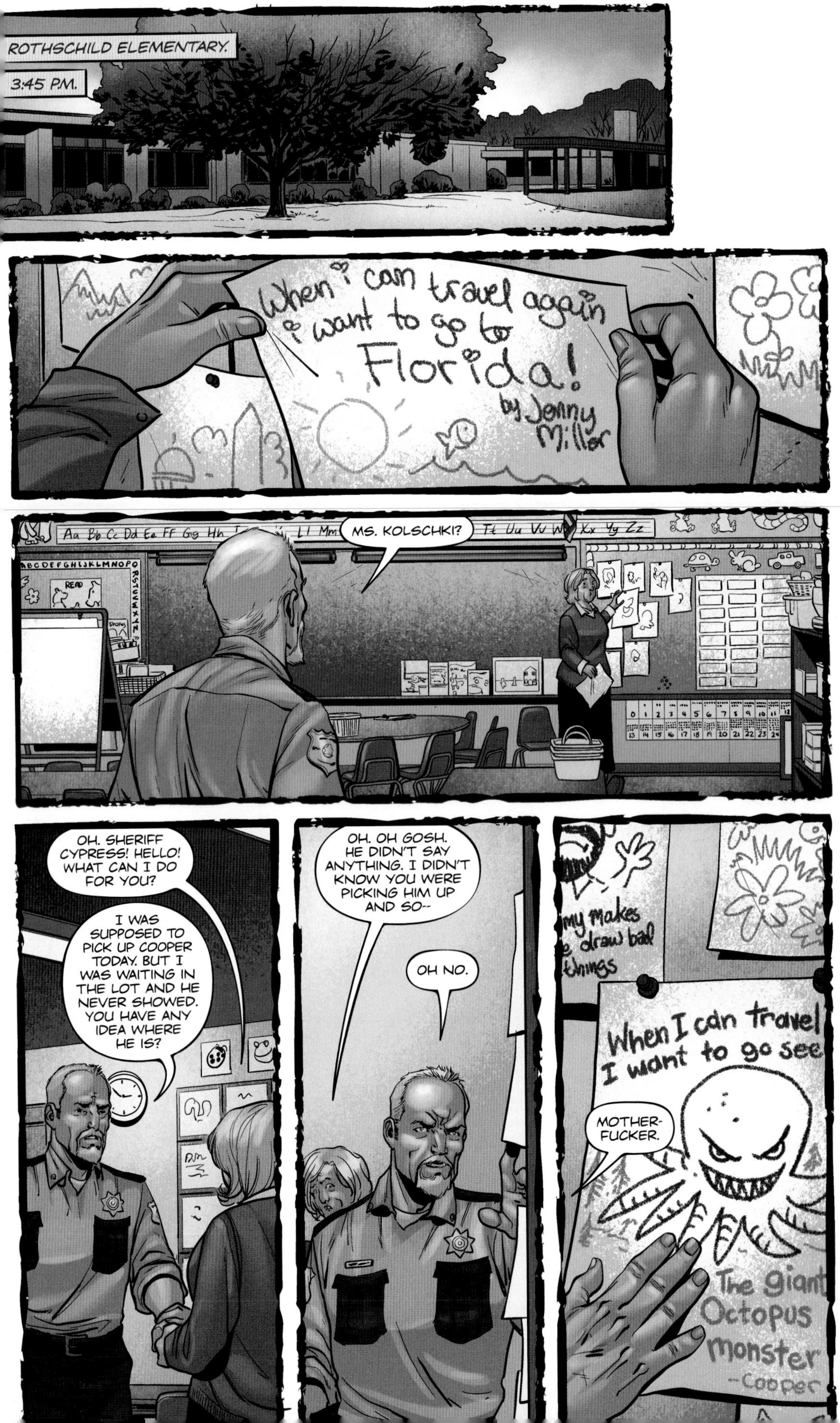
ROTHSCHILD ELEMENTARY.
3:45 P.M.
When i can travel again i want to go to Florida! by Jenny Miller
MS. KOLSCHKI?
OH. SHERIFF CYPRESS! HELLO! WHAT CAN I DO FOR YOU?
I WAS SUPPOSED TO PICK UP COOPER TODAY. BUT I WAS WAITING IN THE LOT AND HE NEVER SHOWED. YOU HAVE ANY IDEA WHERE HE IS?
OH. OH GOSH. HE DIDN'T SAY ANYTHING. I DIDN'T KNOW YOU WERE PICKING HIM UP AND SO--
OH NO.
When I can travel I want to go see
MOTHER-FUCKER.
The giant Octopus monster -Cooper

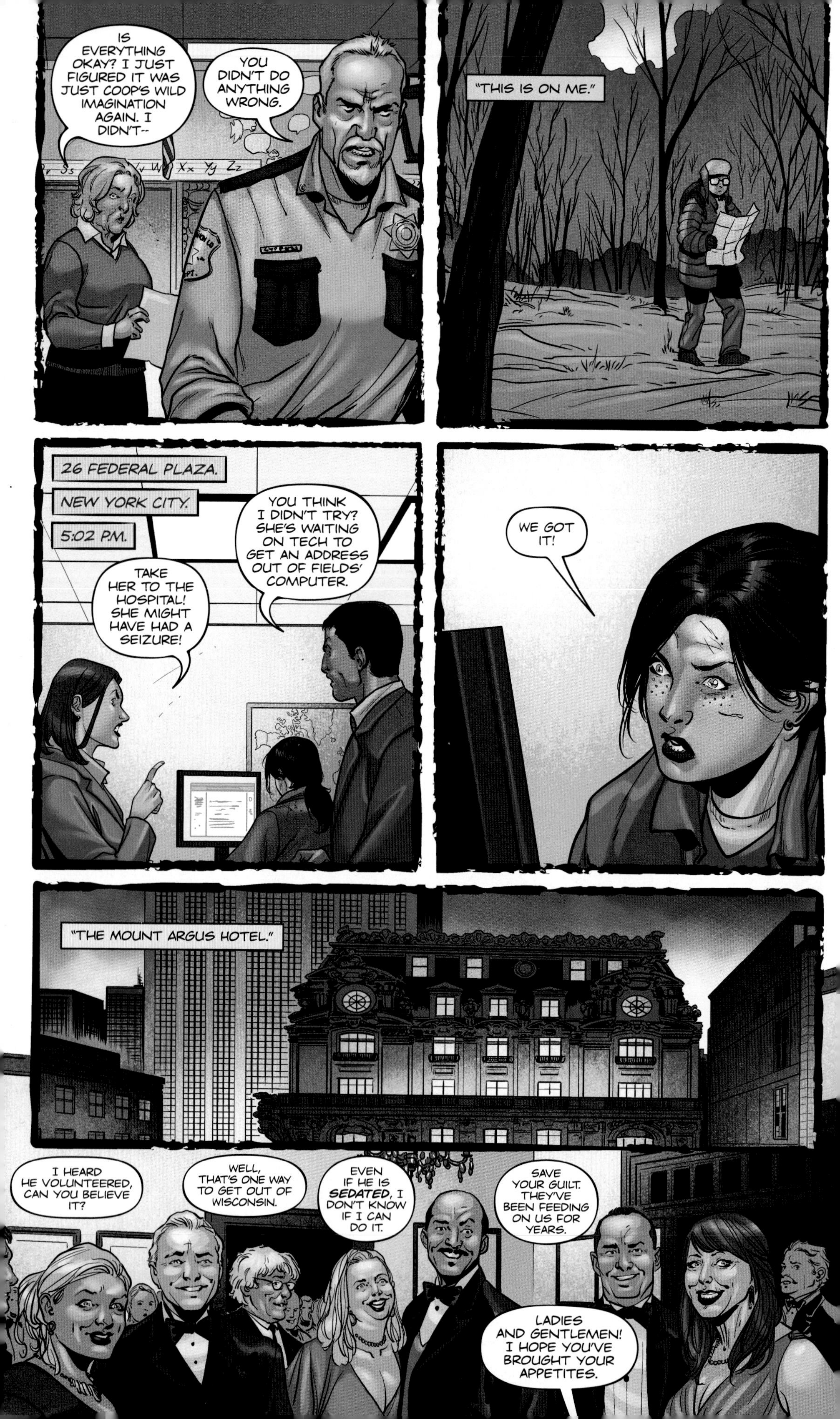

IS EVERYTHING OKAY? I JUST FIGURED IT WAS JUST COOP'S WILD IMAGINATION AGAIN. I DIDN'T--
YOU DIDN'T DO ANYTHING WRONG.
"THIS IS ON ME."
26 FEDERAL PLAZA.
NEW YORK CITY.
5:02 P.M.
TAKE HER TO THE HOSPITAL! SHE MIGHT HAVE HAD A SEIZURE!
YOU THINK I DIDN'T TRY? SHE'S WAITING ON TECH TO GET AN ADDRESS OUT OF FIELDS' COMPUTER.
WE GOT IT!
"THE MOUNT ARGUS HOTEL."
I HEARD HE VOLUNTEERED, CAN YOU BELIEVE IT?
WELL, THAT'S ONE WAY TO GET OUT OF WISCONSIN.
EVEN IF HE IS SEDATED, I DON'T KNOW IF I CAN DO IT.
SAVE YOUR GUILT. THEY'VE BEEN FEEDING ON US FOR YEARS.
LADIES AND GENTLEMEN! I HOPE YOU'VE BROUGHT YOUR APPETITES.

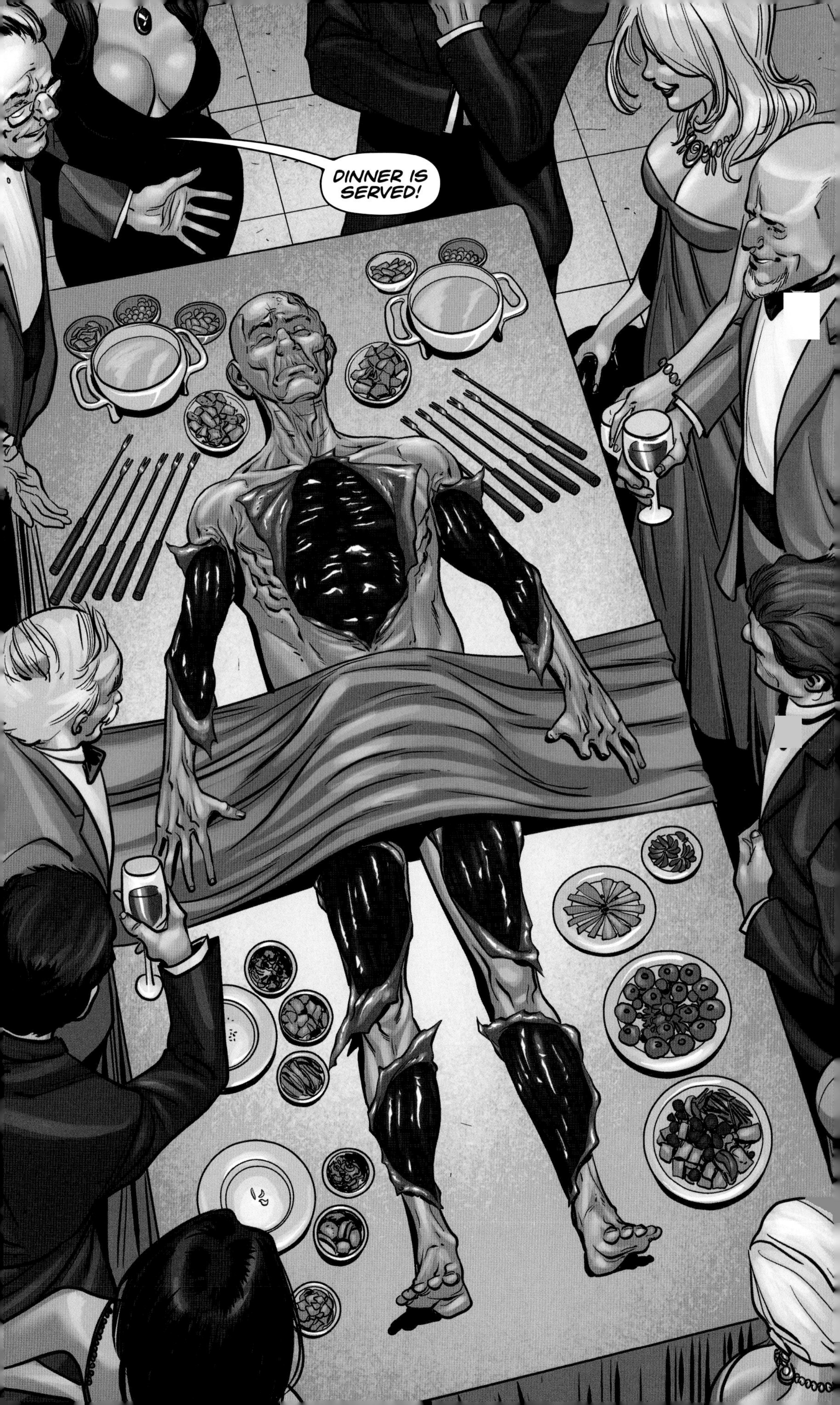
DINNER IS SERVED!

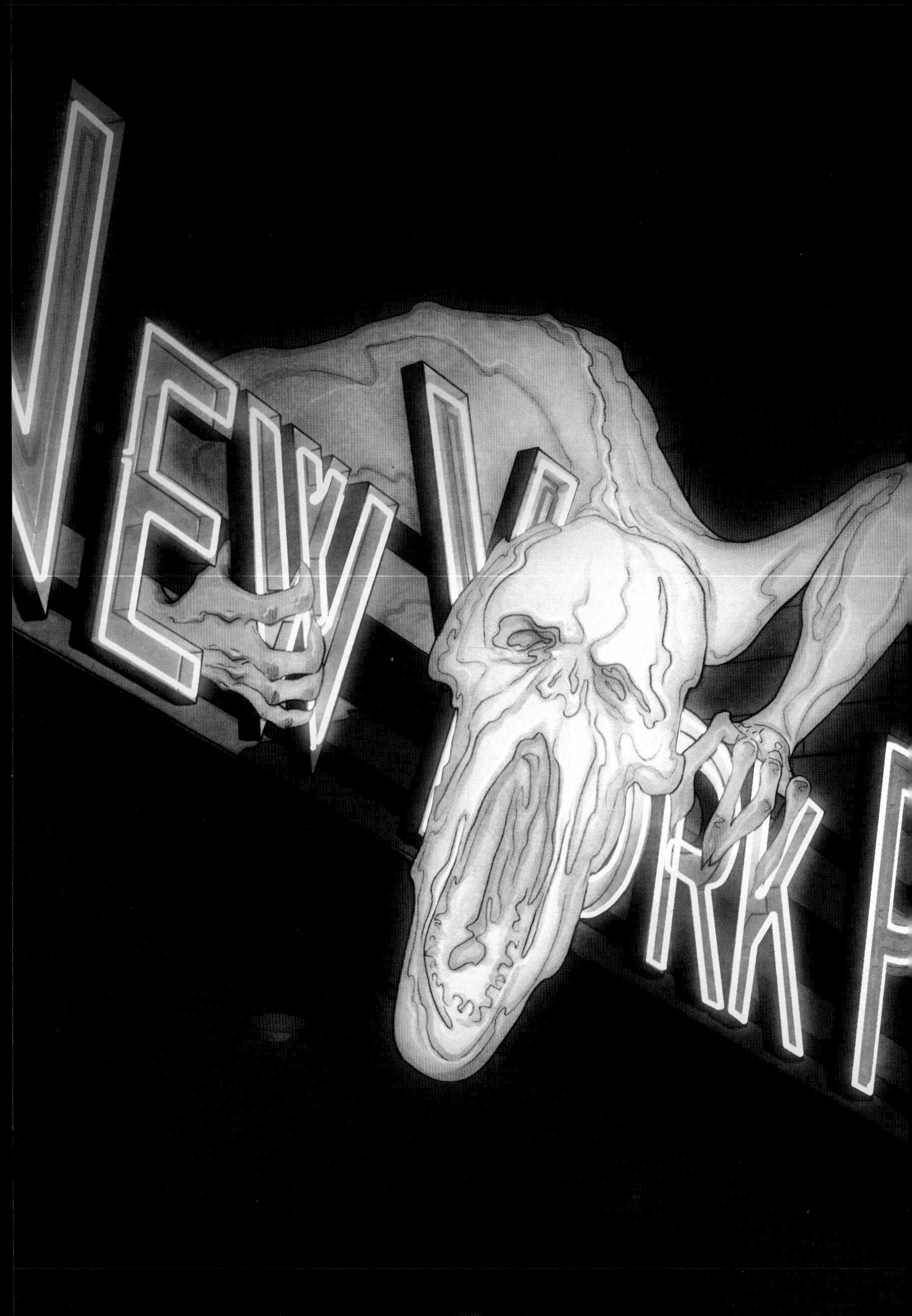

CH. 23

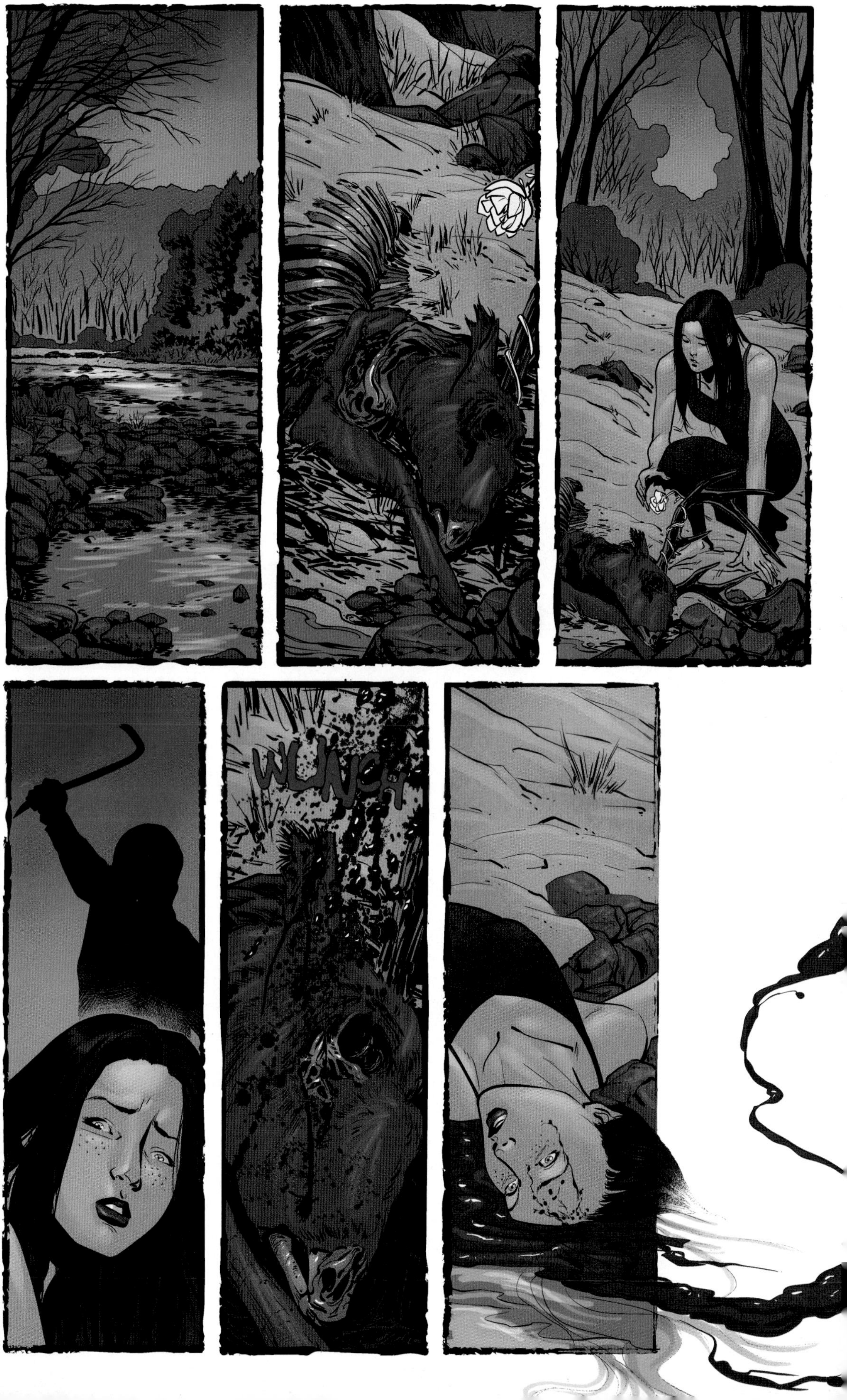
WUNCH

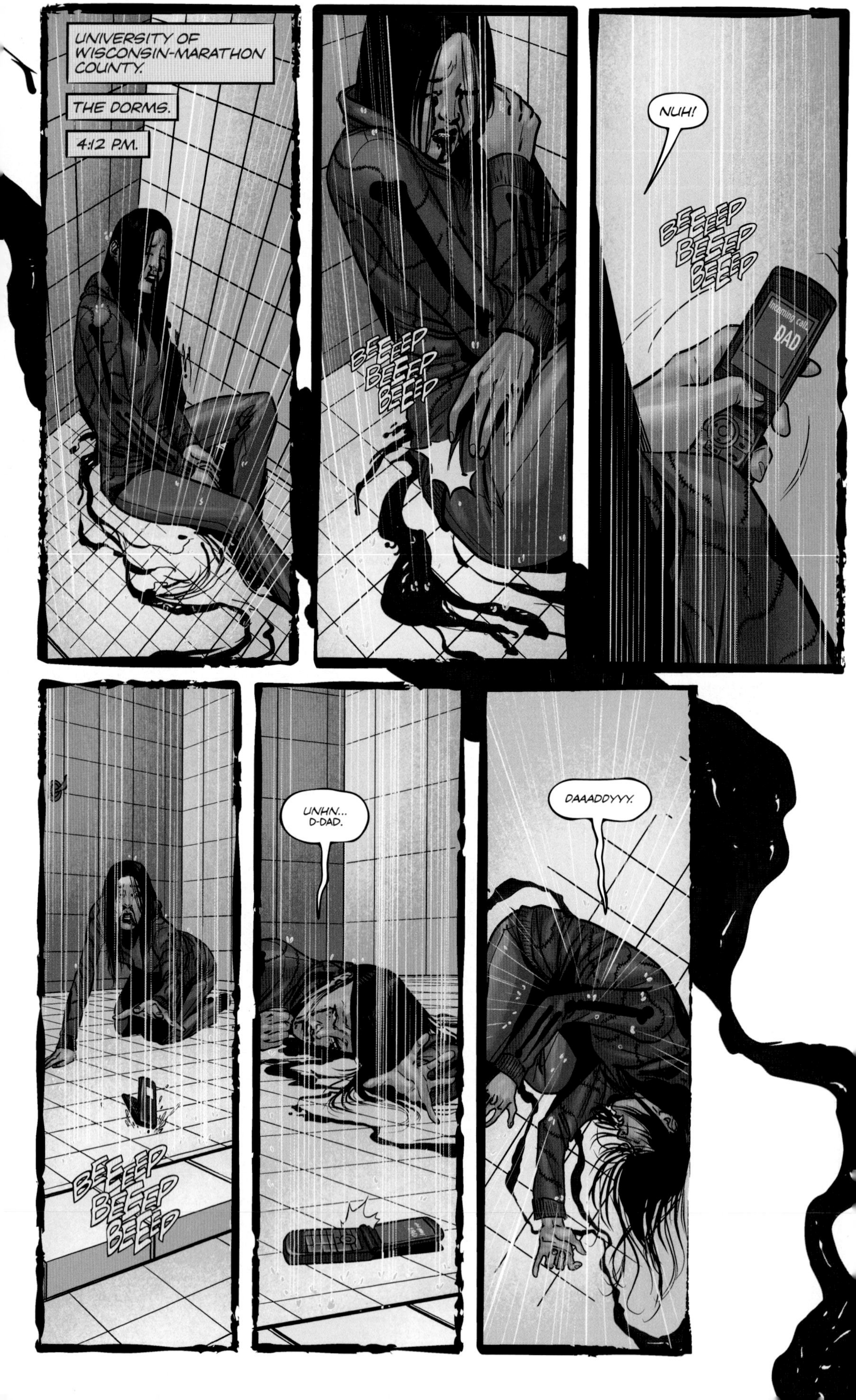
UNIVERSITY OF WISCONSIN-MARATHON COUNTY.
THE DORMS.
4:12 P.M.
BEEEEP BEEEP BEEEP
NUH!
BEEEEP BEEEP BEEEP
DAD
BEEEEP BEEEP BEEEP
UNHN... D-DAD.
DAAADDYYY.

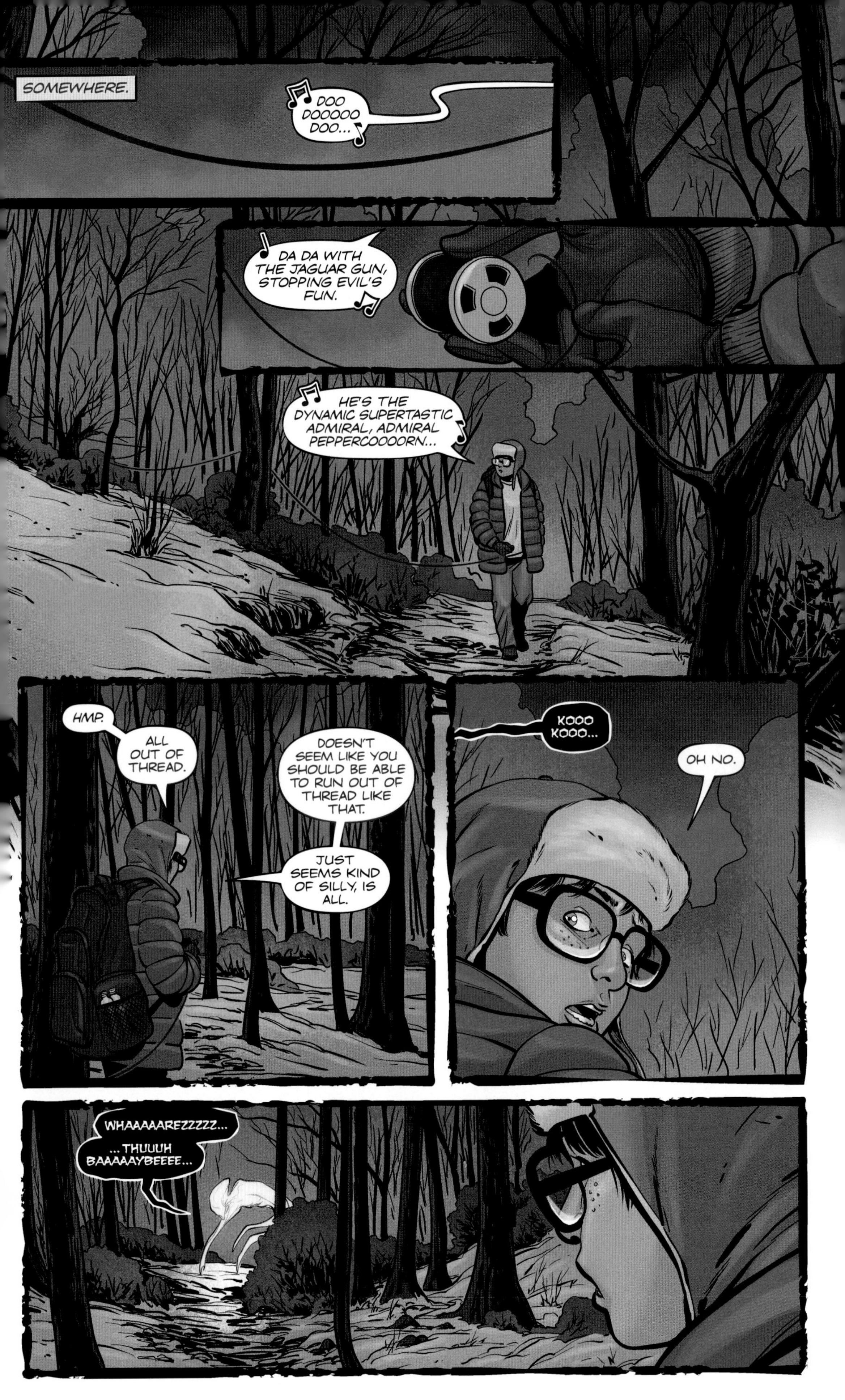
SOMEWHERE.
DOO DOOOOO DOO...
DA DA WITH THE JAGUAR GUN, STOPPING EVIL'S FUN.
HE'S THE DYNAMIC SUPERTASTIC ADMIRAL, ADMIRAL PEPPERCOOOORN...
HMP.
ALL OUT OF THREAD.
DOESN'T SEEM LIKE YOU SHOULD BE ABLE TO RUN OUT OF THREAD LIKE THAT.
JUST SEEMS KIND OF SILLY, IS ALL.
KOOO KOOO...
OH NO.
WHAAAAAREZZZZZ...
...THUUUH BAAAAAYBEEEE...

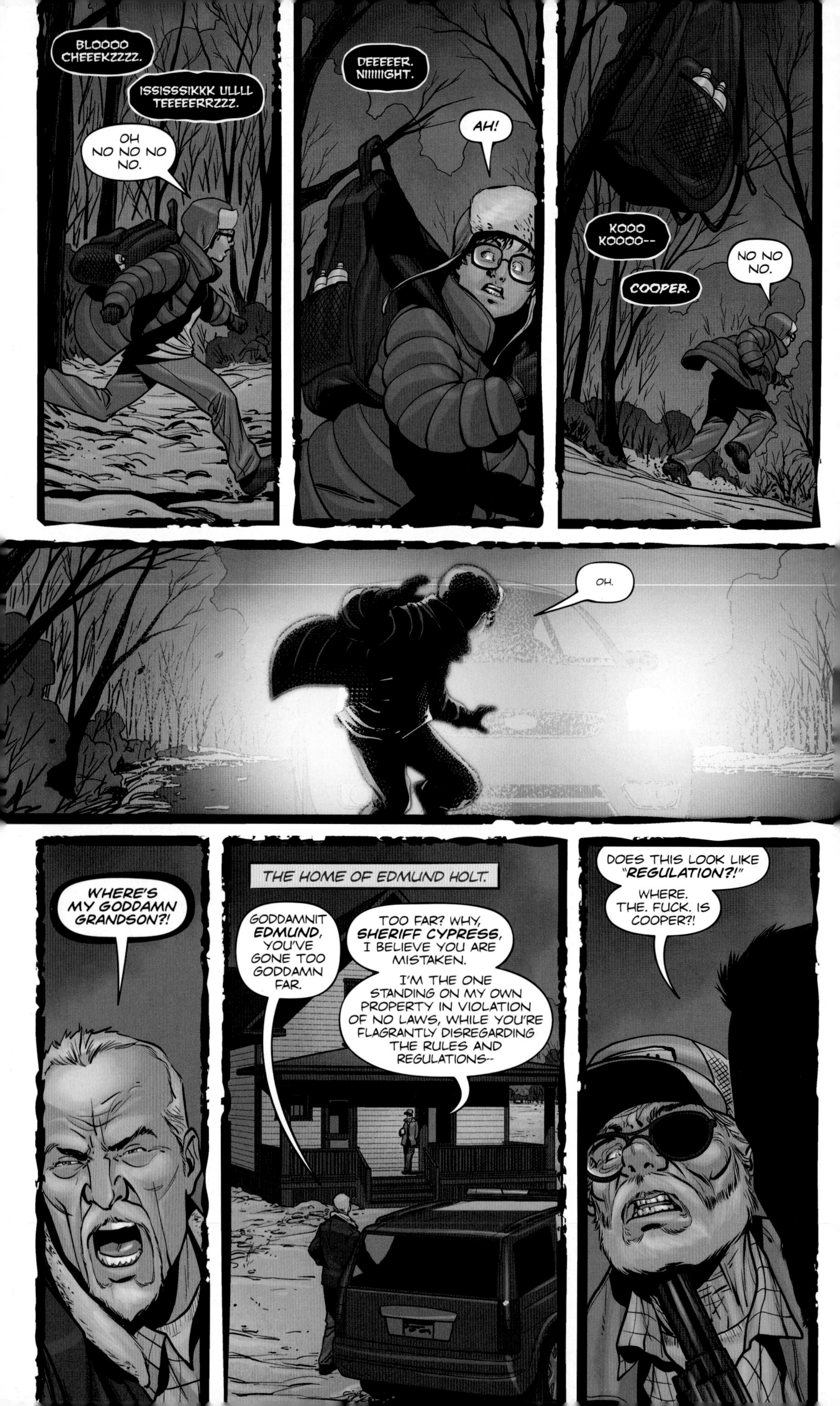

BLOOOO CHEEEKZZZZ.
ISSISSSIKKK ULLLL TEEEEERRZZZ.
OH NO NO NO NO.
DEEEEER. NIIIIIGHT.
AH!
KOOO KOOOO--
COOPER.
NO NO NO.
OH.
WHERE'S MY GODDAMN GRANDSON?!
THE HOME OF EDMUND HOLT.
GODDAMNIT EDMUND, YOU'VE GONE TOO GODDAMN FAR.
TOO FAR? WHY, SHERIFF CYPRESS, I BELIEVE YOU ARE MISTAKEN.
I'M THE ONE STANDING ON MY OWN PROPERTY IN VIOLATION OF NO LAWS, WHILE YOU'RE FLAGRANTLY DISREGARDING THE RULES AND REGULATIONS--
DOES THIS LOOK LIKE "REGULATION?!"
WHERE. THE. FUCK. IS COOPER?!

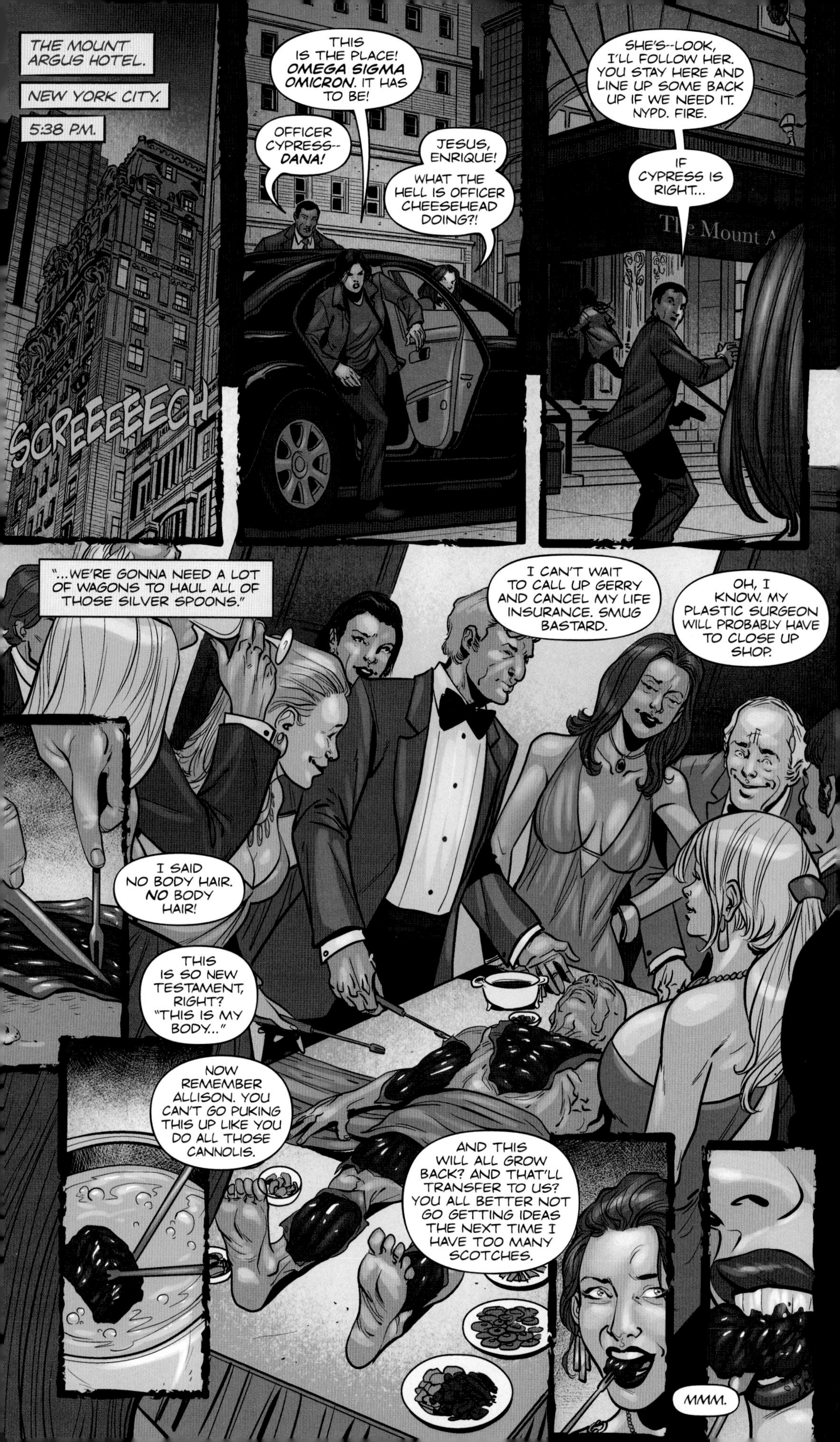
THE MOUNT ARGUS HOTEL.
NEW YORK CITY.
5:38 P.M.
SCREEEEECH
THIS IS THE PLACE! OMEGA SIGMA OMICRON. IT HAS TO BE!
OFFICER CYPRESS-- DANA!
JESUS, ENRIQUE!
WHAT THE HELL IS OFFICER CHEESEHEAD DOING?!
SHE'S--LOOK, I'LL FOLLOW HER. YOU STAY HERE AND LINE UP SOME BACK UP IF WE NEED IT. NYPD. FIRE.
IF CYPRESS IS RIGHT...
The Mount A
"...WE'RE GONNA NEED A LOT OF WAGONS TO HAUL ALL OF THOSE SILVER SPOONS."
I CAN'T WAIT TO CALL UP GERRY AND CANCEL MY LIFE INSURANCE. SMUG BASTARD.
OH, I KNOW. MY PLASTIC SURGEON WILL PROBABLY HAVE TO CLOSE UP SHOP.
I SAID NO BODY HAIR. NO BODY HAIR!
THIS IS SO NEW TESTAMENT, RIGHT? "THIS IS MY BODY..."
NOW REMEMBER ALLISON. YOU CAN'T GO PUKING THIS UP LIKE YOU DO ALL THOSE CANNOLIS.
AND THIS WILL ALL GROW BACK? AND THAT'LL TRANSFER TO US? YOU ALL BETTER NOT GO GETTING IDEAS THE NEXT TIME I HAVE TOO MANY SCOTCHES.
MMM.

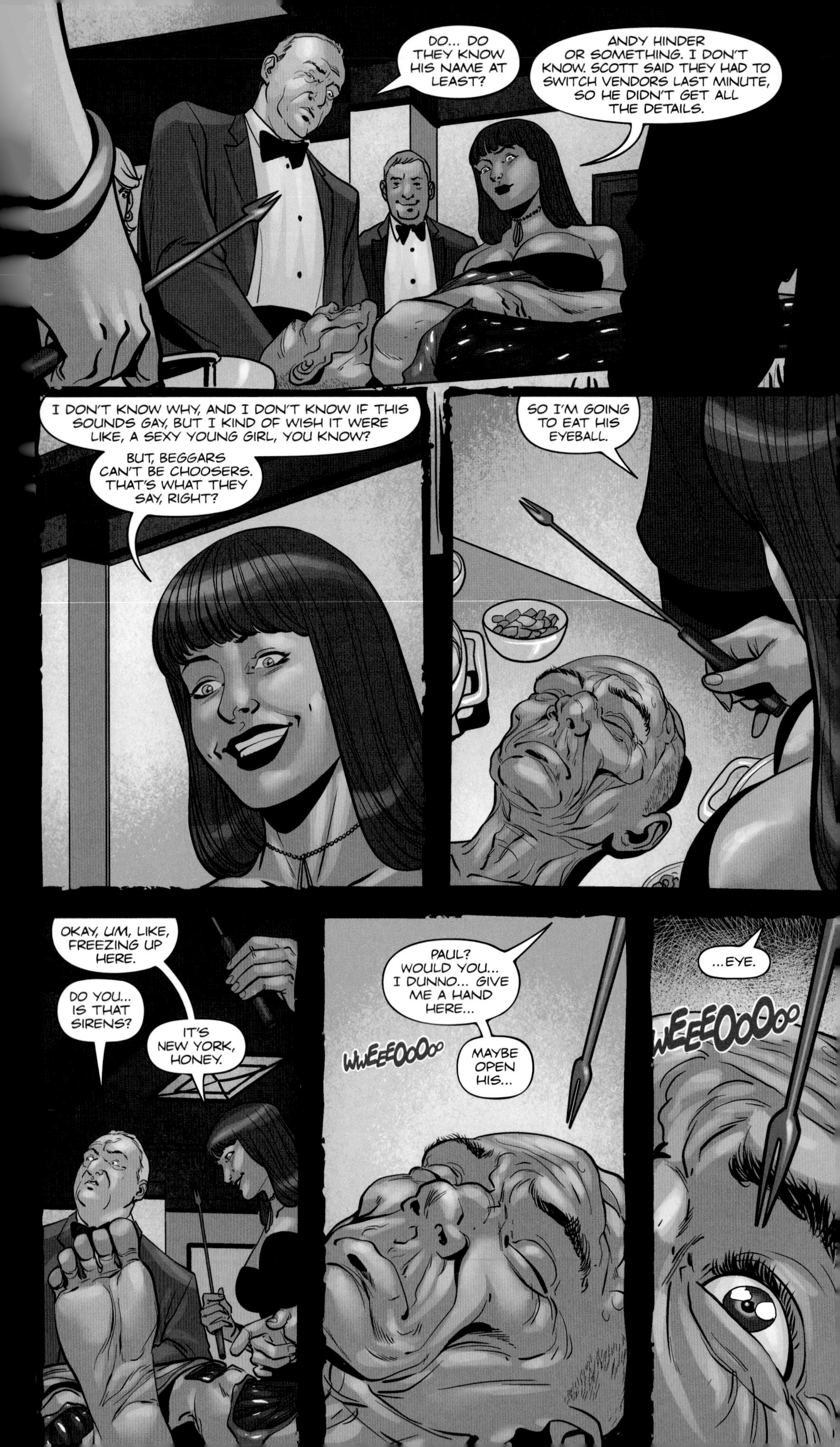
DO... DO THEY KNOW HIS NAME AT LEAST?
ANDY HINDER OR SOMETHING. I DON'T KNOW. SCOTT SAID THEY HAD TO SWITCH VENDORS LAST MINUTE, SO HE DIDN'T GET ALL THE DETAILS.
I DON'T KNOW WHY, AND I DON'T KNOW IF THIS SOUNDS GAY, BUT I KIND OF WISH IT WERE LIKE, A SEXY YOUNG GIRL, YOU KNOW?
BUT, BEGGARS CAN'T BE CHOOSERS. THAT'S WHAT THEY SAY, RIGHT?
SO I'M GOING TO EAT HIS EYEBALL.
OKAY, UM, LIKE, FREEZING UP HERE.
DO YOU... IS THAT SIRENS?
IT'S NEW YORK, HONEY.
PAUL? WOULD YOU... I DUNNO... GIVE ME A HAND HERE...
WWEEEOOOOO
MAYBE OPEN HIS...
...EYE.
WEEEOOOOO

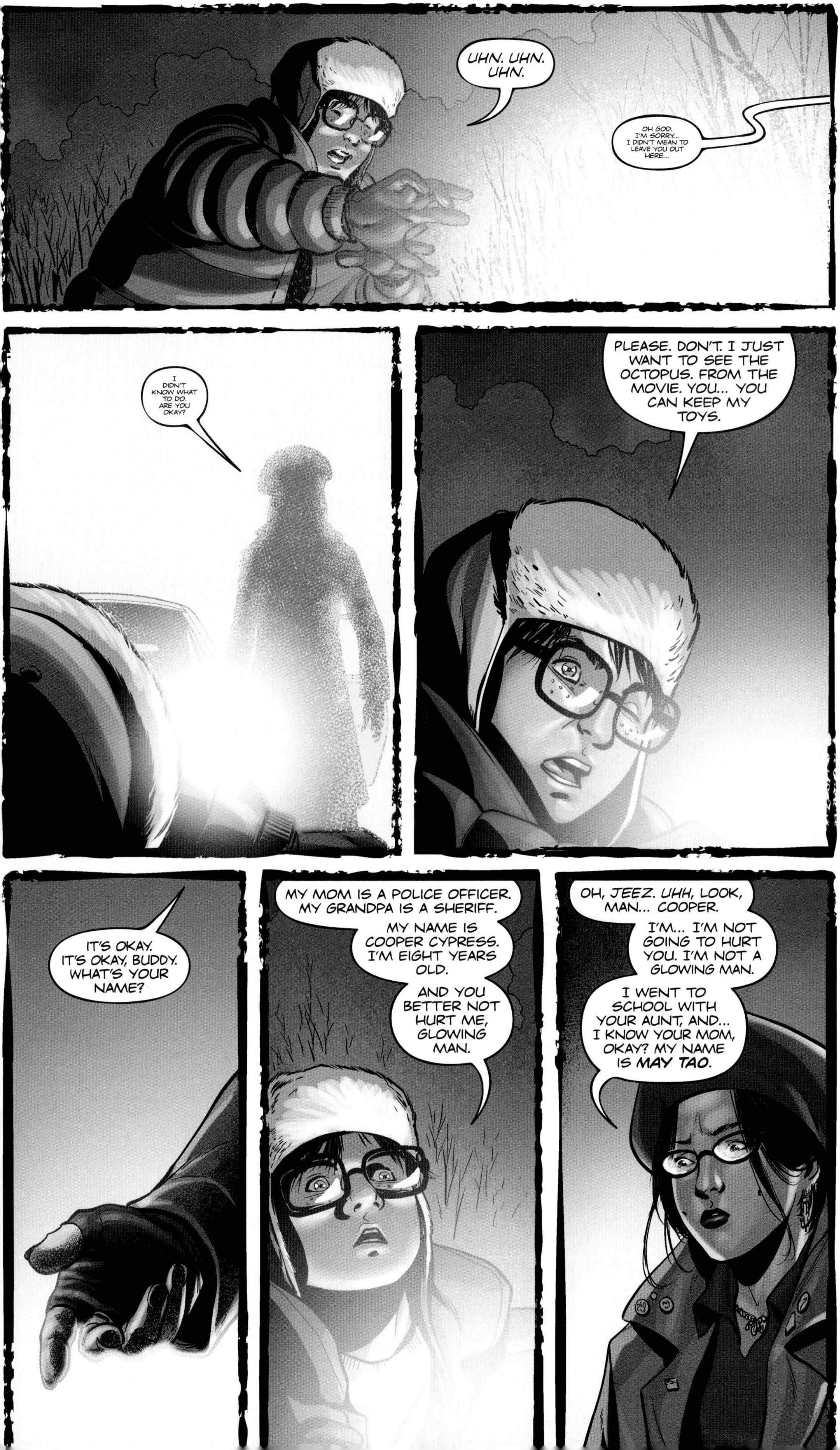
UHN. UHN. UHN.
OH GOD. I'M SORRY... I DIDN'T MEAN TO LEAVE YOU OUT HERE...
I DIDN'T KNOW WHAT TO DO. ARE YOU OKAY?
PLEASE. DON'T. I JUST WANT TO SEE THE OCTOPUS. FROM THE MOVIE. YOU... YOU CAN KEEP MY TOYS.
IT'S OKAY. IT'S OKAY, BUDDY. WHAT'S YOUR NAME?
MY MOM IS A POLICE OFFICER. MY GRANDPA IS A SHERIFF.
MY NAME IS COOPER CYPRESS. I'M EIGHT YEARS OLD.
AND YOU BETTER NOT HURT ME, GLOWING MAN.
OH, JEEZ. UHH, LOOK, MAN... COOPER.
I'M... I'M NOT GOING TO HURT YOU. I'M NOT A GLOWING MAN.
I WENT TO SCHOOL WITH YOUR AUNT, AND... I KNOW YOUR MOM, OKAY? MY NAME IS MAY TAO.

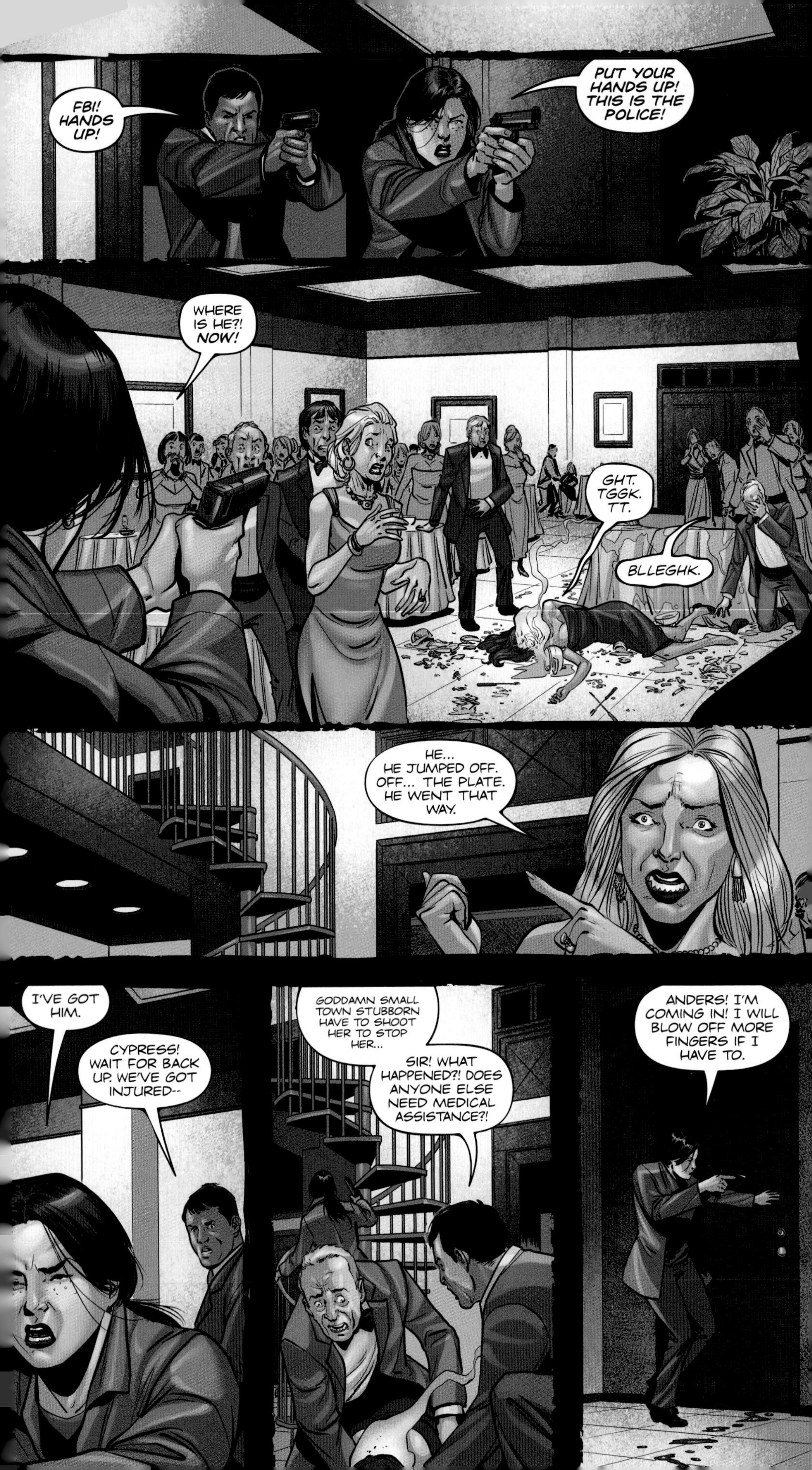
FBI! HANDS UP!
PUT YOUR HANDS UP! THIS IS THE POLICE!
WHERE IS HE?! NOW!
GHT. TGGK. TT.
BLLEGHK.
HE... HE JUMPED OFF. OFF... THE PLATE. HE WENT THAT WAY.
I'VE GOT HIM.
CYPRESS! WAIT FOR BACK UP. WE'VE GOT INJURED--
GODDAMN SMALL TOWN STUBBORN HAVE TO SHOOT HER TO STOP HER...
SIR! WHAT HAPPENED?! DOES ANYONE ELSE NEED MEDICAL ASSISTANCE?!
ANDERS! I'M COMING IN! I WILL BLOW OFF MORE FINGERS IF I HAVE TO.

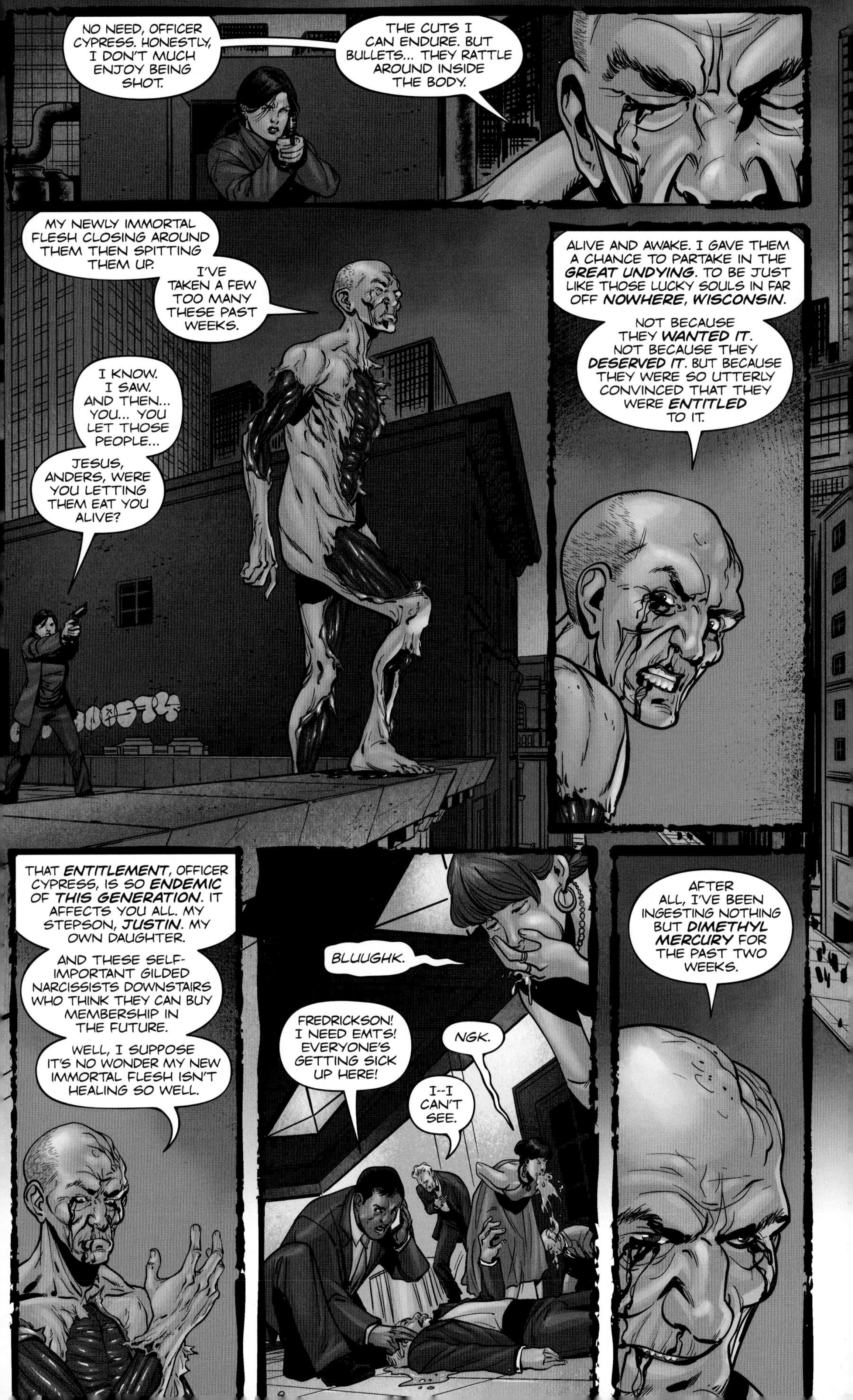
NO NEED, OFFICER CYPRESS. HONESTLY, I DON'T MUCH ENJOY BEING SHOT.
THE CUTS I CAN ENDURE. BUT BULLETS... THEY RATTLE AROUND INSIDE THE BODY.
MY NEWLY IMMORTAL FLESH CLOSING AROUND THEM THEN SPITTING THEM UP.
I'VE TAKEN A FEW TOO MANY THESE PAST WEEKS.
I KNOW. I SAW. AND THEN... YOU... YOU LET THOSE PEOPLE...
JESUS, ANDERS, WERE YOU LETTING THEM EAT YOU ALIVE?
ALIVE AND AWAKE. I GAVE THEM A CHANCE TO PARTAKE IN THE GREAT UNDYING. TO BE JUST LIKE THOSE LUCKY SOULS IN FAR OFF NOWHERE, WISCONSIN.
NOT BECAUSE THEY WANTED IT. NOT BECAUSE THEY DESERVED IT. BUT BECAUSE THEY WERE SO UTTERLY CONVINCED THAT THEY WERE ENTITLED TO IT.
THAT ENTITLEMENT, OFFICER CYPRESS, IS SO ENDEMIC OF THIS GENERATION. IT AFFECTS YOU ALL. MY STEPSON, JUSTIN. MY OWN DAUGHTER.
AND THESE SELF-IMPORTANT GILDED NARCISSISTS DOWNSTAIRS WHO THINK THEY CAN BUY MEMBERSHIP IN THE FUTURE.
WELL, I SUPPOSE IT'S NO WONDER MY NEW IMMORTAL FLESH ISN'T HEALING SO WELL.
BLUUGHK.
FREDRICKSON! I NEED EMTS! EVERYONE'S GETTING SICK UP HERE!
NGK.
I--I CAN'T SEE.
AFTER ALL, I'VE BEEN INGESTING NOTHING BUT DIMETHYL MERCURY FOR THE PAST TWO WEEKS.

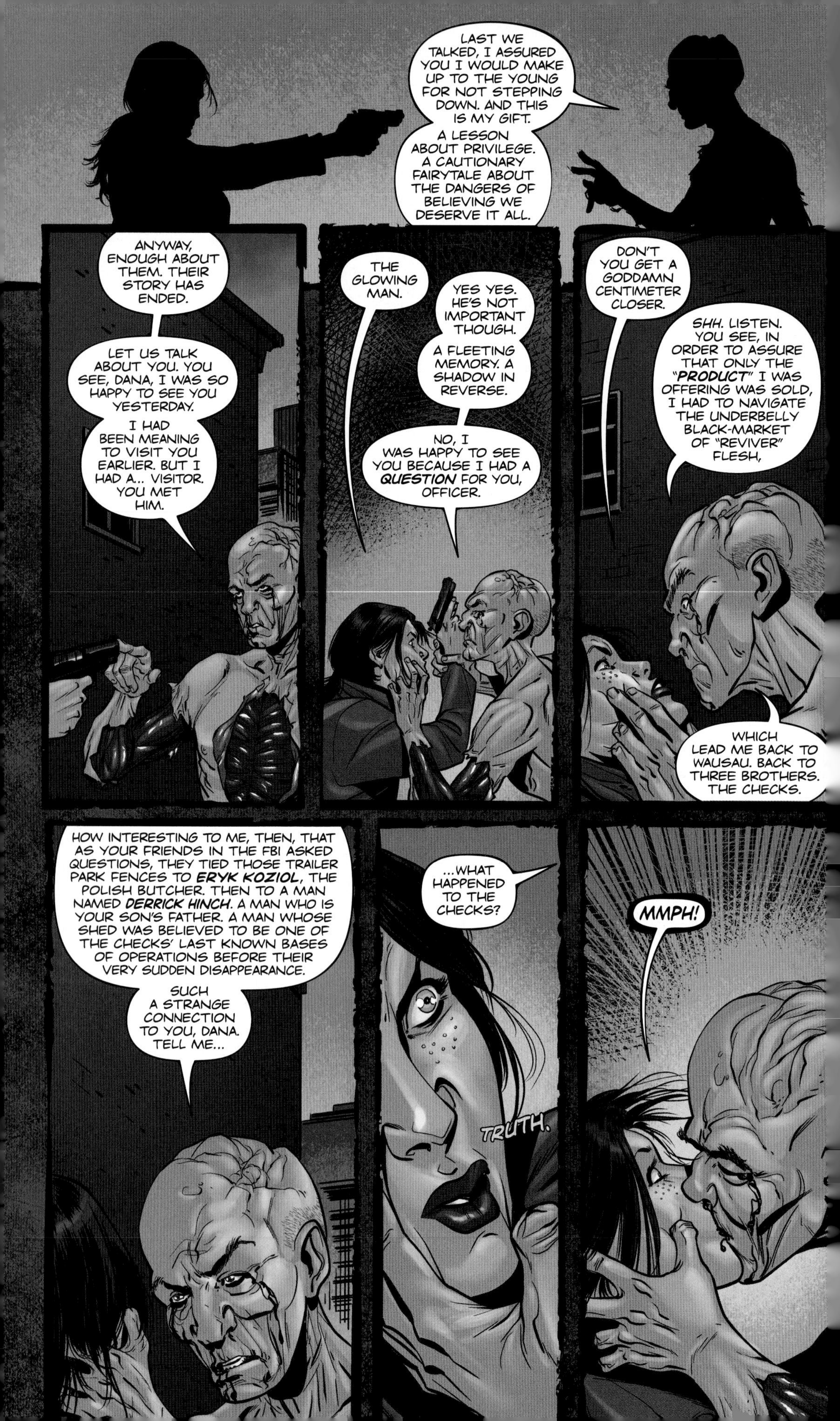
LAST WE TALKED, I ASSURED YOU I WOULD MAKE UP TO THE YOUNG FOR NOT STEPPING DOWN. AND THIS IS MY GIFT.
A LESSON ABOUT PRIVILEGE. A CAUTIONARY FAIRYTALE ABOUT THE DANGERS OF BELIEVING WE DESERVE IT ALL.
ANYWAY, ENOUGH ABOUT THEM. THEIR STORY HAS ENDED.
LET US TALK ABOUT YOU. YOU SEE, DANA, I WAS SO HAPPY TO SEE YOU YESTERDAY.
I HAD BEEN MEANING TO VISIT YOU EARLIER. BUT I HAD A... VISITOR. YOU MET HIM.
THE GLOWING MAN.
YES YES. HE'S NOT IMPORTANT THOUGH.
A FLEETING MEMORY. A SHADOW IN REVERSE.
NO, I WAS HAPPY TO SEE YOU BECAUSE I HAD A **QUESTION** FOR YOU, OFFICER.
DON'T YOU GET A GODDAMN CENTIMETER CLOSER.
SHH. LISTEN. YOU SEE, IN ORDER TO ASSURE THAT ONLY THE "**PRODUCT**" I WAS OFFERING WAS SOLD, I HAD TO NAVIGATE THE UNDERBELLY BLACK-MARKET OF "REVIVER" FLESH,
WHICH LEAD ME BACK TO WAUSAU. BACK TO THREE BROTHERS. THE CHECKS.
HOW INTERESTING TO ME, THEN, THAT AS YOUR FRIENDS IN THE FBI ASKED QUESTIONS, THEY TIED THOSE TRAILER PARK FENCES TO **ERYK KOZIOL**, THE POLISH BUTCHER. THEN TO A MAN NAMED **DERRICK HINCH**. A MAN WHO IS YOUR SON'S FATHER. A MAN WHOSE SHED WAS BELIEVED TO BE ONE OF THE CHECKS' LAST KNOWN BASES OF OPERATIONS BEFORE THEIR VERY SUDDEN DISAPPEARANCE.
SUCH A STRANGE CONNECTION TO YOU, DANA. TELL ME...
...WHAT HAPPENED TO THE CHECKS?
TRUTH.
MMPH!

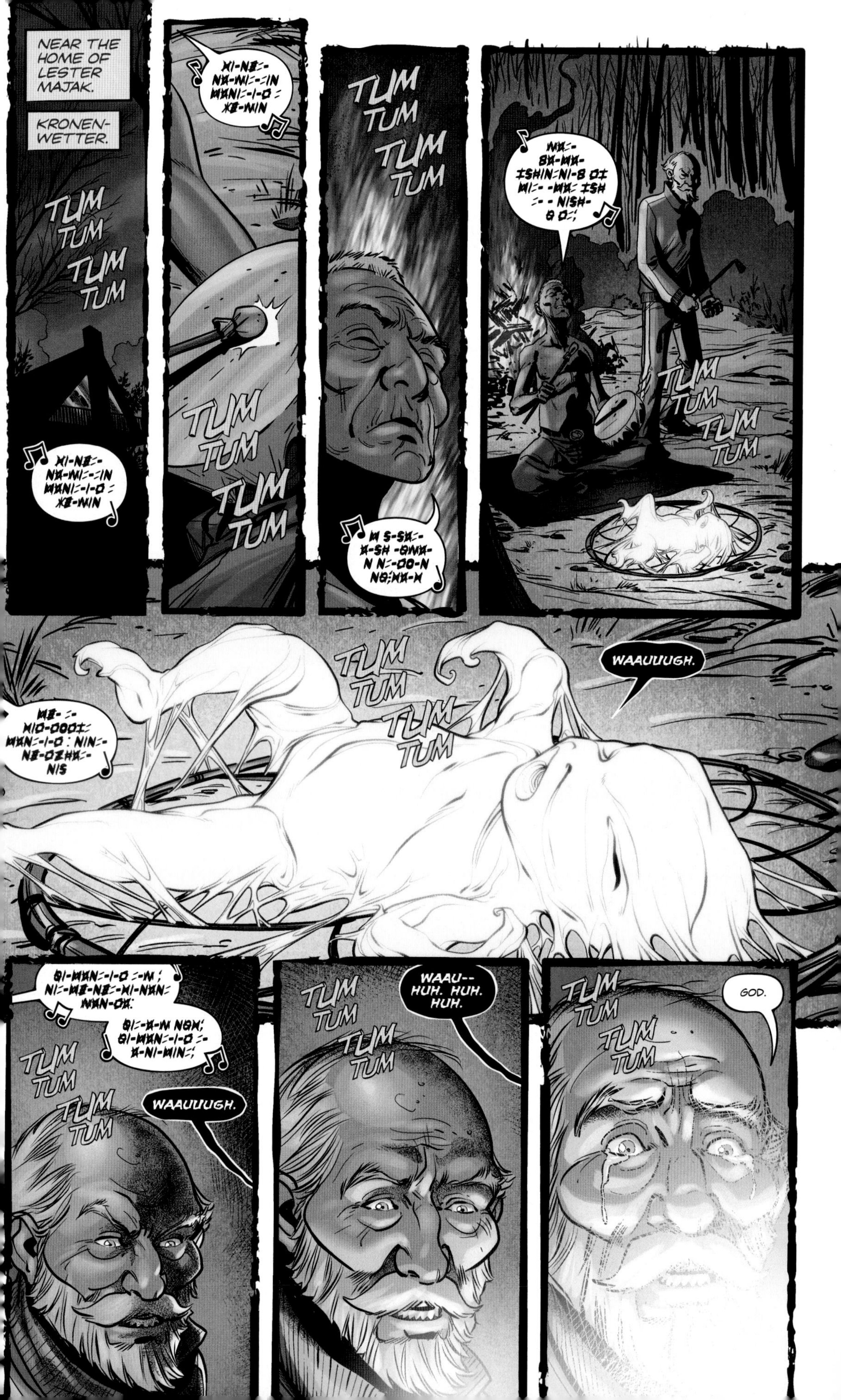
NEAR THE HOME OF LESTER MAJAK.
KRONENWETTER.
TUM TUM TUM TUM
TUM TUM TUM TUM
TUM TUM TUM TUM
TUM TUM TUM TUM
TUM TUM TUM TUM
WAAUUUGH.
TUM TUM TUM TUM
WAAUUUGH.
TUM TUM TUM TUM
WAAU-- HUH. HUH. HUH.
TUM TUM TUM TUM
GOD.

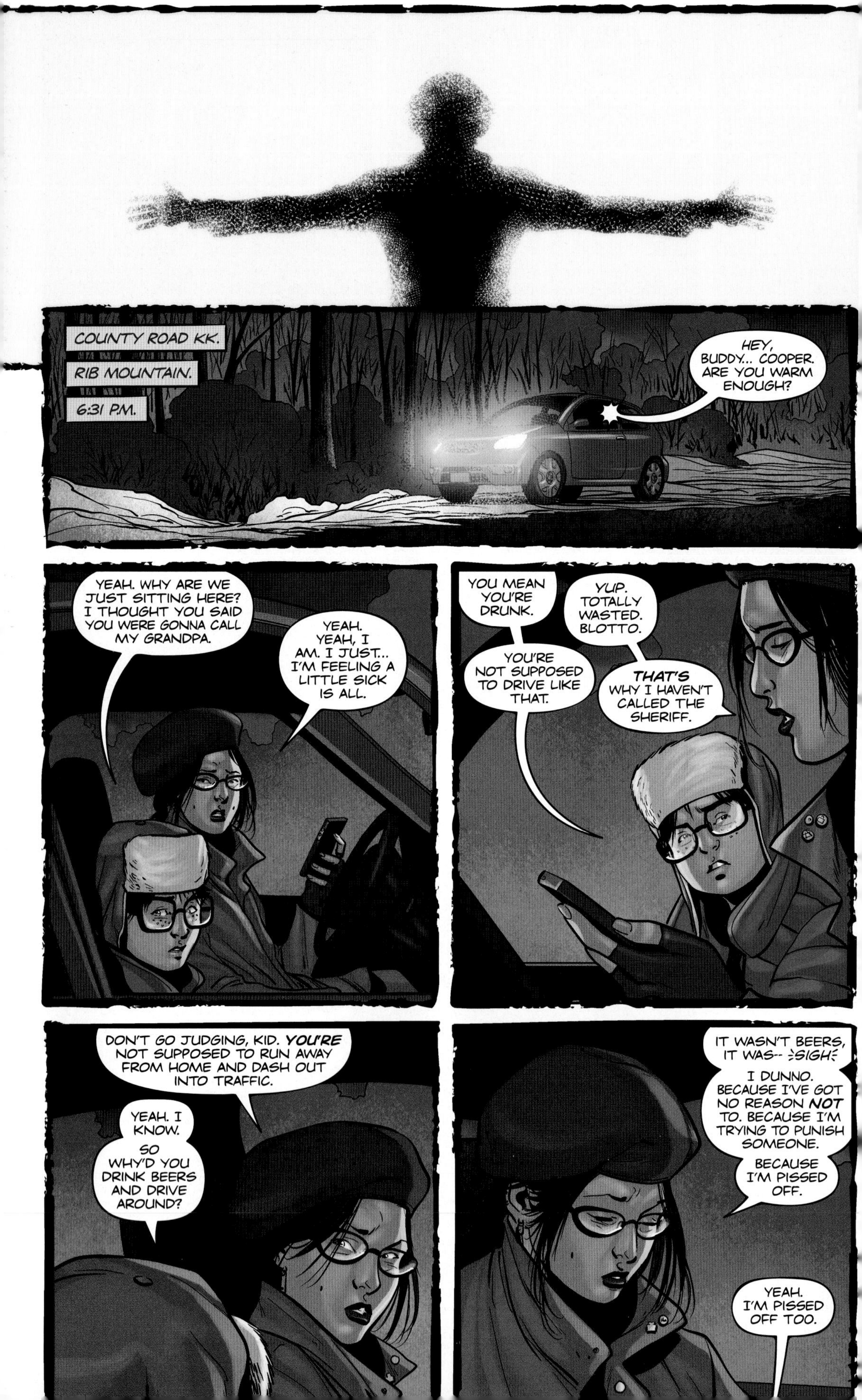
COUNTY ROAD KK.
RIB MOUNTAIN.
6:31 P.M.
HEY, BUDDY... COOPER. ARE YOU WARM ENOUGH?
YEAH. WHY ARE WE JUST SITTING HERE? I THOUGHT YOU SAID YOU WERE GONNA CALL MY GRANDPA.
YEAH. YEAH, I AM. I JUST... I'M FEELING A LITTLE SICK IS ALL.
YOU MEAN YOU'RE DRUNK.
YUP. TOTALLY WASTED. BLOTTO.
YOU'RE NOT SUPPOSED TO DRIVE LIKE THAT.
THAT'S WHY I HAVEN'T CALLED THE SHERIFF.
DON'T GO JUDGING, KID. YOU'RE NOT SUPPOSED TO RUN AWAY FROM HOME AND DASH OUT INTO TRAFFIC.
YEAH. I KNOW.
SO WHY'D YOU DRINK BEERS AND DRIVE AROUND?
IT WASN'T BEERS, IT WAS-- SIGH
I DUNNO. BECAUSE I'VE GOT NO REASON NOT TO. BECAUSE I'M TRYING TO PUNISH SOMEONE.
BECAUSE I'M PISSED OFF.
YEAH. I'M PISSED OFF TOO.

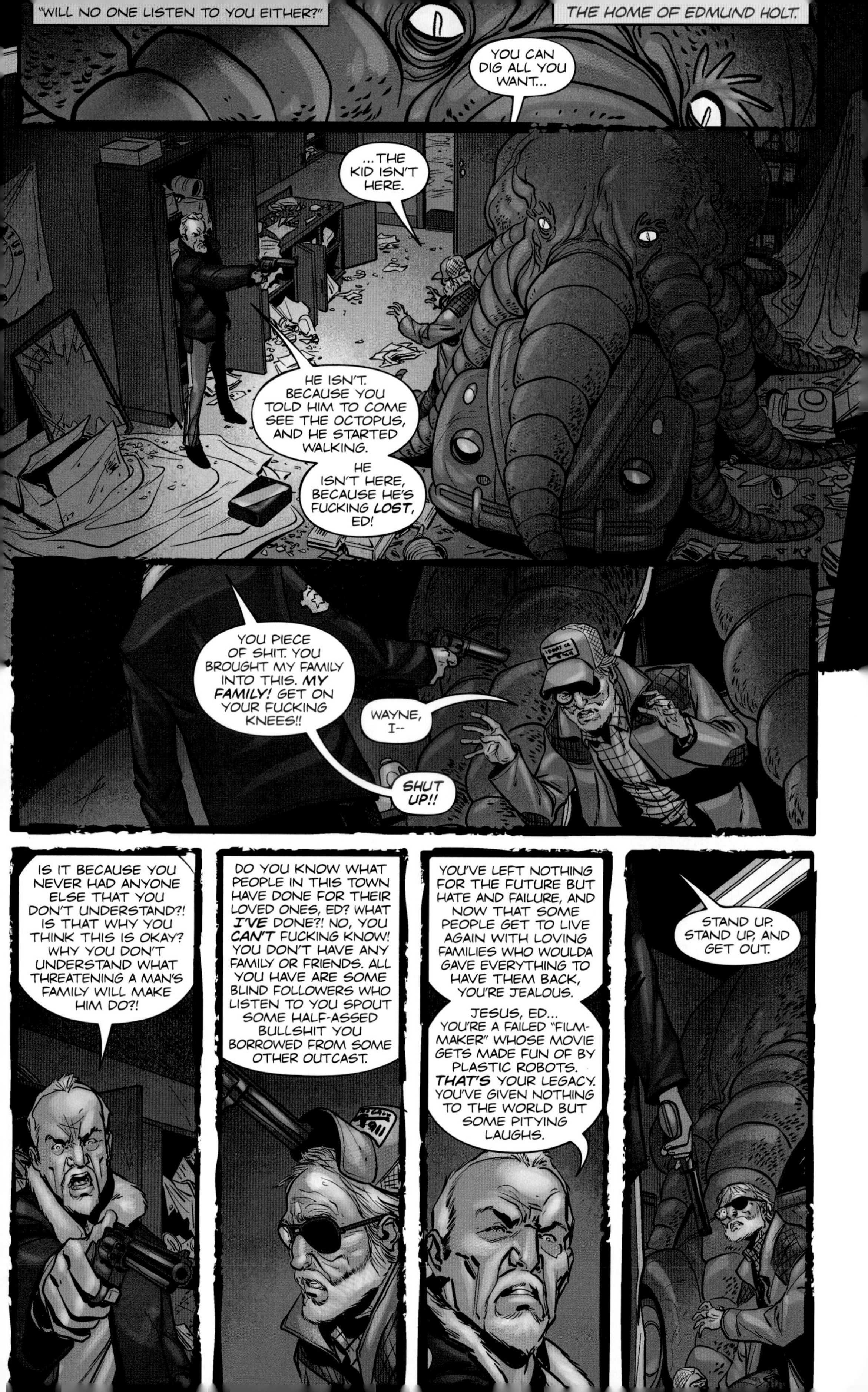

"WILL NO ONE LISTEN TO YOU EITHER?"
THE HOME OF EDMUND HOLT.
YOU CAN DIG ALL YOU WANT...
...THE KID ISN'T HERE.
HE ISN'T. BECAUSE YOU TOLD HIM TO COME SEE THE OCTOPUS, AND HE STARTED WALKING.
HE ISN'T HERE, BECAUSE HE'S FUCKING LOST, ED!
YOU PIECE OF SHIT. YOU BROUGHT MY FAMILY INTO THIS. MY FAMILY! GET ON YOUR FUCKING KNEES!!
WAYNE, I--
SHUT UP!!
IS IT BECAUSE YOU NEVER HAD ANYONE ELSE THAT YOU DON'T UNDERSTAND?! IS THAT WHY YOU THINK THIS IS OKAY? WHY YOU DON'T UNDERSTAND WHAT THREATENING A MAN'S FAMILY WILL MAKE HIM DO?!
DO YOU KNOW WHAT PEOPLE IN THIS TOWN HAVE DONE FOR THEIR LOVED ONES, ED? WHAT I'VE DONE?! NO, YOU CAN'T FUCKING KNOW! YOU DON'T HAVE ANY FAMILY OR FRIENDS. ALL YOU HAVE ARE SOME BLIND FOLLOWERS WHO LISTEN TO YOU SPOUT SOME HALF-ASSED BULLSHIT YOU BORROWED FROM SOME OTHER OUTCAST.
YOU'VE LEFT NOTHING FOR THE FUTURE BUT HATE AND FAILURE, AND NOW THAT SOME PEOPLE GET TO LIVE AGAIN WITH LOVING FAMILIES WHO WOULDA GAVE EVERYTHING TO HAVE THEM BACK, YOU'RE JEALOUS.
JESUS, ED... YOU'RE A FAILED "FILM-MAKER" WHOSE MOVIE GETS MADE FUN OF BY PLASTIC ROBOTS. THAT'S YOUR LEGACY. YOU'VE GIVEN NOTHING TO THE WORLD BUT SOME PITYING LAUGHS.
STAND UP. STAND UP, AND GET OUT.

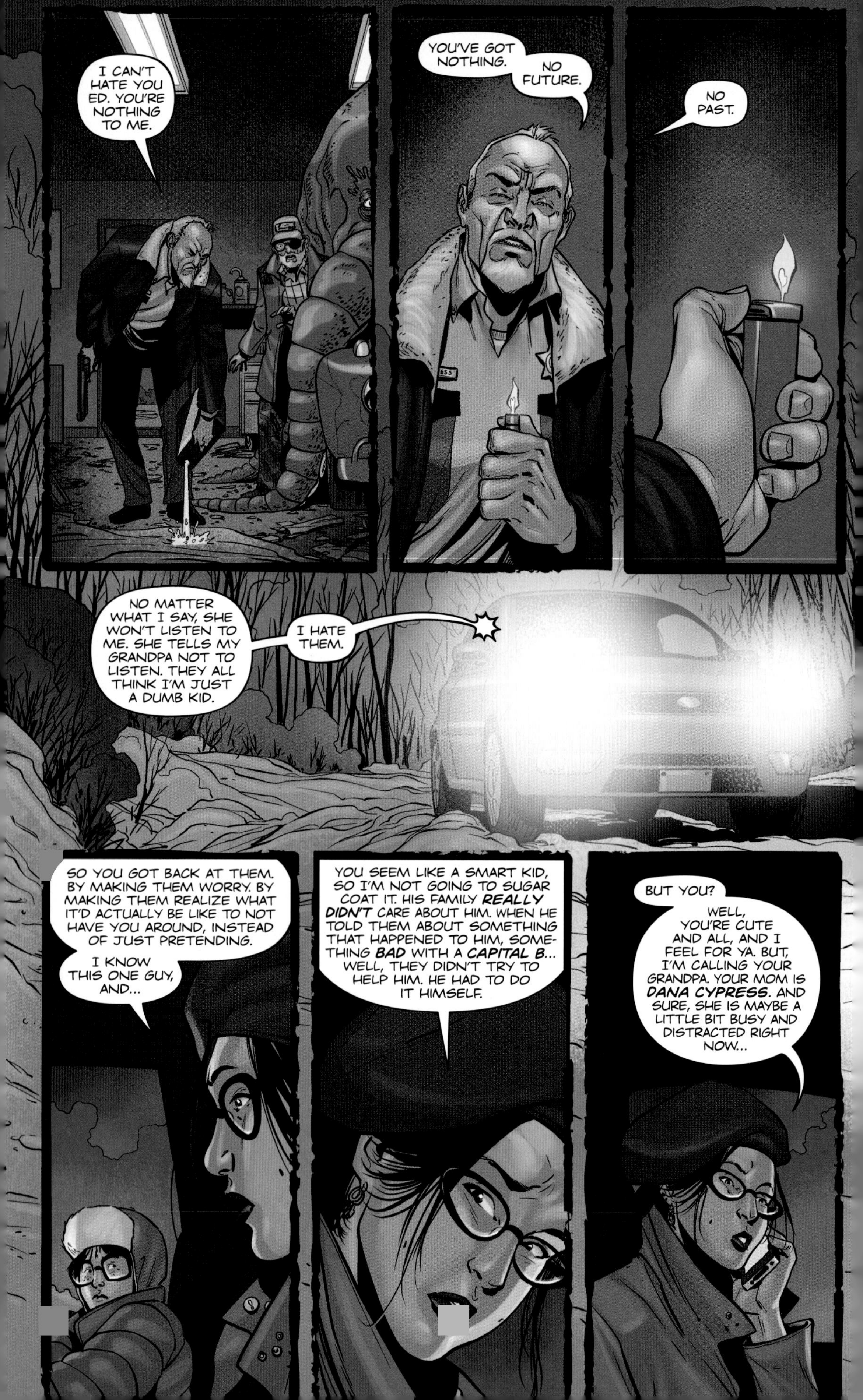
I CAN'T HATE YOU ED. YOU'RE NOTHING TO ME.
YOU'VE GOT NOTHING.
NO FUTURE.
NO PAST.
NO MATTER WHAT I SAY, SHE WON'T LISTEN TO ME. SHE TELLS MY GRANDPA NOT TO LISTEN. THEY ALL THINK I'M JUST A DUMB KID.
I HATE THEM.
SO YOU GOT BACK AT THEM. BY MAKING THEM WORRY. BY MAKING THEM REALIZE WHAT IT'D ACTUALLY BE LIKE TO NOT HAVE YOU AROUND, INSTEAD OF JUST PRETENDING.
I KNOW THIS ONE GUY, AND...
YOU SEEM LIKE A SMART KID, SO I'M NOT GOING TO SUGAR COAT IT. HIS FAMILY **REALLY DIDN'T** CARE ABOUT HIM. WHEN HE TOLD THEM ABOUT SOMETHING THAT HAPPENED TO HIM, SOMETHING **BAD** WITH A **CAPITAL B**... WELL, THEY DIDN'T TRY TO HELP HIM. HE HAD TO DO IT HIMSELF.
BUT YOU?
WELL, YOU'RE CUTE AND ALL, AND I FEEL FOR YA. BUT, I'M CALLING YOUR GRANDPA. YOUR MOM IS **DANA CYPRESS**. AND SURE, SHE IS MAYBE A LITTLE BIT BUSY AND DISTRACTED RIGHT NOW...

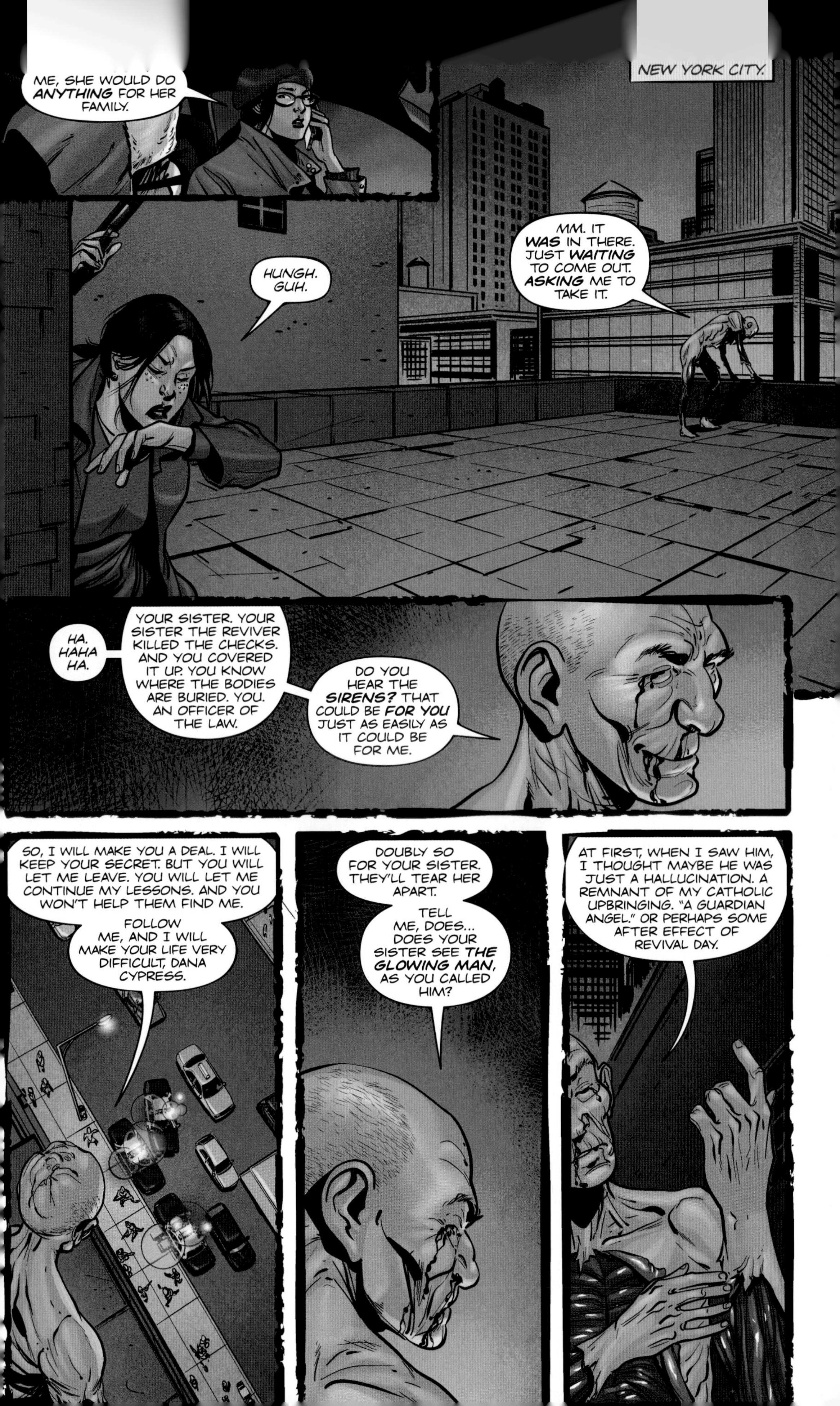
ME, SHE WOULD DO ANYTHING FOR HER FAMILY.
NEW YORK CITY.
HUNGH. GUH.
MM. IT WAS IN THERE. JUST WAITING TO COME OUT. ASKING ME TO TAKE IT.
HA. HAHA HA.
YOUR SISTER. YOUR SISTER THE REVIVER KILLED THE CHECKS. AND YOU COVERED IT UP. YOU KNOW WHERE THE BODIES ARE BURIED. YOU. AN OFFICER OF THE LAW.
DO YOU HEAR THE SIRENS? THAT COULD BE FOR YOU JUST AS EASILY AS IT COULD BE FOR ME.
SO, I WILL MAKE YOU A DEAL. I WILL KEEP YOUR SECRET. BUT YOU WILL LET ME LEAVE. YOU WILL LET ME CONTINUE MY LESSONS. AND YOU WON'T HELP THEM FIND ME.
FOLLOW ME, AND I WILL MAKE YOUR LIFE VERY DIFFICULT, DANA CYPRESS.
DOUBLY SO FOR YOUR SISTER. THEY'LL TEAR HER APART.
TELL ME, DOES... DOES YOUR SISTER SEE THE GLOWING MAN, AS YOU CALLED HIM?
AT FIRST, WHEN I SAW HIM, I THOUGHT MAYBE HE WAS JUST A HALLUCINATION. A REMNANT OF MY CATHOLIC UPBRINGING. "A GUARDIAN ANGEL." OR PERHAPS SOME AFTER EFFECT OF REVIVAL DAY.

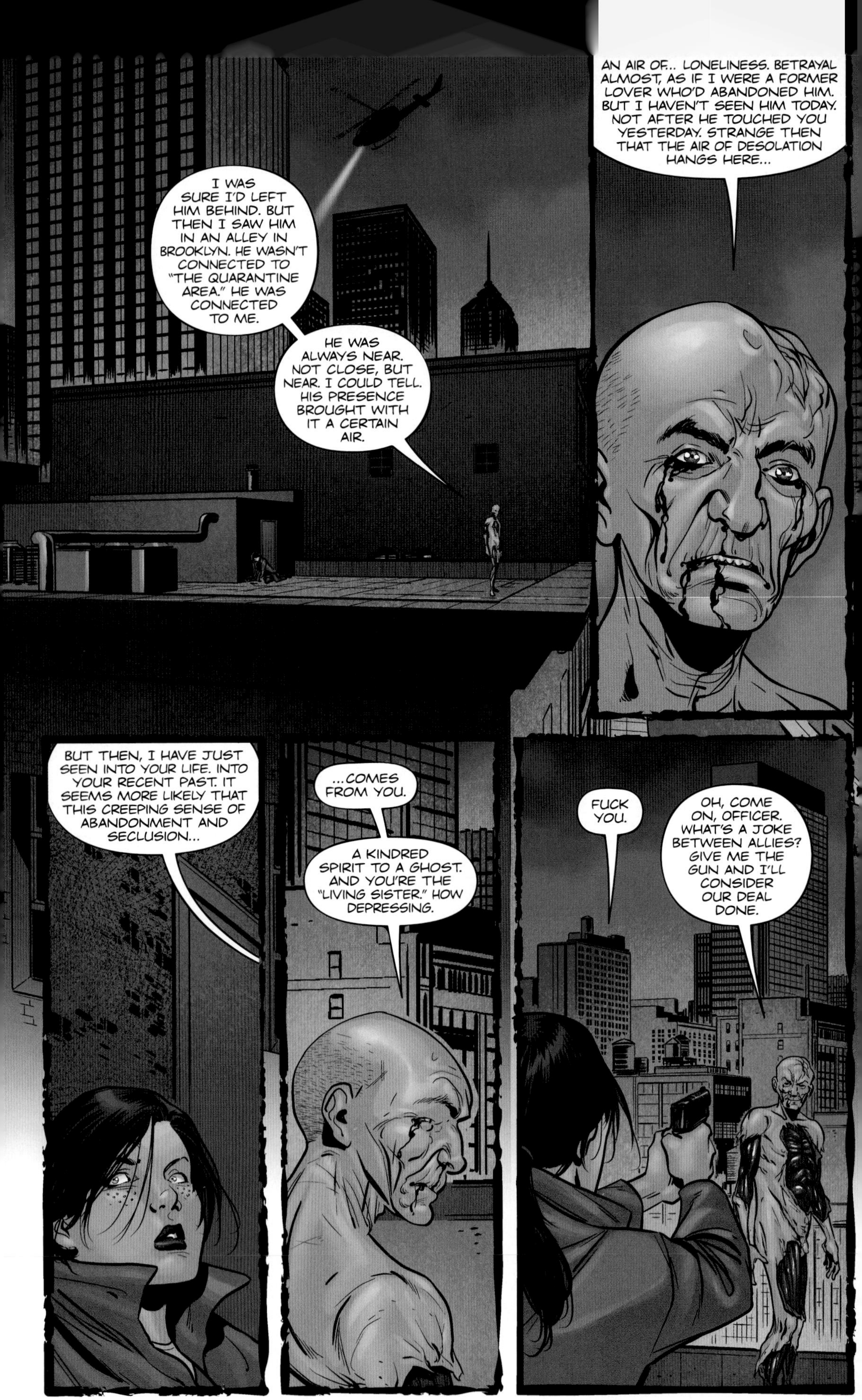
I WAS SURE I'D LEFT HIM BEHIND. BUT THEN I SAW HIM IN AN ALLEY IN BROOKLYN. HE WASN'T CONNECTED TO "THE QUARANTINE AREA." HE WAS CONNECTED TO ME.
HE WAS ALWAYS NEAR. NOT CLOSE, BUT NEAR. I COULD TELL. HIS PRESENCE BROUGHT WITH IT A CERTAIN AIR.
AN AIR OF... LONELINESS. BETRAYAL ALMOST, AS IF I WERE A FORMER LOVER WHO'D ABANDONED HIM. BUT I HAVEN'T SEEN HIM TODAY. NOT AFTER HE TOUCHED YOU YESTERDAY. STRANGE THEN THAT THE AIR OF DESOLATION HANGS HERE...
BUT THEN, I HAVE JUST SEEN INTO YOUR LIFE. INTO YOUR RECENT PAST. IT SEEMS MORE LIKELY THAT THIS CREEPING SENSE OF ABANDONMENT AND SECLUSION...
...COMES FROM YOU.
A KINDRED SPIRIT TO A GHOST. AND YOU'RE THE "LIVING SISTER." HOW DEPRESSING.
FUCK YOU.
OH, COME ON, OFFICER. WHAT'S A JOKE BETWEEN ALLIES? GIVE ME THE GUN AND I'LL CONSIDER OUR DEAL DONE.

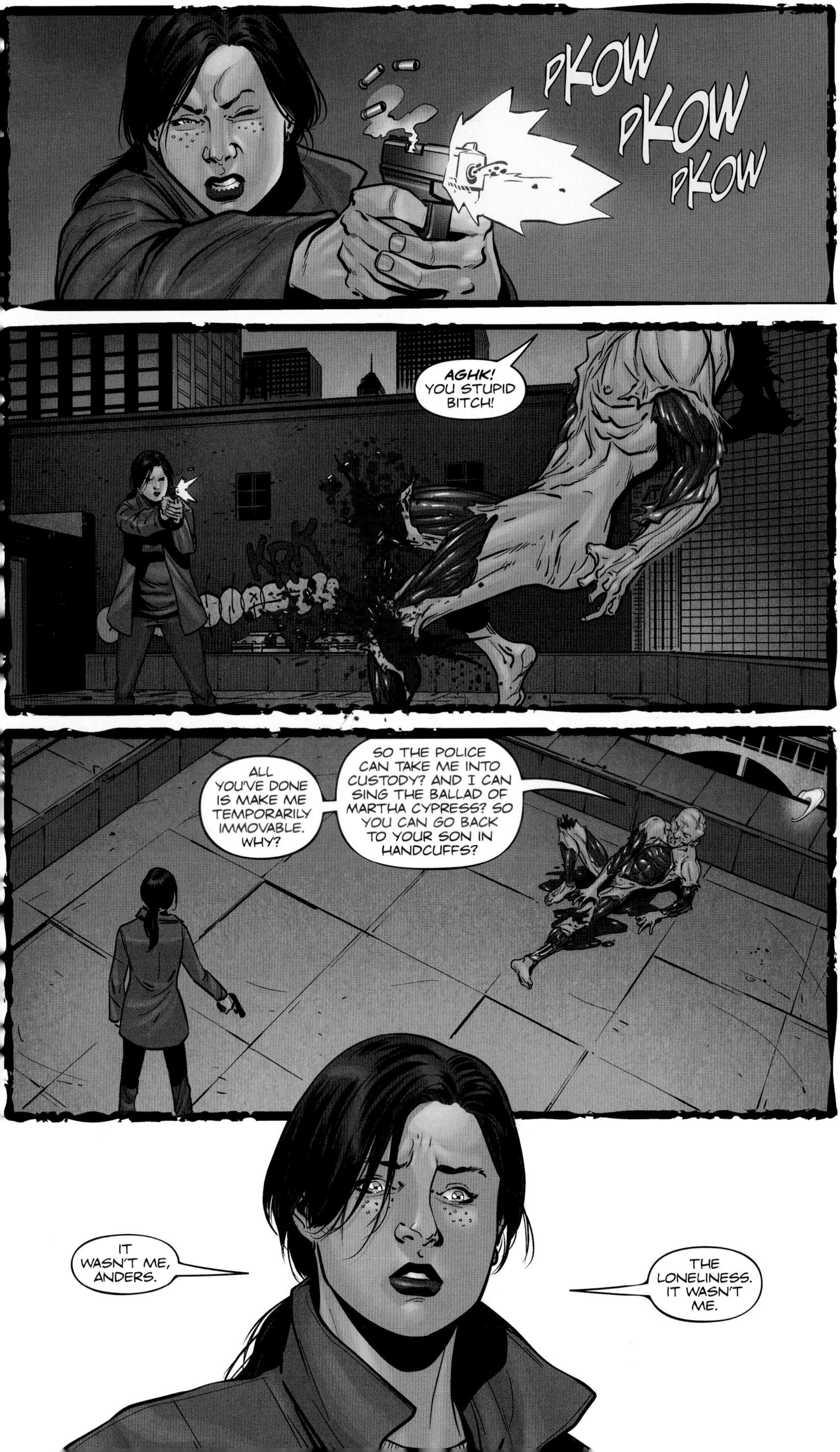
PKOW
PKOW
PKOW
AGHK! YOU STUPID BITCH!
ALL YOU'VE DONE IS MAKE ME TEMPORARILY IMMOVABLE. WHY?
SO THE POLICE CAN TAKE ME INTO CUSTODY? AND I CAN SING THE BALLAD OF MARTHA CYPRESS? SO YOU CAN GO BACK TO YOUR SON IN HANDCUFFS?
IT WASN'T ME, ANDERS.
THE LONELINESS. IT WASN'T ME.

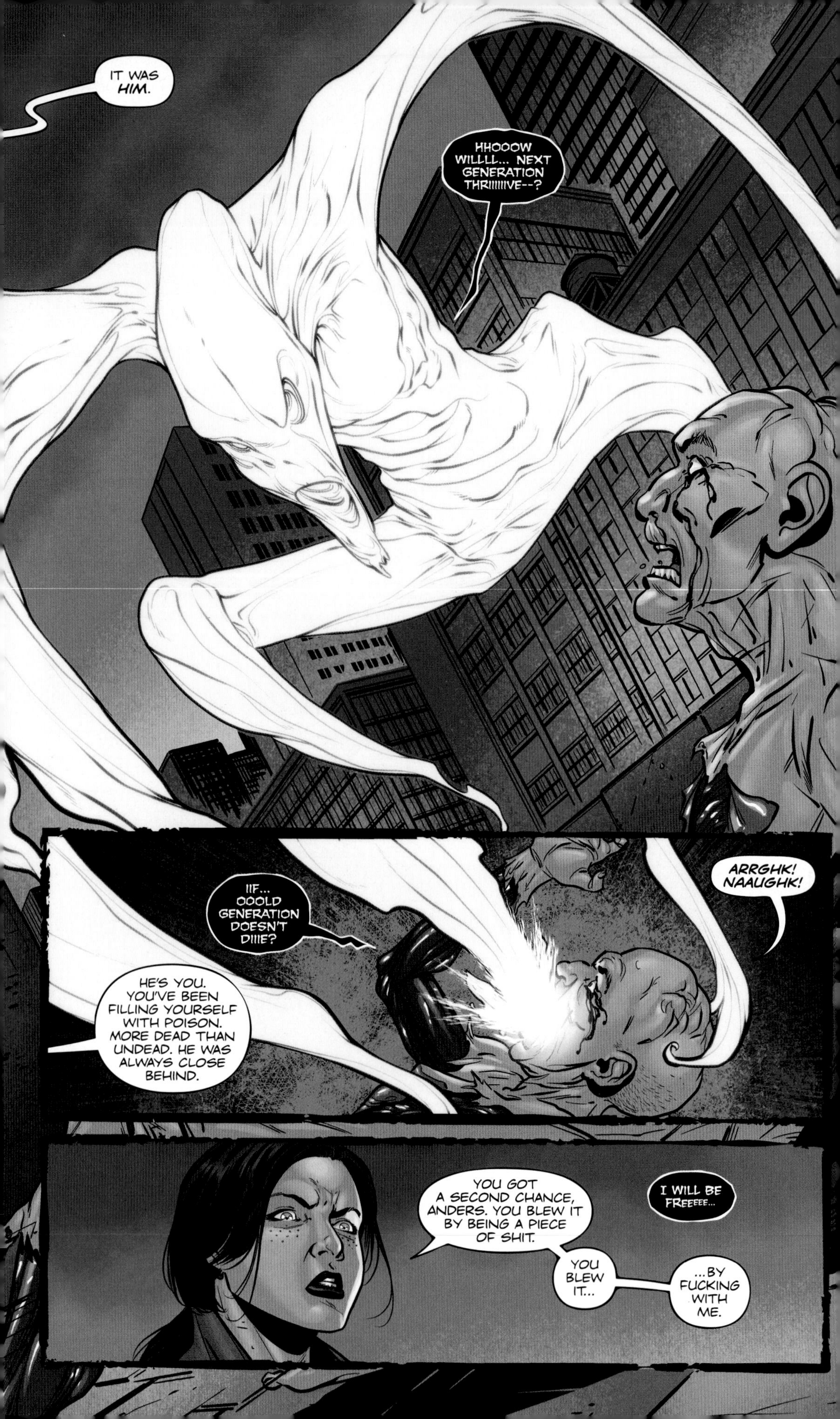
IT WAS HIM.
HHOOOW WILLLL... NEXT GENERATION THRIIIIIIVE--?
IIF... OOOLD GENERATION DOESN'T DIIIE?
ARRGHK! NAAUGHK!
HE'S YOU. YOU'VE BEEN FILLING YOURSELF WITH POISON. MORE DEAD THAN UNDEAD. HE WAS ALWAYS CLOSE BEHIND.
YOU GOT A SECOND CHANCE, ANDERS. YOU BLEW IT BY BEING A PIECE OF SHIT.
I WILL BE FREEEEE...
YOU BLEW IT...
...BY FUCKING WITH ME.

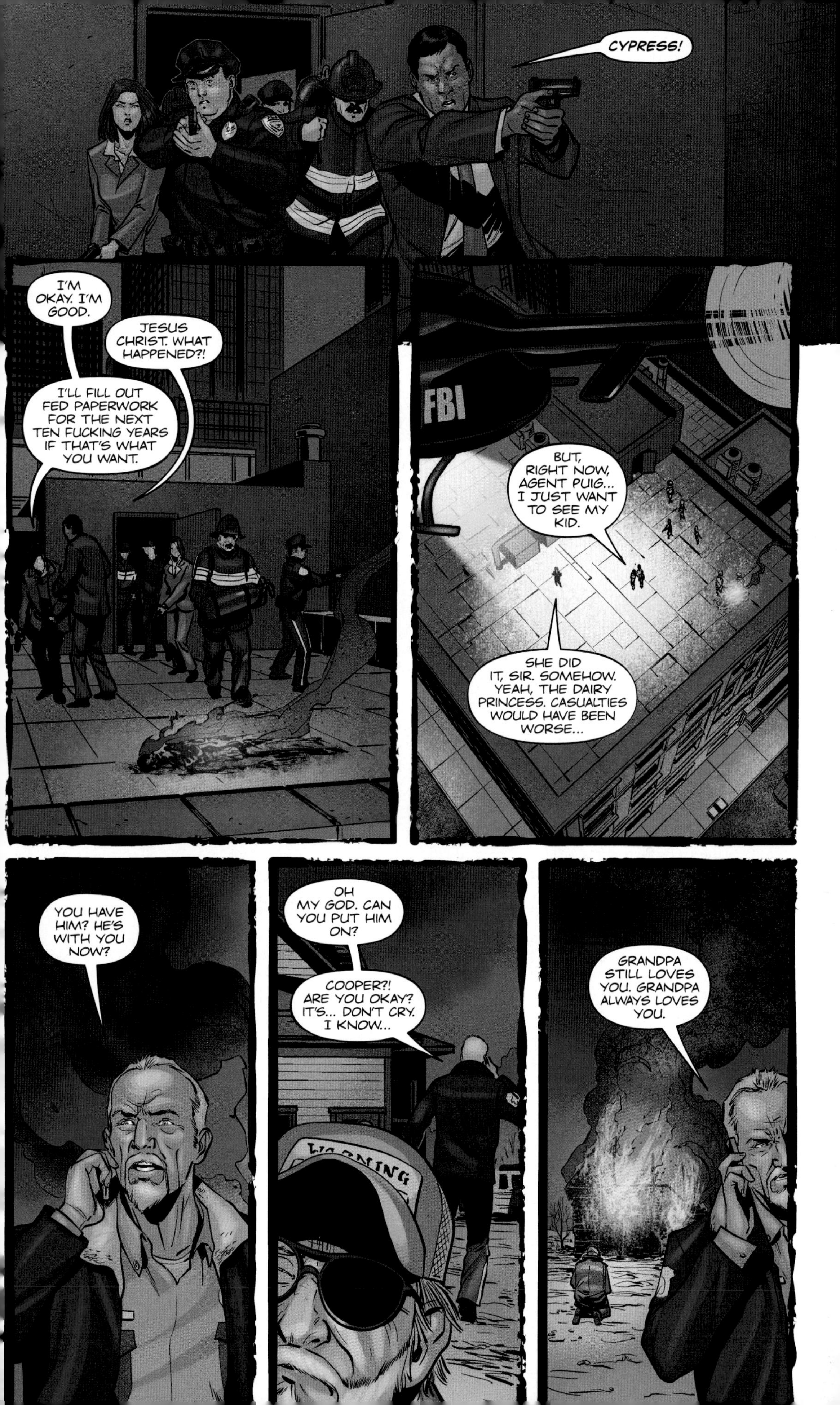
CYPRESS!
I'M OKAY. I'M GOOD.
JESUS CHRIST. WHAT HAPPENED?!
I'LL FILL OUT FED PAPERWORK FOR THE NEXT TEN FUCKING YEARS IF THAT'S WHAT YOU WANT.
FBI
BUT, RIGHT NOW, AGENT PUIG... I JUST WANT TO SEE MY KID.
SHE DID IT, SIR. SOMEHOW. YEAH, THE DAIRY PRINCESS. CASUALTIES WOULD HAVE BEEN WORSE...
YOU HAVE HIM? HE'S WITH YOU NOW?
OH MY GOD. CAN YOU PUT HIM ON?
COOPER?! ARE YOU OKAY? IT'S... DON'T CRY. I KNOW...
GRANDPA STILL LOVES YOU. GRANDPA ALWAYS LOVES YOU.

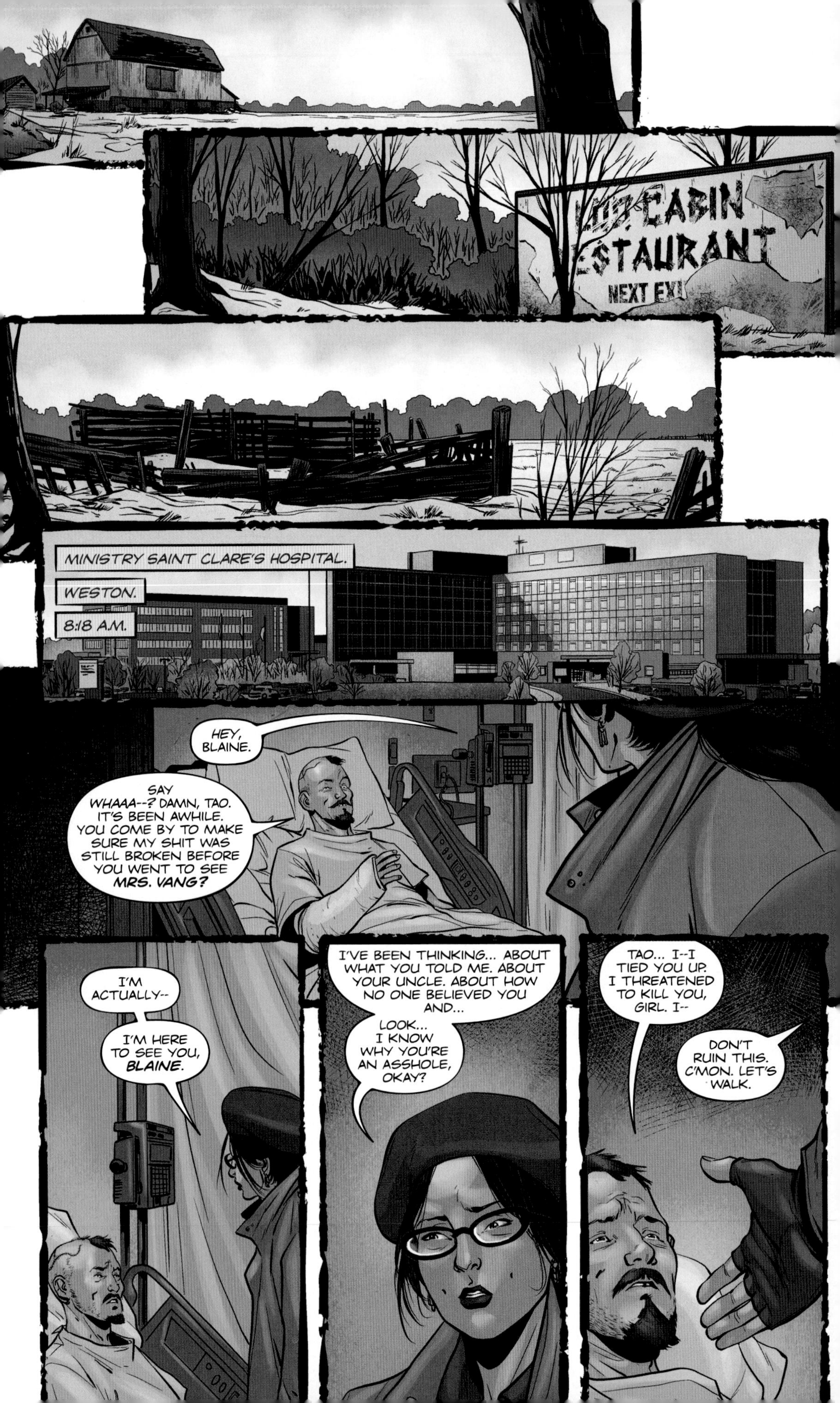

CABIN
ESTAURANT
NEXT EXI
MINISTRY SAINT CLARE'S HOSPITAL.
WESTON.
8:18 A.M.
HEY, BLAINE.
SAY WHAAA--? DAMN, TAO. IT'S BEEN AWHILE. YOU COME BY TO MAKE SURE MY SHIT WAS STILL BROKEN BEFORE YOU WENT TO SEE MRS. VANG?
I'M ACTUALLY--
I'M HERE TO SEE YOU, BLAINE.
I'VE BEEN THINKING... ABOUT WHAT YOU TOLD ME. ABOUT YOUR UNCLE. ABOUT HOW NO ONE BELIEVED YOU AND...
LOOK... I KNOW WHY YOU'RE AN ASSHOLE, OKAY?
TAO... I--I TIED YOU UP. I THREATENED TO KILL YOU, GIRL. I--
DON'T RUIN THIS. C'MON. LET'S WALK.

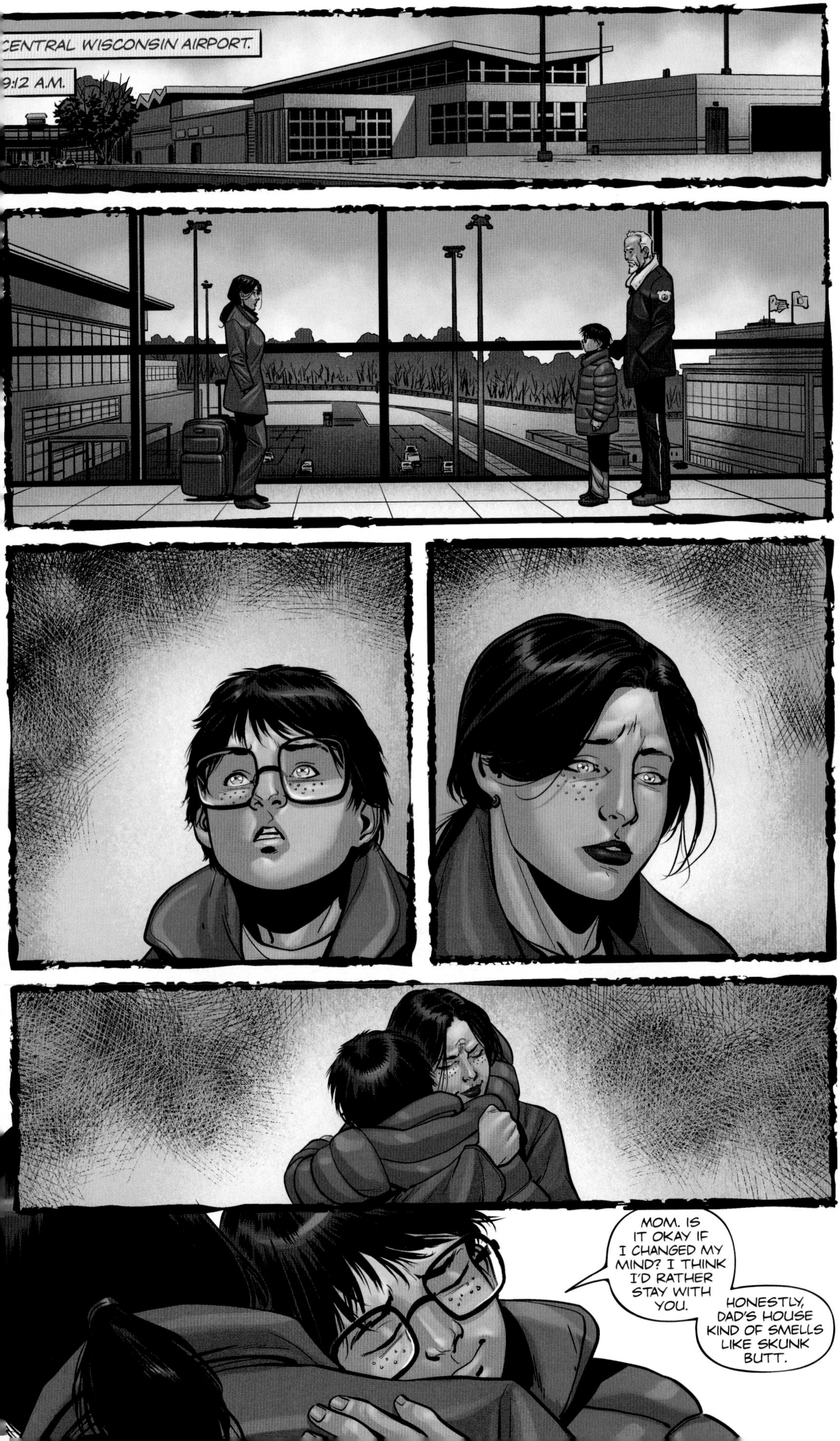
CENTRAL WISCONSIN AIRPORT.
9:12 A.M.
MOM. IS IT OKAY IF I CHANGED MY MIND? I THINK I'D RATHER STAY WITH YOU.
HONESTLY, DAD'S HOUSE KIND OF SMELLS LIKE SKUNK BUTT.

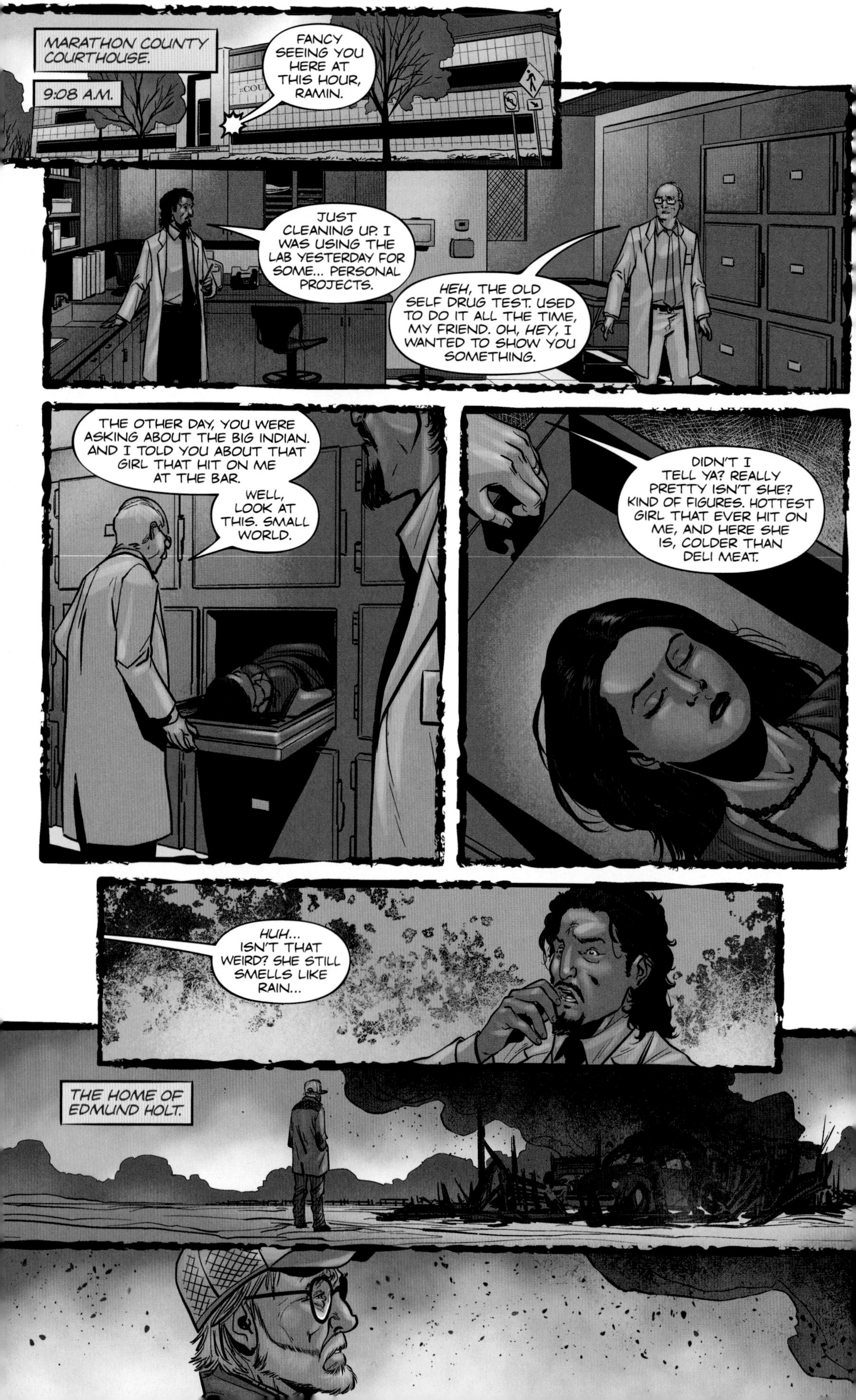
MARATHON COUNTY COURTHOUSE.
9:08 A.M.
FANCY SEEING YOU HERE AT THIS HOUR, RAMIN.
JUST CLEANING UP. I WAS USING THE LAB YESTERDAY FOR SOME... PERSONAL PROJECTS.
HEH, THE OLD SELF DRUG TEST. USED TO DO IT ALL THE TIME, MY FRIEND. OH, HEY, I WANTED TO SHOW YOU SOMETHING.
THE OTHER DAY, YOU WERE ASKING ABOUT THE BIG INDIAN. AND I TOLD YOU ABOUT THAT GIRL THAT HIT ON ME AT THE BAR.
WELL, LOOK AT THIS. SMALL WORLD.
DIDN'T I TELL YA? REALLY PRETTY ISN'T SHE? KIND OF FIGURES. HOTTEST GIRL THAT EVER HIT ON ME, AND HERE SHE IS, COLDER THAN DELI MEAT.
HUH... ISN'T THAT WEIRD? SHE STILL SMELLS LIKE RAIN...
THE HOME OF EDMUND HOLT.

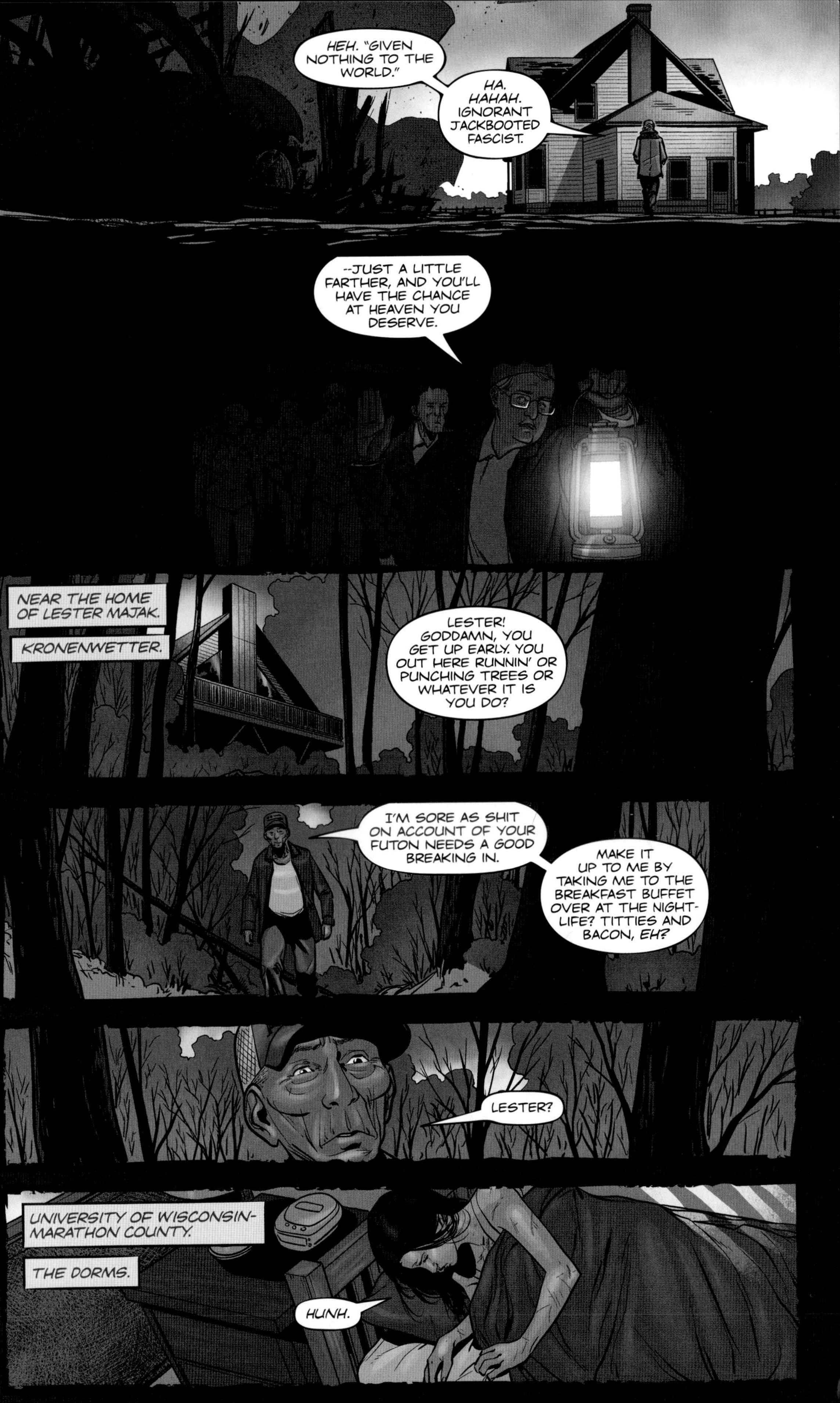
HEH. "GIVEN NOTHING TO THE WORLD."
HA. HAHAH. IGNORANT JACKBOOTED FASCIST.
--JUST A LITTLE FARTHER, AND YOU'LL HAVE THE CHANCE AT HEAVEN YOU DESERVE.
NEAR THE HOME OF LESTER MAJAK.
KRONENWETTER.
LESTER! GODDAMN, YOU GET UP EARLY. YOU OUT HERE RUNNIN' OR PUNCHING TREES OR WHATEVER IT IS YOU DO?
I'M SORE AS SHIT ON ACCOUNT OF YOUR FUTON NEEDS A GOOD BREAKING IN.
MAKE IT UP TO ME BY TAKING ME TO THE BREAKFAST BUFFET OVER AT THE NIGHT-LIFE? TITTIES AND BACON, EH?
LESTER?
UNIVERSITY OF WISCONSIN-MARATHON COUNTY.
THE DORMS.
HUNH.

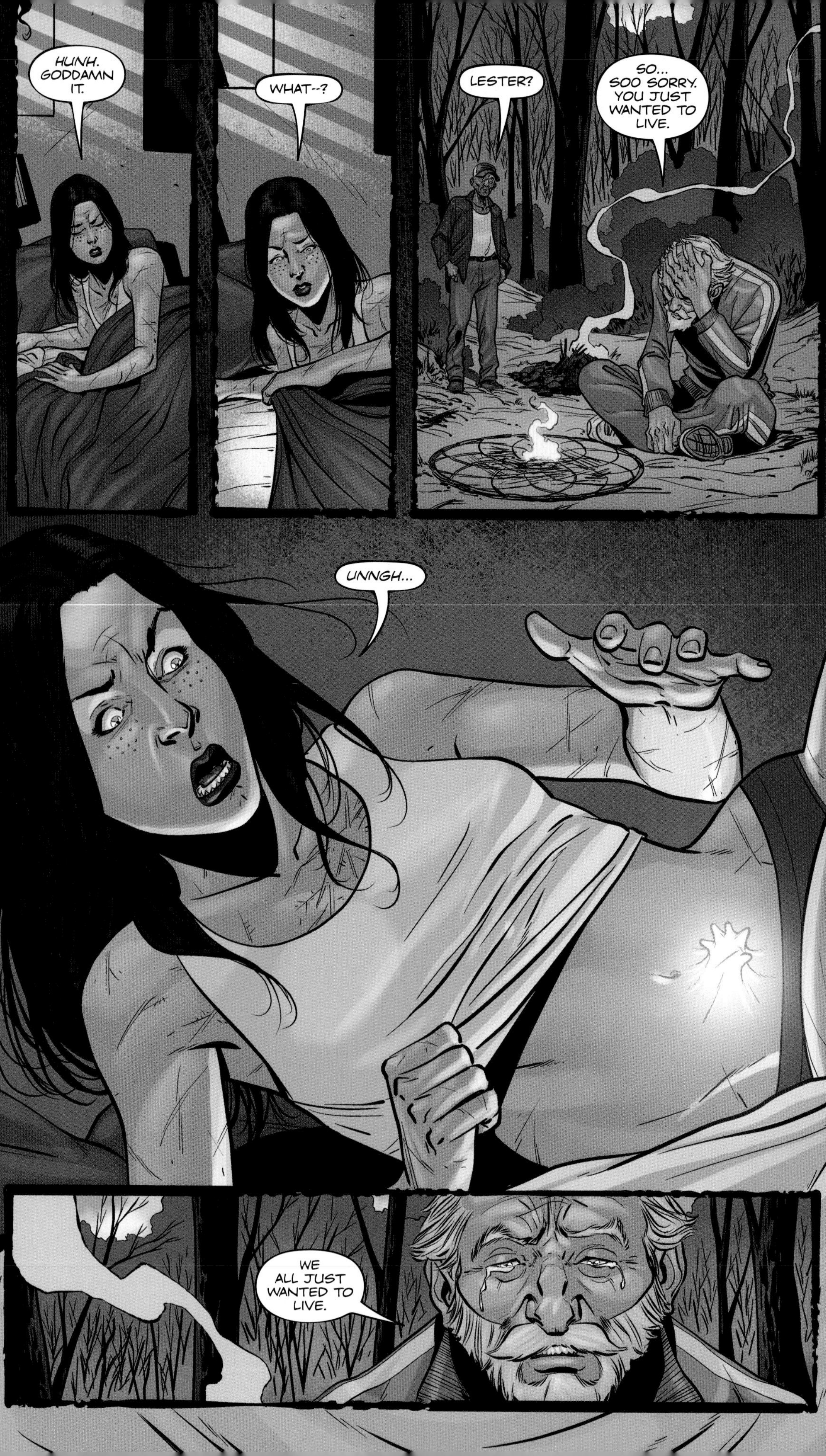
HUNH. GODDAMN IT.
WHAT--?
LESTER?
SO... SOO SORRY. YOU JUST WANTED TO LIVE.
UNNGH...
WE ALL JUST WANTED TO LIVE.

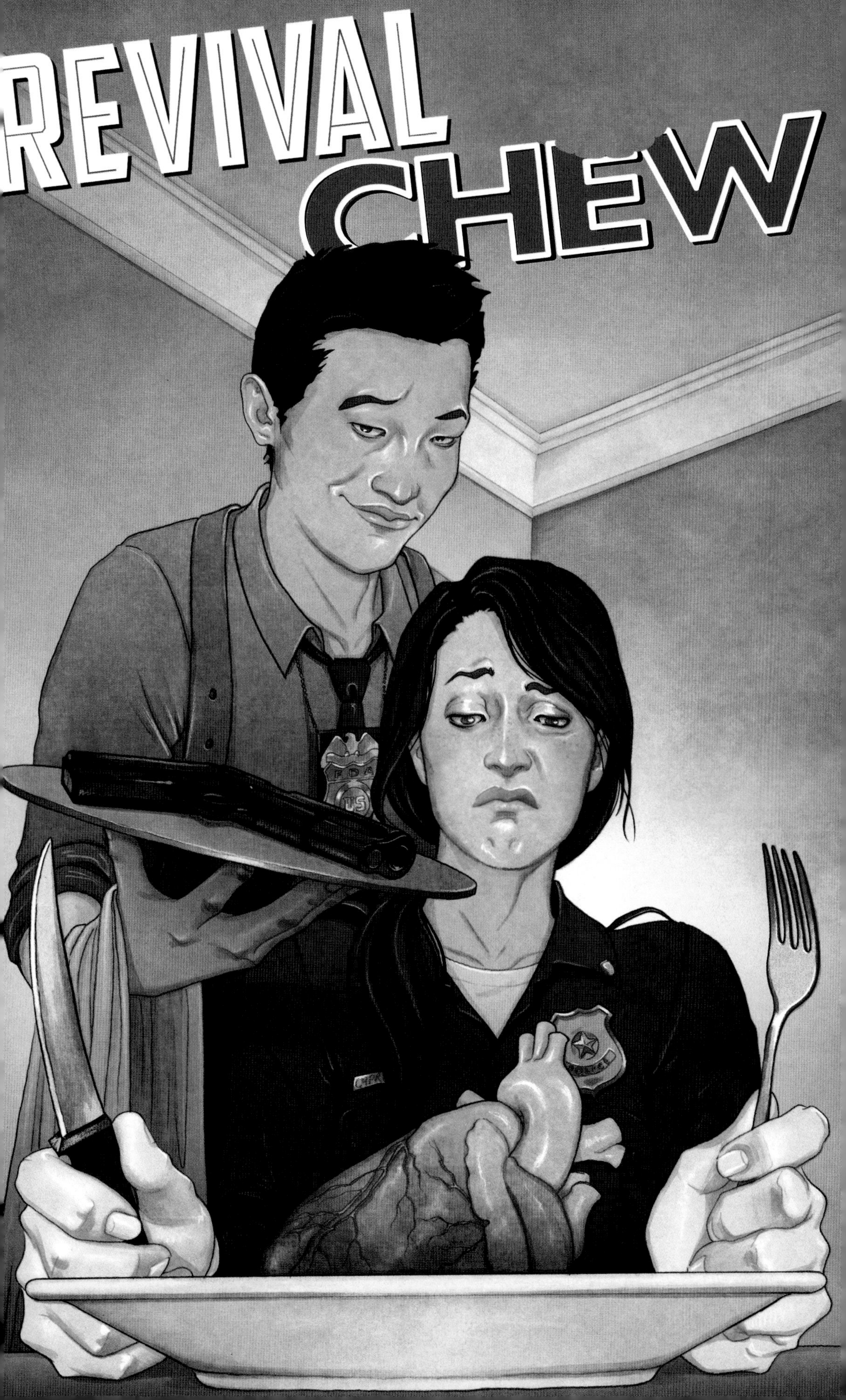

REVIVAL
CHEW

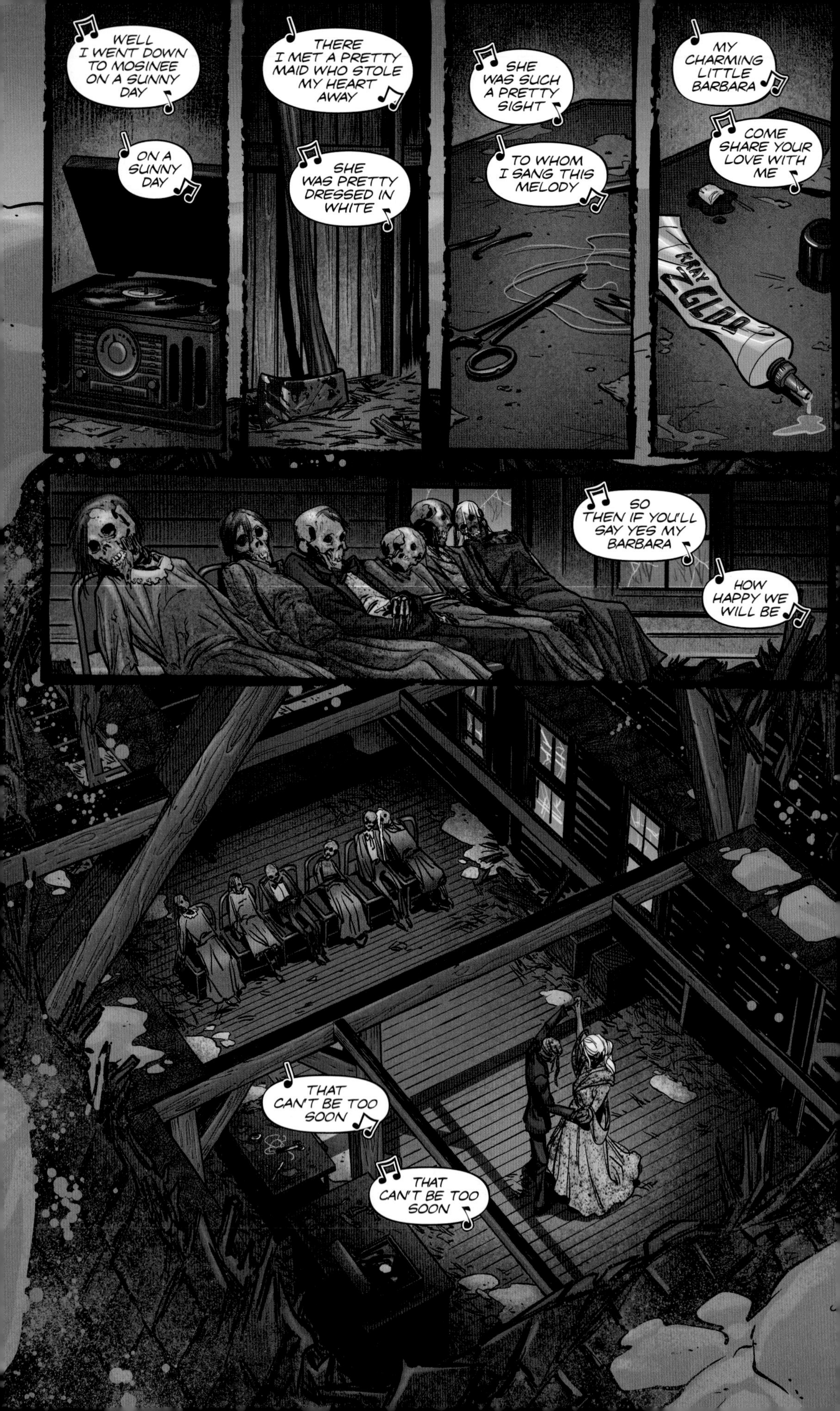
WELL I WENT DOWN TO MOSINEE ON A SUNNY DAY
ON A SUNNY DAY
THERE I MET A PRETTY MAID WHO STOLE MY HEART AWAY
SHE WAS PRETTY DRESSED IN WHITE
SHE WAS SUCH A PRETTY SIGHT
TO WHOM I SANG THIS MELODY
MY CHARMING LITTLE BARBARA
COME SHARE YOUR LOVE WITH ME
K-RAY ZGLUE
SO THEN IF YOU'LL SAY YES MY BARBARA
HOW HAPPY WE WILL BE
THAT CAN'T BE TOO SOON
THAT CAN'T BE TOO SOON

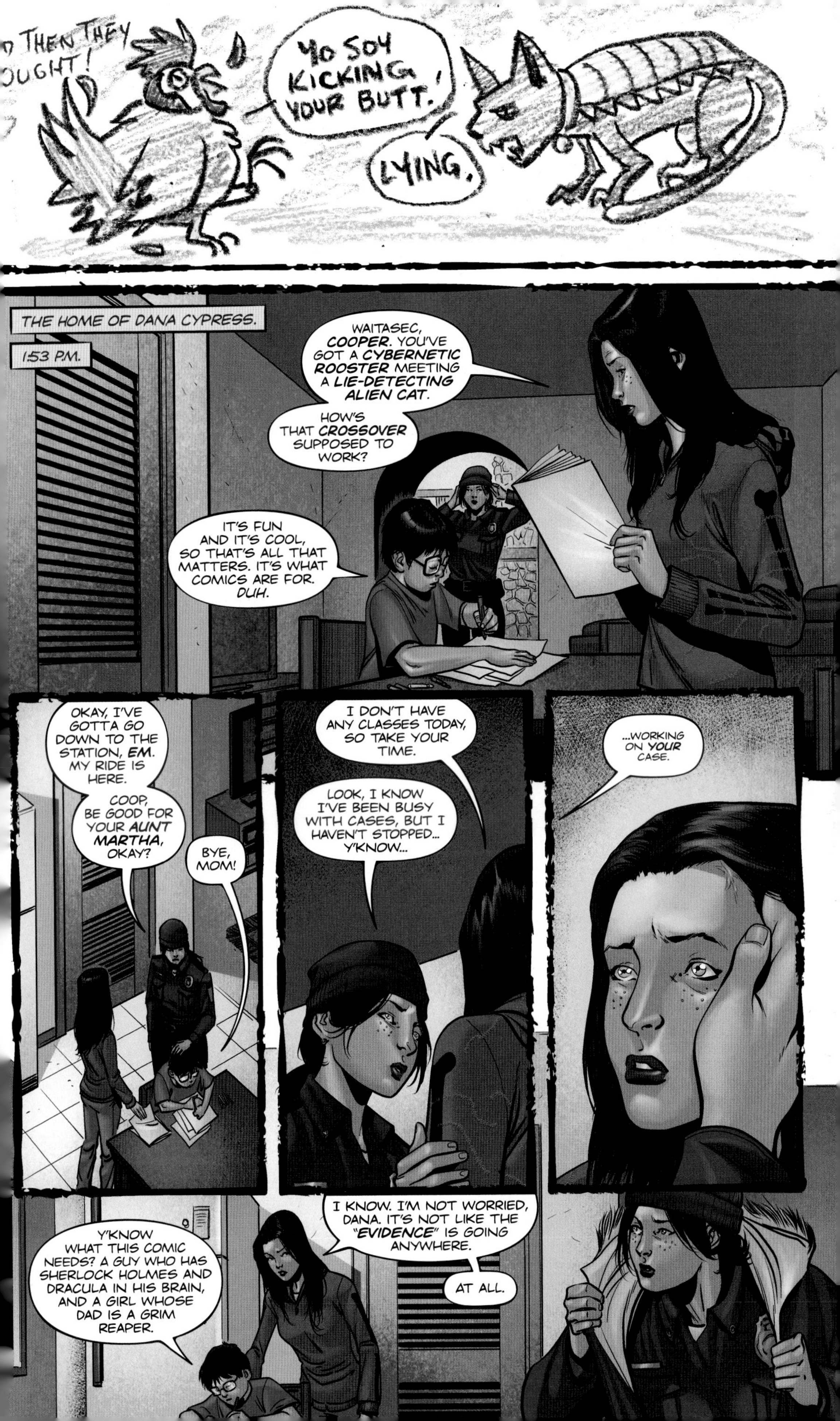
D THEN THEY
OUGHT!
YO SOY KICKING YOUR BUTT.
LYING.
THE HOME OF DANA CYPRESS.
1:53 P.M.
WAITASEC, COOPER. YOU'VE GOT A CYBERNETIC ROOSTER MEETING A LIE-DETECTING ALIEN CAT.
HOW'S THAT CROSSOVER SUPPOSED TO WORK?
IT'S FUN AND IT'S COOL, SO THAT'S ALL THAT MATTERS. IT'S WHAT COMICS ARE FOR. DUH.
OKAY, I'VE GOTTA GO DOWN TO THE STATION, EM. MY RIDE IS HERE.
COOP, BE GOOD FOR YOUR AUNT MARTHA, OKAY?
BYE, MOM!
I DON'T HAVE ANY CLASSES TODAY, SO TAKE YOUR TIME.
LOOK, I KNOW I'VE BEEN BUSY WITH CASES, BUT I HAVEN'T STOPPED... Y'KNOW...
...WORKING ON YOUR CASE.
Y'KNOW WHAT THIS COMIC NEEDS? A GUY WHO HAS SHERLOCK HOLMES AND DRACULA IN HIS BRAIN, AND A GIRL WHOSE DAD IS A GRIM REAPER.
I KNOW. I'M NOT WORRIED, DANA. IT'S NOT LIKE THE "EVIDENCE" IS GOING ANYWHERE.
AT ALL.

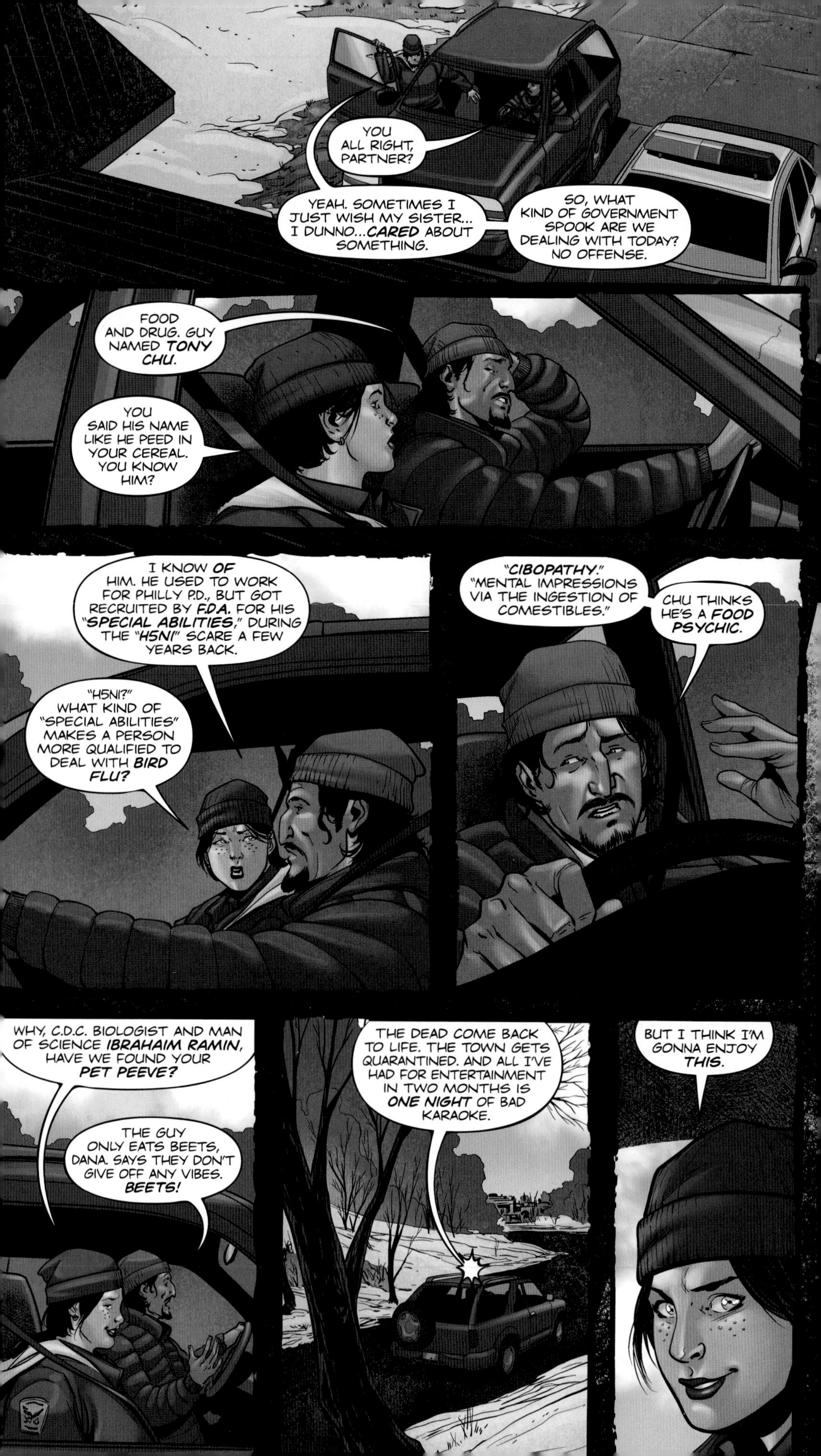
YOU ALL RIGHT, PARTNER?
YEAH. SOMETIMES I JUST WISH MY SISTER... I DUNNO...CARED ABOUT SOMETHING.
SO, WHAT KIND OF GOVERNMENT SPOOK ARE WE DEALING WITH TODAY? NO OFFENSE.
FOOD AND DRUG. GUY NAMED TONY CHU.
YOU SAID HIS NAME LIKE HE PEED IN YOUR CEREAL. YOU KNOW HIM?
I KNOW OF HIM. HE USED TO WORK FOR PHILLY P.D., BUT GOT RECRUITED BY F.D.A. FOR HIS "SPECIAL ABILITIES," DURING THE "H5N1" SCARE A FEW YEARS BACK.
"H5N1?" WHAT KIND OF "SPECIAL ABILITIES" MAKES A PERSON MORE QUALIFIED TO DEAL WITH BIRD FLU?
"CIBOPATHY." "MENTAL IMPRESSIONS VIA THE INGESTION OF COMESTIBLES."
CHU THINKS HE'S A FOOD PSYCHIC.
WHY, C.D.C. BIOLOGIST AND MAN OF SCIENCE IBRAHAIM RAMIN, HAVE WE FOUND YOUR PET PEEVE?
THE GUY ONLY EATS BEETS, DANA. SAYS THEY DON'T GIVE OFF ANY VIBES. BEETS!
THE DEAD COME BACK TO LIFE. THE TOWN GETS QUARANTINED. AND ALL I'VE HAD FOR ENTERTAINMENT IN TWO MONTHS IS ONE NIGHT OF BAD KARAOKE.
BUT I THINK I'M GONNA ENJOY THIS.

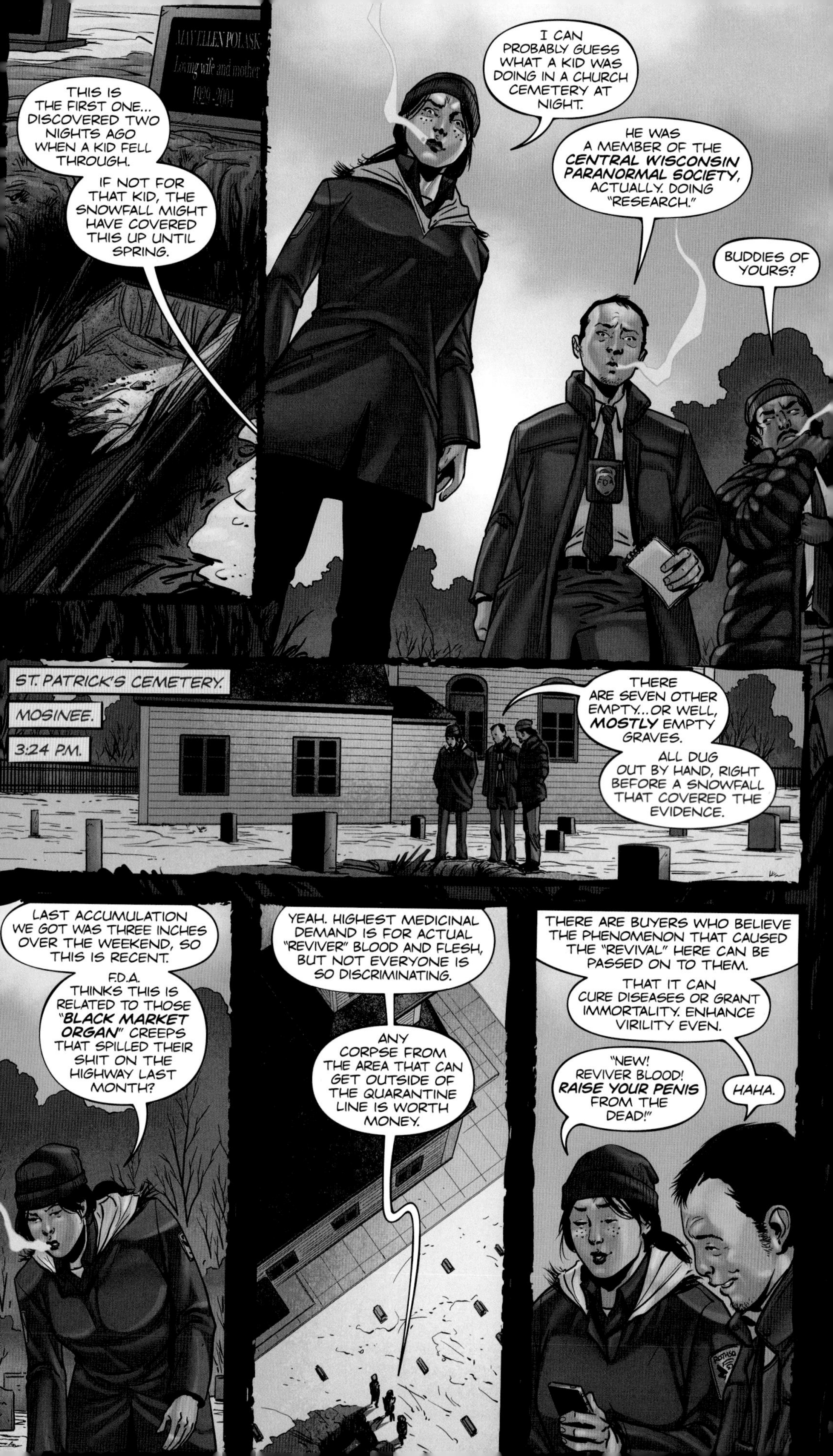
MAY ELLEN POLASK
Loving wife and mother
1920-2004
THIS IS THE FIRST ONE... DISCOVERED TWO NIGHTS AGO WHEN A KID FELL THROUGH.
IF NOT FOR THAT KID, THE SNOWFALL MIGHT HAVE COVERED THIS UP UNTIL SPRING.
I CAN PROBABLY GUESS WHAT A KID WAS DOING IN A CHURCH CEMETERY AT NIGHT.
HE WAS A MEMBER OF THE **CENTRAL WISCONSIN PARANORMAL SOCIETY**, ACTUALLY. DOING "RESEARCH."
BUDDIES OF YOURS?
ST. PATRICK'S CEMETERY.
MOSINEE.
3:24 P.M.
THERE ARE SEVEN OTHER EMPTY...OR WELL, **MOSTLY** EMPTY GRAVES.
ALL DUG OUT BY HAND, RIGHT BEFORE A SNOWFALL THAT COVERED THE EVIDENCE.
LAST ACCUMULATION WE GOT WAS THREE INCHES OVER THE WEEKEND, SO THIS IS RECENT.
F.D.A. THINKS THIS IS RELATED TO THOSE "**BLACK MARKET ORGAN**" CREEPS THAT SPILLED THEIR SHIT ON THE HIGHWAY LAST MONTH?
YEAH. HIGHEST MEDICINAL DEMAND IS FOR ACTUAL "REVIVER" BLOOD AND FLESH, BUT NOT EVERYONE IS SO DISCRIMINATING.
ANY CORPSE FROM THE AREA THAT CAN GET OUTSIDE OF THE QUARANTINE LINE IS WORTH MONEY.
THERE ARE BUYERS WHO BELIEVE THE PHENOMENON THAT CAUSED THE "REVIVAL" HERE CAN BE PASSED ON TO THEM.
THAT IT CAN CURE DISEASES OR GRANT IMMORTALITY. ENHANCE VIRILITY EVEN.
"NEW! REVIVER BLOOD! ***RAISE YOUR PENIS*** FROM THE DEAD!"
HAHA.

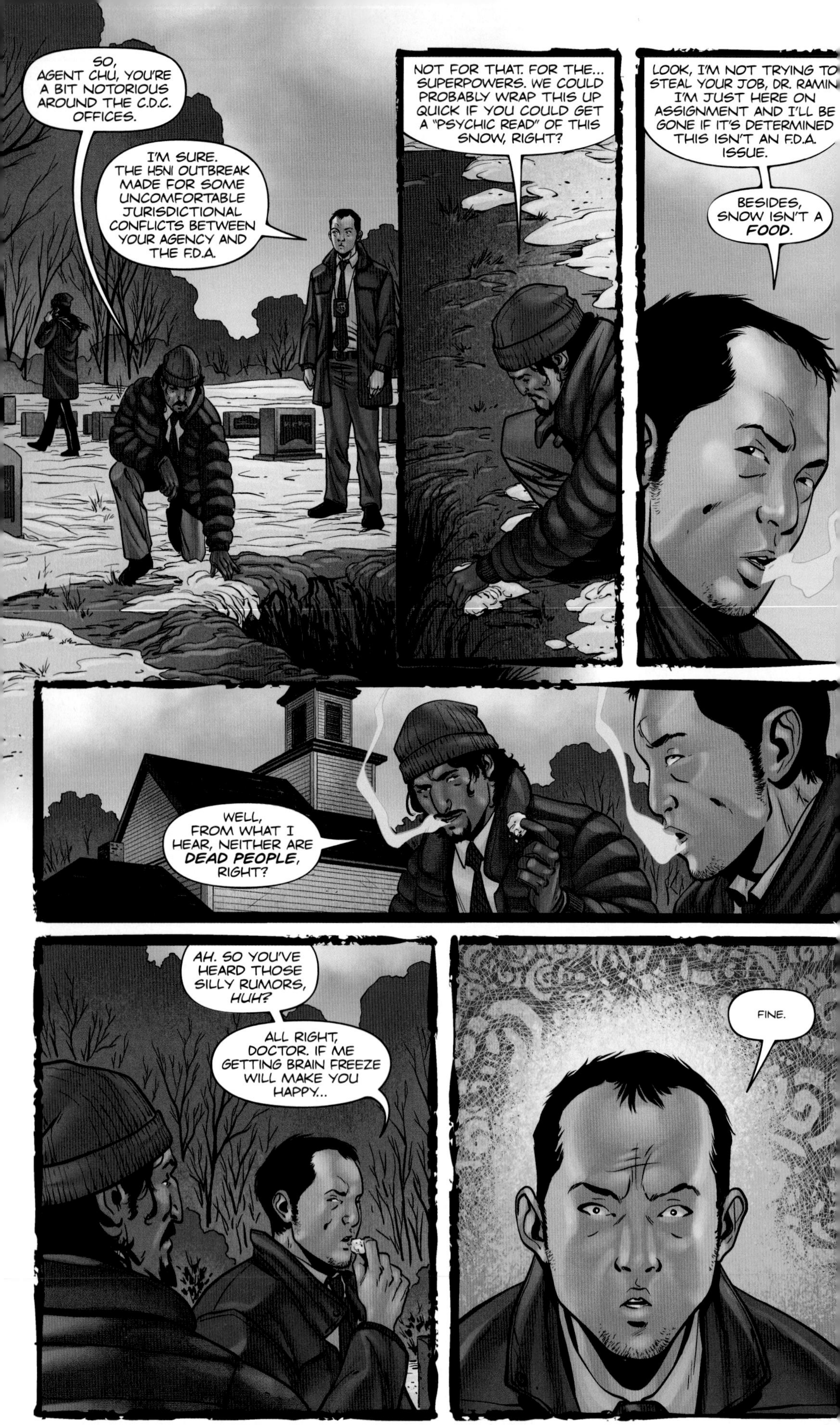
SO, AGENT CHU, YOU'RE A BIT NOTORIOUS AROUND THE C.D.C. OFFICES.
I'M SURE. THE H5N1 OUTBREAK MADE FOR SOME UNCOMFORTABLE JURISDICTIONAL CONFLICTS BETWEEN YOUR AGENCY AND THE F.D.A.
NOT FOR THAT. FOR THE... SUPERPOWERS. WE COULD PROBABLY WRAP THIS UP QUICK IF YOU COULD GET A "PSYCHIC READ" OF THIS SNOW, RIGHT?
LOOK, I'M NOT TRYING TO STEAL YOUR JOB, DR. RAMIN. I'M JUST HERE ON ASSIGNMENT AND I'LL BE GONE IF IT'S DETERMINED THIS ISN'T AN F.D.A. ISSUE.
BESIDES, SNOW ISN'T A **FOOD.**
WELL, FROM WHAT I HEAR, NEITHER ARE **DEAD PEOPLE**, RIGHT?
AH. SO YOU'VE HEARD THOSE SILLY RUMORS, HUH?
ALL RIGHT, DOCTOR. IF ME GETTING BRAIN FREEZE WILL MAKE YOU HAPPY...
FINE.

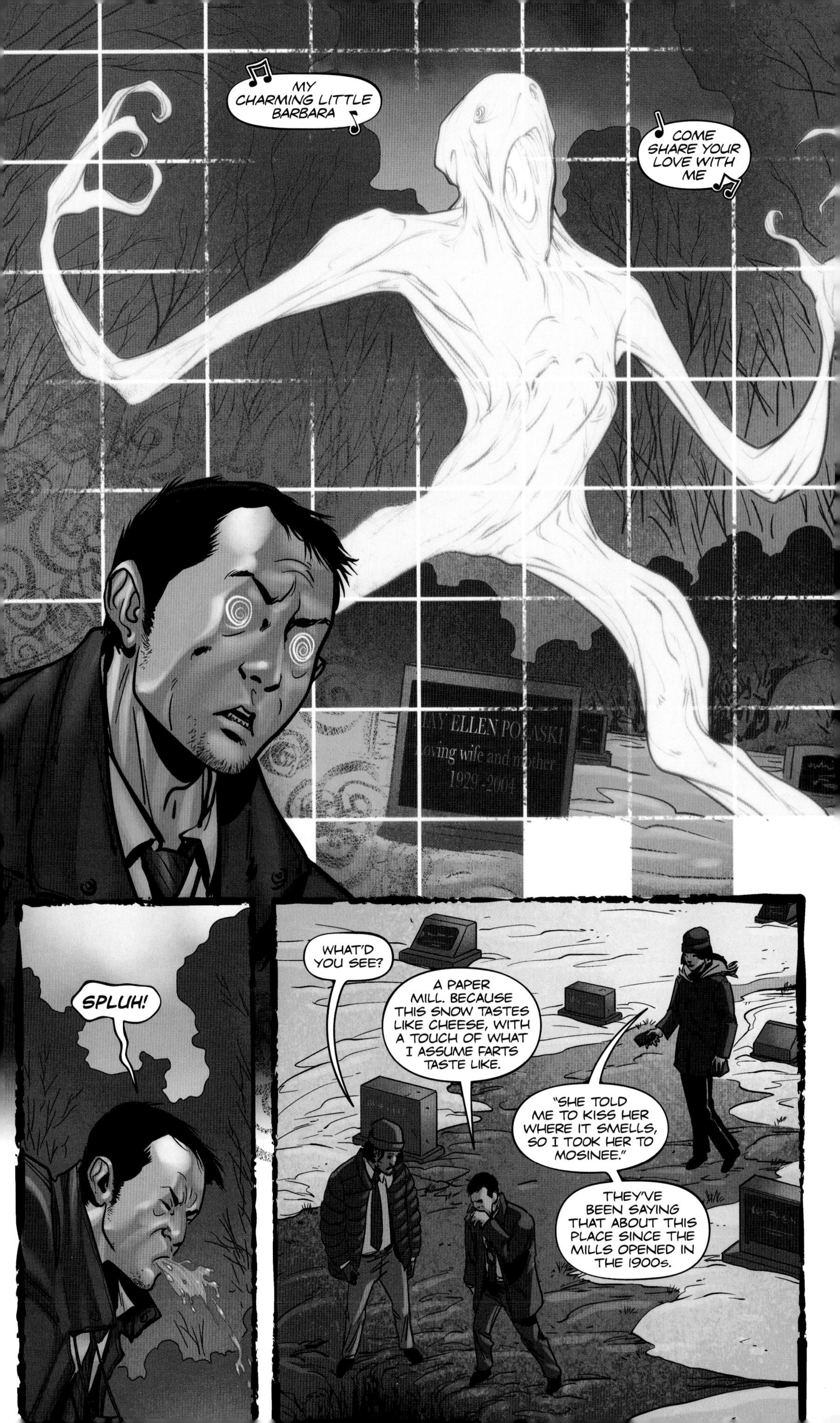
MY CHARMING LITTLE BARBARA
COME SHARE YOUR LOVE WITH ME
MAY ELLEN POLASKI
Loving wife and mother
1929 - 2004
SPLUH!
WHAT'D YOU SEE?
A PAPER MILL. BECAUSE THIS SNOW TASTES LIKE CHEESE, WITH A TOUCH OF WHAT I ASSUME FARTS TASTE LIKE.
"SHE TOLD ME TO KISS HER WHERE IT SMELLS, SO I TOOK HER TO MOSINEE."
THEY'VE BEEN SAYING THAT ABOUT THIS PLACE SINCE THE MILLS OPENED IN THE 1900s.

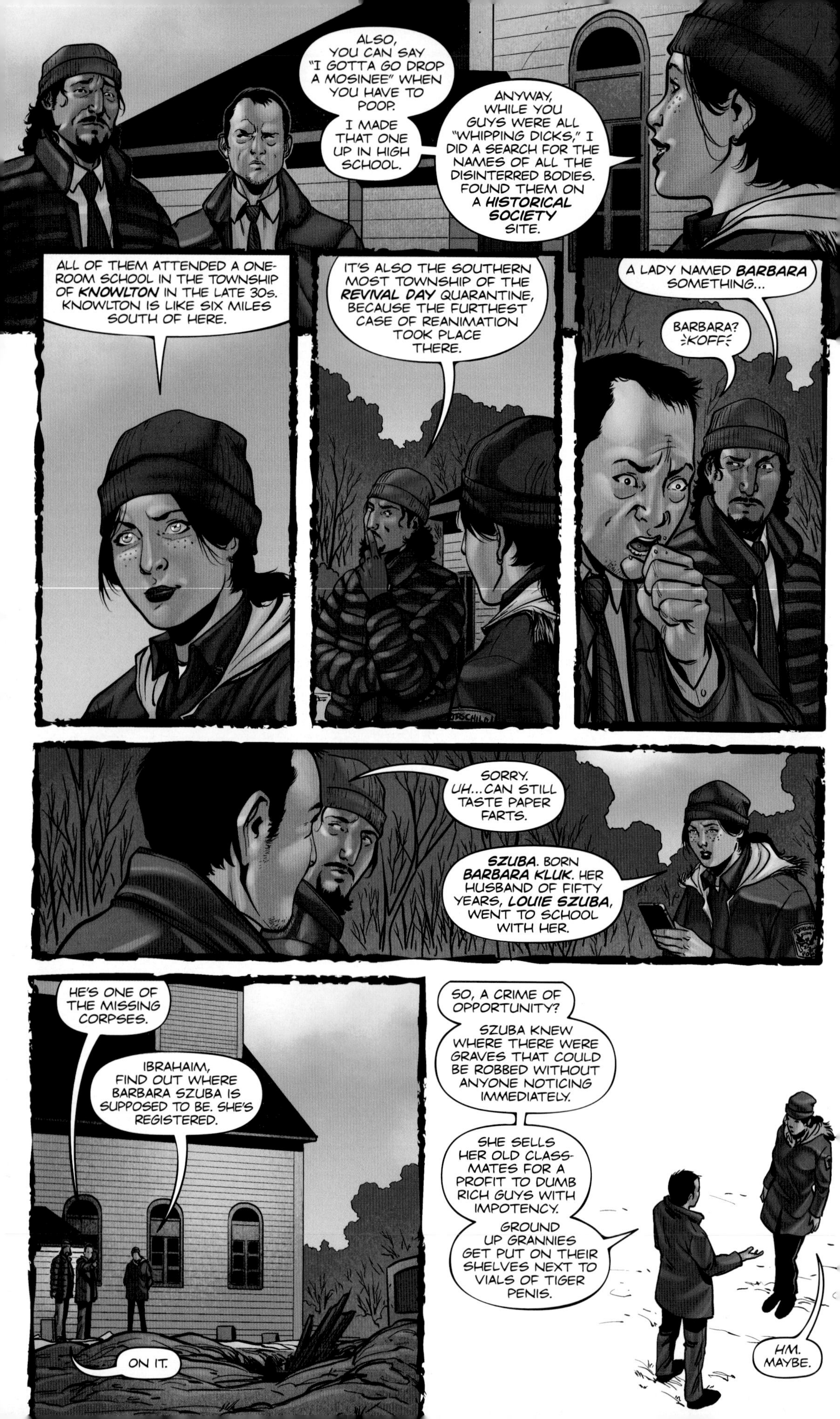

ALSO, YOU CAN SAY "I GOTTA GO DROP A MOSINEE" WHEN YOU HAVE TO POOP.
I MADE THAT ONE UP IN HIGH SCHOOL.
ANYWAY, WHILE YOU GUYS WERE ALL "WHIPPING DICKS," I DID A SEARCH FOR THE NAMES OF ALL THE DISINTERRED BODIES. FOUND THEM ON A HISTORICAL SOCIETY SITE.
ALL OF THEM ATTENDED A ONE-ROOM SCHOOL IN THE TOWNSHIP OF KNOWLTON IN THE LATE 30s. KNOWLTON IS LIKE SIX MILES SOUTH OF HERE.
IT'S ALSO THE SOUTHERN MOST TOWNSHIP OF THE REVIVAL DAY QUARANTINE, BECAUSE THE FURTHEST CASE OF REANIMATION TOOK PLACE THERE.
A LADY NAMED BARBARA SOMETHING...
BARBARA? KOFF
SORRY. UH...CAN STILL TASTE PAPER FARTS.
SZUBA. BORN BARBARA KLUK. HER HUSBAND OF FIFTY YEARS, LOUIE SZUBA, WENT TO SCHOOL WITH HER.
HE'S ONE OF THE MISSING CORPSES.
IBRAHAIM, FIND OUT WHERE BARBARA SZUBA IS SUPPOSED TO BE. SHE'S REGISTERED.
ON IT.
SO, A CRIME OF OPPORTUNITY?
SZUBA KNEW WHERE THERE WERE GRAVES THAT COULD BE ROBBED WITHOUT ANYONE NOTICING IMMEDIATELY.
SHE SELLS HER OLD CLASS-MATES FOR A PROFIT TO DUMB RICH GUYS WITH IMPOTENCY.
GROUND UP GRANNIES GET PUT ON THEIR SHELVES NEXT TO VIALS OF TIGER PENIS.
HM. MAYBE.

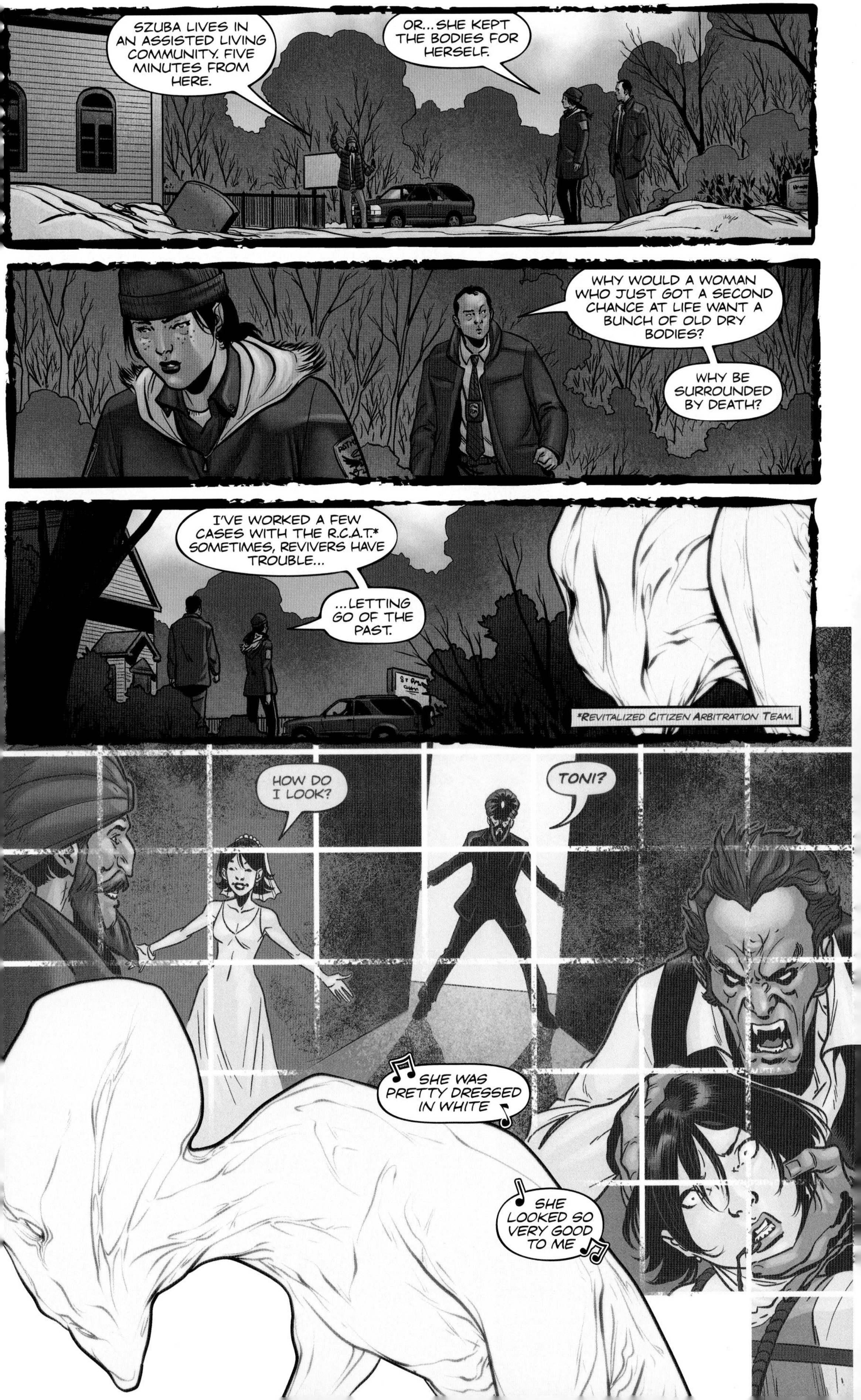
SZUBA LIVES IN AN ASSISTED LIVING COMMUNITY. FIVE MINUTES FROM HERE.
OR...SHE KEPT THE BODIES FOR HERSELF.
WHY WOULD A WOMAN WHO JUST GOT A SECOND CHANCE AT LIFE WANT A BUNCH OF OLD DRY BODIES?
WHY BE SURROUNDED BY DEATH?
I'VE WORKED A FEW CASES WITH THE R.C.A.T.* SOMETIMES, REVIVERS HAVE TROUBLE...
...LETTING GO OF THE PAST.
*REVITALIZED CITIZEN ARBITRATION TEAM.
HOW DO I LOOK?
TONI?
SHE WAS PRETTY DRESSED IN WHITE
SHE LOOKED SO VERY GOOD TO ME

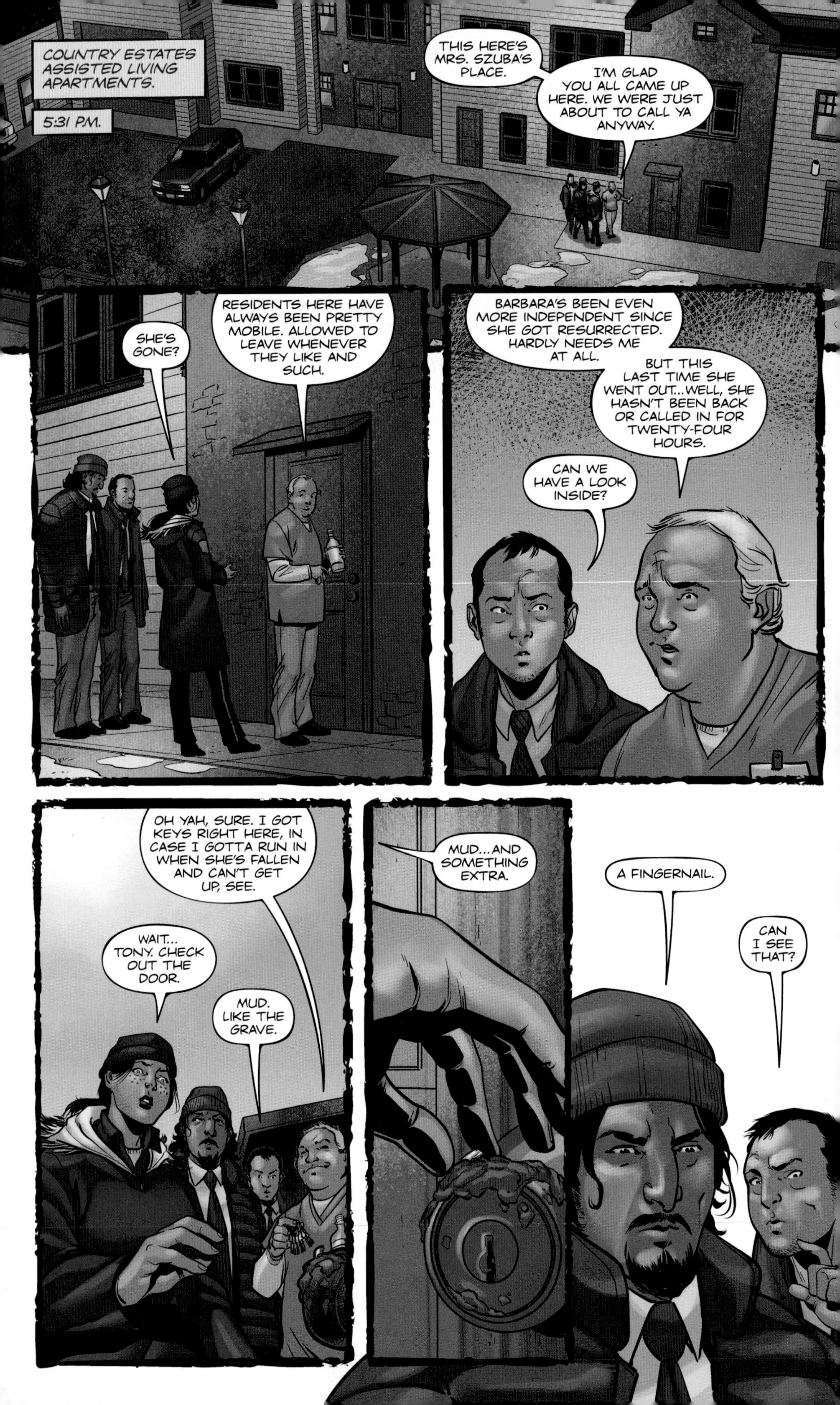

COUNTRY ESTATES ASSISTED LIVING APARTMENTS.
5:31 P.M.
THIS HERE'S MRS. SZUBA'S PLACE.
I'M GLAD YOU ALL CAME UP HERE. WE WERE JUST ABOUT TO CALL YA ANYWAY.
SHE'S GONE?
RESIDENTS HERE HAVE ALWAYS BEEN PRETTY MOBILE. ALLOWED TO LEAVE WHENEVER THEY LIKE AND SUCH.
BARBARA'S BEEN EVEN MORE INDEPENDENT SINCE SHE GOT RESURRECTED. HARDLY NEEDS ME AT ALL.
BUT THIS LAST TIME SHE WENT OUT...WELL, SHE HASN'T BEEN BACK OR CALLED IN FOR TWENTY-FOUR HOURS.
CAN WE HAVE A LOOK INSIDE?
OH YAH, SURE. I GOT KEYS RIGHT HERE, IN CASE I GOTTA RUN IN WHEN SHE'S FALLEN AND CAN'T GET UP, SEE.
WAIT... TONY. CHECK OUT THE DOOR.
MUD. LIKE THE GRAVE.
MUD...AND SOMETHING EXTRA.
A FINGERNAIL.
CAN I SEE THAT?

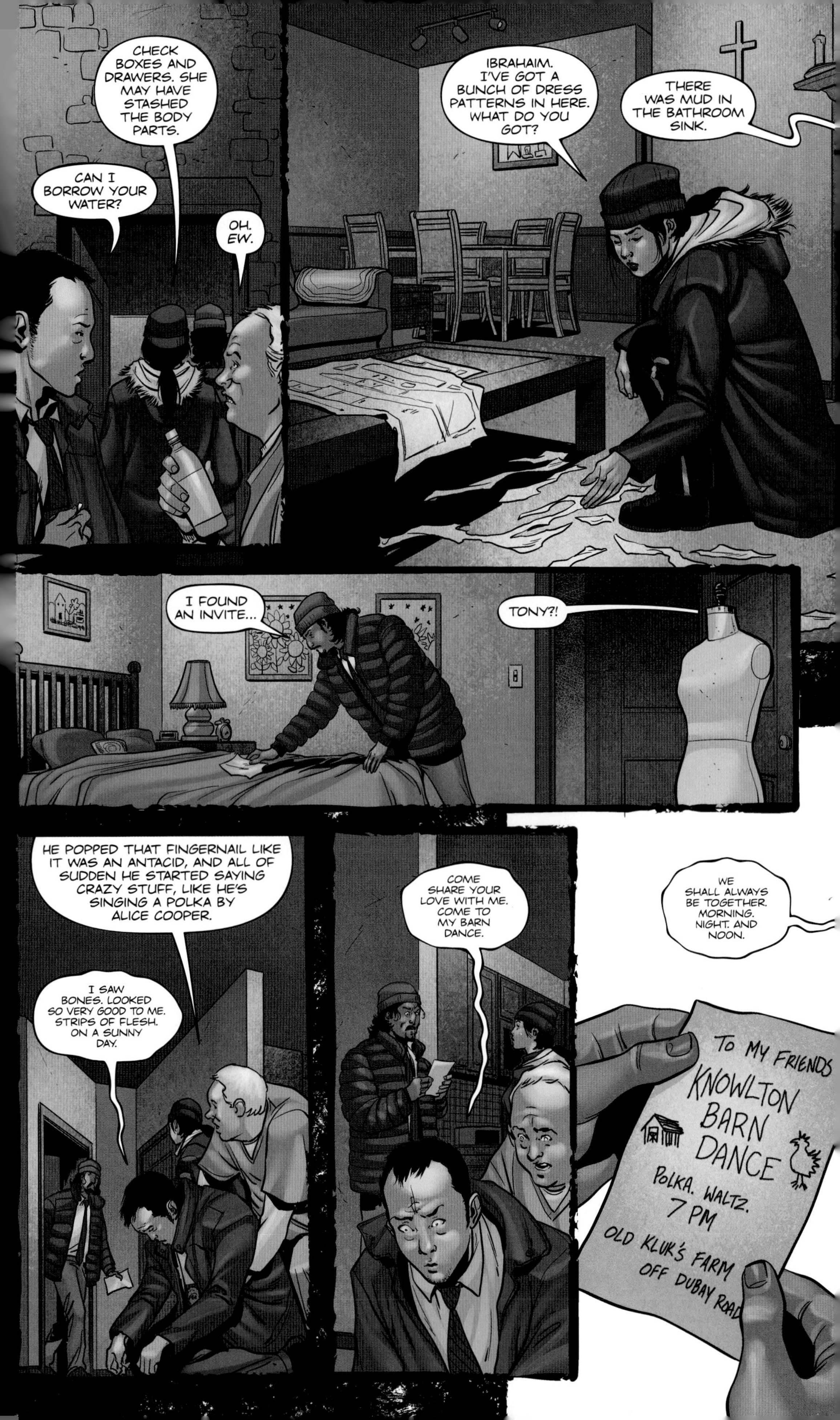
CHECK BOXES AND DRAWERS. SHE MAY HAVE STASHED THE BODY PARTS.
CAN I BORROW YOUR WATER?
OH. EW.
IBRAHAIM. I'VE GOT A BUNCH OF DRESS PATTERNS IN HERE. WHAT DO YOU GOT?
THERE WAS MUD IN THE BATHROOM SINK.
I FOUND AN INVITE...
TONY?!
HE POPPED THAT FINGERNAIL LIKE IT WAS AN ANTACID, AND ALL OF SUDDEN HE STARTED SAYING CRAZY STUFF, LIKE HE'S SINGING A POLKA BY ALICE COOPER.
I SAW BONES. LOOKED SO VERY GOOD TO ME. STRIPS OF FLESH. ON A SUNNY DAY.
COME SHARE YOUR LOVE WITH ME. COME TO MY BARN DANCE.
WE SHALL ALWAYS BE TOGETHER. MORNING. NIGHT. AND NOON.
TO MY FRIENDS
KNOWLTON BARN DANCE
POLKA. WALTZ.
7 PM
OLD KLUK'S FARM OFF DUBAY ROAD

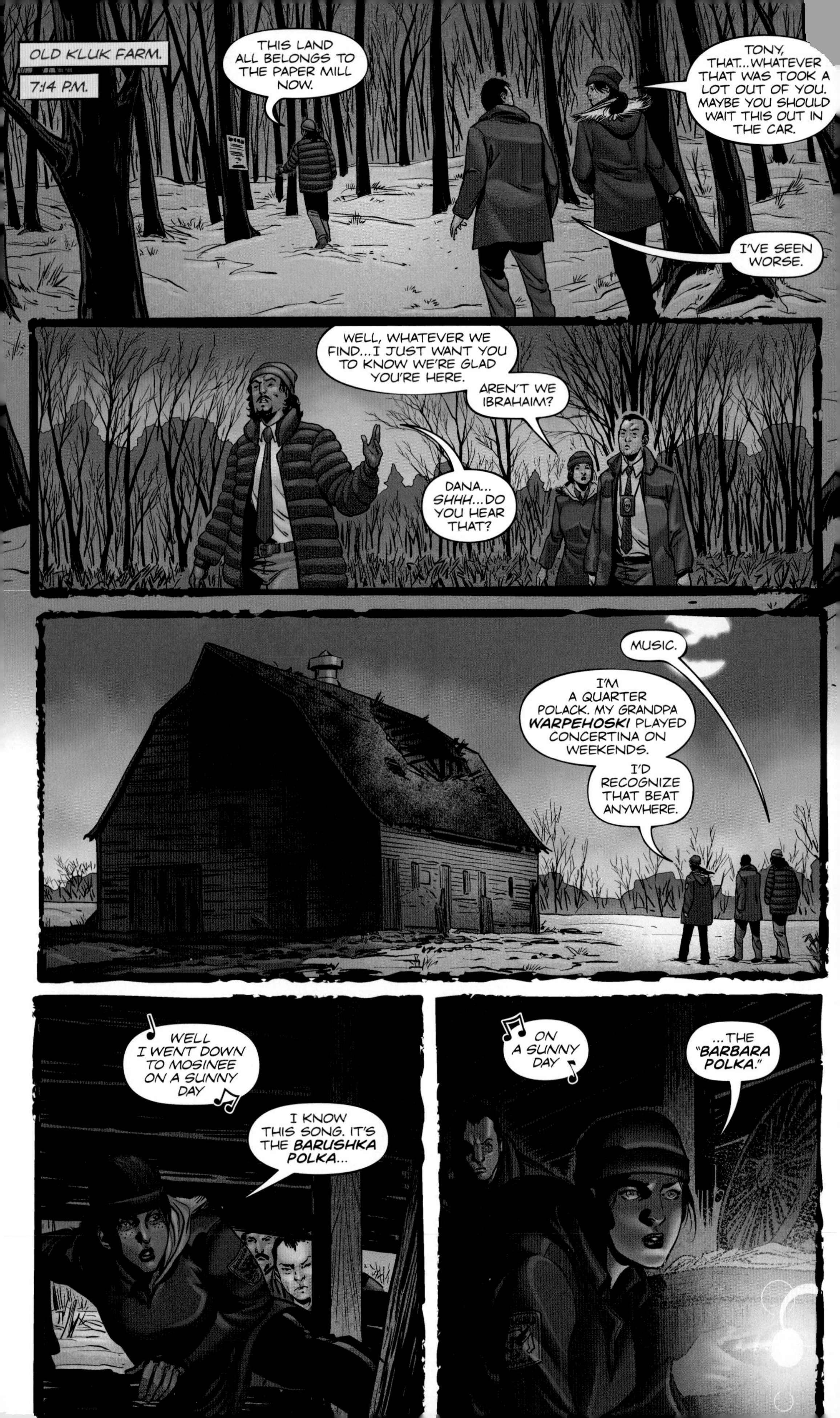
OLD KLUK FARM.
7:14 P.M.
THIS LAND ALL BELONGS TO THE PAPER MILL NOW.
TONY, THAT...WHATEVER THAT WAS TOOK A LOT OUT OF YOU. MAYBE YOU SHOULD WAIT THIS OUT IN THE CAR.
I'VE SEEN WORSE.
WELL, WHATEVER WE FIND...I JUST WANT YOU TO KNOW WE'RE GLAD YOU'RE HERE.
AREN'T WE IBRAHAIM?
DANA... SHHH...DO YOU HEAR THAT?
MUSIC.
I'M A QUARTER POLACK. MY GRANDPA WARPEHOSKI PLAYED CONCERTINA ON WEEKENDS.
I'D RECOGNIZE THAT BEAT ANYWHERE.
WELL I WENT DOWN TO MOSINEE ON A SUNNY DAY
I KNOW THIS SONG. IT'S THE BARUSHKA POLKA...
ON A SUNNY DAY
...THE "BARBARA POLKA."

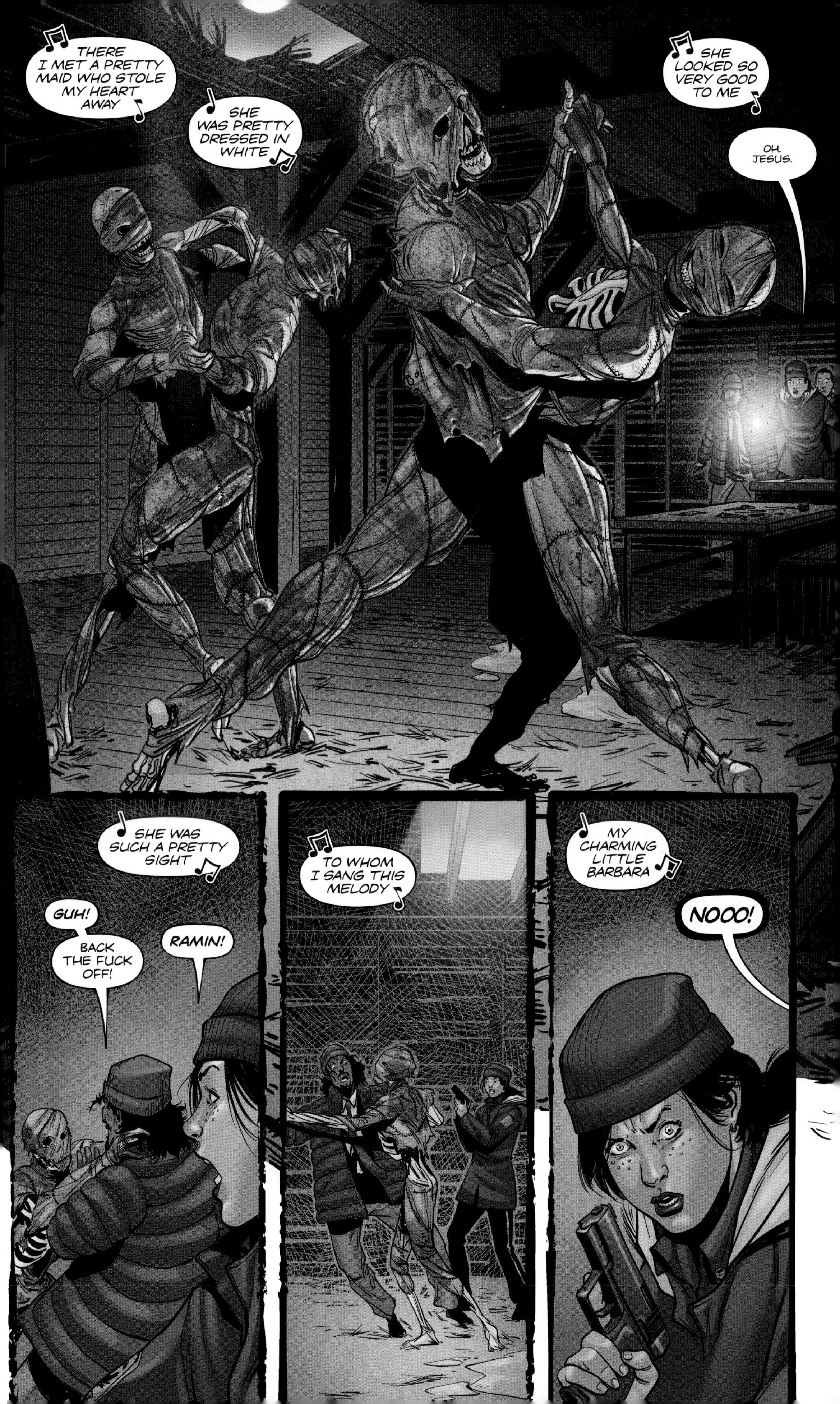
THERE I MET A PRETTY MAID WHO STOLE MY HEART AWAY
SHE WAS PRETTY DRESSED IN WHITE
SHE LOOKED SO VERY GOOD TO ME
OH. JESUS.
SHE WAS SUCH A PRETTY SIGHT
GUH!
BACK THE FUCK OFF!
RAMIN!
TO WHOM I SANG THIS MELODY
MY CHARMING LITTLE BARBARA
NOOO!

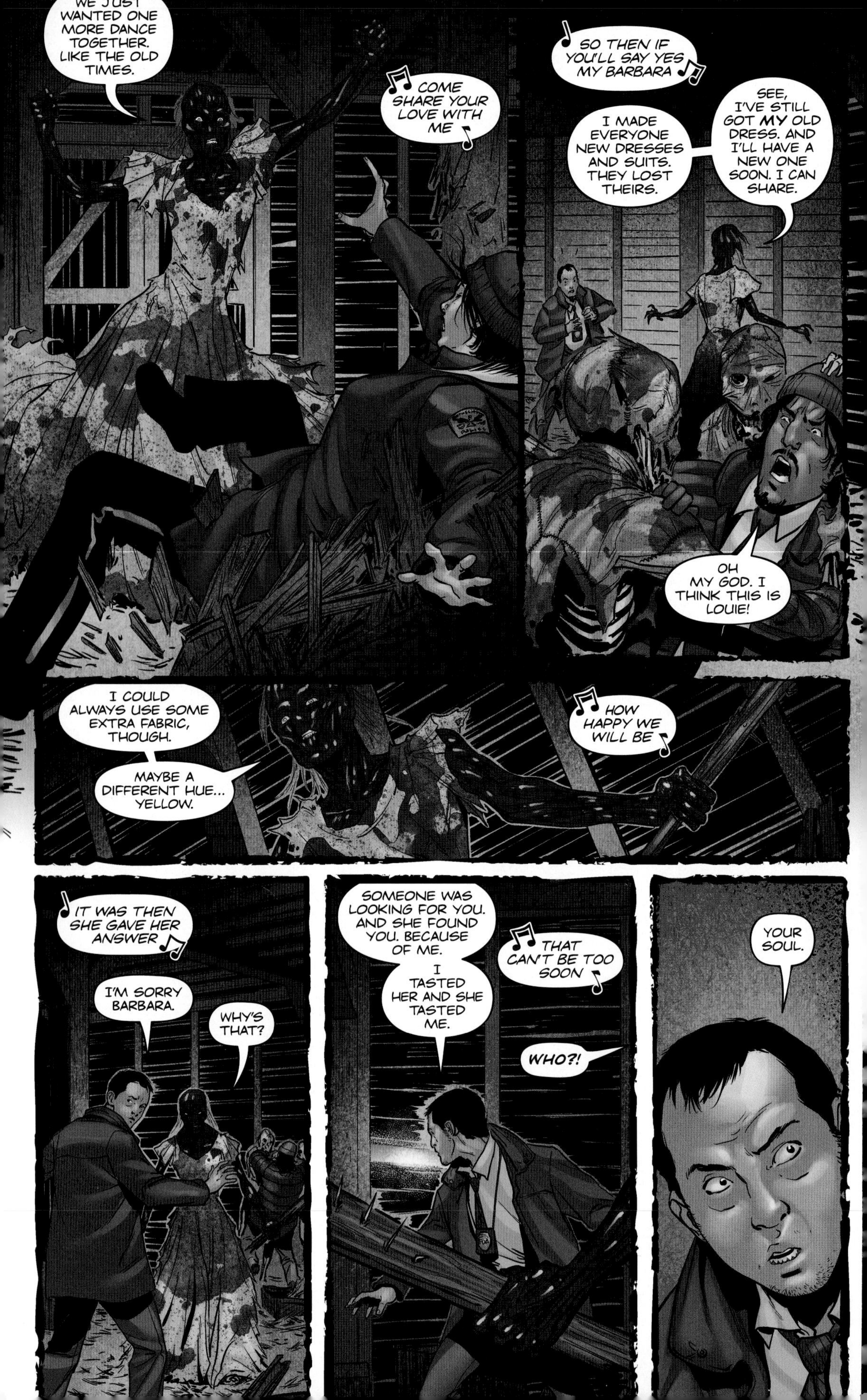
WE JUST WANTED ONE MORE DANCE TOGETHER. LIKE THE OLD TIMES.
COME SHARE YOUR LOVE WITH ME
SO THEN IF YOU'LL SAY YES MY BARBARA
I MADE EVERYONE NEW DRESSES AND SUITS. THEY LOST THEIRS.
SEE, I'VE STILL GOT MY OLD DRESS. AND I'LL HAVE A NEW ONE SOON. I CAN SHARE.
OH MY GOD. I THINK THIS IS LOUIE!
I COULD ALWAYS USE SOME EXTRA FABRIC, THOUGH.
MAYBE A DIFFERENT HUE... YELLOW.
HOW HAPPY WE WILL BE
IT WAS THEN SHE GAVE HER ANSWER
I'M SORRY BARBARA.
WHY'S THAT?
SOMEONE WAS LOOKING FOR YOU. AND SHE FOUND YOU. BECAUSE OF ME.
I TASTED HER AND SHE TASTED ME.
THAT CAN'T BE TOO SOON
WHO?!
YOUR SOUL.

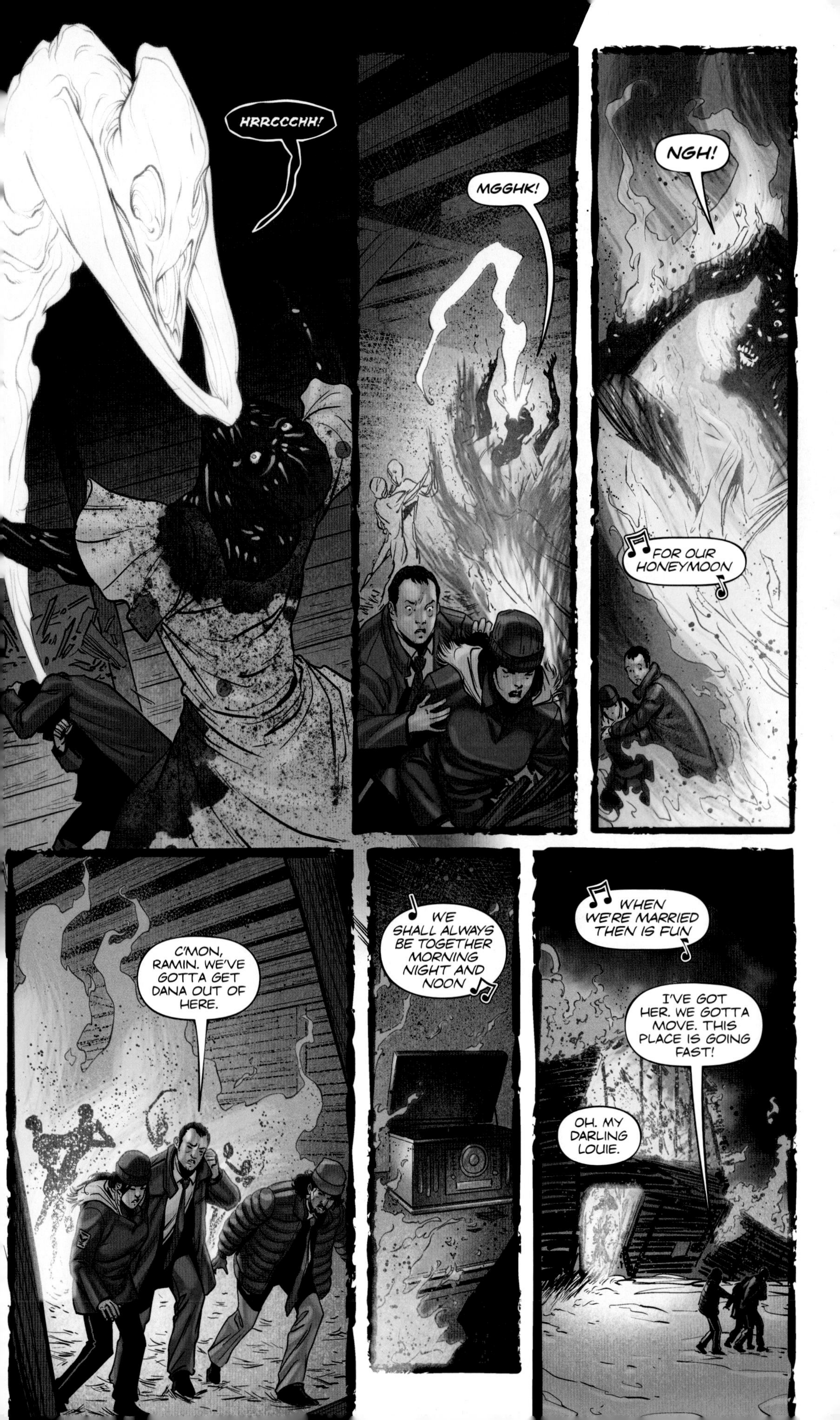
HRRCCCHH!
MGGHK!
NGH!
FOR OUR HONEYMOON
C'MON, RAMIN. WE'VE GOTTA GET DANA OUT OF HERE.
WE SHALL ALWAYS BE TOGETHER MORNING NIGHT AND NOON
WHEN WE'RE MARRIED THEN IS FUN
I'VE GOT HER. WE GOTTA MOVE. THIS PLACE IS GOING FAST!
OH. MY DARLING LOUIE.

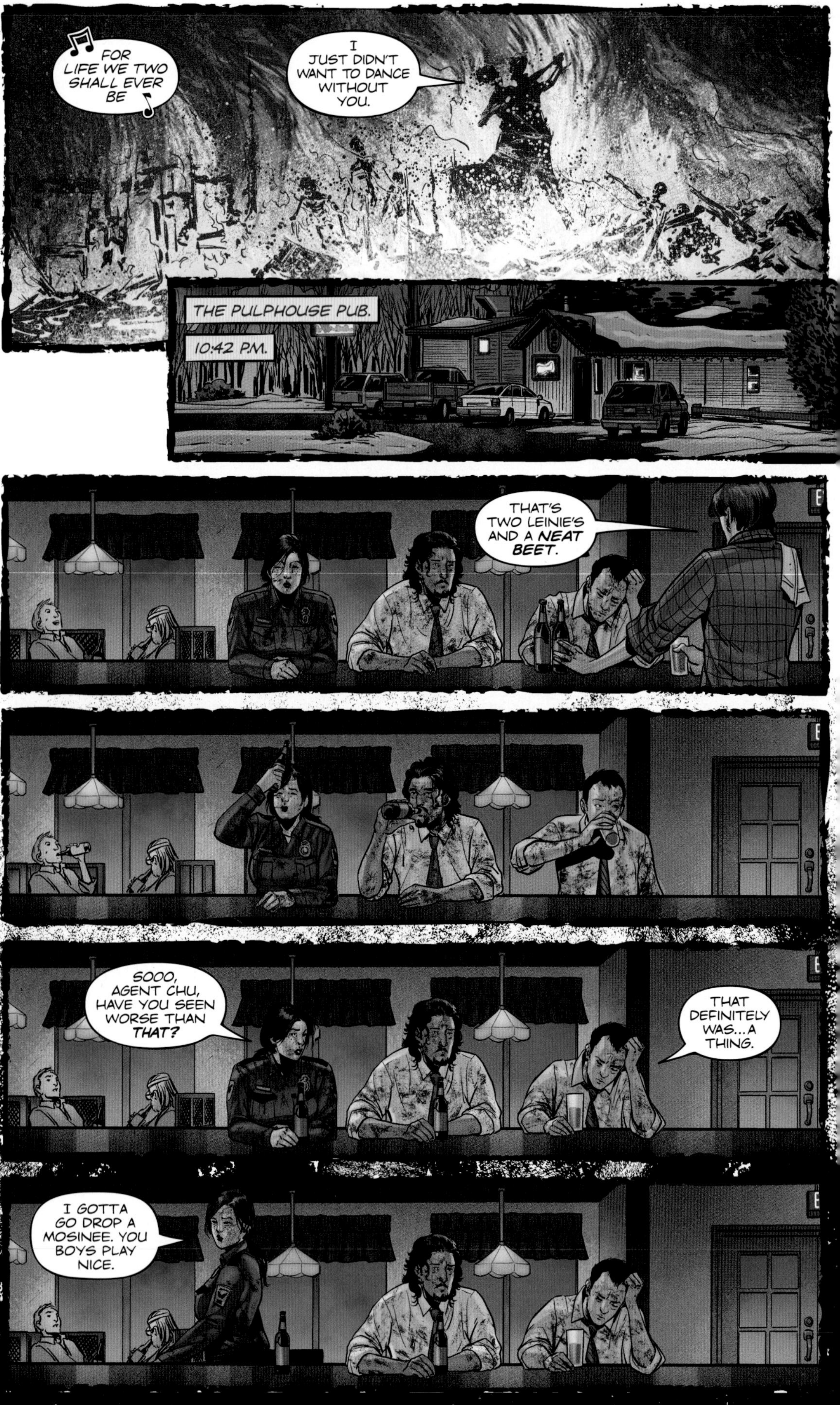
FOR LIFE WE TWO SHALL EVER BE
I JUST DIDN'T WANT TO DANCE WITHOUT YOU.
THE PULPHOUSE PUB.
10:42 P.M.
THAT'S TWO LEINIE'S AND A *NEAT BEET*.
SOOO, AGENT CHU, HAVE YOU SEEN WORSE THAN *THAT?*
THAT DEFINITELY WAS...A THING.
I GOTTA GO DROP A MOSINEE. YOU BOYS PLAY NICE.

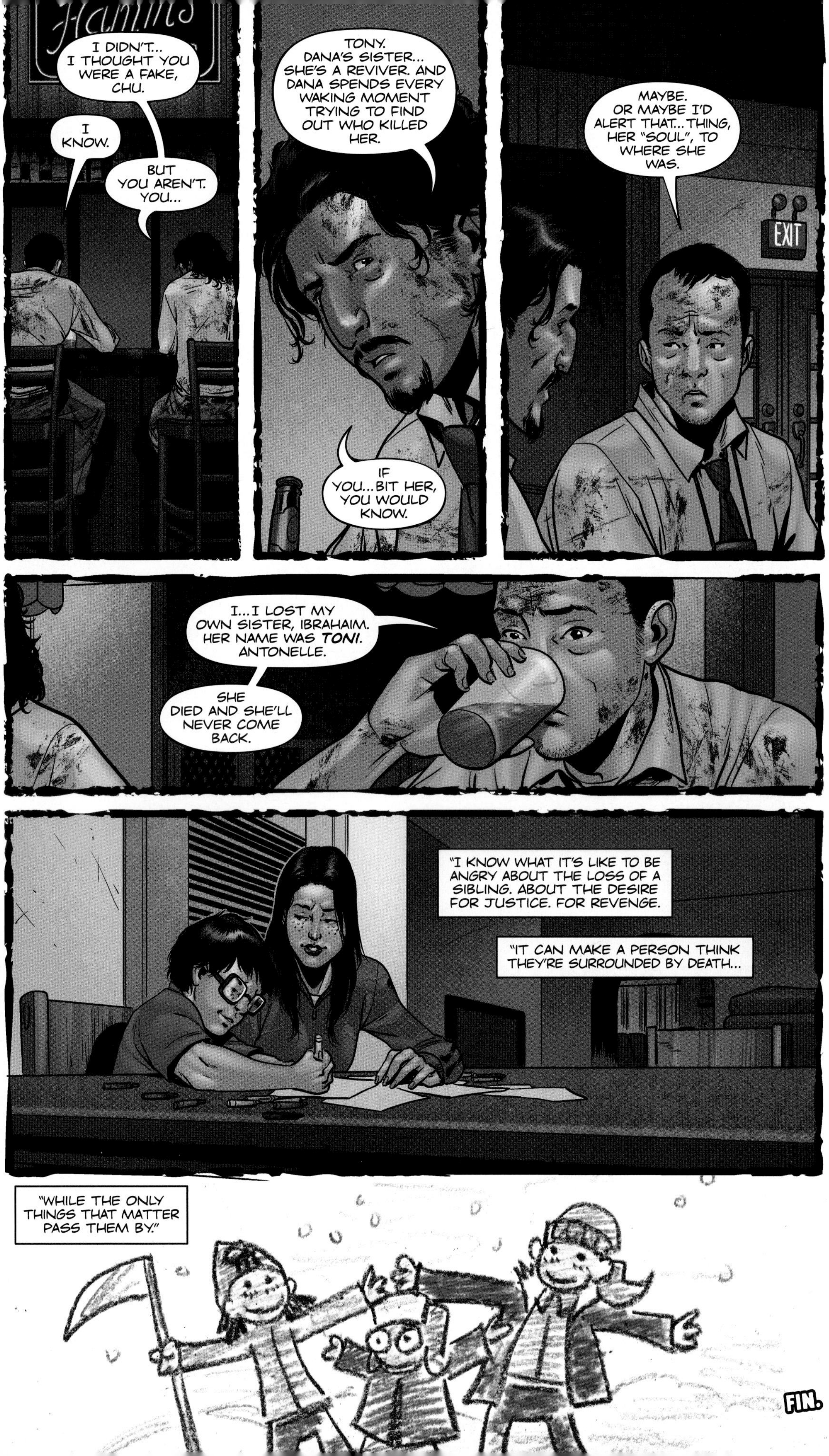
I DIDN'T... I THOUGHT YOU WERE A FAKE, CHU.
I KNOW.
BUT YOU AREN'T. YOU...
TONY. DANA'S SISTER... SHE'S A REVIVER. AND DANA SPENDS EVERY WAKING MOMENT TRYING TO FIND OUT WHO KILLED HER.
IF YOU...BIT HER, YOU WOULD KNOW.
MAYBE. OR MAYBE I'D ALERT THAT...THING, HER "SOUL", TO WHERE SHE WAS.
EXIT
I...I LOST MY OWN SISTER, IBRAHAIM. HER NAME WAS *TONI*. ANTONELLE.
SHE DIED AND SHE'LL NEVER COME BACK.
"I KNOW WHAT IT'S LIKE TO BE ANGRY ABOUT THE LOSS OF A SIBLING. ABOUT THE DESIRE FOR JUSTICE. FOR REVENGE.
"IT CAN MAKE A PERSON THINK THEY'RE SURROUNDED BY DEATH...
"WHILE THE ONLY THINGS THAT MATTER PASS THEM BY."
FIN.

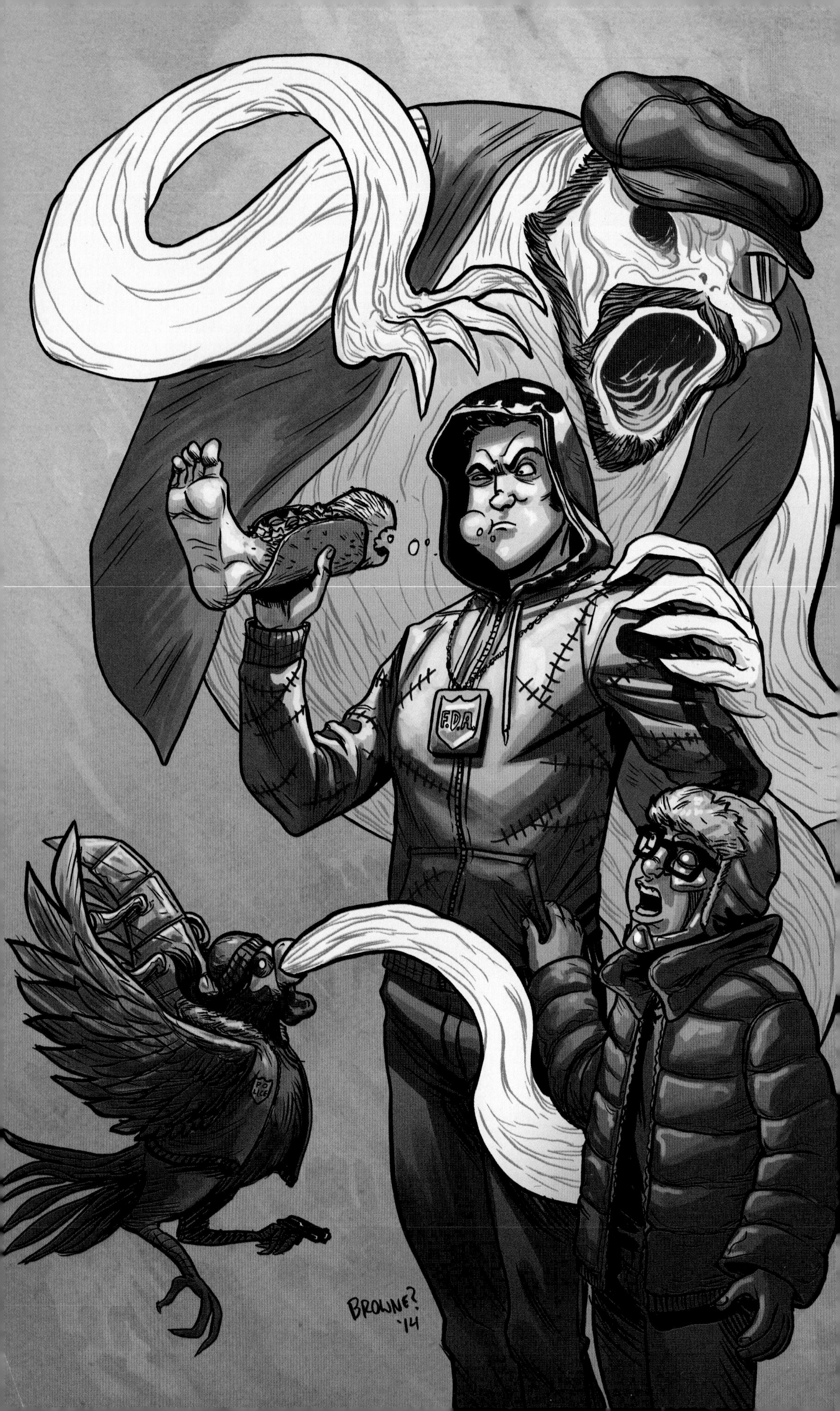
F.D.A.
BROWNE?
'14

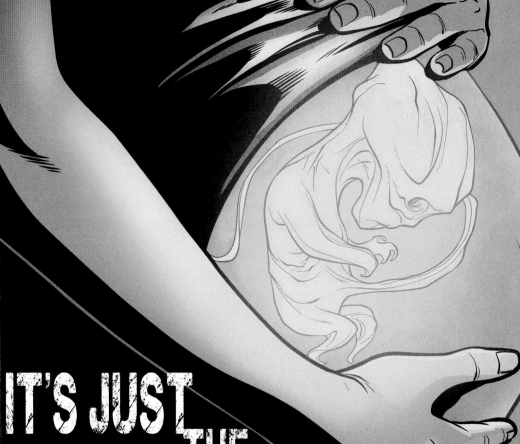

DEATH IS NOT THE END.

IT'S JUST THE BEGINNING.

A RURAL NOIR BY TIM SEELEY + MIKE NORTON

REVIVAL

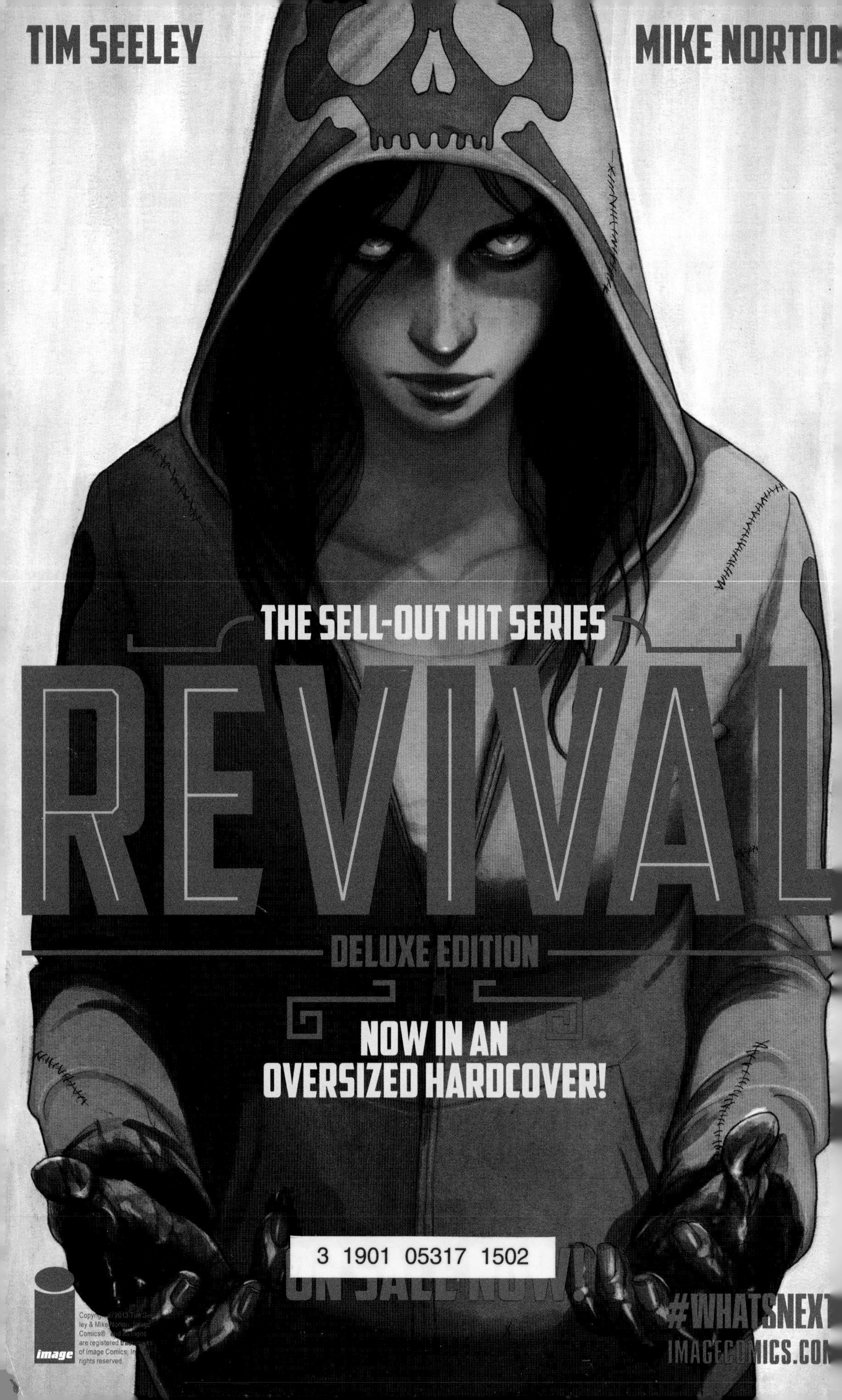
TIM SEELEY
MIKE NORTON
THE SELL-OUT HIT SERIES
REVIVAL
DELUXE EDITION
NOW IN AN
OVERSIZED HARDCOVER!
#WHATSNEXT
IMAGECOMICS.COM
image